ACCLAIM

"Amanda Wright uses classic fantasy tropes like good versus evil and chosen one as she weaves a story about realm walkers, daughters of stars, and hidden kingdoms. She doesn't shy away from the horror of war, but leaves a glimmer of hope for the reader. An excellent read for those looking for their next fantasy novel."

—MORGAN L. BUSSE, award-winning author of the Ravenwood Saga and *Winter's Maiden*

"I was hooked from the first paragraph! *Darkfell* is filled with chilling evil, soaring triumphs, and the hero everyone wants to root for."

—AJ SKELLY, author of *Of Flame & Frost* and *An Alliance of Ash & Jade*

"*Darkfell* is an action-packed fantasy with memorable characters who've been forced in to battle across multiple realms to defend their loved ones and their lives. The storyline clearly has more secrets to reveal, and more battles ahead for the unassuming

Realm Walker hero. I truly enjoyed the writing style, the world-building, and the characters. I'm waiting for the sequel."

—R. J. LARSON, author of *Books of the Infinite* and *Realms of the Infinite*

"*Darkfell* is a faith-filled fantasy adventure that is perfect for classic fantasy fans. I was transported into the world Amanda Wright created and didn't want to leave! The adorable romance combined with magic and high stakes held me captive from the start and all the way through the end. Loveable characters are sure to live in the mind and hearts of readers long after the final page. Additionally, the messages of faith, hope, and light woven throughout the story make this a refreshing and uplifting read. Don't miss this one!"

—ASHLEY BUSTAMANTE, author of the Color Theory trilogy

"There are many things to love about Amanda Wright's debut novel, *Darkfell*—spiritual warfare, epic battles, dragons, daring adventures, a sweet romance—this classic Christian fantasy has everything. But the heart and soul of the book comes from the relationship between brothers Thom and Puck, as they try to navigate a world that's suddenly far larger and more complex than either of them ever suspected, threatening to tear apart everything they hold dear."

—AMBER KIRKPATRICK, author of *Until the Rising* and the Changed duology

"This epic tale of one man's journey to become a Realm Walker and defeat an ultimate evil being in the name of his Creator kept me on the edge of my seat. Wright's ability to portray the darkness of evil and the heroism which rises against it was mesmerizing. *Darkfell* left an impression on me and I find my mind wandering back to it time and again. If you like Donita K Paul or Frank Perreti, you will also enjoy *Darkfell*."

—DAWN FORD, award-winning author of The Firebird series

"*Darkfell* follows an unlikely hero thrown into war where he battles monsters both dark and strange. Filled with witty banter and well thought out characters, Wright weaves a gripping tale of friendship, love and faith that will pull you in and lead you down mystical paths that you won't soon forget."

—SARA K. ANDERSON, author of the Mind Hunters duology

"Capturing you within the first paragraphs, *Darkfell* mirrors the works of Patrick Carr and Bryan Davis in the world building and prose. This epic adventure of good vs. evil, epic love, and ultimately the triumph of hope will leave you longing for more!"

—ANNA AUGUSTINE, author of *By Blood & Blade* and *By the Sun & Stars*

"Tender, humorous, yet unafraid of tough questions, offers readers sweet romance and page-turning adventure in a fantasy realm full of surprises."
—L. G. MCCARY, author of *That Pale Host*

"Perfect pacing and great tension make this debut novel from Amanda Wright shine. *Darkfell* reads like a classic fantasy with all the right vibes—heroism, loyalty, faith, magic, beasts, and an epic battle of good vs. evil. Wright created the perfect cast of characters to tell this story: a reluctant hero who just wants to enjoy his books and maps; his snarky best friend who loyally fights by his side; and a girl he meets in his dreams who is connected to the stars. This adventurous journey through perilous realms, as well as the inner journey of faith and surrender, will have readers turning pages to the very end."
—CRYSTAL D. GRANT, award-winning author of The Gateway trilogy

DARKFELL

DARKFELL

Quill & Flame
PUBLISHING HOUSE

AMANDA WRIGHT

To my Lord and Savior, Jesus Christ, who has
never refused to call me His own.

And to my son, whose heart inspired
the character of Thom Darkfell.

PROLOGUE

Titus, immortal master of the realm of Zakar, stood in the center of his courtyard. Gore pooled about his leather boots as his eyes probed the huddle of human slaves. A bone dagger twirled through his pale fingers. Nearly three hundred years had passed since fresh human prey had graced his realm. Titus inhaled. Palpable and intoxicating, the odors of their terror rushed up his nostrils.

"My lord!" A sharp voice cut through the panic-laden air.

Titus's focus snapped to the source, as Slager, Realm Walker and commander of the Zakarian hordes, stalked into the courtyard and halted at the edge of the sweeping space.

"Not now," Titus snarled, lethal impatience stabbing like a poison-tipped blade toward his commander.

Despite once being human, little was left of that weakened race in Titus's steely-eyed Realm Walker. Slager's blood-soaked soul bore no resemblance to the ambitious young man Titus had coaxed away from the Creator's grasp long ago. It hadn't been hard. El'Ohim's gifts of peace and love were a weak substitute for Titus's promises of power.

Indecision warred across Slager's face for a moment before he ignored Titus's command and started across the courtyard, his dark cloak stirring about his muscular frame. "My lord, I must speak to you."

Titus's fingers tightened around the hilt of his blade. "What is it?"

No pity dwelled in Slager's stony countenance as he strode by the men he'd captured and brought to Zakar. A weeping male, stripped naked to the waist, reached out to grasp Slager's pant leg.

Titus's lips curved into a satisfied smile as Slager's boot came down on the man's fingers, and he ground his heel into the slave's flesh. Nearly as satisfying as the crunch of bone and tendon was the agonized cry that ripped from his throat. Bloodlust pulsed through Titus's veins as the slave, clutching his mangled hand, wailed. His voice dropped to a low purr. "Bring me that one."

Slager grunted in annoyance but obeyed, stooping to grab the man by his black hair and drag him forward. He threw him down at Titus's feet.

Titus seized the squalling male by the throat and lifted him to his knees. *Ah, I've missed this.*

Supplications spewed frantically from the human's mouth, and the aroma of fear intensified as urine splashed onto the cobblestones.

Prayers, perhaps? Not that those held power in Zakar.

"Shh," Titus crooned. His dagger gently kissed the side of the man's cheek, and a single droplet of crimson blood pooled on the edge of the blade.

He caught Slager's eye. "Now you hear him..." Titus sliced the tongue from the babbling mouth.

The man fell to the ground. Writhing. Blood gushing from his soundless, gaping maw.

"Now you don't." Titus sighed, the sound almost wistful. "Magical."

He dragged a finger through the blood on the blade and rubbed it thoughtfully between his thumb and index finger before reverently licking the stain. A rush of metallic flavor exploded across his tongue. Heady.

"My lord…" Impatience edged Slager's voice as he glanced at the bleeding slave and then back at his master. "The king of Abadonia has agreed to an alliance with you in exchange for the kingdom of Lomair. He has pledged his entire army. What answer would you have me give?"

Titus chuckled darkly and flicked a lock of blond hair from his eyes. "A measly human king thinks he can make demands of me?" Like a striking viper, Titus's mood swung, and rage reddened his face. "I am a god!"

"We are not yet at our full strength," Slager cautioned. "Spill the blood of his men first."

"And whose fault is that?" Titus asked, a deadly and unpredictable calm masking his anger. The urge to throw his dagger and watch it sink into Slager's chest was almost too much to resist.

But I need him. For just a little longer. The thought galled.

Titus stalked closer to Slager, the manacles around his ankles tugging as the enchanted chain dragged through the puddles of human blood and refuse. "Tell me. How much longer until you breach the wall?" The impenetrable barrier circling his realm was his eternal punishment for attempting to take over El'Ohim's precious Human Realm.

Slager moistened his lips. "It is nearly done. A week or two more, and it will fall."

"For your sake, it had better." Hatred for his maker and thirst for revenge broiled in Titus's gut. "And what of my shackles? Have you made any progress there, mighty Realm Walker?" If the wall hadn't been enough, the manacles were El'Ohim's final surety that Titus would forever be bound to Zakar, his magic muted.

A flicker of nervousness passed through Slager's gaze. "Perhaps they will break with the wall, sire."

"Perhaps?" Danger coiled around that single word as Titus's eyes narrowed to slits. "You have been feeding me excuses for too long."

Slager eased away. "I am close. I was able to bring you back slaves last time, was I not?"

A growl rumbled from Titus's chest. "One success does not negate years of ineptitude."

A muscle beside Slager's eye spasmed. "Breaking through El'Ohim's enchantments is not easily done. I've hunted down countless magic-containing artifacts and hundreds of witches and sorcerers to get as far as I have. It takes time."

"Three hundred years, apparently," Titus mocked. "Now leave me and tell that king he will get his reward."

"Truly?"

Titus rolled his eyes skywards. "Of course not, you fool. But tell him what he needs to hear. In the end, I will have the Human Realm. All of it."

"Yes, my lord." Slager bowed low and, with a quick flick of his hand, opened a blood-red portal and hastened through.

The
Hidden
Realm
(Silmea)

Northern Mountains
Wiise River
Great Woods
Knor
Iron Forge
Lomair
Abadonia
Border Keep
Nomad Tribes
Sea
Human
Realm

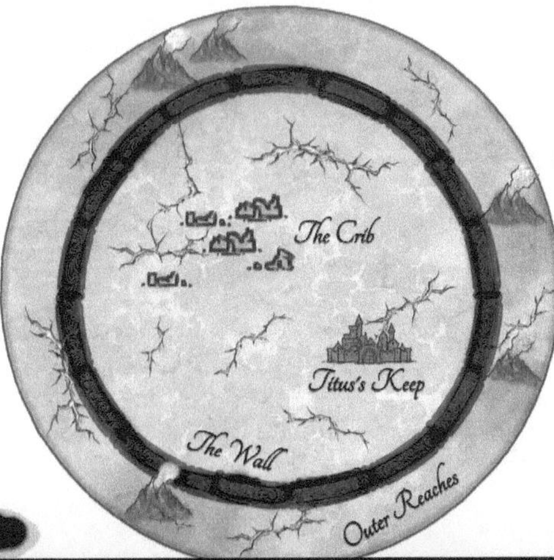

The Crib
Titus's Keep
The Wall
Outer Reaches
The Realm
of Zakar

Chapter 1
From Quills to Blades

By Decree of his Royal Majesty King Xerses of Lomair,
all males aged thirteen to forty years of age
are hereby conscripted into His Majesty's army.
Report by dawn tomorrow.
No exemptions unless by written decree of the king.

Thom stared at the notice hanging askew on his beloved library door and scanned the badly scrawled words again. *All males. Conscripted. No exemptions.* Pressing his lips into a hard line, he tore the parchment off the door and crushed it in his fist.

For ten years, war had raged against the land-hungry Abadonians to the south. Ten long years of blood spilled to defend Lomair's borders. And now, mere months after the passing of his mentor and his subsequent appointment as the official royal librarian and advising cartographer, he was being called off to war.

Thom twisted the ornate doorknob and stepped out of the castle hallway into the majestic library. He inhaled a deep breath, steadied by the scent of parchment from the vast array of books, maps, and manuscripts that filled the shelves. Light filtered in through the low stained-glass windows, casting a soft glow on the rows of well-organized spines. In a shadowed corner, away from the damaging effects of sunlight and disturbance, sat his work desk, where an old map waited patiently for his attention.

Thom dropped the draft notice into the waste bucket and sat heavily in his chair, the aged movement belying his twenty years. He'd received notices before, but his had always come with a written exception.

Why not this time?

Did the king no longer need a resident cartographer? Had his usefulness truly run out? Thom closed his eyes and drew in a long breath. He'd meticulously copied hundreds of maps for the war effort. Many candles had met their end in his library as he'd worked late into the night, scouring the texts for information on the Abadonians and the geography of their lands.

I'm...going to war. The thought beat unrelenting through his mind.

Thom picked up his quill, the cool instrument trembling in his fingers. He stared at the map in front of him, but his mind refused to focus.

I'm a scholar. Not a warrior. I can't kill a man.

His stomach churned, and Thom dipped his quill in the black ink, willing the tremor in his hand to disappear. Clinging to the comfort of routine, Thom hunched over his desk. With careful strokes, he outlined the borders of Knor, the capital of Lomair, before moving on to darken the harsh lines of the Northern Mountains. The tension in his shoulders eased. There was nothing like the feel of parchment skimming his fingertips or the smell of his library. To be truthful, he enjoyed the company of his books over that of most other people. His friend Puck, his brother in every way that counted, accused him of being dull, but Thom preferred to think of his lifestyle as peaceful.

"Here you are!" a voice boomed.

Thom startled, his quill streaking aggressively across the map. "Saints above, Puck!" He hadn't heard him come in.

The blond, thick-chested young man in question sauntered across the library. "What're you still doing in here?"

"Working." Thom tried valiantly to lift the fresh ink stain, groaning as it smudged. "Look what you made me do!"

Puck peered over Thom's shoulder and winced. "Ouch." He rocked back on his heels, everything about him exuding barely contained energy. "Did you hear the news?"

Thom curled over his desk, doing his best to ignore Puck and his question. Could he blend the line into the forest? Make it look like part of the trees?

"Thom!"

"I heard you." Thom set down his quill. "Yes. I got a notice."

"So, why're you here? Shouldn't you be packing? We leave at dawn."

We? Eyes widening, Thom turned in his seat. "Wait...what? You were drafted too?"

Puck's eyes flashed with excitement. "Aye! Finally."

Thom's brow puckered in confusion. "You didn't get an exemption?"

As the only son of the Royal Baker and his sole assistant, Puck had always been excluded from the drafts, much like Thom.

"Nope." Puck grinned. "Pa checked right away, and the recruitment officer said neither of us were getting an exemption. But I figured I'd still find you here. You're as predictable as Pa's yeast."

"Am not," Thom grumbled. Puck arched a brow. Thom shrugged and straightened the items on his desk. "Nothing wrong with being organized."

"Except it's boring," Puck said. His gaze grew thoughtful as he regarded Thom. "Maybe this will be good for you."

Thom shot him a dark look. "You know I won't last a minute on the battlefield."

Not to be subdued, Puck countered, "Oh, I'd give you at least two minutes."

"Donkey."

A jarring knock sounded on the door of the library, and Thom's chin hit his chest in defeat. *Must everyone come in here today?* A library was supposed to be a place of silence. Peace. Learning. But apparently not today.

Puck strode to answer the door, and Thom heard the telltale creak of the hinges. "Well, hello there," said Puck.

By the tone of Puck's voice, Thom knew instantly that it was a girl. He slunk deeper into his chair and peeked over his left shoulder. Oh no...Marla. The chattiest and loudest kitchen maid he'd yet to meet. Thanks to Puck, he'd unfortunately met them all. Girls flocked to Puck like chickens to grain. It was terrifying.

Thom ducked his head and busied himself trimming the end of his quill, praying that she wouldn't pay him any notice. Marla's shrill laughter grated on his ears, and today was no exception as her voice pitched an octave higher at something Puck said. An object hit the ground with a thud, and Thom cringed, his fingers strangling his quill. It sounded like a book. A moment later, Marla's clomping footsteps approached his desk, and Thom reluctantly looked up. She stopped just to his left, his breakfast tray precariously balanced in one hand and a large book in the other. A grin split her face.

"You want this on the table like usual?"

The tray tilted dangerously. Thom's eyes widened, and he scarcely had time to splutter an incoherent warning before Puck snatched it from Marla's hands.

"Careful there, beautiful," said Puck with a chuckle.

She let out an embarrassed laugh, her cheeks blushing pink. "Oh, oops! Almost had a little spill, didn't I?" She handed Thom the leather tome. "Sorry about your book."

"It's fine," Thom mumbled, accepting the abused manuscript. This was far too much excitement for one day, let alone a barely hatched morning. For an unsettling moment, the thought of leaving these grand halls for the open air sounded appealing.

Puck set the food laden tray on a side table, far from Thom's documents, and escorted Marla out of the library. Relieved, Thom pushed out of his chair and approached his breakfast. There was a mug of brewed tea and a steaming bowl of oat porridge sprinkled with dried fruit. He inhaled appreciatively. Cinnamon. His favorite.

Hungry, Thom picked up the bowl of porridge and retreated once more to his chair. Grasping the wooden spoon, he ate, vaguely aware of Puck and Marla still speaking in the hall. The earthy flavors of boiled oats, dried cranberries, and cinnamon spread comfortingly across his tongue. Years ago, an older kitchen matron had started bringing him breakfast in the library when she noticed him skipping staff meals in favor of his work. Somehow, the tradition had continued even after she'd left her employment.

The conversation outside the library gradually trickled to a halt, and a single set of footsteps faded down the hall. Thom looked up to see Puck still standing in the doorway. By the expression on his friend's face, he was contemplating going after Marla.

Why? What could he possibly see in her?

If Thom was critical about it, he could appreciate the smattering of freckles across the girl's cheeks, the cute upturn of her nose, and the fact that Marla was always smiling—a rare trait in the war-weary city. She wasn't an unattractive girl nor was she unkind, but there was nothing about her or any of the other palace maids that made Thom want to hoof it down the hall after them. He'd yet to meet a girl with enough depth to warrant such a pursuit, and even if he did, Thom wasn't sure he'd have the nerve to talk to her like Puck undoubtedly would.

Puck ambled back over and leaned against a shelf.

"How do you do that?" Thom gestured with his spoon at the space Marla had occupied a minute before.

"Do what?"

"Talk to girls like that?"

Puck shrugged. "No different than talking to a man, I suppose." He winked. "Except they're prettier."

"Exactly."

Puck chuckled. "You might find it easier to talk to girls if you practiced talking to people in general."

Thom grunted and focused on his porridge. "I talk to you all the time."

"Other people."

Thom shook his head. "I'd rather read words than speak them."

"The Creator took an odd turn when he made you, my friend." Puck crossed his arms. "I'm heading home to pack. You coming?"

His anxiety returning, Thom shook his head. "I'll meet you there. I want to finish this piece."

Puck turned to go, and then paused, his face growing serious. "Don't even think about running, Thom. They'll kill Ma and Pa if you do."

"I know." Thom fidgeted with his spoon, not able to meet Puck's eyes. "I'll see you at home."

When he was alone again, Thom leaned further into his chair, rocking it onto its two rear legs. If it weren't for Puck's mother and father, the couple who'd taken Thom off the streets just after his eighth birthday, he might have tried to flee the draft. Puck was right, though. The military didn't bother hunting down deserters. No, they simply killed someone close to them—an effective, if not brutal, solution to the recent uptick in young men escaping the drafts. During the war's infancy, men had lined up to join the effort. However, over the last three months, rumors of unbelievable horrors and mass casualties had been finding their way north, and men were no longer volunteering to join.

But who was he kidding? Even if he had no one he cared about and found a way to slip out of the city, Thom was quite certain he wouldn't survive a week out in the wild. It had been too long since he'd been forced to scrape survival out of nothing.

Thom rose and began the soothing task of replacing the books piled on his trolley. Few patrons frequented the library these days, so most of the collections left out were because of him. The business of serving the war effort, finding enough food to fill their bellies, and grieving their young men had stolen most citizens' desire for knowledge. What abundance of free time could there be when work grew and young men didn't return from the front lines? Needled by restless thoughts, Thom swept the floor and set the breakfast tray out in the hall where one of the castle maids would collect it.

When his space was put back in order, Thom returned to his desk. He selected a fine-tipped quill, dipped it in ink, and got to work. With a steady hand, he carefully filled in the faded lines of the Wiise River to the northeast of Knor. Next, he outlined the forests to the south before moving to the nasty blot on the map. With precise strokes, he blended it into the forest until the stain almost looked like it belonged.

Cartography had always fascinated him. Perhaps, if he were less averse to the outdoors, he would have applied himself to learning the practical aspects of the trade more in depth—like his father before him. As it were, he satisfied himself with the academic side of maps, where he was less liable to get stuck in a bog, chewed on by mosquitos, or forced to live in a canvas tent for months on end. He loved studying the layout of the land and tracing the rivers, valleys, and roads of Lomair with his quill. In a way, it felt like he'd travelled the entire kingdom many times over.

Over the years, Thom had compared the castle's countless maps with the rough sketches and verbal descriptions he'd received from the army. Blending the information into accurate documents had made him an asset to the king. It was unlikely there was another in the kingdom with as much knowledge of the geographical nature of Lomair's changing borders as him. Odd that his usefulness had worn out.

With a sigh, Thom lost himself in the restoration of the time-faded map, and before he knew it, the familiar rattle of the evening food carts being pushed past the library on their way to the royal dining hall greeted his ears. Was it that time already? The map would have to be good enough.

Thom carefully stowed his supplies in a little wooden box. He started to put the map away and then stopped. No. He'd leave it on his desk, and when he was done with the war, he would walk through the library doors, pick up his quill, and put the final touches on it. Somehow, it felt like a promise that he would one day return.

With nimble fingers, he rolled up the stack of other maps and tucked them mindfully inside their leather canisters. Their turn on the restoration desk would have to come later. With no reason left to dally and no patrons to help, Thom closed the library and left the castle by the servants' exit.

Long shadows stretched across the narrow lane that led to the main road, and Thom lengthened his stride. Ma would not be pleased if he was late for dinner. He dodged a muddy hole in the broken cobblestones. The city of Knor was tired. A decade of war had starved the capital of healthy trade and skilled laborers. The signs of the city's distress were everywhere, from the buildings themselves to the people who lived in them. Paint peeled from the wooden walls of businesses. Vendors' shelves boasted precious few wares. And as for the folk themselves? Hems of dresses were frayed, jackets boasted more patches than actual fabric, and lines of worry had carved permanent furrows into far too many brows. The bitter tang of war had touched every corner of the once-grand capital city.

It was a brief walk home. The shop where Puck and his Pa worked was tucked right beside a small courtyard which led into their humble home. Their location near the castle was enviable but intentional, as it ensured the bread could be delivered fresh and hot every morning. Thom arrived just as Pa was shutting the door of his bakery.

"Evening, Thom." Pa was a man of few words but solid companionship, both traits Thom appreciated immensely.

"Evening."

Thom pushed open the gate. Together, they walked across the small courtyard and up the three steps to the front door. Sounds echoed: plates hitting the table with steady thuds, Ma scolding Puck to be more careful, and Puck's quick verbal defense. Pa's lips twitched as he shared an amused glance with Thom. The look vanished as Ma whirled around the corner, ladle in hand and apron swirling. Her round face was rosy from standing over the hot ovens all day and bustling about her kitchen.

"There you two are! I thought you'd be late!" Ma said.

"Never, my dear." Pa stooped to brush a kiss across her floured cheek as they entered. The low rumble and gentle cadence of his voice could pull the tension out of any space and dry the tears of the most anxious child. Ma was no exception. Her eyes softened as she looked up at her husband.

A clatter came from the dining room, and Ma stiffened. "Puck Pearcely, mind my dishes!" She abandoned her husband in the hall, hurrying to rescue her endangered cookware.

Thom smothered a smile as he hung his coat on its hook and then followed Pa into the small dining room. Chairs scraped against the scuffed wooden floor as they all pulled out their seats and sat. Puck reached for a fresh roll at the same moment Thom lifted his cup.

"Boys," Ma said. That single word, spoken in the tone only mothers can master, froze both young men.

Thom set his cup down and drew his hands into his lap. He shot a quick look at her face, her disapproving frown making him wince. "Sorry, Ma."

Puck groaned, his fingers still hovering over the platter. "Aww, Ma. I'm starving!"

She arched a brow at him. "You are most definitely not starving, young man."

Pa cleared his throat, and Puck slouched, crossing his arms as his father spoke the ritual words over their meal. "Creator, the land and seas and skies are Yours. The blessings of their bounty are Yours. We give as You have given to us."

Pa took the extra plate that sat on the table and served a helping of each dish onto the plate. He then handed it to Ma, who went to the door and set it outside on the step, as was the custom, and returned to her chair.

Thom watched the familiar rite he now knew by heart since coming to live with the Pearcelys. They worshiped the Creator, as did most of Lomair, and His laws of blessing ensured that the orphans and those less fortunate would not starve. The Creator provided for all who were His. Sipping his tea, Thom's mind drifted to his early years when he'd survived off plates such as the ones the Pearcelys left on their doorstep every evening.

"Merciful heavens, slow down, Puck!" Ma scolded.

Thom's gaze snapped to Puck, who, with cheeks bulging, was already reaching for another roll.

"I'm hungry, Ma," Puck said, his words muffled around a mouthful of food. He grabbed two more rolls.

She swatted his hand away with the ladle, guarding the plate. "Save some for Thom!"

It was a familiar conversation. The "lack of meat on his bones" was a source of personal consternation for Ma. Thom chose a roll and sank his teeth into the light brown crust. The flavor of freshly baked bread was one of his favorites.

Ma scooped a generous portion of stew into everyone's bowls, and Thom took a sip. The homey blend of potatoes, carrots, and spices spread across his tongue. "Ma, this is amazing."

Her face brightened. "Thank you, darling." She turned to her son. "Puck, how did the fields look today?"

Puck dunked his roll into his stew. "I'm no farmer, but they looked to be growing all right. The miller said the harvest should be in by the next full moon, and he'll make a delivery then."

Ma nodded. "Hopefully sooner, or we won't have bread by autumn with how fast they're burning our crops to the south."

Pa grunted. "No war talk."

The table fell silent for an awkward beat before Puck spoke. "Ma, I heard today that Josy and Karl down the street are expecting another babe this winter."

Thom lifted his spoon and gave Puck a subtle salute. Masterfully handled. There was nothing like an engagement or a new baby to make Puck's Ma forget everything else. Sure enough, the rest of the meal passed quickly as Ma peppered Puck with questions, to which he had few answers. No one else brought up the war or the unspoken certainty that Puck and Thom would be leaving in the morning. Dinner was like it was every night, and for that, Thom was grateful.

THUD. THUD. THUD.

Three hard hits rattled the door. Four sets of eyes swung toward it.

"What on earth?" Pa heaved himself to his feet as Ma started for the door. "Hold on, dear. I'll get it," Pa rumbled.

THUD. THUD.

"I'm coming! Keep your britches on!" Pa bellowed.

Puck shot Thom a wary look, before springing up to follow Pa. Thom heard the door hinges creak, then a soft cry from Ma. The sound of her distress drove Thom to his feet. In four quick strides, he'd crossed the small dining room and joined his family in the crowded entryway. Two capital guards stood in the doorway, dressed in navy cloaks and silver helmets.

"By order of the king," the soldier, who boasted a wicked scar across his face, began, "all men between the ages of thirteen to forty years are ordered to report for military duty." His gaze swept the interior of the home and landed on Puck and Thom. The scar-faced man spoke to his companion, "There are two here, besides the baker."

The second soldier stepped forward, a book in his hand. "Names."

Puck subtly maneuvered himself between the soldiers and the rest of the family. "Sir, we were told to report in the morning."

The book-wielding officer frowned. "And you will." His green eyes flashed. "Name."

"Puck Pearcely," Puck replied, his voice even, and Ma let out a muffled gasp.

Thom slipped an arm around her, hugging her close. "It'll be okay." Sweat slicked his palms. It was happening. The draft was really happening.

"You there. Name!" the officer barked, addressing Thom.

"Thom Darkfell." His sire's name. The only thing Thom had ever received from a man he barely recalled. According to Thom's mother, he'd been a cartographer, traveling extensively around Lomair and Abadonia, mapping the countryside. His trips were lengthy, and somewhere between Thom's third and fourth birthday, he'd failed to return home. Not long after, creditors had seized their home and forced Thom and his mother to the streets.

Those memories were bleak. Filled with hunger. Dark shadows. And fear. For reasons unknown to his young mind, Thom's mother had kept them moving from village to village, city to city, always restless and constantly looking over her shoulder. She'd never explained why they'd leave a place or how she'd choose their next destination, but Thom knew they ran from something. Or *someone*. For five years, they'd eked out a meager survival, until Thom's mother had fallen ill and died. Puck's ma had found him shortly thereafter. *Thank the Creator.*

The scarred guard spoke again, jarring Thom. "Report to the south gate by dawn." He gave them both a hard look that warned them not to defy his words and left.

Puck shut the door and bolted it. The silence in the small home was deafening as they all stared at each other. The façade of normalcy they'd maintained over dinner was gone. Puck and Thom were going to war.

"Leave the dishes." Ma's voice cracked. "We best get you boys packed."

Chapter 2

Star Daughter

Norealle crouched in a treasure trove of wild herbs, picking the best ones to season her mother's dinner with. The savory aromas of dill, sage, and rosemary were making her hungry. She hastened her clippings.

A lyrical voice startled her. "Would you like to visit the stars with me, daughter?"

Sheepishly, she smiled up at the radiant woman. "I didn't hear you coming, Mother."

A soft laugh, reminiscent of starlight and dreams, tinkled from her mother's pale pink lips. "You were very absorbed." Merriment danced in her gray eyes.

Affection washed over Norealle. "I'd love to come with you." She paused snipping off another piece of dill. "Are we going right now?"

"How about after dinner? You can join me in the dance tonight."

Her heart leapt. "Oh, yes, please!" She made no effort to hide her excitement as a grin spread across her face.

The dance! It was set in the grand ballroom of the darkened heavens, overseen by Silmea's twin moons, Ethos and Caris. The stars, in all their sparkling glory, twirled the night away across their expansive stage, their joyful dance lighting the worlds far beneath them. For as long as Norealle could remember, her mother had sung about and told her stories of the starlit dance. How Norealle had dreamed of joining her one day, but alas, as only a half-star, she'd never grown strong enough to soar the firmament alone. Instead, her mother occasionally bore her to the heavens and twirled her across the night skies in her arms. Even though she was now a grown woman of nineteen, she still loved to go.

Norealle watched as a warm breeze stirred her mother's hair, causing the cascading white waves to ripple on their way down to her bare feet. Even beneath the sun, light emanated from every pore of her mother's body. She was dazzling. For her part, Norealle took after her father, a man of soil and forests. Her hair was the color of a dark oak and her eyes an earthy brown, but she had the willowy figure and snow-kissed complexion of the stars.

A maternal hand gently touched her cheek.

"I'll see you at home soon?" her mother asked.

Norealle bobbed her head. "Yes, I'm nearly finished."

Her mother glided away, her feet barely kissing the forest floor as she walked. Dropping her attention to the herbs, Norealle finished the task, anticipation hurrying her hands. It had been weeks since she'd attended the starlit dance.

A feminine scream rent the air.

Norealle sprang to her feet, herbs fluttering to the ground. "Mother?" Her voice pitched high, carrying through the trees. Her dark eyes darted, probing the leafy foliage. What could have possibly caused her mother to cry out? The valley where they lived was a peaceful sanctuary.

An anguished wail, farther away this time, cut through the forest. Norealle broke into a run. Her leather-shod feet flew across the ground as grass slapped her bare shins, and branches snagged her loose hair. "Mother!" The call tore from her throat as she ran. There was no answer.

Norealle burst out of the woods into the sweeping green meadow that bordered their mountain home. Several paces away, a creature of darkness stood, her mother's limp body dangling from its saliva-encrusted jaws. Its scaled talons bit into the earth, and its crimson eyes bored into her. The stench of blood and sulfur hit her nostrils.

She screamed. And screamed.

"Norealle!" Someone shook her. "Wake up, daughter."

Dazed, Norealle felt herself lifted out of the dark mire of her mind. Her father's bearded face hovered over hers, his sorrow-creased eyes peering worriedly down at her. Grief had carved deep shadows beneath his eyes. "Was it the same dream?"

Norealle slowly sat up and rubbed her eyes. "Yes," she whispered weakly.

Her lips trembled, and despite her effort to hold them at bay, tears trickled down her cheeks. Rough fingers tenderly brushed them away, and she miserably met her father's gaze. "I miss her so much."

"As do I." His soft timbre pulled her in, and Norealle leaned forward, curling into her father's barrel chest. Strong arms wrapped around her, pulling her close.

Nearly three months had passed since her mother had gone alone to visit the stars and never returned. Through his gift of Sight, her father had discerned that the dark inhabitants of Zakar had broken through the wall El'Ohim had built hundreds of years ago. The stars had confirmed that Norealle's mother had fallen trying to stop the breach. At first, Norealle had refused to believe she was dead, but it had been months. Hope was no more.

"Do you want to go for a walk?" her father inquired tenderly.

Turning her face against his leather vest, Norealle peered toward the entrance of their cave. It was still dark outside. Dawn had not yet painted the skies with her palette of pinks and yellows. "No. I don't want to see them."

By "them," she knew her father understood what she meant. The stars. She couldn't bear to look upon their glimmering light knowing that her mother was no longer among them. A deep sigh rumbled out of her father's chest as he gazed into her face.

"You can't avoid the darkness forever, daughter."

"I know."

But darkness without light was unbearable, and without her mother, there was no light. Even El'Ohim's presence, a comforting warmth that resided in her soul, seemed dim and far away.

Chapter 3

Worn Boots & Tired Men

It was well before dawn, but shuffling footsteps and the odd bump and clatter from the kitchen warned Thom that Ma was already up. Rising from his comfortable bed, Thom tugged on a pair of hand-knit wool socks Ma had made him and a matching brown sweater. Both were thick and warm. Unlike Puck who was strapped with muscle and never complained about being cold, Thom was lean, and the icy winds from the north had a way of nipping straight at his bones.

Across the room, Puck tugged a shirt over his head and shuffled out the door to the kitchen. Thom cast his eyes about the small room he'd shared with Puck since they were boys. There was a bed on each side, hand carved by the carpenter two streets over, topped with straw-filled mattresses. A single wardrobe, made from light pine, contained both their clothes. The room was simple, but the memories it held were priceless—like the char mark in the middle of the floor where Puck had once tried to light a campfire while they were pretending to be explorers.

"Thom?" Ma's voice beckoned him from the kitchen.

"Coming!"

Thom blew out a quick breath and left the room, shutting the solid wood door behind him. Ma was bustling about the kitchen, but to Thom's surprise, Pa, who was usually in the bakery at this hour, was standing near the door talking to Puck. Ma hurried over to Thom and pressed a cloth-wrapped offering into his hand that smelled suspiciously like cinnamon-flavored rolls—his and Puck's favorite.

Worry wrinkled her brow and filled her voice. "Here you are, in case they don't feed you breakfast this morning. You best get going. Better to be early than late."

"I'm sure they'll feed us," Thom reassured her. "Hungry men can't fight well."

"Still..." Her voice trailed off. She looked near tears.

Thom shifted his gaze. If she started to cry...

He retreated to his bag and tucked the pastries inside while Puck did the same. Out of the corner of his eye, Thom saw Ma clasp her work-worn hands to her mouth. Candlelight flickered across her face, revealing the teary glisten on her cheeks. Puck marched over to his Ma and folded her into a hug. He held her for a long moment before moving to his father.

Thom took his place. *For pity's sake, don't cry,* he mentally begged himself, but a shuddering breath escaped his lungs as Ma wrapped him in her warm embrace. Dropping his head, he pressed his face against her soft shoulder. In an instant, he was transported to another time when she'd held him like this. He'd been an eight-year-old orphan, wounds still fresh from losing his mother, and terrified of the world he'd been left alone in. The tang of fear tasted the same then as it did now.

"I don't want to go, Ma," Thom choked out. He knew he should be braver, stronger...but *war*?

"I know," she murmured. "But you will do well. You always do things better than you think you will. And I will pray for you. Every day."

Her hand stroked up and down his back, and Thom squeezed his eyes shut. The lavender scent of her hair and the aroma of freshly baked bread that clung to her skin drifted comfortingly up his nose. For twelve years, she'd been his Ma, and this had been his home. He wasn't ready to leave it.

Behind him, he could hear Puck shoving his feet in his boots. Ma's arms tightened around Thom, and he swallowed hard.

"Let's go, Thom!" Puck huffed impatiently.

Slowly, Thom released Ma. Pa moved into his blurry line of vision and enfolded him in a quick, hard hug. Neither spoke. Thom pulled away, shoved on his boots, and grabbed his cloak. Pa handed him his bag, and Thom slung it over his shoulder.

Drawing in a deep breath, he stepped outside into the chilly morning air. Despite the crisp breeze that stirred from the north, the musty smells of the tired city still lingered. Puck shifted from foot to foot on the bottom step, eagerness evident in every line of his fit body.

"You boys take care of each other, you hear?" Pa spoke gruffly from the doorway, cradling Ma's hand as she valiantly held back her remaining tears.

"Aye," said Thom thickly. "We will."

Puck grinned. "Don't worry. Thom will make sure we don't have any fun."

"And you mind him, Puck Pearcely! And listen to your officers!" said Ma.

A wink was all the answer Ma got from Puck before he grabbed Thom's arm and tugged him down the walkway. Dawn was fast approaching. They both paused at the gate to wave and then headed south down the cobblestone street. Their feet carried them past the residence of the tailor, and beneath the low-hanging placard of an inn that traveling merchants used to frequent in droves before the war had dried up trade routes. In the last few years, its beds were rarely filled to capacity. The next block contained the livery, and Thom frowned as the strong odor of horses, manure, and moldy hay assaulted him. Next was the smithy, conveniently located beside the stables, followed by the tanner. No business prospered. Every storefront they passed desperately needed a fresh coat of paint and a healthy restocking of wares.

They reached the south gate as the first tendrils of dawn stretched across the sky. Thom's steps slowed. *This is it.*

The desire to drop his sack and run spasmed through Thom's chest. Beyond that wall was the start of his new life. A life he'd never wanted and never asked for. His steps faltered.

"Keep walking," Puck warned grimly. "Shoulders back. Head up. Don't let them see you as weak." Puck jutted his chin in the direction of the gate. A small group of guardsmen watched them.

Thom squared his shoulders, forcing his body to obey Puck's commands. His pulse thundered in his ears. As they approached, the haggard appearance of the soldiers became obvious; the night guard had not yet changed.

Puck spoke first, confidence ringing in his tone. "Puck Pearcely, reporting for duty."

A gray-haired soldier with a tobacco-stained beard sized them both up. "Here a bit early, aren't you?"

"I'm used to early mornings," Puck answered easily.

The grizzled soldier chuckled. "When you get to be my age, you take every moment of sleep you can." As he spoke, he consulted a roll of parchment before making a notation, then settled his tired gaze on Thom. "And you are?"

"Thom Darkfell," said Thom quietly.

The soldier glanced at his parchment again before gesturing them through the gate. "Unit Three under Lieutenant Commander Drayen. Follow the road out, then head east. Units one through seven are on the east side, eight to fourteen on the west. You'll find it."

Subdued, Thom followed Puck beneath the rough-hewn timbers of the archway and over the wooden drawbridge that spanned the algae-filled moat. Their footsteps echoed dully on the travel-worn bridge, and after about fifteen paces, their boots landed on the dirt road.

Thom paused, taking in the foreign scene stretching out before him. The fall sun, its position on the horizon notably lower than it had been a mere month ago, crested the rolling hills to the east. Long shadows, cast from the quarry-hewn stones of Knor's walls, stretched down the Southern Road. Vast fields, dotted by small farming hovels, textured the land as far as his eyes could see to the south and west. To the north lay the grazing hill country, which would eventually give rise to the towering mountains of the far north.

"Come on, Thom," Puck urged, already a half dozen paces down the dusty road.

"Sorry," Thom called and hastened to catch up. "The camp is bigger than I thought."

"Aye. It's about a mile wide. They had to expand it with the latest draft."

Thom stared, easily believing Puck's estimate. Knor's recruitment site now occupied the entire strip of farmland that fanned out directly from Knor's walls. The earth was badly trampled, and nothing remained of the crops except stubble and dirt. The sprawl of canvas and leather tents covered every available foot of ground.

How many men did the draft pull in?

Despite the early hour, the war camp was already waking. Men's voices and the clanging of equipment carried up to the Southern Road.

"Well, let's find Unit Three." Puck veered off the road and followed a set of wagon ruts into the encampment. The crude path branched. Puck took the larger one, but Thom paused at the fork.

"East is this way," he called.

Puck pivoted and doubled back. "Right."

"More like left."

Puck chortled and took the lead. All around them, men sleepily emerged from large rectangular tents. They passed row after row of barracks, mess tents, smithies, and other tent structures which Thom could only guess as to their purposes. As they walked, the true vastness of the war camp became evident.

Overwhelmed, Thom darted a worried look at Puck. "How are we going to find Unit Three in all of this?"

Amusement sparked in Puck's blue eyes as he slid Thom a sideways glance. "You *ask*." He grabbed the elbow of a scrawny soldier who couldn't have been much over thirteen. "Kid, where do we find Unit Three?"

"Keep headin' straight," the lad pointed directly east, shaking off Puck's grip, "and you'll bump right into it."

"There you have it," Puck declared and barreled forward.

Thom followed, absorbing his surroundings. Twice someone stumbled around Puck's hulking frame, only to bump into Thom's narrower one.

Puck snorted a laugh. "There it is."

Sure enough, there was a square white tent with a number three painted in black across the door flap. A red-haired lad in a baggy uniform sat on a bucket in front of the tent with a creased parchment in hand. Like the quill dangling carelessly in his fingers, the lad with drooping eyes looked ready to tumble off his perch.

"I guess that works," said Thom dryly as they approached.

"Is this Unit Three?" Puck's voice jolted the poor sap out of his almost slumber. The bucket wobbled, and Thom was certain the boy would land on his bottom.

"Aye," the lad squeaked. His pimpled cheeks reddened, and he gripped the parchment in both hands, showing how it had come by all its wrinkles. "Names?"

Thom edged forward to spare the boy more of Puck. "I'm Thom Darkfell, and this is Puck Pearcely. We were told to come to Unit Three."

"Well, you found it," he mumbled before leaning forward to squint at the parchment. His lips moved, clearly trying to decipher the letters.

Thom glanced at the upside-down document and tapped his finger on his and Puck's names. "Right there, and that's not how you spell Unit Three. Here, hand me that quill."

"Don't matter how it's spelt," the lad groused.

Thom frowned. Inaccuracies always mattered.

A tall man, with the black uniform of an officer and the bright-blue epaulets of a lieutenant commander, leaned out of the tent behind the lad.

His gaze settled on Thom. "You read?"

"I do." Thom answered.

Despite an appearance that suggested he was only in his mid- to late twenties, the lieutenant commander was highly decorated, with the number of campaign bars sewn over his heart numbering at least twenty.

He must have joined the army right when the war started.

"You there." The lieutenant commander stabbed a finger at the boy. "Stop crumpling that list and give it to him."

The lad's eyes lit up, and he joyfully shoved the offending document and worn quill into Thom's unsuspecting hands.

Thom's new commanding officer gestured at the parchment. "Mark off the recruits as they arrive and send them to the wagon to get a uniform. Let me know when everyone is here." Orders given, he disappeared back into his tent.

Bewildered at the odd turn of events, Thom sat stiffly down on the bucket, the worst sort of work desk there ever was. Nonetheless, he felt absurdly thankful for the quill in his hand and parchment on his lap.

Puck shook with silent laughter. "You're in the army for ten minutes, and you already have a quill in your hand. Come find me later." Still chuckling to himself, Puck sauntered to the uniform wagon.

Thom stared down at the long list of names. He was going to be here a while. But at least he didn't have a sword in his hand. Yet.

Hours passed. Thom's rear grew numb. Apparently, "arrive at dawn" had a variety of meanings ranging from the first rays of light to nearly noon for some folk. Thom sighed as he finally struck the last name off the list and pointed the recruit in the direction of the uniform wagon. The motions had become rote. Thom's stomach growled. He'd finished the warm cinnamon roll Ma had sent with him hours ago, and it was long past the time he typically had his oatmeal and tea. Stiff, he stood.

"Sir?" he called into the tent.

A moment later, the lieutenant commander pushed aside the tent flap and held out his hand. Thom passed him the list of crossed-out names and quill. Up close, Thom could see that Lieutenant Commander Drayen was at least as tall as Puck, but far thinner. His cheeks were hollow in a way that suggested a lack of food, not just an intense amount of physical exertion. Dark smudges of exhaustion smeared purple beneath his eyes, and weariness creased his face. His appearance didn't bode well for Thom's future.

"Everyone came?"

"They did."

The lieutenant commander rolled up the parchment. "Good. Get in uniform, then come back here. I have another job for you."

"Yes, sir."

Hopefully not another job that involves sitting on a bucket for hours.

Rotating his shoulders to work the stiffness out of them as he walked, Thom approached the wagon. It was propped up on a rock to support a missing spoked wheel. The wood on its side was charred, and the mound of clothing and boots piled inside didn't look to be in much better shape than the vessel that held them. A blond-haired soldier leaned against the wagon, picking at his fingernails.

"Are these the uniforms for the third division?" Thom questioned. He certainly hoped so, since he'd been sending men here all morning.

"Yep." The soldier reached into the pile and grabbed a long-sleeved shirt, a pair of pants, and a vest. He tossed them unceremoniously at Thom who caught them with a frown. They looked used and more than a little soiled. He lifted them to his nose and sniffed. Urine.

Disgusting.

"Excuse me, is there anything clean?"

The young man grunted and waved his hand at the cart. "Probably not, but you can look for yourself."

Thom hoisted himself into the bed of the wagon and began the unsavory task of rifling through the load of clothes and other belongings. The entire pile reeked of sweat and some nameless stench. Some garments were torn, others had blood on them, and Thom had the sinking suspicion that these were uniforms removed from soldiers who would not be needing them anymore. Was their army truly in such a dire situation that they were clothing their new recruits in the gear of their fallen men?

Thom finally found a matching set of brown pants and shirt which looked mostly clean and roughly his size. With a jump, he leapt off the creaking wagon. The soldier shoved a pair of tall leather boots, coated with dried mud and badly scuffed, into Thom's arms along with a belt.

Thom glanced around. "Where do we change?"

The soldier let out a guffaw. "Wherever you pretty well please." He pointed to Thom's right. "Barracks are that way, but don't expect no privacy. Can't even take a pee in private here."

Thom headed in the direction of the barracks, his mind racing. His stomach growled again, giving him something to focus on.

I'll change, and then I need to find some real food.

Locating an empty tent, Thom ducked under the rawhide flap. Rumpled mats and worn bags lined both sides. With the soldier's warning ringing in his ears, he hastily changed into his uniform. The pants were too loose, but the belt held them in place. He kicked off his own shoes, dropped them in his sack, and shoved on the tall boots he'd been given. To his relief, they fit well. Thom stepped over to a broken piece of glass someone had propped against a pallet, next to a box holding several shaving blades, and peered in.

His own serious brown eyes, set above the shadowy scruff that he hadn't bothered to shave off that morning, stared back at him. Thom straightened the collar of his uniform, hardly recognizing the soldier in the mirror. The garments fit loose on him, but that was expected. He'd always been lean despite Ma's daily attempts to change that. Thank the Creator he wasn't also short.

Thom touched the empty bar over his chest. Either the person who'd worn the uniform before him had died in their first battle, or the uniform people had stripped the campaign bars off before throwing the shirt in the wagon.

How long until they strip it off my dead carcass? The woeful thought settled heavily in his mind.

His stomach gave another snarl of hunger, and he gritted his teeth, shoving the depressing thought away. *Buck up. Time to find food. Then return to the lieutenant commander.*

Thom threw his old clothes into his bag and followed his nose. A minute later, he found himself in the doorway of a smoky tent. Several men were chopping vegetables, kneading bread, and scrubbing dishes. At one end of the table sat a large basket of crusty-looking buns with burnt edges.

He edged closer to one of the cooks. "Excuse me."

The man's hands didn't slow, his knife thudding rhythmically into the board as he chopped a potato.

Thom cleared his throat.

Still no response.

He raised his voice. "When is the noon meal?"

The man stopped chopping and shot Thom an annoyed look. "Two meals, lad. Breakfast and supper. Grab a bun and get out."

Thom snagged a bun and backed away. "Thanks."

He bit into it, chewing as he walked. The bun was hard and salty, but it would fill the empty void in his stomach. Reaching the tent with the painted three, Thom shoved the last of the morsel into his mouth and pushed inside.

"There you are." Lieutenant Commander Drayen looked up from a square desk as Thom entered. "I was starting to think you'd gotten lost."

Thom shook his head and swallowed, suddenly unsure if he should have sought out the mess tent. "No, sir."

The man's grave eyes assessed him, and Thom had the feeling he didn't miss anything.

"What's your training?"

Eager to redeem himself, Thom spoke quickly. "I read and write fluently in both our language and that of the Abadonians. I'm skilled at document restoration as well as basic cartography. I managed the Royal Library in Knor and have been providing geographical research for the war effort over the last few years."

The lieutenant commander looked mildly surprised but pleased. "You'll do nicely, then. My last assistant was killed. I am Lieutenant Commander Drayen, and you will work for me."

Thom paled. "Killed...in battle, sir?"

"No. Plague." Drayen stood. "There are a lot of ways to die in the army." He handed Thom a small stack of papers. "I need these all copied five times each. Share what you read with anyone, and I'll permanently station you on the front line." He paused. "Your name?"

Thom blinked. "Understood." He took the papers. "And it's Thom, sir."

"Come find me on the training grounds when that's done." Drayen swept the door aside. "And use the desk."

The flap slapped closed behind him, leaving Thom alone in the dimly lit tent. Gripping the papers, Thom sat and picked up the commander's finely carved quill. He scanned the words quickly.

"Greetings, Lieutenant Commander Drayen Ward,

We are in retreat and pray that we can reach Knor by month's end. Our situation is dire. We have lost many men to the cursed abominations employed by the Abadonians. We will fall back to the capital and make our defense there. Be ready, for our enemy pursues our every step. Please inform the king.

—General Cain"

Month's end...but that was in ten days. Thom's mouth grew dry as he stared at the paper. The war was coming here? To the very capital? With quick, even strokes, Thom copied the letter onto five separate pieces of browned parchment. It did not take long to finish the task.

Ten days. The knowledge beat through Thom's brain like a drum in a rhythm of doom. Snatching up the papers, he left the tent at a jog. Finding the training grounds was simple: he followed the sounds of shouting and cursing. Sure enough, just beyond the last line of tents, hundreds of men were practicing with swords or engaging in hand-to-hand combat. They looked like bumbling fools.

This was the army that would defend their king and capital city? Unease tightened Thom's chest. The latest draft had conscripted the sad remnants of Lomair's men. Even to his untrained eye, it was clear that the training field was filled with the too young, the too old, farmers, scholars, and those that were previously unfit to serve in the army.

None of us will be battle ready in ten days.

The grave realization clouded his mind as Thom scanned the uneven lines of sparring men before spotting the lieutenant commander's black uniform with its blue epaulets amidst the flood of brown. Thom hurried over, dodging scuffling fighters and men slashing swords.

"Lieutenant Commander Drayen?" Thom called.

The man turned at his name, surprise flickering across his face. "You can't be done already?"

Thom handed him the papers. "Aye, sir."

A brief smile twitched at the corners of the commander's mouth, then he gestured at a wagon filled with weapons. "Grab a sword, scholar."

"A real one?" *Surely not.*

Drayen's expression turned grim. "Aye, there's no time to train with wooden toys. You've got to learn the weight and feel of your blade as quickly as possible."

So much for hoping his penmanship would save him from wielding anything other than a quill. With the noose of dread tightening around his throat, Thom moved on heavy feet to select a sword. He had no clue what he was looking for in a weapon, so he simply chose one that looked straight and had a solid-looking handle.

A tool of death. Thom's fingers tightened on the hilt as he stared down at the long, chipped blade. *So I can kill.*

Woodenly, he joined the line of practicing recruits.

"You! Sword up. Spread those feet!" A captain stomped toward him, and Thom hastily lifted his sword.

"It's not a flagpole, you ninny! It's a sword. Here, like this." The man grabbed Thom's sword out of his hand and demonstrated the stance before thrusting it back against his chest. Thom grabbed it.

"Now swing," the captain barked. "Get the feel of the weight. Faster!"

Two hours later, Thom stood fighting to catch his breath, sweat dripping down his face. Evidently, working in a library did not build strong muscles or endurance. His arm shook as he lifted his weapon for what felt like the thousandth time and executed the unfamiliar motions of stabbing, swinging, and blocking.

All around him, men carved their swords in similar patterns. It was a miracle they hadn't accidentally decapitated each other. Nearby, a captain shouted at an unfortunate soldier. Thom clenched his jaw and swung his blade again before stabbing it at an imaginary foe. The sun beat down on his sweat-plastered head.

"All right men, grab a partner and let's try it again," a captain ordered.

Thom awkwardly sheathed his sword before planting his hands on his knees, panting for breath. *Hell. This is hell.*

"Thom!"

He looked up to see Puck striding toward him with an exuberant grin on his face, the blade at his side lending him a swagger that Thom could only envy.

Thom straightened and headed towards Puck, his scabbard slapping against his leg with every step and tilting his balance uncomfortably to the right. "Unbelievable," Thom grumbled, thrusting his hand onto the hilt to leverage the weapon away from his legs. He couldn't even walk with the blighted thing!

Puck stopped in front of Thom and studied his slipping sword belt with a frown. "Can you cinch that up tighter?"

"Any tighter and I won't be able to walk at all."

Puck snorted. "Fair enough. Let's practice."

The rest of the afternoon passed painfully, with every drill designed to maximize Thom's misery—or so it felt. One of the captains finally ordered them off the field for dinner just as the sun began to set. They joined the line of hungry, stinky men, and after a long wait, found themselves with a bowl of nameless chunky soup. Puck eyed it like it might bite him, but Thom was too tired to care what it looked like or even what it tasted like. For better or worse, it didn't taste like much, and he gulped the whole bowl down without complaint.

The missive from earlier drifted hauntingly through his brain. *Ten days*. Could any of them be ready in that amount of time? A cold breeze that warned of winter's impending arrival moved through the camp, and he shivered. What he wouldn't do for a warm hearth, a cup of tea, and a book. As it was, he'd settle for a sturdy canvas tent to cut the wind.

"Hurry up and finish," Thom groused at Puck. "It's getting cold out here."

Puck swallowed the rest of his soup and stood. "Yeah, let's find our tent before there are no good spots left."

Thom wasn't sure what a "good" spot looked like, but he followed Puck as they retrieved their bags and located their assigned barracks.

"Welcome home," Puck chuckled as they stopped in front of the drooping structure.

The tent looked like it had been through a war, which Thom reckoned it had. The once white canvas was stained brown, and soot discolored the dipping roof. Rips ran down the flanks of the tent and its frayed edges flapped in the breeze. With wide eyes, Thom noted the tent pole that had been replaced by a gnarled tree branch. Overall, the structure didn't look like it would be able to withstand someone bumping into its side, let alone a significant wind or rainfall.

Thom cautiously ducked inside. The interior was a haze of smoke as men lounged, puffing on wooden pipes. He blinked as his eyes began to tear, and he gritted his teeth to hold back a cough. Ahead of him, Puck picked his way down the aisle between the makeshift beds until he came to the empty ones. He dropped his gear and flopped down onto a mat as if he slept in an army camp every night.

Thom unbuckled his sword. With every muscle protesting, he sat and unlaced his boots.

"Leave 'em on, lad," a gruff voice to his left spoke. "There are rats in the camp, and ye' don't want them chewing on yer' toes."

Just like when I lived on the streets.

Memories Thom had long ago smothered rose to the forefront of his mind as he retied his boots. He was going to have to remember the skills he'd learned as a homeless child and forget the comforts he'd grown accustomed to.

Troubled, Thom tugged his small sack of belongings close and lay down.

Chapter 4
Feast of Flesh

Slager strode through the victorious Abadonian army, consisting of tens of thousands of muscular, hard-eyed men garbed in leather armor. Many leaned on their cruelly-tipped spears and others stood, feet widely planted, with callused hands still gripping the hilts of their thick broadswords and battleaxes. Sweat soaked their brows, and the blood of their enemies dripped from their weapons.

The Abadonians shifted away from him, their gazes following him distrustfully. Slager ignored them and set his course for the heart of the battlefield. The soldiers of Lomair had fallen like wheat beneath a scythe under the combined strength of his Zakarian errgoths and the Abadonian warriors. They'd successfully taken most of Lomair over the last three months. All that lay between them and victory was the final stronghold of Knor, and it would not stand against the coming onslaught.

Titus, lord of Zakar, was pleased.

Reaching the site of the battle, Slager crossed his arms and watched as the errgoths feasted on the slain. Their large, reptilian forms crouched over the bodies, their teeth and fangs ripping and tearing as they gorged themselves, impartial to whether the flesh was Lomairian, Abadonian, or even one of their own.

The men behind him shifted restlessly. He could feel their rage and fear as they mutinously watched the errgoths devour their kin. Slager's lips twisted into a dark smile. They feared the loss of their death rites and the accompanying offerings to their deities. The petty gods of wood and stone they worshiped would not save them from the emptiness of death, even if their ridiculous rites were performed. How little they knew.

Fools.

"I thought we agreed that they would not desecrate our dead!" a furious voice roared from behind him.

Slager did not turn. The thundering manner gave away the speaker. It was the hulking leader of the Abadonians. King Scaul. A mountain of a man who led by brute force.

"I'm afraid you misunderstood, Your Highness," Slager answered smoothly as he pivoted to face the king.

"You told me you would control your monsters!" Spittle flew from the king's lips as he clenched his fists. Rage burned in the depths of his black eyes.

Slager regarded the king with contempt. "I believe I said I would keep them from eating your men."

"Exactly!"

Slager's eyes glinted. "And I have. Those are no longer men. They are corpses. Unless you wish to go argue with my errgoths?"

King Scaul's face flushed scarlet, and a vein bulged on his forehead. "I've about had enough of you and your...your..." He waved a hand at the beasts that prowled the ravaged battlefield, as if the mere sight of them numbed his brain into a complete state of paralysis.

Slager moved like a viper, fingers curling around the king's throat as his dagger pressed against the larger man's jugular. He snapped open a crimson portal. With startled shouts, the king's guards leapt forward, their blades ringing from their scabbards. Slager threw wide another portal, and the men fell into oblivion, their screams swallowed by the darkness. The remaining soldiers stumbled back, their wide eyes flickering between their king and Slager.

Pressing the king to the brink of the portal, Slager snarled, "If you wish to betray the lord of Zakar, I will let you tell him yourself. He will take great pleasure in carving your flesh to ribbons."

King Scaul swore, eyes flashing pure hatred. "Release me!" His fingers wrapped around Slager's wrists, and he muscled the blade away from his throat.

The men stumbled apart, eyeing each other like two predators circling for a kill.

"Keep your monsters off my men," said King Scaul. "Or your lord, or whatever he calls himself, can forget his deal."

A spasm of panic twanged through Slager's warped soul as a tendril of his control slipped. He didn't have enough errgoths to destroy Knor without the Abadonian army. Not yet.

Slager widened his portal, leaning on his threat. "I could drop your whole army into the abyss for your insolence."

King Scaul's mouth pressed into a hard line. "You won't. You need us."

Not for much longer. Then we'll see who is smiling when Titus has his blade to your throat and your people enslaved!

With a sneer, Slager unfurled a strand of magic and laid a path through The Inbetween, the space between the worlds, and stomped out of the Human Realm to update his master.

Chapter 5

Eldehein

"Up and at it, men!"

The booming voice jarred Thom from the light sleep he'd finally succumbed to. Between the cold and the way his bones had protested every position he tried to find solace in, he hadn't slept much. Apparently, years of a comfortable bed had weakened his ability to sleep on the ground. Thom labored to his feet. Beside him, Puck was already up and eagerly strapping on his sword belt.

Right. The sword.

Thom picked it up, not even trying to hide his frown. The blasted thing felt twice as heavy as it had the day before, and his blistered hands protested the mere idea of gripping the hilt. His movements decidedly less enthusiastic than Puck's, he strapped the blade to his hip and followed the other yawning recruits as they shuffled out of the tent.

Caught in the slow-moving tide of men, Thom found himself in a long line stretching to the mess tent. The first fingers of dawn crept over the eastern hills as they waited, but the meager light did nothing for the night chill that still clung relentlessly to the air. Thom shivered and shoved his hands into his pant pockets. He puffed out a breath of frosty mist, and it hung in the air for a moment before dissipating. The line slowly shrank, and Thom gratefully accepted the mug and bowl that were shoved into his hands by a harassed-looking cook in a worn leather apron.

The soldier in front of Thom muttered, "My blasted chickens eat better than this slop."

Thom didn't reply. The mug was filled with plain hot water, and the bowl held a hunk of bread thrust into mushy oats.

Better than starving.

Thom glanced around for a place to sit. The ground was covered in hard frost, and there were no empty benches. Leaving the glut of grumbling men, he found a vacant spot beside an empty wagon. Propping his hip against it, he set his bowl down on the running board and took a sip from his mug. The hot liquid flowed down his throat and thawed his chilled insides.

Puck joined him a minute later. He was frowning. Curious, Thom watched his friend pick up the piece of bread like it was a dead rodent and pinch it between his thumb and forefinger.

"It's *stale*," Puck choked out, aghast.

Dipping the bread into his gruel, Thom let it absorb some moisture before crunching into it. "Just soak it."

Stale bread and mushy porridge were a king's portion compared to what he'd scrounged off the streets as a child. Years of eating well at the Pearcelys' table hadn't erased those early memories.

Puck ignored him and continued to examine the offensive offering miserably. "It's at least two days old." He reluctantly took a nibble and his face contorted into a grimace.

"I'd say at least three or four days old," Thom countered. Unwilling to go hungry, he tore off another chunk of bread and chewed with the required vigor.

"It's not edible!"

A smiled ghosted across Thom's face. "We've been drafted, are sleeping on the ground with the rats, and you're worried about stale bread?"

Puck finally mimicked Thom and plowed his bread moodily through the questionable slop, forcing it to soak up moisture. "Food's not a laughing matter," he muttered, before taking an overly large bite of his breakfast.

Thom shook his head. The military rations, while bland and begging for some of Ma's spices, were far better than going hungry.

"Get your lazy lumps off the ground! Breakfast is over," a voice, likely one of the captains, barked. "To the training grounds. Hurry your hides!"

Thom threw the last piece of bread into his mouth and swallowed it with a swig of water. Dumping his clay mug and wooden plate into an overflowing box made of wagon panels, Thom followed the other recruits to the trodden field. Beside him, Puck had apparently recovered from his traumatic breakfast and was eagerly eyeing the field of torture. A long row of straw targets stood like sentinels, and a pile of bows and arrows lay at the feet of each impatient captain. Thom's heart sank.

Now we can maim each other from a distance. Brilliant.

As it turned out, Thom was worse at archery than he was with the sword. Not far into the training session, he managed to fire an arrow and nearly hit the captain standing *behind* him. An hour later and Thom was still unable to fire the arrow further than he could huck the thing. The captain working with him looked about ready to strangle Thom—or himself—with the bowstring. To their mutual relief, the lieutenant commander summoned Thom around midafternoon to take a missive to the castle.

Parchment in hand, Thom strode down the main cobblestone road within Knor. Dressed in his brown military uniform with his sword belted to his hip, Thom hardly recognized himself in the murky reflections of the shop windows. A mere day had passed since he'd walked through the southern gate of Knor, and already it felt like a different lifetime ago.

The temptation to stop by his library was almost irresistible, but Thom pushed it from his mind. Instead of using the servants' plain doorway on the west side of the castle like he normally did, he hurried up the stone steps of the front entrance. Guards blocked his path, forcing Thom to explain his errand. Once satisfied, they pushed open the towering oak doors and allowed him inside.

Thom tried not to gawk. Impressive wooden beams hung beneath mighty stone arches, and intricate stained-glass windows painted the stone floor with a dazzling array of color. Giant pillars, carved in the images of bears, wolves, and stags lined the hall. He'd never been inside the grand entrance chamber before.

Footsteps interrupted Thom's staring. A wiry man, who Thom vaguely recognized as one of the king's aides, approached him. He swept Thom with a dismissive glance. "What do you want?"

"I have a missive for the king."

"From?"

"Lieutenant Commander Drayen." Thom extended the parchment, pushing down his annoyance. Was he so unrecognizable?

"Hmm." The aide plucked the missive from Thom's outstretched hand and paused. A seed of confused recognition flickered over his face.

Thom didn't bother to offer an introduction. It hardly mattered anymore.

The aide waved a hand at the door. "See yourself out."

Feeling oddly at loose ends, Thom left the castle the same way he had arrived. Almost on their own accord, his feet carried him to Ma and Pa's door. Twisting the handle, he stepped inside.

"Ma?"

A startled cry came from the kitchen, and a moment later, Ma flew into the entryway. "Thom!" She abruptly halted, her eyes growing wide. "Is everything all right?"

Thom pulled her into a bear hug, her familiar scent enveloping him as he reassured her. "Everything's fine. I had to drop a parchment off at the castle, and I wanted to see you."

"Oh, you dear boy." She wrapped her arms around him and leaned up to press her lips to his cheek. "Are you both faring well?"

Thom shrugged. "Aye. Puck hates the food, but he's keen on all the training."

Ma laughed, her eyes sparkling with amusement. "That sounds like Puck. He's wanted to be in the army for years. Here, let me pack you some food."

Thom held up his hands. "No, Ma. I don't want them to know I stopped. I should probably get going."

Ignoring him, she bustled to the kitchen and reappeared a moment later with a cinnamon bun. "Then you quickly eat this while you walk." She pressed it into Thom's hand and reached up to cradle his face. "Be careful, sweetheart. And come see me again."

Thom cinched her into a tight hug and pressed a quick kiss to her cheek. "I'll try."

"I love you!" she called after him as Thom hastened to the street. Without delay, he sank his teeth into the pastry, the delicious flavors of the warm dough, cinnamon, and sugar making him moan. He might have nearly shot a captain with an arrow and been unrecognizable to the king's aide, but at least he had Ma and her baking.

Puck would kill me if he knew I was eating Ma's food.

Smiling to himself, Thom downed the tasty treat and sucked the last bits of sugar from his fingers as he passed the livery and made his way to the south gate. The guards took one look at Thom's uniform and let him pass without question.

Convenient.

He headed directly to Lieutenant Commander Drayen's tent. Already, the layout of the camp and the different units were mapping themselves in his head.

Knocking on a tent flap was a ridiculous notion, so he halted right outside the tent and simply spoke. "Sir, I delivered the letter. Is there anything else you'd like me to do?"

Drayen's voice responded from inside. "That will be all for now. Head to the training grounds."

Thom bit back a sigh. "Yes, sir."

When evening finally arrived, the captains released the men from the practice field. Thom wasn't the only one limping as the new units dragged themselves to their assigned mess tents. The lineup for food was silent as the men shuffled forward. No one had the energy to talk. A grizzled man with a splotchy, red beard thrust a bowl of chunky stew into his hands. Spotting Puck in the line behind him, Thom waited for Puck to join him and then headed to a bare patch of ground.

Gingerly, Thom sat. "I'm *sore*." It was shocking how much his body hurt.

Puck grinned as he sprawled on the ground, stretching out his legs. "That's because you lift books instead of grain." He punched Thom lightly in the arm, making him wince. "Maybe now you'll finally get some meat on your bones and stop looking like an underfed rooster."

"I don't look like a rooster."

"You've got little chicken legs."

Thom snorted. "At least I don't have a chicken brain."

"Brains don't get the gals, these do." Puck flexed, completely unperturbed.

Thom rolled his eyes, lifted the bowl to his mouth, and took a large gulp. From what he'd seen, Puck was excelling in combat. It made sense. While he'd grown up in the library, Puck had spent many of his twenty-one years kneading massive batches of dough and carrying heavy bags of flour. If that weren't advantage enough, Puck was a full head taller than most of the men in their unit. It was good that *one* of them could handle a sword. Maybe Puck would make it home when the war was over.

"Thom Darkfell?"

Someone shouted his name over the sea of heads. Thom craned his neck. The voice belonged to one of the captains. With a grimace, he stood, his leg muscles screaming at the effort.

"Here, sir!"

The officer beckoned him to come and strode away.

Puck chuckled. "And that's what you get for having too much learning. I'll take your stew."

Thom chugged the last couple of mouthfuls and dropped the empty dish into his friend's lap. "Have at it." He walked away with Puck's indignant "Hey!" ringing in his ears.

Unsurprisingly, the captain led him to the lieutenant commander's tent and gestured for him to enter. Thom ducked inside. The smell of burning candles hit his nostrils, and soft light flickered across the tent walls. Drayen stood beside his desk, his attention focused on something in the far corner.

Thom followed the direction of his gaze and startled. A tall stranger, dressed in dark clothing with shoulder-length black hair, stood tucked within the shadows. Purple circles stained the skin beneath his eyes, and the bones of his cheeks angled sharply upward. And his eyes...they cut into Thom like twin knives, assessing in a sharp glance, before turning back to the commander to grunt out a single word.

"Food?"

Drayen picked up a bowl of stew from his desk and handed it to the dark stranger. The man took it, not even bothering with the spoon, and slurped it down.

Thom stood uncomfortably near the entrance, unsure what he was supposed to do with himself.

Who is he? And why am I here?

The stranger finished the stew. "Anything to drink?" The words rasped hoarsely from his throat.

Drayen handed him his own flagon, and the man drank deeply. His eyes briefly flickered to Thom once more. "You trust him?"

Drayen trained steely eyes on Thom, and it was all Thom could do not to squirm under their combined scrutiny. "Aye, he knows the punishment for wagging his tongue." Drayen paused then added, "And he's a Darkfell."

The stranger's brows lifted. "Interesting. Does he know?"

Drayen shrugged. "I haven't asked."

Know what? Confused, Thom frowned, his gaze bouncing between the two men.

Drayen motioned to the desk. "Thom, write everything he says."

Wary, Thom sat down and settled the quill between his sword-blistered fingers. The stranger began to speak.

"Your Royal Highness, King Xerses. I have found a path to the Realm of Zakar and can confirm that the wall has been breached. A horde from that foul place, led by the Realm Walker Slager, has joined forces with the Abadonians." The man's fists clenched as he spoke. "The nature of these creatures cannot be contended against with the forces we currently possess. As Lomair's Realm Walker, I am invoking my right to act as an emissary to the Hidden Realm. I will keep you informed of my progress." Thom thought there might've been a steady breath indrawn before the man concluded, "Eldehein, Realm Walker."

Thom wrote feverishly, questions roaring through his mind. *What is the Hidden Realm? Or Zakar?* He'd restored dozens of maps from the royal archives, and he'd never seen anything with those names.

"Did you get it all?" Drayen's voice cut in.

Thom quickly wrote the last line. "Aye. Would you like another copy?"

"No. One will do."

Drayen's shoulders drooped. "Eldehein..." He seemed to be searching for words. "You've told me that finding the Hidden Realm is impossible. Father hunted for years. What makes you think you can do it now?"

The stranger, Eldehein, slumped into a chair. "Because there is no other way, brother. Monsters from Zakar are in our realm, and another Realm Walker is at play. Someone powerful. I'm positive it's Slager. We need help."

Brother? There were similarities between them, but not enough that Thom would have guessed they were related.

"But that's impossible! He cannot still live!" Drayen protested.

Eldehein shook his head. "I've found countless paths between here and Zakar. Paths I know weren't there a year ago. I've traveled them and seen the wall with my own eyes. Zakar is no longer bound. Who else would be strong enough to do this? It must be Slager. Plus, everyone else is dead."

"He'd be hundreds of years old," Drayen argued.

"Titus is powerful," Eldehein countered. "It's entirely possible Slager lives. What other option is there?"

"Another Realm Walker survived the killings? But that's almost as unlikely as Slager still being alive." Defeat lined Drayen's face.

Eldehein sighed, fatigue weighing down his words. "I know what I saw. Paths now exist between our realm and Zakar, and only a Realm Walker of great power could perform such a feat. Who else could it be but Slager?"

"Where will you search?"

Eldehein frowned. "If any paths remain to the Hidden Realm, they will be in the Northern Mountains."

"Father searched for years up there and found nothing."

Eldehein's eyes flashed as he leaned forward, his hands gripping the arms of his chair. "What else would you have me do?"

Silence descended.

They both seemed to remember that Thom was in the tent at the same moment. Two sets of eyes swung to him, and he offered them a weak smile.

"I know how to keep quiet." He nodded respectfully to his commanding officer, but in a sudden moment of courage, Thom pressed, his academic curiosity demanding he seek answers. "But where are Zakar and the Hidden Realm? I've been drawing maps of Abadonia and Lomair for years, and I've never seen these places you mentioned."

"You work with maps?" asked Eldehein.

"I do," Thom sat straighter. "I've been restoring the royal archives for years, and lately taking the geographical information from the military to update the king's battle plans."

"I'm surprised they put you in the army. Those are valuable skills," Eldehein mused.

Thom wasn't sure how to answer that. Apparently, he hadn't been valuable enough for an exemption from the ranks. He swung the conversation back to his original query. "Where are these places?"

"You won't find them on any map they'd let you see. Hundreds of years ago, King Fraucis of Lomair ordered every record of the other two realms wiped from our history after the master of the Hidden Realm accused him of stealing something infinitely precious."

"What did the king take?"

Eldehein shrugged. "No one knows, but after that, every path that led to the Hidden Realm disappeared. No one has been there since."

"But you mentioned the Northern Mountains?"

Eldehein assessed him. "You don't miss much, do you? Yes, I'm hoping to find a path there."

He keeps mentioning paths.

"I take it these aren't normal paths." When Eldehein merely winked, Thom asked, "How do you know all this?"

The two men exchanged a quick glance, but it was Drayen who answered. "The eldest son in our family has always been a Realm Walker. It's a power that is gifted from one generation to the next at the giver's time of choosing—and rarely to someone outside our family." He gestured to Eldehein. "My brother can walk the magical faerie trails that run through our realm, and apparently the paths that stretch to Zakar." He stared hard at Thom. "Are you familiar with any of this?"

Thom shook his head, his mind scrambling and refusing to accept the onslaught of information that conflicted with everything he'd ever been taught. "There are no other realms, and there is no such thing as magic."

Eldehein fixed tired eyes on Thom. "You're *almost* right. There is precious little left in our realm, and our bloodlines have grown weak." He pushed himself to his feet and looked at his brother. "You'll make sure the king gets this tonight?"

"I will." Worry creased Drayen's brow. "You're not planning to leave now, are you?"

Eldehein smiled, though with his exhaustion, it looked more like a toothy grimace. "I must. We're running out of time. I'll return tomorrow or the next day. You'll still be here?"

"No. We're moving to the edge of the Great Woods at dawn. The king does not wish to have a battle fought at his walls unless there is no other choice."

Eldehein frowned. "That is unwise. The fight is coming here, whether he likes it or not. Your men must defend the capital."

"I am not the king," Drayen replied simply. "Be careful."

Eldehein briefly clasped his brother's forearm. "Aren't I always?" He nodded to Thom. "Next time I see you, I have a map I'd like you to look at."

Eldehein nodded to his brother before gesturing with his hand. Green light flared from his fingertips before expanding into a magic-rimmed portal.

Thom shouted, nearly tumbling from his chair.

The lieutenant commander arched a brow at him, a wry smirk tugging at his lips. "No such thing as magic, hmm?"

With a chuckle, Eldehein waved his hand again and the glowing sphere disappeared, as if it had never been. He winked and slipped out of the tent.

Mouth gaping, Thom gripped the desk as if it were the only thing anchoring him to his world. It was a long moment before he found his voice. "This...changes everything."

"Knowledge has a way of doing that," the lieutenant commander agreed. "Tell no one what you've seen or heard."

Mouth dry, Thom rasped, "I won't."

Not that anyone would believe me, even if I did.

"Get some sleep. We march tomorrow."

Chapter 6
The Shadows of Forests

The next morning, the army was ordered to break camp. Thom was confident that the citizens of Knor heard the cursing and shouting as the officers showed the new recruits how to tear down the tents. The morning was half gone before Thom got his first taste of marching. It was slow, dusty work that rapidly turned monotonous. The miles dragged by beneath the steady thudding of their boots. However, the mindlessness of marching gave Thom valuable time to think.

Eldehein had literally formed a ball of magic right in front of him.

Magic that shouldn't exist.

They'd spoken of Realm Walkers, a concept he still didn't fully understand, and places he'd never heard of.

Zakar. The Hidden Realm.

General Cain's missive had stated that the army was pursued by abominations and was in retreat. Eldehein had made no secret that Lomair's plight was desperate. The king had drafted every available lad and man from his country to fight.

What was coming for them?

What did it all mean?

Thom itched to tell Puck everything he'd learned the night before, but he didn't. He'd given his word.

"Thom." Puck's voice broke through his tumultuous thoughts in the late afternoon. "Look at that!"

Thom's gaze followed Puck's pointed finger, and he stumbled. A soldier behind him cursed, and Thom muttered a quick apology before correcting his step.

"The Great Woods!" Thom gasped. He knew them from his maps.

His thoughts veered from Eldehein and Drayen's conversation to the intimidating line of green that marked the forest. All around Thom and Puck, men were whispering and gesturing at the nearing wall of wood and leaf.

"Incredible," Puck breathed. "How are they so tall? We're still miles off."

"They've never been cut," Thom answered reverently.

Hundreds of years prior, builders had harvested every tree for leagues around Knor for the construction of the new capital city. The barren fields were never reclaimed by the Great Woods but instead planted with wheat, oats, and barley. With every step, Thom felt his anticipation growing. He wanted to walk among the giant trunks. To understand what it would have felt like to live when the forests had covered the plains of Lomair.

However, the miles were unbothered by his eagerness, and they passed slowly, one footstep at a time, until the towering wall of incomprehensibly large trees blocked the way and the captains ordered a halt. Thom could only marvel. How many times had he sketched the trees onto a map with no clear idea of their magnitude or how intimidating it was to stand before them? Men broke formation as the captains shouted orders for setting up camp. Tearing his gaze away from the looming forest, Thom worked quickly, his eyes finding any excuse to stare at the trees that towered over their camp.

"Big, hey?" Puck paused beside him, a load of supplies in his arms.

"Aye."

"Big" did not do them justice. They were *magnificent*. Puck drifted away, but Thom stayed where he was. All around him he could hear men getting their food, sparring with their swords, arguing, or performing various duties.

Almost of their own volition, his feet moved. Before he was truly aware of what he was doing, Thom found himself passing the first of the expansive trunks as he entered the dark shadows of the forest. Awed, he let his fingers drift over the rough bark. He tilted his head back to stare through the heavy layers of branches suspended high above his head.

Utterly magnificent. And to think this stretches for fifty miles.

He circumnavigated a tree, murmuring to himself. "One, two, three..." He got to eight. Eight steps to walk around the width of a single tree. Disbelief swirled through him, and Thom wandered deeper in. The light from the setting sun faded faster in the forest, and though the camp was basking in the evening glow of the sun, where he stood was already dipped in shadow.

Thom inhaled deeply. The forest scent was unlike anything he'd ever smelled before. It was old, musty, yet there was a tang of life that he could only attribute to the trees. He crouched down, his fingers pressing the needles of a small tree between thumb and forefinger. Aye, that was the smell of freshness that made him want to fill his lungs again and again.

"Thom!" An annoyed shout that suggested it wasn't the first time Puck had called broke the peace.

"Here!" Thom spun on his heel and headed in the direction of camp.

As soon as Puck saw him, relief flooded his face. "There you are."

"What? I was just checking out the trees."

Puck grimaced, his voice lowering. "For a second, I thought you might be making a run for it."

"No...no, of course not." Thom furtively glanced around. "Why'd you think I was deserting?"

Puck shifted uncomfortably. "You've been pretty miserable the last couple days."

"We've been drafted into the army, Puck. And unlike you, swinging a sword around all day and marching isn't my idea of fun."

"Actually, that is why I was looking for you. We need to practice."

What? No. "I'm tired."

"Just a few rounds. Come on," Puck urged and then switched tactics. "For Ma?"

"That's not fair," Thom complained, but he grasped his sword. At least he'd gotten used to walking with it over the course of the day. He hefted his blade, like he'd been coached, and planted his feet squarely beneath him. Standing normally was a good way to get knocked over, a lesson he'd already learned the hard way.

Puck began, his feet and sword moving through patterns Thom recognized from the day before. Thom jabbed his weapon to the left and right, trying to keep Puck's blade from getting through his weak defenses. He lasted for a few swings before Puck sent his sword sailing through the air.

"Good," Puck encouraged him. "Again."

Thom made a face but stooped to pick up his fallen blade. Puck carved a slow arc toward Thom's left side. He blocked it with an exaggerated thrust. Puck took a quick step, brought his blade up, and drove the tip straight at Thom's chest.

Thom leapt back and knocked Puck's sword away. He realized too late that the stab was a feint, and as his momentum carried him to the right, Puck's sword swept down and then up, pricking him in the shirt above his heart.

"Again," Puck ordered.

With his muscles still sore from the hours of training he'd endured over the past couple of days, Thom wearily took up the defensive position. Puck responded. *Strike, strike, thrust, parry, strike...*

Thom moved his feet, doing his best to remember what he'd been taught and stay out of reach of Puck's sword as he countered the blows. A moment later, his heel caught on a rock, and he toppled backward, his arms windmilling as he fell. He hit the ground with a grunt, and a familiar sword tip touched his neck.

"Dead," Puck proclaimed. "Again."

Thom made no effort to get up. "I'm done."

Puck frowned. "We just started."

Annoyed, Thom pushed himself up on his elbows. "I know. But I'm tired and sore and hungry." He shoved his hands in Puck's direction, palms up. "And I have blisters on my blisters, and they're bleeding. I'm done." *And I have no intention of killing anyone with this sword.*

Puck looked about ready to argue, and then he flopped down beside Thom. They were quiet for a while. Finally, Puck spoke. "You're doing better than I thought you would."

Thom laughed under his breath as he stretched out on the grass. "That doesn't say much for your opinion of me."

Puck snorted and nudged him with his toe. "No. I mean that you're trying."

Thom shrugged. "If I can defend myself, I will. I'm not keen on dying, if I can help it."

"Isn't that the truth," Puck muttered.

Neither of them spoke for a long minute, then Thom broke the silence, giving voice to his trepidations. "I can't shake the knowledge that we're practicing to kill someone." He sat up, kicking a lump of grass. "I'm not sure I can do that."

"It's war. Men die." Puck spread his arms wide, palms facing up.

Irritation thrummed through Thom. "But why? Why do we have to slaughter each other to solve this? It makes no sense. The Creator made us all. Why can't we live in peace?"

Puck frowned. "Because the Abadonians don't want peace. They want Lomair. And if we do nothing, they'll take it. Violence is the only thing they understand."

"But killing is wrong," Thom argued.

Puck flipped over and propped himself on his elbows. His brows slanted down. "Let me put it to you this way. If someone were attacking Ma, and the only way to save her was to kill her attacker, and you chose not to, are you right for sparing the attacker's life? Or wrong for not killing him and sentencing Ma to die?"

Thom swallowed hard, struggling to formulate an answer.

"Hey, you two louts!" A voice boomed from behind them, causing both Thom and Puck to spring upright.

"You." The officer pointed at Puck. "Go help unload the rest of the wagons. And you." He ran an assessing gaze over Thom's thin stature. "Go dig latrines with that lot over there."

Puck turned, but not before Thom noticed his grin.

"Shut it," Thom muttered to Puck. He headed back to the border of the woods where three other men were already digging small holes in a straight line.

So much for privacy.

A spare shovel leaned against a tree. Thom grabbed it and began to dig. Head and shoulders bent, he focused on his task and tried to ignore the blisters on his hands. By the time a captain inspected the makeshift latrines and declared the job finished, the sun was setting over the horizon, and Thom had worked up a fresh sweat. With a sigh, he rammed the shovel into the loamy earth. The other men drifted toward camp—undoubtedly in search of a meal—but Thom waited until they were swallowed up by the tents and slipped into the woods.

His eyes roved over the gnarled trunks and sprawling branches. The forest lay deep in dusky shadows, the last rays of golden sun casting an enchanting glow on the glimmering air. He allowed it to draw him deeper and deeper in. Soon, all sounds from the war camp faded away, and Thom found himself relaxing in the peaceful silence. It reminded him of his library.

A strange sensation prickled his skin.

Thom lifted his gaze just in time to see the air in front of two twisted trees ripple like disturbed water. An instant later, it split like a ripping seam, and green light burned along the edges of a large opening. In the center, an inky void yawned from the gaping hole. A familiar figure, with a drawn sword clenched in his fist, leapt from the portal. Recognition flared. It was Eldehein.

Eldehein's gaze collided with Thom's and his eyes widened. "Run!"

Thom stood transfixed. From within the void a horned creature, with more legs than he could number, lunged at Eldehein. Paralyzed with horror and disbelief, Thom gaped.

With a fierce war cry, Eldehein forced the portal shut and drove his blade into the monster's spiny back. The creature shrieked and struck at him. Eldehein swung, severing one of its slashing legs. It roared. Ducking, Eldehein rolled to the side as the beast lowered its horns and charged.

Thom drew his sword, his fingers strangling the hilt as he stared desperately at the warring figures. They moved in a nightmarish blur. The creature lunged again, its maw impossibly wide, and clamped down on Eldehein's waist. Thom watched, mortified, as it shook the Realm Walker like a rabbit caught in a wolf's jaws.

"No!"

Bravery that Thom didn't know he possessed surged through him, and he ran forward with a yell. Gripping his weapon with both hands, he brought it slicing down onto the creature's scaly tail. His sword pinged off, the reverberations ringing through his hands, and Thom nearly dropped the blade.

The action worked...of a kind. The monster dropped Eldehein and faced Thom, its legs curling up to its torso like a praying mantis.

Thom brandished his weapon. "Back! Get back!"

The monster pounced, and Thom crashed to the side, barely avoiding the slashing claws. On his hands and knees, he scrambled behind the nearest tree. The oak groaned as the beast hurtled itself against it, its claws slicing the trunk and missing Thom by a hand's width. His heart pounded, rushing filling his ears.

A shower of bark and branches pelted Thom's head and back as the monster raked its claws down the tree. The cool, moist soil pressed against Thom's body as he lay in the foliage, shadowed by bushes and debris. Thom's lips parted, his breaths coming in shallow pants, as he tightened his grip on his sword. A saliva-encrusted snout rooted through the underbrush, its bloodied teeth bared, as it hunted for its prey. Thom stopped breathing altogether.

I'm going to die.

He closed his eyes, expecting to feel the agony of a hundred razor-sharp teeth sinking into his flesh at any moment.

The monster suddenly roared.

Thom's eyes snapped open, and he stared as the beast reared back, a sword protruding from its scaly throat. Black blood gushed from the wound. Scrambling to his feet, Thom hefted his blade. The monster staggered, its countless legs twitching erratically. It turned its head, its reptilian eyes locking on Eldehein.

Doubled over, an arm clenched around his middle, Eldehein dodged clumsily as the beast lunged.

Jerking forward, Thom stabbed his blade into the muscular thigh of one of its hind legs. Its tail lashed, catching Thom in the back of the knees and sending him sprawling. With a guttural snarl, the monster snatched Eldehein in its jaws and hurled him into the bushes. The beast lurched, its legs spasming in death throes, before toppling over with a ground-shaking thud. Leaves and other debris exploded into the air.

"Eldehein!" Thom pushed to his feet, dodging the creature's contracting legs as he searched for the fallen warrior.

A weak movement caught his eye. Eldehein lay crumpled against a log with his hand clamped to his middle. Crimson blood poured from his torso.

Creator above...

Thom fell to his knees, pressing his hands to the wound to try and slow the flow.

So much blood.

Eldehein's body listed to the side. Thom caught his shoulders and eased him carefully to the ground. "Hold on." He fought to keep the panic out of his voice. "I'll go get your brother."

"Too late," Eldehein gasped, his face ashen gray. He lifted a bloodied hand and grabbed Thom's shirt in a fierce grip. His chest heaved as blood trickled from his mouth, his gaze wild with desperation. "There is a...Key Keeper...in the...Hidden Realm."

Thom's gaze darted, searching in vain for something he could use to stem the flow of blood. The warm liquid spurted through his fingers, mocking his attempts to halt its deadly gushing.

A nightmarish gurgle rattled out of Eldehein's throat. Thom stilled at the sound, his body chilling with foreboding.

Eldehein pressed a trembling hand against Thom's forehead as he struggled, breaths wheezing through his drowning lungs, to perform a final act. Slowly, a green glow enveloped his body. A bolt of pain slashed through Thom's skull. He flinched, gasping as Eldehein's hand dropped away.

Fingers slick with his own blood, Eldehein fumbled inside his chest pocket, withdrew a leather-bound parcel, and thrust it shakily into Thom's hands. "Take...map." He wheezed. "Close...Zakar." His body went limp.

Panic jolted through Thom. "No!" Eldehein's blood still flowed between his fingers. He pressed harder against the wound, but the man's chest no longer moved. The air was silent. Breaths no longer wheezed in and out of his bloodied mouth. Bile pooled in Thom's mouth, and his hands trembled. "Eldehein!"

There was no response.

"Eldehein!" He grasped his shoulders, giving them a hard shake. Eldehein's head rolled to the side. Lifeless.

Thom rocked back on his heels and let his bloodstained hands fall away.

Eldehein was dead.

Chapter 7

Whispers of a Call

Something had awoken her. Norealle threw off her fur blanket and stood. Restlessness coursed through her limbs, and an uncertain feeling settled in her soul. On edge, she trudged out of the cave and emerged beneath starlit skies.

Her father was planted on the rocky ledge outside their cave, his gaze fixed on the heavens. It was a position she'd seen him in countless times since she was a small child.

He spoke without turning to look at her. "The heavens are uneasy tonight."

So am I. She pressed her lips together, keeping the thought to herself. Steps hesitant, she joined him. The silence stretched between them, uncomfortable for her but likely unnoticed by her father. His attention remained riveted on the sparkling lights overhead.

"What do you see?" she finally asked.

"Change."

The word landed heavily on her ears, and she flinched. "Good or bad?" For the first time in months, she reluctantly looked up at the moons and stars.

"Only El'Ohim knows, but a light, one I have not seen for many eras, has appeared tonight." His craggy finger pointed to the heavens.

A small orb, with a streaking tail of murky white, hung in the night sky, its path blazing toward the red haze of Zakar.

The feeling of apprehension deepened, and Norealle backed away from her father. "I'm going for a walk."

He didn't answer. His focus had already returned to the stars. Swallowing her loneliness, Norealle picked her way down the mountain and headed for the meadows below.

Chapter 8
A Task Unlike Any Other

There was blood everywhere.

Thom leaned to the side and vomited, his body heaving until there was nothing left of his bygone breakfast rations. Trembling, he climbed heavily to his feet, eyeing the hulking form of the monster. The beast shuddered, and Thom snatched up his sword, aiming it for the creature's eye. The blade shook, the hilt slick in his bloodied hands.

Be dead. Please be dead.

Tense moments passed. It didn't move again. Thom backed away from the bodies, fighting a second visceral reaction to the carnage. He needed the lieutenant commander. Thom sheathed his gore-covered sword, and surveyed his surroundings, trying to get his bearings.

How do I get back?

Stepping gingerly around the fallen creature, he forced his mind to recall the direction he'd been heading. Two inter-twined trees caught his eye.

Camp is that way. Thom started forward, then stopped. *El-dehein...*

He'd never be able to lead the lieutenant commander to his fallen brother in the dark. Gritting his teeth, Thom hurried to Eldehein's body and noticed the leather-bound parcel laying in the leaves. He picked it up and shoved it in his pocket before grasping Eldehein under the armpits. The man was not light.

With a grunt, Thom began the arduous task of dragging him back to camp. Undergrowth and prickly branches snagged at both hair and clothing, and several times he was forced to carry Eldehein over fallen logs and through dense thickets of tangled brush. Gradually, Thom became aware of the sounds of camp. They were almost there. Delving deep for strength, he ignored his burning muscles and hauled Eldehein into the meadow, well clear of the forest's shadowy grip.

Panting, Thom lowered Eldehein to the ground. A movement caught his eye. A soldier, coming back from the latrine.

"You!" Thom stabbed a finger at him. "Get Lieutenant Commander Drayen, Unit Three. Quickly!"

The man obeyed instantly, breaking into a run and beelining into the heart of the camp.

Alone once more, Thom sank to his knees. Crickets chirped, heralding the night, and evening birds darted across the sky. Exhaustion clung to every fiber of his being, but worse than the physical pain was the chaos in his mind. Shouts echoed through the camp, but he blocked them out and stared with vacant eyes at the tenebrous forest. Green shimmers oscillated through his field of vision. He blinked, a dull ache spreading across his brow.

A cry of unspeakable pain tore through the clearing.

Thom whipped his head up to see Drayen barreling toward him. The man fell to his knees and hauled Eldehein against his chest with a wail of anguish. Men, with swords drawn, fanned out around them. The lieutenant commander gripped his brother fiercely as savage grief consumed him.

Fear and guilt spasmed through Thom as he eased back. He opened his mouth to say something—anything—but nothing came out. The peaceful sounds of the night were lost to Drayen's tortured weeping. Thom sat motionless, unable to offer comfort or flee.

Long minutes passed before Drayen dragged in a ragged breath. His body ceased shaking, and no more sounds came forth for several painful minutes. When he looked up, his gaze was wretched. "What. Happened."

Thom's heart pounded at a frenetic pace. He'd never beheld such fury and pain in one countenance. "He used some sort of magic, like last night, but he came through it. And there was a terrible beast behind him."

Thom could hear himself speaking, his tone even but detached, as if it belonged to someone else. He lifted a trembling hand and ran it through his hair, realizing too late it was covered with Eldehein's blood. Bile rose in his mouth. His gaze fell to Eldehein's broken body, his gore-soaked garments, and then to his own blood-encrusted hands.

"I tried to help," his voice cracked, "but it was too strong. He managed to kill it, but not before it got him in its jaws."

"How many beasts?" Drayen croaked.

The men surrounding them leaned in, straining to hear. Thom lowered his voice to a hoarse whisper. "One."

"It is dead?"

"Yes."

The circle of soldiers eased a little closer as they tried to discreetly discern for themselves what had happened.

Drayen wheeled on his men. "Back away!"

They obeyed, retreating a respectful distance off. Thom exhaled shakily.

Gently, Drayen rested Eldehein on the grass. Grief contorted his features as he hauled in a ragged breath before speaking, "Did my brother say anything to you...before he died?"

Thom nodded.

Anguish tightened Drayen's words. "What did he say?"

Thom's mouth felt dry as sand, and he licked his lips before answering, anxiety twisting through his gut. "He said to find the Key Keeper in the Hidden Realm. And close Zakar."

Drayen grew still, and his voice came out eerily calm. "Who was to do this task?"

"I..." Thom paused. He had simply assumed Eldehein had meant him. Hadn't he? "I don't know."

Even in the dim light, Thom could see Drayen paling. "Thom, did he give you his powers?"

What? Thom's thoughts flashed back, dread filling him. "He...touched my forehead with some sort of magic." His fingers traced the place where Eldehein's power had seared him. Where his head still pounded.

"So, it's done then."

The hollowness in Drayen's voice did nothing for Thom's frayed nerves. "Sir?"

"He gave you his Realm Walker abilities." Drayen closed his eyes once more, as if the news rivaled that of his brother's death. "You have no training. No experience." His chin hit his chest. "Darkfell or not, we're finished."

Why does being a Darkfell seem to matter?

Thom trembled as he stared down at Eldehein's broken body—a form that had been wreathed in magic a scant hour before and wielded both power and sword like a master. Eldehein was dead, and even with his lack of knowledge, Thom innately knew this spelled a type of doom he could only imagine.

Climbing heavily to his feet, he withdrew as Drayen's muffled sobs filled the air once more. Thom shoved his bloodstained hands deep into his pockets. He wanted to close his eyes and push every memory since meeting Eldehein out of his mind. But he couldn't. The images of the nightmarish beast, of the battle that followed, of the gurgling sounds that had come out of Eldehein's chest in those last moments... There was no shutting off the torrent of images nor turning back time to when his world did *not* consist of other realms, magic, or unspeakable monsters.

The moon rose above the forest, and Drayen ordered a grave dug for Eldehein. Without hesitation, Thom grasped a shovel and dug like a madman until sweat soaked his shirt and the blisters on his hands bled freely. Still, he dug, the physical pain a wanted distraction. When the rim of the grave was over his head, he and the other soldier were lifted out. With great care, Eldehein's body was lowered in. In a halting voice, the lieutenant commander spoke a prayer to the Creator over his brother, and the hole was filled. Thom knew he'd go to his own grave remembering the sounds of each shovelful of dirt landing on Eldehein's broken form.

Hungry, exhausted, and barely standing under his increasing headache, Thom nevertheless remained by his commander's side even after all the others were sent away. Numb, Thom stared at the fresh grave. None of it felt real—just last night Eldehein had been talking to them and dictating a missive to the king. How was he now dead?

Eventually, Drayen retreated from his brother's grave. Something in his lost expression made Thom grasp his elbow. "Let's get you to your quarters, sir." Expression blank, Drayen didn't protest as Thom led him into the camp. Realizing he had no idea where Unit Three had been set up, Thom asked lowly, "Sir, where is your tent?"

Drayen gestured straight ahead, and they found the large tent, with its rough three painted on the flap.

Thom ushered Drayen inside, trying to ignore the pain stabbing behind his eyes. "Sir, do you have a lamp?"

Drayen shuffled through his belongings, and a few moments later light illuminated his dirty and drawn face. He lit several other small lamps and candles before hoarsely speaking, "Your powers will arrive tonight."

Is that what's causing this awful headache? Thom pulled out Drayen's chair and gestured for him to sit. "We'll worry about that later. You need to sit down."

Drayen ignored him. "Did he give you his map?"

Silently, Thom reached into his stained jacket and retrieved the leather-bound packet Eldehein had given him. He offered it to Drayen.

The lieutenant commander shook his head. "It's yours. Open it."

Now? We both just need to get some sleep.

Thom drew in a slow breath, bracing against the aching in his head and fortifying his patience. Blinking back the blurriness that kept clouding his vision, he examined the package. With care, for the parcel looked old, Thom withdrew a map and unfolded it. His pain and fatigue faded. It was unlike any map he'd ever seen before.

"Lieutenant commander, is this—"

"Drayen."

"Excuse me, sir?"

"Call me Drayen. By all accounts, you outrank me now." He gestured at the map. "It's all three realms. The best my family has, anyway."

Outrank him? Thom disregarded the bizarre statement as grief-fueled confusion and focused on the parchment in his hands. Eyes devouring the map, his academic heart sped in wonder. The images painted on the parchment dismantled every conception he had of his own reality. Drawn onto the worn papyrus were three distinct globes.

Drayen spoke again, his voice barely audible. "It should have been me. I was the one who pushed us to join the war. He wanted to stay out of it."

"No." The word was thick in Thom's throat, and he looked up from the tantalizing document, his voice grim. "Everyone is in the war now. If you hadn't joined, you would have been drafted. At least by joining up early you learned to fight properly."

"How am I going to tell my mother?"

The heartsick words were like a punch to Thom's gut. He had no answer.

Drayen walked heavily to his chair and collapsed into it. "You will need to continue his quest."

"Sir, we don't have to discuss this now." Thom's fingers begged to tighten on the paper. "We can talk tomorrow."

"No," Drayen growled. "There's no time." He fisted his hair, elbows resting on his knees as he sat hunched in his chair. "Study the map, scholar. See if you can find something my brother missed." Grief mixed with bitterness soured his words.

Shaken, Thom returned his focus to the map in his hands. It was intricate and boasted far too many features to absorb in one study. There were three spheres, and within each sphere were indications marking mountains, lakes and rivers. The sphere in the center he was familiar with. While not all the lines were the same, it was a reduced version of the map he'd worked on just before leaving Knor. It was the kingdom of Lomair, of which Knor was the capital, with the Abadonian Kingdom to the south. The two kingdoms made up his known world. The other two spheres contained details of places he'd never documented on any of his projects. The names "Hidden Realm" and "Zakar" had been stroked onto the map beneath those unknown spheres.

"This Hidden Realm." Thom's finger touched the sphere. "This is where I need to go first?"

"That's what my brother was convinced of."

Green dots swam before Thom's vision, followed by a fresh wave of pain. He blinked. They did not go away. The room tilted dangerously. Staggering, he dropped the map onto the desk and stumbled outside the tent. Hands braced on his knees, he dry-retched.

"Thom!"

Thom groaned and waved Puck away as his friend skidded to a halt beside him. He retched again, but nothing except bile expelled from his empty stomach.

Creator above...

Slowly, Thom straightened, the pounding inside his skull screaming against even that small movement.

Strain lined Puck's face. "I've been looking everywhere for you! Are you hurt?"

"No," said Thom hoarsely, the sickening taste of vomit fouling his mouth. His vision wavered, and he lurched unsteadily on his feet.

Puck grabbed his elbow, steadying him. "Hell's teeth, Thom! What's wrong? You're covered in blood!"

"Not mine," Thom groaned.

Drayen appeared. "Get him in here."

"He needs a healer," Puck lashed out, his stance shifting as he planted himself protectively beside Thom.

Thom shook his head. Green dots exploded across his vision. *Bad idea.*

Drayen helped him into the tent and onto a mat. Puck hovered on the edges of his wavering vision. He could vaguely hear them speaking, but he didn't care what was being said. The pain was too bad. Pulling his knees up, Thom curled into a fetal position. It felt like a monster was trying to beat its way out of his head with an axe.

Drayen crouched down in front of him and rested his hand on Thom's shoulder. "Your powers are coming. Try not to fight it."

Thom groaned and curled into a tighter ball. He just wanted the pain to stop. From somewhere outside the haze of agony, Thom heard Puck snarl, "What's happening to him?"

"He took my brother's powers."

Thom wanted to protest that he hadn't *taken* anything, but another blaze of white-hot fire, followed by a rapid series of flashing lights, flared behind his closed eyes. He cried out in pain, unable to help himself.

"You need to help him!" Puck shouted.

"No one can help him now."

The grim words hammered into Thom. Pain, unlike anything he'd ever felt before, gripped his head. A strangled groan grated past his clenched teeth. Puck let out a fresh stream of curses.

Thom was vaguely aware of Puck leaving and returning. A cold cloth was draped across his brow, and Puck's voice spoke from somewhere beyond the pain-filled fog, "Thom, I brought you some ale and food."

Thom didn't even have the strength to grunt "no." He tried to open his eyes, but all he could see was a blaze of green. Someone propped him up, and he yelled. The green flared, and it felt like his brain was being sliced to ribbons. A burning drink was dribbled into his mouth. He choked, then swallowed.

"A few more sips, okay?"

The voice was far away, but Thom obeyed, his body somehow still responding to his cues as he drank the molten liquid. The blaze of swirling green now haunted his vision whether his eyes were open or closed.

The agony. It wouldn't stop. It was an inferno he couldn't escape. A scream ripped from his chest. He wanted to die. An instant later, he was falling into oblivion and plummeting through utter blackness. There was no top or bottom. The only thing he was aware of was falling.

Forever falling.

And then nothing.

Thom slowly became aware of a firm surface beneath him. His fingers curled into something damp at his sides. A chill cut through the thin material of his uniform. Groaning, he eased his eyes open as he sat up.

He was outside. Grass waved in an endless plain all around him, and dark clouds moved slowly across a nearly blackened sky. It was impossible to tell if the faint light was from the coming of dawn or the fading of dusk. Thom rubbed his head. The pain was a mere whisper of what it had been. A howl cut eerily through the night air.

Where am I?

Thom climbed to his feet. A rumble shook the ground, and his gaze lifted to the jagged peak that towered above him. Fire burned from the mountain, and another tremor rocked the earth. He stumbled, planting his feet wide to avoid being toppled.

"Who are you?" a female voice demanded from behind him.

Thom spun. A young woman, with a slender sword gripped in her hand, stood several paces away. His mouth grew dry and words refused to come.

She advanced, wariness underlying the challenge in her tone. "Who are you?" she repeated.

Am I dreaming? Despite the weapon in her hand, Thom found himself staring. She was lovely. The wind stirred her long, dark hair against her fair skin, drawing his attention to her eyes. They flashed at him, intensity blazing from their bottomless depths.

The girl took another step closer, her blade lifting. This time when she spoke, there was no missing the tremor in her voice. "I feel El'Ohim's power in you. Why are you here?"

Thom finally found his voice. "I...I don't know."

She frowned.

"I'm Thom," he added stupidly.

The glinting steel lowered a little. "Norealle," she whispered.

He moistened his lips, his heart hammering. He couldn't look away from her. "Where am I?"

Confusion flared in her gaze. "How do you not know?"

Thom shook his head and opened his mouth to answer, but her face blurred. He could feel himself drifting away, as if his presence was being carried off by the breeze. Her surprised eyes followed him as her world faded from view. Everything grew dark once more, and Thom was once again falling through the vast emptiness.

Falling.

A blinding, searing light scattered the blackness. Thom threw his arm across his face. The next moment, his feet landed on a solid but soft surface. The light intensified, and he fell to his knees and covered his head. It blazed through the bones of his skull and into his very brain. He felt *seen*. As if every aspect of himself had been laid bare.

"My child." A voice spoke within him. Through him. Around him. It had no source. No direction. It just *was*.

The light. Heavens above, the light was everywhere.

"Nothing that happens is ever out of My hands. You are chosen by Me. Be of courage. The darkness will come for you, but call on My name, and you will overcome it."

Terror flooded Thom. "Who are you?"

"I crafted you in your mother's womb. I have been with you since the day of your birth. I have seen you in your library. I was there when the creature of Zakar attacked. And I will be with you now. I am El'Ohim."

A deep sense of knowing filled Thom. "Creator."

"Yes."

The light faded enough for Thom to lift his head. He was kneeling on something soft. Five creased pillars curved around him, their peaks ending in rounded points. His brain struggled to decipher why they looked familiar. Then it hit him.

He was resting in the palm of a giant hand.

Then suddenly, the hand was gone, and he was falling once more.

Chapter 9

The Birth of a Realm Walker

Thom woke with a yell, his arms thrashing to the sides as he tumbled into confused awareness.

"Thom!" Drayen barked.

Disoriented, Thom's eyes swung wildly back and forth around the confines of the dimly lit tent. Had it all been a dream? *It felt so real.* His heart thundered in his chest. Kicking the tangled blanket off his legs, Thom sat up.

Puck stared at Thom like he'd grown another head. "Fates above, Thom. You're *green!*"

Thom looked down at his hands. Sure enough, they glowed like Eldehein's had.

"Easy there." Drayen crouched beside Thom, lantern in hand. "How are you feeling? The transition took my brother days. You were only out a couple of hours, but it looked rough."

Thom groaned and dragged a hand over his face. He felt wrung out and shaken, and there was something undeniably foreign coursing through his veins. "Thirsty."

Drayen stood and filled a mug with the pitcher on the desk before handing it to Thom.

Cool water sloshed down Thom's parched throat as he drank greedily. "Thank you," he croaked.

Drayen retreated to his mat. "Try and get some rest. The worst should be over now."

Only the worst? Wrung out, Thom slowly lay down on the mat. Shadows flickered across the canvas roof from the candle that still burned on Drayen's desk. The visions replayed through his mind. The girl. The light. The voice.

El'Ohim.

Even thinking the name made the hair on the back of his neck stand on end and his skin prickle with an unspeakable power.

Puck scooted closer, his voice strained with barely contained panic. "Thom, what's going on?"

Thom threw a glance toward the far end of the tent where Drayen lay on his cot. He kept his voice low. "I saw the commander's brother get killed by a monster in the woods."

Puck stiffened. "A bear?"

"No. Nothing of this world. It was the size of this tent, with horns and a half dozen legs and jaws big enough to eat a horse."

Puck cursed then added, "The rumors are true."

"It would seem so. What have you heard?"

"That there're beasts with dozens of heads, flying monsters, creatures that can eat an army in one mouthful...Everyone's whispering about it. They think our troops to the south have been obliterated, and that's why they had to draft all of us."

Thom pressed a hand to his aching head. "Our troops to the south are retreating to Knor. They'll be here by month's end with the enemy close behind."

Puck frowned. "I haven't heard that."

Thom's conscience gave a tug, but he pushed it aside. After everything he'd seen and heard, sharing this seemed like a small thing. "I read it in a missive."

Another foul oath fell from Puck's lips.

The ache in his head was getting worse. Thom shifted uncomfortably. "You better stop all that swearing. Ma's going to have a fit when you get back."

"*If* we get back." Puck growled, uncharacteristic fear burning in his eyes. There was a long beat of silence before he asked, "Do you think the beasts can consume an army like they say?"

Thom shook his head slowly. "If they could, I think we'd be dead already, but what I saw was terrifying enough."

"I wonder where they came from."

Thom grimaced. "From another world."

"I'm serious, Thom."

"So am I."

Puck stared at him. "Stop joking."

"The commander's brother could travel magical pathways between worlds, or something like that. That monster that killed him followed him here from somewhere else. I watched it happen."

"What do you mean, *travel between worlds*?" Puck's voice came out sounding half strangled.

Not that Thom could blame him. He stared down at his skin, still shimmering with green magic that he had no idea how to control. "It has something to do with magic." Thom flexed his fingers experimentally—nothing happened.

Puck was silent for a long moment, staring at Thom's hands. "I'd think you'd been hit on the head or eaten some crazy mushrooms if I wasn't sitting here, watching you glow green."

"I wish it was just mushrooms," Thom groaned.

"Your condition," Puck gestured at Thom's hands, "is it permanent?"

"I don't know. Eldehein, the commander's brother, glowed green like this before he used his magic."

Puck's eyes widened, and he regarded Thom like he might vanish at any moment.

"I don't know how to use it," said Thom. "Maybe it won't work with me."

"Well, let's hope not. I don't like the idea of you traveling to some other world with monsters on your tail."

I couldn't agree more. Thom stifled a yawn, noting that the glow was fading from his skin. "I need to sleep," he mumbled. "I'll show you the map tomorrow."

"What map?"

"Tomorrow."

"Wake up, dumb-dumbs!" A high-pitched voice screeched from somewhere above Thom's head.

Thom's eyes snapped open and locked with a pair of beady black orbs. "Ahh!" The shout ripped from his throat.

A winged creature hovered inches from his nose. Thom scrambled away, swatting at it like a maniac. The thing blurred past Puck's face, eliciting a shout of alarm, before landing on Thom's shoulder. Exploding to his feet, he slapped it off.

With a shrill cry, the small beast shot into the air with an indignant, "Why, I never!"

It talks!

"Kill it!" Wild eyed, Puck raised his sword.

The creature landed on the floor, snapping its teeth at Puck.

"No! Don't!" Drayen's voice sliced through the pandemonium.

Heedless of the order, Puck dove and landed on the little beast. It shrieked like a tortured banshee. They tumbled across the floor in a tangle of wings and limbs. Puck let out a howl and rolled to the side, holding a bleeding hand. The squat creature spat at him, and its entire form puffed up like a bird. Bat-like wings protruded from its furry body, and its bulbous eyes glared at them all.

"It bit me!" Puck accused.

A tiny fist punched the air. "You *attacked* me!" Its long, pointy ears pinned against its skull, and its arms crossed grumpily across its black chest.

Thom jumped between Puck and the *thing*. "What are you?"

"Don't talk to it!" said Puck.

The creature stuck out its tongue at Puck and flew a rapid circle around Thom's head, tugging his hair as it did so. "I'm a faergo, you dumbleheads." It hovered just out of reach, its wings beating hard to keep its chubby body afloat.

"Impossible," Thom breathed, but at the same time, the creature was hardly the oddest thing he'd seen in the last day. He couldn't decide if it looked more like a bat, bird, overfed piglet, or offended squirrel. Perhaps a combination of all of them. Oddly, the "faergo" was too bizarre to not be real, and Thom's imagination wasn't that good.

"Impossible," the faergo mocked in a singsong voice.

"Should I kill it?" Puck growled.

The little creature bared its teeth again, and Puck responded by aiming his blade threateningly.

"Big dumb-dumb!" it snipped. "You're too slow to hurt Traell!"

"And I thought this day couldn't get any stranger," Thom muttered. "Put the sword down, Puck."

Puck reluctantly lowered his weapon but didn't put it away. The faergo snickered.

"Who are you?" Thom asked warily.

"I'm Traell," he answered proudly and bowed at the waist. His pudgy stomach bulged over an odd belt buckled around his middle.

"Thom." He bowed back awkwardly.

Traell let out a shrill stream of laughter, as if the action was the funniest thing he'd ever seen. "Realm Walker, bowing to Traell." It dropped to the floor and rolled about, snickering.

Thom frowned.

Puck stepped forward, his hard gaze never leaving the creature as he gripped his sword hilt. "What are you doing here?"

The creature ignored him and zipped toward Drayen. The lieutenant commander stood his ground and merely arched a brow. "We meet again, Traell."

The faergo buzzed so close that its pointy nose almost touched Drayen's before it spoke, "Funny hair, icky little ears, stubby nose..." It sniggered. "You look just like him."

A dangerous light entered Drayen's eyes. "Like. Who." The softly breathed words brandished a lethal edge.

"Edy-Edy-Eldeheeeein," the faergo sang in an obnoxious voice. Drayen lunged for him with a snarl, but Traell zoomed out of reach. Ignoring the murderous commander, Traell glowered at Thom. "Now I have to train a new one, Big Voice says." He landed with an indelicate flop on the floor and stalked over to Thom. Glancing at Puck, he whined, "Why'd He give me the scrawny one?"

"Look here," Puck growled, and in a shockingly fast motion, he had the small creature in his fist. He wrapped his fingers around the pointy snout and snappy teeth. "You fly in here, scare us half to death, and insult us." His eyes flashed. "Give me one good reason not to kill you."

Traell wriggled fiercely and finally managed to pop out of Puck's hand. He flew angrily around Puck's head and gave a vicious tug on a lock of his hair. Puck swiped at him. Traell hissed. Winging to Thom, he settled on his shoulder, strands of Puck's hair gripped tightly in his angry little fist.

Traell waved at the commander. "Ask him!" Strands of Puck's hair floated lazily to the floor as he dismissively began admiring his own paws.

Drayen glared at Traell. "This obnoxious creature appeared shortly after my brother became Realm Walker. He is a tutor of sorts. And not a very good one, from what I remember."

The little beast's head shot up indignantly. "Traell is the bestest of teachers!"

Thom leaned his head to the side, trying to put some space between his face and the temperamental oddity. "You're my...teacher?"

Traell sent him a look, that even on another species, Thom could identify as long-suffering. "Traell wouldn't have to be if you dumbleheads would quit dying."

The commander let out a low growl from the other end of the tent.

"I don't care what you are. I'll toss you out if you don't stop speaking ill of Eldehein," Thom warned.

Traell stuck out its lower lip in a pout, but said nothing more.

A rumble from Thom's stomach broke the brief silence. Thom frowned. "I don't think we ate yesterday except for breakfast, did we?"

"No, I ate." Puck gestured to a plate of food sitting on Drayen's desk. "I brought you food while you were ill, but you didn't want any." He picked up the plate and offered it to Thom.

There were two cold biscuits and a bowl of congealed stew. Thom opted out of the stew and grabbed a biscuit. He'd scarcely picked it up when Traell launched himself onto the plate.

"*Give me!*" Traell shrieked.

"Get off!" Puck bellowed, swatting at him.

Traell let out a howl and lashed at Puck's hand with a set of sharp claws. Instinctually, Thom tore off a piece of his biscuit and held it up. Traell snatched it and dove into the corner. Shocked, Thom stared as the little beast hunched over the morsel, his grubby racoon-like paws shoveling the crumbs into his bulging cheeks as fast as he could.

Traell was downright feral.

Wary, Thom retreated to where Drayen and Puck were standing. He took a bite of his biscuit, keeping an eye on the unpredictable beast. All three men watched wordlessly as Traell finished the biscuit in record time and brushed the last remnants off his belly.

With a belch, Traell hefted himself to his feet and marched over to Thom, his paw perched on his hip. "Time to go. Wall is broken, world is ending, blah blah blah." He gestured at Thom. "Open a portal, skinny."

"My name is Thom," he ground out. "Not 'skinny.' Not 'dumb-dumb.'"

Traell blinked up at him, his long snout twisting into a deviously delighted smirk. "Ooh, sensitive Realm Walker, this one is!"

Thom growled, fighting an uncharacteristic flare of temper. "If you want a portal, you'd better show me how to make one. And we aren't going anywhere until morning."

"You can't be serious. You're honestly going to leave with that thing?" Puck's hands balled into fists as if he could fight the change that was coming with his bare hands.

Traell glared at the commander, his voice rising in pitch. "Dumb-dumb knows nothing?"

Drayen shook his head.

Traell let out a torrent of shrill chatter in a language that Thom was grateful he couldn't understand. A moment later, a disturbingly serene expression overlaid Traell's fury, and he began to speak.

"You're the Realm Walker." He gestured at Thom with a flourish of his paw. "A mere mortal, but one who can see the fibers that connect the realms." He smirked. "That is, if you can figure it out."

Thom crossed his arms. "Realms?" He wanted to know what Traell knew.

Traell already looked bored with his role as teacher. "Boring Human Realm with dumblehead Realm Walkers, The Inbetween, Glorious and Most Wonderful Hidden Realm, Nasty Ugly Zakar Realm..." He ticked them off.

Puck choked on what almost sounded like a laugh. "Glorious and Most Wonderful Hidden Realm?"

Traell puffed himself up like an affronted porcupine. "It *is* glorious, and far better than anything you humans have."

Deciding that it would be wise not to ruffle the creature until he gleaned what he needed out of him, Thom dipped his head respectfully. "Of course," he agreed, and Eldehein's last words slipped through his mind. "How do we get to the Hidden Realm?"

Traell frowned. "Tricky tricky. There used to be so many beautiful paths." He eyed Thom darkly before continuing. "When you humans made Hidden Realm angry, all the paths got lost, except one."

He only needed one. Thom crossed his arms. "I need to get there. Do you know where the path is?"

Traell shrugged. "It's lost now too."

Thom swallowed a groan of frustration and tried a different angle. "Well, are you from there? How'd you get here?"

Traell suddenly looked uncomfortable. "Is there more biscuit?" He began to root around for food.

Realization dawned. "You've never been there, have you?"

Traell ears twitched and he glared. "Unlucky faergoes got stuck in yucky Human Realm when paths disappeared. Long time ago. So Traell here."

Drayen spoke up. "The paths have been lost for hundreds of years. A small remnant of creatures from the other realms still exists in our world."

Traell found a crumb and popped it into his mouth. "Long, long time," he agreed.

Thom raked a hand through his hair. "Have Realm Walkers been searching for this lost route to the Hidden Realm the whole time?" Worry knotted his stomach.

"Aye," Drayen confirmed grimly.

Fantastic. "And I need to find this path in the next few days."

Drayen sat. "Yes."

Thom began to pace. "The Key Keeper. That's what Eldehein said. I'll have to locate him too, then get to Zakar. All before month's end."

Drayen chuckled darkly. "Don't forget learning to use your magic."

"Thom, you can't be serious about all this," Puck interjected, something akin to pleading in his voice.

Thom let out a slow breath, images from his vision flooding his mind. Of the light. Of the promise. He swallowed hard. "Eldehein gave me this task. I must try."

Grief contorted Drayen's face. "I need a moment." Without another word, the commander stood and left the tent.

There was a long, awkward beat of silence before Puck asked, "Traell, what's The Inbetween?"

Traell, not at all bothered by Drayen's abrupt departure, grinned and clapped his paws. "The gap between realms where new ones get born!" He cackled. "Empty. Dark. You fall until you dead if no path."

Thom winced. It reminded him of his dream. Of the endless descent. "And what of Zakar?" he inquired, almost reluctantly. Simply saying the name out loud made the room feel colder. If the monster he'd seen was any indication, he had a good idea of what Zakar contained.

Traell shuddered. "Evil. Nasty. Ugly. Horrid. Smelly."

Thom nodded. "Got it."

Traell eyed him. "I won't go there."

"I think we have to," Thom answered quietly.

Puck swore. "Thom. You're no hero."

Thom flushed and spun to face him. "Don't you think I know that? I know exactly what I am, Puck. But if I don't try, then in eight days, the Abadonians will be here with more of those monsters that killed Eldehein, and we will all die. I didn't ask for this power, but I got it. I have to do something."

There was a long moment of silence.

"You're right. I'm sorry." Puck mumbled.

Traell was still sniffing around on the floor, picking up bits and pieces of food. He sat on his haunches and preened his wings.

Puck gestured at the faergo. "So, all our fates are tied to that fat little thing."

"No." Thom gave a self-depreciating grin. "To a librarian who hates adventure."

He could only hope that the words spoken to him in his dream were real, and that El'Ohim somehow knew what was happening and had a plan for all of this.

Chapter 10
The Sparks of Changes

Norealle poked the iron into the fire and watched as sparks danced around the spot she'd just disturbed. She couldn't stop thinking about the startled young man in the strange dream she'd had the night before. She'd seen him as clearly as the flames now flickering in the fire at her feet. It had felt so real, from the confusion reflected in his eyes to the hesitancy in his tone when he'd offered her his name and asked where he was.

Thom.

She poked at the fire again. Agitated. Why couldn't she shake the feeling that his appearance boded change? Though whether for good or ill, she knew not.

"Would you like to talk, or are you going to keep stabbing that poor fire?"

The rumbling of her father's deep baritone jarred Norealle out of her own thoughts. With a sigh, she set down the poker and glanced at her father. Between them sat her mother's chair. Empty. Exactly where she'd left it.

Norealle's shoulders slumped. She'd hardly spoken to her father since her mother had left. The pain was too much, and some bizarre part of her was angry that he hadn't foreseen her mother's fall and somehow prevented it. What was the point of having the gift of Sight if he couldn't even protect his own wife? But the silence between them was lonely, and the burdens on her heart grew heavier with each passing day, not lighter like she'd hoped.

"You know you can talk to me. If you wish." His tone had gentled even further, and a single tear trickled down Norealle's cheek in a traitorous path. She swiped it away.

"I had a dream last night." The words were mumbled, but he did not comment on that. Instead, her father just listened, and Norealle knew he was patiently waiting for her to continue.

She cleared her throat, her mind struggling to decide how she wanted to put her experience into words. "I was outside in the meadow, and this boy appeared. He wore strange clothing, and he asked where he was. He said his name was Thom. We spoke, as easily as you and I are right now. And then he vanished, and I woke up here." She fidgeted. "It's probably nothing."

Her father curled his index finger slowly through his beard and frowned thoughtfully. "Was there anything else?"

Norealle let her gaze drift to the fire and hesitated for a few seconds before speaking. "It sounds silly, but I felt like El'Ohim's presence was with him. It was so *real*."

Her father made a hum deep in the base of his throat as he considered her words. "Dreams are often simple driftings of the mind through lark and folly." He paused, his wise eyes studying her. "But this sounds like something else."

Yes. And that's what is bothering me.

Norealle sighed, releasing a portion of the tension she'd been holding. Relief eased her heart. Her father didn't think she was ridiculous.

"It won't leave my mind," she admitted. "And it's been bothering me all day."

"Don't let it rob you of your peace. If it is of El'Ohim, He will not keep His purpose hidden from you. That is not His way," he cautioned.

"I know," Norealle whispered. *But it's easier said than done.* She felt her father watching her, and she lifted her eyes to meet the dark, warm depths of his gaze. "Thank you for listening."

The corners of his eyes wrinkled as his lips curved into a smile beneath his bushy beard. He reached across her mother's chair to squeeze her hand. "It is my honor. I love you, daughter."

A thick knot formed in her throat, and she choked out, "I love you too."

He withdrew his hand, and Norealle stood. "I'm going to try and get some sleep. Can I get you anything before I do?"

"I'm fine. Rest well, daughter."

Her heart lighter from sharing, Norealle stepped away from the hearth, her skin immediately missing the warmth. The flickering light of the fire cast dancing shadows across the craggy walls and ceiling of the cave they called home. It was sparse but provided everything they needed. The fireplace gave them heat and a way to cook their food, and a high wooden counter built into the rocky wall with shelves above it served as their kitchen. A smaller table, with three hand-hewn stools, was set a few feet away from the kitchen. Norealle had shared many animated conversations and meals with her parents there.

To the side of the cave, her father had built an L-shaped wall out of carefully stacked stone for him and his wife to sleep behind. Norealle, preferring to be able to see the light of the fire, had her straw-stuffed mattress laid against the far wall. Her father had made her a little wooden shelf, where she proudly displayed her few worldly treasures: some beautiful pebbles she'd found while wandering the mountains and exploring the creeks and lakes, a hand-carved flute her mother had helped her make as a child, and a glimmering necklace the stars had given her the first time her mother had taken her to join the heavenly dance. Their life had always been simple and filled with love and joy, a fact Norealle hadn't known to appreciate. Now, the simplicity remained, but the joy was harder to find.

She lay on her bed and pulled the blanket her mother had woven for her over her shoulders. Her restless thoughts kept her awake for a long while, but eventually she drifted off to sleep.

Chapter 11

A Cruel Master

Slager stepped through the crimson-rimmed portal into the land of Zakar. He'd chosen to enter near the rear entrance of Titus's red-stone keep, a spot where he'd likely be able to steal into his chambers unnoticed. He wanted to be alone.

Self-preservation warned against admitting to Titus that his control over the Abadonians and the errgoths was slipping. Despite what he'd told King Scaul, Slager hadn't meant for the errgoths to go half mad with bloodlust after the battle and hurtle themselves at every dead and half-dead thing on the battlefield. Pure luck had kept them from turning on the Abadonian army during the battle.

A fact King Scaul would never know.

Slager eased open a brittle wooden door, an artifact from long ago when trees had grown in Zakar, and padded on silent feet down the short stone corridor to his room, his thoughts burdened. He was losing control. The errgoths' rampaging hatred and desire for human flesh was insatiable. They were a true embodiment of their dark maker, and they needed their master to take them in hand.

But Titus remained chained to Zakar.

With a groan, Slager collapsed on a brittle seat covered with a decaying cushion, sending a cloud of dust into the dimly lit room. Moodily, he stared out the window at the orange, dusky light that seemed to never lighten nor fade in this cursed land. His forays to the Human Realm reminded him how grim Zakar truly was.

Mere months ago, he'd finally managed to bring down a portion of El'Ohim's wall around Zakar—a nearly impossible feat—but Titus's chains hadn't broken as Slager had hoped.

He massaged his temples, anxiety making it hard to breathe. He needed to speak to Titus and figure out how to force the errgoths into compliance, but the mere thought of entering the throne room of his unstable lord made his teeth grind.

Titus had stabbed him through the gut when he'd learned that breaching the wall hadn't loosened his chains. A painful wound, but sadly nothing Slager's immortally-cursed body couldn't mend. Titus's rage had yet to dim, and Slager had no desire to feel the edge of his blade again.

Bitterly, he glared at the barren landscape. *I've done nothing but do his bidding for hundreds of years. I've scoured every inch of his realm and that of the Human Realm to find a way to break his curse, while he does nothing but insult and ridicule me.*

He'd exhausted every lead. Nothing had freed Titus from El'Ohim's enchanted manacles. A seed of conscience, a foreign and unwelcome feeling, pricked at Slager. Did he even want to?

Fool!

Of course he did. Titus was his lord. His master.

Admittedly, he was ruthless, but without Titus, Slager's bones would have long-ago faded to dust. Titus had enhanced his natural abilities far passed anything El'Ohim had ever permitted. In exchange for his loyalty and service, Titus had granted him immortality and an ability to bend paths between worlds unlike any Realm Walker before or after him. Slager owed it to him to free him.

One day, Titus will recognize my worth. And then I will rule by his side.

Chapter 12

If Only It Could Be Learned from a Book

Despite Traell's insistence that they leave immediately, Thom staunchly refused. It was the middle of the night, and his head still ached from the power that had viciously entered his body. He needed sleep and a hearty meal.

As it was, Thom slept badly. Nightmares haunted his dreams, and the unblinking eyes of the monster that had attacked Eldehein lurked behind every shadow. About an hour before dawn, he rose and nudged Puck awake.

"Ugh," Puck grunted. "Is it morning already?" The words were muffled by the cloak he'd wedged under his head for a pillow.

"Nearly," Thom hedged, feeling mildly guilty for the exaggeration.

He heard a rustling from the other side of the tent, and in the dim light of the low-burning lantern, he could see Drayen sitting up. The only one still sleeping was the outrageously snoring little beast that had claimed the commander's chair.

"Sorry to wake you," Thom whispered to Drayen, the remains of sleep thickening his voice.

"You didn't."

Thom believed him. Drayen's face was haggard, and he looked awful.

"Thom, you need to write a letter to the king informing him of your identity and your intentions of following through with Eldehein's plan."

"Why?"

Drayen grimaced. "Though Realm Walkers answer to no one, my brother worked closely with King Xerses in recent years. You might want to as well, considering what is at stake. If there was more time, I'd suggest you go meet with him directly."

"Oh" was all Thom managed. It was too early for this kind of news. Preparing documentation for the king's advisors to present to him was one thing, meeting directly with Lomair's monarch was quite another. The mere idea of standing in the same room as King Xerses made Thom feel ill. "I need tea," he muttered.

"I half expected you to need ale," Drayen replied heavily. "I'll see what I can do, and I'll send men to gather supplies for your journey."

Drayen motioned for a sleepy-eyed Puck to follow, and they left the tent. Thom shuffled to the desk and bent over a piece of parchment. He didn't dare move the antagonizing faergo taking up the chair.

What did he write? *Greetings, I'm your librarian. Or I was. Until you sent me to war. And now I have magical powers. Thought you should know.*

Truth, it was a tempting script. Thom fidgeted the quill between his fingers. King Xerses was a man reputed to be withdrawn and stern. With a sigh, he moistened his fever-cracked lips and began to write.

Your Royal Highness,

I am Thom Darkfell, previously employed by your majesty as a librarian and cartographer, and currently a recruit under Lieutenant Commander Drayen. The Realm Walker, Eldehein, has been killed. Upon his death, he passed his power to me. I will continue Eldehein's mission to find the Hidden Realm, which he believed was the only way to defeat the realm of Zakar.

Your loyal subject,

Thom Darkfell, Realm Walker

Thom felt like an imposter writing such words, but there was nothing to be done about it. Like it or not, he was a Realm Walker, and apparently that title came with a host of different responsibilities. Mindful of his fingers, he used the blunt end of the quill to nudge Traell. The little beast swatted at the quill but did not wake.

Thom nudged him again. "Traell."

The faergo grunted and opened a single black eye to glare at Thom. "Traell was having a good biscuit dream," he groused.

That's what he dreams about? Biscuits? Thom struggled to keep a straight face. "It's almost morning. I need to know where we're going and how to use some of these powers."

Traell closed his eyes. "Biscuit."

"Food is on the way," Thom coaxed.

"Biscuit."

"I'll see what I can do. Now, about this Realm Walker business?"

With a long-suffering sigh, the little beast sat up and spread his bat-like wings wide, then did the same with all four of his limbs. Thom waited quietly until he had finished. Finally, Traell flapped his wings hard and propelled himself up on top of the desk. He studied Thom until Thom grew uncomfortable.

"Stop that," Thom grumbled.

"What?" The voice was far too smug.

"That...staring."

Traell made a snorting sound. "You don't look like a Realm Walker."

Irritation pricked Thom. "And you don't look like a teacher."

Traell chortled.

"They'll be back soon." Thom glanced at the tent door. "Can we get started?"

Traell grunted and plopped down on his hindquarters. "Close your eyes, dumb-dumb."

Half expecting Traell to fly over and pull his hair, Thom reluctantly obeyed. Surprisingly, Traell tried no such mischief, but his decidedly bored voice proclaimed his disinterest. "Feel your magic."

"How?"

"Inside you, dumb-dumb. Even Traell senses it."

Thom exhaled slowly and then inhaled again through his nose. *Just feel it?* He relaxed his shoulders and focused. *What does magic feel like?*

"You think too much, Realm Walker."

Thom ignored him. He'd felt the power tearing through his body before he'd passed into the visions, but where was it now? Holding his breath, he searched for any residue of the raging magic. *There.* In his chest. A sense of otherness within.

Thom gasped. "I can feel it." He opened his eyes.

"Good," Traell crowed. "Where is it?"

"My chest."

"Yes, yes. Let it grow. Ask it to flow out of you."

"Like a river flowing from a lake?" Thom asked.

"Traell does not know about magic rivers, but dumb-dumb can try."

Thom focused on the magic inside of him. It moved and expanded, turned and twisted, but always it stayed just above his heart. Not really knowing what he was doing, he willed a tendril of it to flow away from the main source. To his shock, he felt it respond willingly to his command.

"Ah, Traell feels it move. Yes, yes. Now take little piece and send it out of you," Traell ordered.

Thom nodded. He let out another slow breath before imagining breaking off the piece of magic he'd somehow isolated. It severed and sat there, drifting aimlessly in his chest. He tried to picture pushing it out. Nothing happened. It simply floated there. He tried again, mentally shoving it.

"Magic doesn't like to be bullied." Traell cackled.

Thom grunted but took another breath and forced the tension out of his shoulders. He refocused on the small bundle of power and this time, simply breathed it out. His skin prickled. To his amazement, a glimmering ball of green magic floated in front of him.

"Hmmm." Traell's eyes widened in surprise. "Now pull it open."

Thom frowned. "Like a doorway?"

"Why Realm Walker say these things? Like a river? Like a doorway?" Traell chittered impatiently. "Open, like a portal."

Lifting his hands, not sure why he felt like he needed a physical gesture, Thom focused on the sphere. "Can I touch it?"

"Many Realm Walkers do when they are learning," Traell confirmed.

Thom touched the sphere. A current of energy ran over his fingers, but it was not unpleasant. He mimed forming a portal, but his hands simply passed through the green sphere.

Traell's impatient voice chimed in. "Feel!"

Thom let his hands fall to his sides and simply stared at the floating orb. He willed it to open. To his shock, the green sphere expanded, and Thom found himself staring into a black void. He jerked back. It was the same blackness the monster had sprung from the night before.

Panic broiled in his chest. "How do I close it?" he yelled.

Bored, Traell waved a dismissive paw. "Push it into a ball, dumb-dumb."

Thom grabbed the edges and tried to squash it shut.

"Use your mind, Realm Walker!"

All Thom could see was the gaping darkness. He panted and wrestled with the immaterial rim, trying to force the edges to close.

Traell was suddenly in his face, his bat-like wings beating rapidly as he hovered in front of him. "Back, get back! You can't do it like that. It's not a cow you can tow about by its nose!"

"We need to get it closed! What if another monster comes through?"

Traell looked at the sphere and cocked his head. "There are no paths. Nothing can come through, dumblehead."

"Nothing?" It was repetitive, but it would take a long time before the memory of the monster leaping through Eldehein's portal dimmed in Thom's mind. Everything about the dark portal, hanging suspended before him, radiated danger.

Traell snorted, unbothered by Thom's distress. "Not even stinky monsters of Zakar can walk The Inbetween without a path."

He could hear what Traell was saying, but that didn't immediately quell the panic squeezing Thom's chest. Bracing himself, he studied the empty portal. Traell was right, nothing lurked in the darkness except deep emptiness. Thom forced himself to calm. "Then that blackness is The Inbetween?"

Traell let out an excited chirp. "Yes, yes. The void between our worlds."

"Incredible." The word escaped Thom's lips without thought. His academic mind filled with questions. He was looking into the literal space between worlds. It was beyond anything he'd ever fathomed could exist. "Can you ever see the other realms from here?"

"No, you need a path to carry you to the doorways of the other realms." Wistfulness filled Traell's tone. "Close the portal, Realm Walker. And then try again. And relax."

Thom slowly exhaled. The foreign tendrils of his new gift stirred within him, and he could feel the portal before him. Waiting.

Relax. He focused on the portal and the tether-like pull it exerted upon him. *Come back,* he willed. There was a subtle tug in his chest and the portal vanished. He'd done it.

"Again," Traell ordered, ignoring Thom's small victory.

Bolstered by his success, Thom obeyed. Again and again, Traell coached him through the process of isolating a piece of his power and opening and closing the portal. The little imp was surprisingly patient...if one ignored the name calling.

Puck and Drayen walked into the tent just as Thom pushed a piece of magic from his body. Distracted, he paused and felt a sharp tug on his hair. "Hey!"

"Focus!" Traell snapped.

Thom glared at the winged menace and rubbed his head. His scalp stung.

Traell returned his glare and bared his teeth. "Distraction will get you dead, dumb-dumb. Again!"

Eldehein's broken body flashed before his mind's eye. The enormity of what he was doing sank into Thom's sleep-deprived brain. He was using magic. To form portals. A skill that had ultimately killed Eldehein. Another sharp tug on his scalp demanded his attention. "Ouch!"

"Again," Traell hissed, his beady eyes flashing at Thom as he hovered in front of his face, strands of Thom's brown hair clutched in his fist.

Focus on the magic. Don't think about Eldehein.

Thom separated off another piece of magic. With an inward push, he willed it outside his body. He studiously avoided looking at Puck or Drayen as he eased the sphere apart to reveal The Inbetween. The sound of something heavy hitting the ground snagged his attention, and Thom glanced to the side. Drayen had dropped a fully loaded pack beside the desk.

"He's learning fast," Drayen commented.

He spoke to Traell, but Thom warmed a little at the words. There had been few successes to celebrate over the last couple of days.

Traell shrugged, already clambering over the supplies. "Traell needs biscuits!"

"Puck has them."

In a flash, Traell was airborne and all over the breakfast tray Puck held in his hands. Puck didn't even react. He stood still, staring at the portal suspended in front of Thom.

Traell took off with an entire roll, but Puck still hadn't moved, his blue eyes fixated on Thom's magic.

Thom closed the portal and glanced at his friend. "Puck? You ok?"

"What was that?"

Thom took the tray and set it on the desk. "A magical portal."

Puck's complexion faded several shades lighter than his normal coloring, leaving him rather pasty. "You weren't kidding." His Adam's apple bobbed. "Do we have to go through that?"

Drayen spoke up. "No. You can't step through a portal into The Inbetween without a path being there. Right now, Thom is just practicing getting a portal to open. Hopefully, they can find an existing path and then use the portals."

Thom was already busy downing a massive serving of plain oatmeal. He finished the bowl and eyed the remaining one still sitting on the wooden tray.

Drayen caught him looking. "Go ahead. I'll get another later."

Not needing any more encouragement, Thom quickly ate the second bowl.

As he finished, Drayen spoke again. "Has Traell told you about the paths yet?"

"A little," Thom answered around a mouthful.

Drayen glanced at Traell, but the little beast was still stuffing his long snout full of food. He shook his head. "We believe that the Creator, El'Ohim, crafted the three realms. To the masters of the Hidden Realm and Zakar, He gifted them immortality and magic to lead their worlds, and to the race of men, He granted unique individuals the ability to create magical pathways within and between the realms."

"Realm Walkers," Thom supplied.

"Yes. Travel through and between realms was common and simple."

"So, what happened?"

"Greed. The realms began to get envious of each other, each thinking that the other realm had more than they, but none more so than Zakar. Titus, master of Zakar, betrayed El'Ohim's trust and sent his subjects to plunder wealth and resources from the other realms. El'Ohim was furious, so He built a wall around the lands of Zakar and broke the pathways that connected it to his other two realms. For a time, there was peace. But then the kingdoms of men began to covet the Hidden Realm."

"Predictable," Thom murmured.

Drayen nodded slightly. "This time, it wasn't El'Ohim who destroyed the paths between here and the Hidden Realm. It was the master of the Hidden Realm, an immortal known as the Key Keeper. Cut off from the other realms, the magic of the Realm Walkers all but disappeared. They could not reform what had been broken."

"If there are no paths left," Thom spoke slowly, "then how do I get from our world to theirs?"

Drayen sighed, despondent. "Therein lies the problem. Eldehein never believed that the Key Keeper destroyed all the paths. He held to the hope that there was one left. And that is what he was searching for."

"How do you search for a path?"

"Not easily. My father and Eldehein traveled all around our realm, opening portals at random, hoping to stumble across the lost path. It was a fool's hope then, and even more so now."

A thought struck Thom. "If there are no paths left, how did that monster get here? And how was Eldehein in a portal?"

Drayen gave him a tired nod. "As I said, the strength of Realm Walkers faded after the connection was broken with the Hidden Realm. The ability to form pathways through The Inbetween was lost."

"Right."

"So, you can imagine our surprise when Eldehein started finding paths through The Inbetween about three months ago." Drayen paused to take a sip from a wooden cup, then continued. "But there is one part I haven't told you yet. After Titus was locked away for plundering our realm, he lured an exceptionally skilled Realm Walker named Slager into his service with promises of power." He tapped his fingers on the desk for emphasis. "Eldehein suspected that the Realm Walker forging these new paths must be Slager. And those were the paths that Eldehein was exploring in hopes of finding a way to the Hidden Realm, but they all led to Zakar."

Thom frowned. "Why does Zakar want the Human Realm? Wouldn't Slager prefer the Hidden Realm? It sounds more his type than us."

Drayen grimaced. "Our realm has men. Both Titus and Slager have always enjoyed twisting and controlling the minds of humans."

"Are there no humans in the Hidden Realm?"

"No, at least not like us."

But what of the girl in my vision? The oatmeal he'd just scarfed felt heavy in Thom's gut. "Where do I begin looking? Do you know where Eldehein already searched?"

Drayen walked to his desk. He opened a worn book, tore out a page, and handed it to Thom. It was a miniature map of Lomair with hundreds of small "X" marks all over it. "All the places my father and Eldehein searched," Drayen confirmed.

"May I keep this?" Thom asked.

Drayen nodded.

Thom slipped the second map into the leather packet Eldehein had given and tucked it in his pocket.

"His goal was to focus on the Northern Mountains again," Drayen continued. "He had explored them, but not completely."

"That's"—Thom ran the figures quickly in his head—"at least a two-week's journey from here on foot."

"Not if you use the faerie trails!" Traell chimed in.

"You can't be serious," Puck muttered and set his bowl down harder on the tray than was necessary.

"Faerie trails?" Thom echoed, wondering if he even wanted to know. How much of his world did he not understand? He was a learned man. A scholar. Yet somehow, he apparently knew next to nothing about the truth of his existence.

"Yes, yes! Sparkly paths through your realm. Fast, fast!" Traell chirped.

Thom shot a questioning glance at Drayen.

The commander took over. "I don't know about *sparkly*, but my brother did take me on several journeys using the faerie trails." He glanced at Puck. "As a non Realm Walker, you won't be able to see them. Only Thom and Traell will."

"Great," said Puck.

"Wait, Puck's coming?" Thom cut in.

Drayen continued, ignoring their interruptions. "The faerie trails stay within our realm and do not venture into The Inbetween. They merely condense the journey."

"Meaning?" Thom asked.

"You walk for five minutes on a faerie trail and cover a distance that would take a full day of travel otherwise."

Thom shook his head in awe.

"Well, at least we won't have to walk for two weeks," Puck grumbled, slightly mollified.

Thom couldn't agree more. He was still tired from the day of marching they'd put in yesterday. Plus, they didn't have two weeks to find the Hidden Realm. They had days.

Thom glanced between Traell and Drayen. "How do I find the faerie trails?"

Traell cackled. "Lots and lots and lots of practice and knowing where they are." He sniffed at Thom. "You would get lost. Lost, lost. But you have Traell. I'll show you the faerie trails."

Drayen grimaced. "Aye, they are a twisting network, and one wrong turn can send you right across the country. It would take a lifetime to learn them on your own."

"Good to know."

Puck surprised them all by picking up his pack and slinging it across his shoulders. "Well, are we going to keep talking, or are we going to march?"

Thom shot him a startled look. "I should probably practice a bit more. I can barely form a portal."

"You don't have time." Drayen tossed Thom a black uniform. "Put these on. You're a mess."

"Thank you," Thom murmured.

Relieved to be rid of his bloodstained clothing, he stripped down to his under garments and quickly donned his new outfit. He could feel the high quality of the fabric against his skin, and unlike his previous clothing, it smelled clean. Retrieving the map from his old shirt, Thom tucked it into his new chest pocket.

Drayen handed Thom his canvas bag. "Puck is right. You can learn from Traell on the way."

Overwhelmed, Thom put on the pack. Drayen handed him his sword, and he secured it to his hip. Ironically, he wished he knew how to use it better. "How long do we have to find the Hidden Realm?"

Drayen grimly handed them both filled water skins. "The Abadonians will be here in eight to twelve days, depending on how hard they march, but every hour Zakar remains unbound, the more creatures enter our realm."

"So, no pressure," Puck drawled.

"Something like that," said Drayen. "Be careful, but hurry."

Thom grabbed Puck's arm. "Puck... This is my journey. I don't know where I'm going, but I know it will be dangerous. If we both don't come back, Ma—"

"Would skin me alive if she knew I'd let you go off on some dangerous mission alone," Puck growled. "Shut it, Thom. I'm coming with you."

"I was about to say the same thing," Drayen interjected, watching them with sad eyes. "You're better off together."

Thom picked up the letter he'd written to the king and handed it to Drayen. "Can you get this to the palace?"

"Aye. It's time to go."

Chapter 13

Faerie Trails

They ducked out of the tent and into a gray world. A heavy mist hung over the camp and lent an eerie feel to the encampment. Dawn was barely upon them, but already men were making their way to the mess tent. Thom and Puck walked heavily, their shoulders braced against the damp chill and weighted with their full packs.

Drayen discreetly draped a cloak over Traell and tucked him under his arm—much to the creature's annoyance—to smuggle him out of the camp. The last thing they needed was a riot due to the otherworldly little beast. With the lieutenant commander as an escort, no one questioned Thom and Puck's large packs laden with provisions or their trajectory out of the encampment.

They passed the last line of Lomairian tents and entered the meadow where Thom had dragged Eldehein the night before. Dirt, piled in a mound, signified the grave. Wordlessly, they all halted.

"Will you mark his grave?" Thom asked Drayen quietly.

Drayen stared down at his brother's final resting place, grief straining his features, and he shook his head. "No. I don't want to risk our enemies searching the grave."

"That's just sick." Indignation straightened Puck's spine.

"I'll give him a proper burial, when the war is over," Drayen's voice trailed off.

"Good," Thom agreed softly, his thoughts circling back to the nightmare of the night before. Eldehein did not deserve to be forgotten in a far-flung field away from his family and friends. But then again, what soldier did? It was wrong. All of it.

Nervously, Thom lifted his gaze to the forest. The mist shrouded his view of the trees, giving an illusion of a dark wall looming behind a sheer curtain. He shuddered.

A squawk from the cloak drew all their attention. Drayen unwrapped Traell, who immediately took to the air and flew straight into the ominous forest.

"Best be after him."

Thom faced the lieutenant commander. "You'll make sure Puck's ma and pa are all right? That we aren't listed as deserters?"

"And if we don't come back, you'll tell them?" Puck jumped in. "My pa is the royal baker."

"I'll make sure no harm befalls them for your absence."

Traell's shrill voice cut through the fog. "Hurry up, Realm Walker! Traell has found the way!"

Drayen clapped them both on the back. "May the Creator's blessings be with you both." He left them then, the mist wrapping him in its embrace and obscuring him from view.

Puck glanced at Thom, his eyes grim. "I'll watch your back. You follow the bat thing."

"Fine," Thom agreed, "but stay close. This fog is thick."

The forest loomed threateningly. The mist deceived Thom's eyes, making him see movement where there was none. On edge, he walked beneath the curving boughs of the first wooden giant.

"Great day for a stroll," said Puck, feigning cheerfulness.

To Thom, it felt like every unseen eye in the forest fixated on them at the sound of Puck's voice. Ridiculous, he knew, but he couldn't shake the feeling that they were being watched.

"I think it best we keep quiet," Thom lowered his voice, glancing around for Traell. There was no sign of the little imp. "Can you see Traell?"

Puck looked around before shaking his head. "No. The foul critter ditched us."

Out of the mist, a dark form streaked toward their heads. Puck cursed, his sword coming halfway out of its scabbard, before he realized it was the object of their discussion.

"Hell's teeth, Traell! I'm gonna cook you in a soup!"

"Traell cook *you* in soup! And eat with biscuits!"

Thom's heart pounded in his chest. He ground his teeth together, taking a moment to rein in the angry words that wanted to spew from his mouth before speaking, his voice strained, "Traell, stick where we can see you."

In lieu of answering, Traell landed heavily behind Thom's head on his pack. "Straight ahead, dumb-dumb. Faerie path is up there."

Shoving down his irritation, Thom strode through the forest, setting a winding course around the massive tree trunks. Just as Traell had said, a bright, sparkling path became visible through the mist, its shimmering form hovering above the forest floor. It reminded Thom of sun glinting off dew drops in the early morning, but there was scarcely any light in the murky forest. The trail itself was giving off the glimmer.

"Remarkable," Thom breathed.

Puck's head swung left and right as he peered into the mist. "What? What am I looking at?"

"You can't see it?"

"See what?" Puck sounded annoyed.

Awed, Thom pointed at the faerie trail. "It's only a few feet in front of your boots. A sparkly path, like Traell said."

Puck took a quick step back, his brow creasing as he squinted at the ground. "There's only sticks and leaves."

"Big dumb-dumb has no magic. He can't see sparkles," Traell chimed in smugly.

Out of the corner of his eye, Thom watched as the little horror stuck his tongue out at Puck.

Ignoring them, Thom squared his shoulders and placed his boot on the faerie trail. The outline of the trees blurred, as if washed by an invisible veil of flowing water. He caught his breath. *Where was Puck?* Thom squinted, finally picking out his friend's diminutive smudge against the indistinguishable haze of rippling green.

From behind his head, Traell spoke. "Must get the big one, Realm Walker, or he will be left behind!"

Thom gave a slow, disbelieving shake of his head. *Unbelievable.* He left the faerie trail, and the trees around him solidified, the individual needles and textures of the bark coming back into focus.

Puck's eyes bulged, and he stumbled back. "Thom! What the..." He gaped. "You...vanished. Right before my eyes!"

Thom let out a slow exhale. "I did? I could still see you. Here, hold on to my pack and follow me."

Puck let out a curse that would have had Ma chasing him with a spoon, but he grabbed on to Thom's pack.

Thom set his feet on the faerie trail once again. Like the last time, everything went hazy except the glittering trail stretching out before him. Thom paused. "Where do I go, Traell?"

"Walk straight. Traell tell you when to turn. Don't leave trail."

To Puck, Thom asked, "Can you see anything or feel anything different?"

"Just feels like there are spider webs all over my skin," Puck grumbled. "And I think I have something in my eyes. It's all blurry."

"It's the trail."

"Spider webs and grit in your eyes?" Puck sounded peeved. "Sounds great."

"Hold on. I don't want to lose you."

"I don't want to lose me either. Unless you see a pub. You can lose me there."

Thom breathed out a quiet laugh, some of his tension drifting away. "Especially one with pretty girls?"

Puck let out a long groan. "Don't even talk to me about lasses. I haven't seen anything but ugly men and this messed-up little fur ball for three full days."

"How have you survived?" Thom replied blandly.

"I ain't. I'm probably dying. That's why the world's gone all blurry and itchy."

Biting back a chuckle, Thom carefully picked his way forward until Traell got annoyed at his pace and flew on ahead, urging them to move faster. For Thom, it was an experience he'd never forget. He was aware of the miles slipping by only in the vague sense that he knew the landscape outside of the trail was passing. After an hour or so of walking, he realized they'd already left the forest and were crossing a vast plain. The sky above was blue, and in the light of day the trail glimmered even brighter than it had in the early dawn hours.

Traell refused to stop for a rest but darted ahead, sometimes flying down one path, only to reappear a moment later to direct them onto another. The faerie trails branched constantly, and Thom could see how easy it would be to get terribly lost. Behind him, Puck maintained a steady grip on his pack.

Without warning, Traell landed on the path in front of them. "Food time." He planted his fists on his pudgy hips.

"Can we eat somewhere not magical?" Puck asked from behind them.

Thom tossed a glance over his shoulder for the first time since starting on the trail. Puck's face was blotchy, and his eyes were red. Thom abruptly halted. "Puck! What's wrong with your face?"

Puck scrubbed his sleeve across his eyes. "Apart from being unspeakably handsome?" He sneezed. "It's this magic grit. Can't get it out of my eyes."

"Can we get off?" Thom asked Traell.

Traell flapped his wings. "Must be careful, don't want to leave the trail over a cliff or a lake." He cackled. "Then no more Realm Walker."

Thom rolled his eyes and peered carefully into the haze that bordered the trail. It looked like they were in low-lying hills. "Traell, can you check it out?"

To his surprise, Traell obeyed and flapped off the trail. A moment later, he reappeared. "It's safe for the humans."

Thom grabbed Puck's elbow. "Brace yourself, I'm not sure how the landing will be."

"Let's just get off this thing."

Puck didn't even wait for Thom. He boldly left the faerie trail, and Thom lurched after him. They exited the magical pathway, and the land around them sharpened into focus. It was almost strange to be able to see individual trees. As it were, their new surroundings weren't terribly different from the one they'd left behind hours before. They were in another forest, though this one was made of much smaller trees and shrubs. Nearby, Puck dropped onto a log and took a deep drink from his canteen. Already he was starting to look better.

Traell landed on top of Puck's pack, and Puck shooed him away.

"Hungry!" The little imp jerked a piece of Puck's hair.

"Traell!" Thom barked. Puck looked ready to skewer the little menace. With a groan, Thom dropped his bag onto the ground. He rolled his shoulders, working out the stiffness before selecting a wrapped parcel of food.

Traell was at his side in an instant. Thom didn't have to wonder what the faergo wanted. Digging around in the food packet, he found a biscuit and held it out. Traell snatched it. The sounds of snuffling, grunting, and mouth smacking soon filled the air as Traell stuffed his face.

"Is that all you eat?" Thom asked the small creature. A thought struck him, and he chuckled. "Imagine what he'd think of Pa's bakery."

Puck's eyes widened, and he shook his head quickly. "That little whelp would destroy the place!"

If Traell got them to the Hidden Realm and home again, Thom had a mind to smuggle him into the bakery regardless of the destruction. "Traell, do you know where we are?"

With crumbs all over his snout and belly, Traell looked up, cheeks bulging, and spoke around a mouthful of food. "In little mountains." He swallowed. "Soon we will get to the big mountains."

Thom's jaw dropped open. "So soon?"

"That's impossible!" said Puck.

Traell sniffed. "Humans and their puny minds."

Puck chucked the remainder of his biscuit at the little beast's head. Traell snatched it out of the air and popped it in his mouth. Thom shook his head.

Their respite was short lived. As soon as Traell finished Puck's biscuit, he harassed them onto their feet. Both grumbling that they hadn't had a chance to properly eat, Puck and Thom nevertheless shouldered their packs and followed Traell back onto the faerie trail.

Even though Thom now knew what to expect, the glimmering beauty and the rapid passing of the land outside was still shocking. Traell drove a hard pace. What felt like hours later, he halted them.

"The faerie trails go no further," he announced, and without further explanation, he flew off the trail.

"He drives me crazy." Puck fisted his hands, glaring at the spot where Traell had disappeared.

Thom gripped the straps of his pack, adjusting the load on his shoulders. "Well, without him we'd be marching for two weeks to get to this point."

"He drives me a little less crazy," said Puck, sighing as if the admission caused him physical discomfort.

Thom led Puck off the trail, being mindful to depart in the exact same spot Traell had exited. The last thing he wanted was to leave the trail miles away from where Traell had. Annoying or not, their guide was essential.

A bitter chill greeted him. Traell had led them into a stubby forest filled with scrawny trees not much taller than Puck. The undergrowth was a thick mossy-type substance, and it gave way beneath his feet, not unlike walking on a cushion. Only a short distance away, towering mountains cut a jagged line against the sky.

Under Traell's impatient eye, Thom and Puck had a quick snack before beginning their march through the spindly forest. The route was challenging, with Traell often leading them up large hills and into overgrown valleys. Despite the cold, sweat soon coated their brows, and their breaths came in ragged puffs as they trudged toward the imposing mountains.

At the top of one such hill, Traell flew at Thom's face, stopping a mere hand's length away. "Realm Walker, open portal. Yes, yes. Check for paths!"

"Why here?" There was nothing significant about the rocky knoll they were standing on.

Traell jerked a strand of Thom's hair.

"Ouch!" Thom yelped.

Traell bared his teeth. "Portal, dumb-dumb. We start searching now."

"Don't do that again," Thom gritted out as he raked his fingers through his hair, his scalp smarting. Irritation curdling, he tried to focus inward on his power, but Traell's hovering presence was too distracting. "I need space."

The request had no effect on Traell.

An uncharacteristic flare of temper ignited within Thom, fuelling his snarl. "Back. Off."

Shockingly, Traell listened and retreated to sit on a nearby rock.

Thom steadied himself. *I shouldn't have yelled at him.*

"I say we cook him for dinner." Puck was making no effort to hide his grin.

Thom's face cracked into a rueful smile. "Always good to have options."

From the rock, Traell squawked, "Traell hears you!"

Puck winked at Thom, and Thom relaxed. Methodically, he walked himself through the steps Traell had shown him that morning. Isolate the power, pull a piece off, send it out, form the portal. The first attempt was clumsy and amounted to nothing, and the second was only marginally better. Finally, on the third try, Thom formed a portal into the emptiness of The Inbetween.

Traell popped up beside him and peered in. "No path." He announced primly and promptly winged down the slope.

For the rest of the waning afternoon, Traell frequently halted Thom and ordered him to form portals. Thom created dozens, each one getting a little easier to do, but all of them were simply black holes into The Inbetween. As they marched, the terrain around them grew rockier, and the scraggly trees thinned. The sun set, and dusk settled over the countryside.

"Portal, Realm Walker," Traell ordered.

If nothing else, he is persistent.

Thom obeyed, and almost without effort, he opened a man-sized portal into the dark void. *Empty.* Mentally exhausted, Thom retracted his power. His head pounded.

"That's enough for today," Puck announced, grabbing Thom's pack and pulling it off his shoulders. He addressed Traell. "It's getting dark, and Thom looks ready to pass out. We need to set up camp at the forest edge where we can get wood for a fire."

"Yes, yes. Fire good!" Traell trilled.

Thom perked up at the idea of a warming flame, and he hurried after Puck who was already striding back towards the tree line.

They reached the dwarfed pines, and Puck tossed their bags on the ground. "Sit."

Thom wanted to argue, but he was mentally and physically spent. Kneeling beside the packs, he made himself useful pulling out their gear while Puck got to work collecting wood for a fire.

Puck returned with an armful of sticks just as Thom was unrolling the bedrolls. Using flint, Puck soon had a small fire going, and they all crowded close as the cool bite of evening edged in. Over the tops of the trees, Thom marveled at the rugged faces of the Northern Mountains, mirroring the many outlines he'd drawn on countless maps. He'd honestly never imagined seeing them for himself.

Dinner was a quick and unappetizing affair consisting of salty jerky and a day-old bread roll each. The only one who was excited about it was Traell, who ripped into his portion with unmatched exuberance. All tired, they readied themselves for bed with minimal talking. Despite the hard ground and the scarce heat their small fire gave off, sleep came quickly.

Chapter 14
When Nothing Is as It Appears

Norealle woke in the meadow and immediately knew she was back in the dream. Her heart pounded. The young man from the night before stood only a few feet away, his brown eyes wide as they met hers. They regarded each other warily for several strained moments before he broke the silence.

"Norealle, right?" he asked hesitantly, his words a mere whisper. He had a nice voice, but his accent sounded strange to her ears.

"Yes." She felt oddly safe in his presence, despite the alarming realization that she was once again in some sort of dream talking to a stranger.

"I'm Thom."

"I know." *How could I forget?*

Red tinged his cheeks. "Oh. Of course." His eyes darted around, but he avoided looking at her. "Do you know where we are?"

"Near my home."

A short chuckle, a sound mixed with nervousness and humor, lurched out of him, and his soft brown eyes lifted to meet hers. "I mean, do you know which realm this is?"

Oh. "This is Silmea."

"Silmea...I'm not familiar with that name."

Norealle once again took note of his strange dress and its odd material. "Where are you from?"

"The Human Realm."

Awe punched through Norealle. Her mother and father had told her stories of that realm and its human inhabitants—beings similar to her own shape and form. As a child, she'd dreamed of finding a secret way to visit the mysterious Human Realm, much to the amusement of both her parents.

"I'm trying to figure out if this is a dream or some sort of vision or…" Thom's voice interrupted her musings, and he gave her a slightly crooked smile.

She liked his smile, and to her own surprise, Norealle found her own lips tilting upwards. "I've been wondering the same thing." She took several steps closer.

Thom stiffened.

Hesitantly, she reached out. Her palm met the solid warmth of his chest, and she heard him catch his breath. Heat rushed through her, and she quickly pulled her hand back. "You feel real."

A startled laugh rumbled out of his chest. "That's good. I hope?"

"Yes." Norealle could feel her face warming.

Thom bent down and ran his fingers through the grass. "You're right, it all feels real." He straightened, considering her thoughtfully. "Unless there is a fourth realm that I don't know about, I think we might call your world the Hidden Realm." A glint of excitement sparked in his eyes.

Norealle frowned. "It's not hidden."

"Well, it is to us. We haven't been able to travel to the Hidden Realm for hundreds of years."

"Oh." That made sense. She remembered her parents telling her the same thing about the Human Realm—a truth that had shattered her childhood fantasies of one day visiting.

"We never leave our realm either," Norealle said. "But my father has told me stories about the old days when humans used to visit."

"Your father has a good memory. That was a long time ago, as I'm told."

"Yes, it was."

Norealle discreetly studied Thom as they spoke. He was taller than her, but not by much. His shoulders were broad but narrow, in a way that suggested he'd yet to fill out. A shadow, hinting of a beard, darkened his cheeks in the dim light and emphasized the strong line of his jaw. His nose was straight, and his brown hair hung in shaggy waves over his ears but not quite to his shoulders. She struggled to not stare; her parents had failed to tell her how nice looking humans were. "I wonder how you are coming here? Even in your dreams? It's very odd."

Thom took in the towering mountains and rolling fields. "Maybe because I'm a Realm Walker?"

"You're a Realm Walker?" Norealle echoed, feeling another thrill of excitement shoot through her. "My father has told me stories about your kind!"

Thom fidgeted with the edge of his cloak. "You probably know more about it than I do," he confessed. "I only became a Realm Walker last night."

"When first I met you?"

He nodded. "Yes. I thought seeing you was part of becoming a Realm Walker."

"I don't think so." She frowned. "Why would I have anything to do with that?"

"I don't know, but I don't believe in coincidences. And after I saw you, the Creator spoke to me."

The Creator? "Who?" asked Norealle.

"You may call him El'Ohim?"

The very air around them crackled at the sound of His name, and the hair on the back of Norealle's arms stood on end.

Thom's mouth fell agape, clearly as affected as she was. "Whoa."

"You spoke to El'Ohim?" Awe filled Norealle. She could only imagine what that would be like. Longing burst from her heart.

"I did," Thom answered softly, his tone reverent. "Which is why I wonder if you're meant to help me, seeing as I had a vision of you too."

"I'm not sure I can do anything for you. This is only a dream...or something."

"But maybe you can," he put in earnestly. "I'm trying to find a way to the Hidden Realm."

Norealle instinctually stiffened, her voice growing wary. "Why?" She remembered clearly the stories her father told her of the pillaging ways the humans had explored their realm.

Thom's eyes widened. "I swear to you, I mean no harm." He rushed to explain. "Monsters from Zakar are destroying the Human Realm, and they will be at my home in days. I've been told that the key to lock them in Zakar may be with an immortal called the Key Keeper in the Hidden Realm."

Norealle felt her blood run cold. *Zakar.* The mere sound of its name stirred her pain and grief to the surface.

"Zakar." She spat the word, the very taste of it on her tongue utterly vile. Tears burned her eyes.

Thom took a cautious step forward, his hand hesitantly brushing her elbow. "Are...are you all right, Norealle?"

Her name rolled smoothly off his tongue, and Norealle closed her eyes briefly against the pain and anger raging through her bleeding heart. She wrapped her arms around her torso, hugging herself. "I lost my mother to those monsters."

Thom blanched. "I'm so sorry."

"You didn't do it," she mumbled.

He shook his head. "It's just a saying. It means I'm sad for you."

"Thank you." The soft word brushed past her lips before she added, "Zakar is evil. You can't let them have your realm."

"I know," Thom responded quietly, his voice sincere. "I will try and stop them, if I can. But I need to get into the Hidden Realm."

His eyes met hers earnestly. There was nothing treacherous or cunning in his gaze. Instead, all she could see was honesty and tentative hope. They were both quiet for a long moment.

Norealle gave a long sigh before speaking. "I'll ask my father if he knows anything that might help you."

Gratitude lit Thom's face. "Thank you, Norealle." His image blurred.

"Goodbye, Thom," Norealle called. Like the night before, he vanished, and she woke up back in her cave with more questions than answers.

Chapter 15

Of Maps & Visions

Thom drifted into full wakefulness and stared up at the night sky, lit with stars and the bright glow of the moon.

What just happened?

The stars blinked back at him, offering no answer. The dreams, which he now highly doubted were merely that, were far too vivid to be conjured by his limited imagination. He was seeing visions; of that, Thom was quite certain. But why? And why had he seen and spoken to the girl again?

Norealle. He let his mouth form her name silently. Norealle, with her trusting eyes and waist-length hair.

Silmea. The other name given to him.

Thom had assumed that the previous visions were a singular event, brought on by the gaining of his Realm Walker powers, but clearly, he'd been wrong. Questions with no easy answers piled up in his mind.

A gust of wind from the mountains swept down the hillside and through their camp. Thom shivered and pulled his blanket tighter around his body. The thin trees around their campsite bent with the wind, their spines creaking like an old man's joints. A deep chill penetrated his bones, and Thom curled into a tighter ball beneath his blanket, grateful for the fur that separated him from the unforgiving ground. Puck's fire no longer held even a spark of life, and morning still looked to be a long way off. With troubling thoughts to keep him company, Thom closed his eyes and tried to fall back asleep, half wishing and half fearing that slumber would carry him to Silmea.

As it were, true rest proved hard to achieve. Thom gave up trying at the arrival of dawn. With his blanket still wrapped around him, he leaned against the trunk of a thin tree and watched as brilliant pinks stained the clouds and the dazzling white streaks of the sun blazed across the crisp mountaintops. The newness of the day lit the sky with power. The peaks stood tall, their rocky spines thrust proudly against the glory of the sun. It was unlike anything he'd ever beheld in his life.

Thom gripped Puck's shoulder, giving it a shake. "Puck, wake up."

"Goway." A muffled reply came from somewhere under the large, man-sized lump of blanket. However, a moment later Puck's head emerged. "What?"

Not bothering with words, Thom pointed at the sky. With a grunt, Puck sat up, his gaze slowly taking in the majesty on display for them.

"I'll have you know, I was having a good dream," Puck eventually spoke.

"Girls?" Thom guessed.

Puck grimaced. "No. Food. Real food. Turkey with gravy and Ma's homemade bread and pickled beets."

From somewhere near Puck's feet, Traell popped out from beneath the blanket, his bat-like ears swiveling in Puck's direction as he licked his snout.

"Traell eat your dream. Eat it all! Yummy yum."

"Oi! Were you under there all night?" Puck yelped.

Traell wrinkled his snout. "Big one has stinky toeses."

"You shouldn't be smelling my toeses!"

"Toeses?" Thom choked on a laugh as he caught Puck's eye. "Really, Puck?"

Puck groaned. "Toes."

Thom watched as Traell scuttled on all fours over to his bag. With a quick downthrust of his wings, the faergo latched on to the fabric and began tugging at the flap.

"I got it, Traell," said Thom.

"Traell needs food!"

Thom shooed him off his bag and unpacked his provisions. He handed Traell half a biscuit, which Traell snatched, devouring it with unbridled enthusiasm. Amused, Thom tossed Puck a piece of salted meat. "Afraid it's not turkey and gravy."

"You owe me a good meal when all this is over," Puck warned.

"At least."

They ate quickly, splitting their attention between the sunrise and Traell's antics. Traell had scarcely licked the last crumb off his paws before he took flight and perched on a short branch. The limb drooped dangerously, but he hung on gamely.

"Up, up! Time to go!"

Puck took another bite of food. "I'm still eating, you little tyrant."

"At least we'll warm up if we're moving," said Thom ruefully.

It was cold, much like it had been in Silmea. Unbidden, No-realle's face drifted through his mind, and his pulse quickened. Thom shoved his blanket back in his bag. He was losing his mind, reacting to a girl he couldn't even be sure was real.

It only took a few minutes to pack up their campsite. Traell leapt off the branch and into the air, the poor greenery snapping back into place. Thom adjusted the straps on his shoulders and followed the faergo with Puck close behind.

The terrain was breathtaking, but despite the beauty, the day passed tediously. Traell drove them at a merciless pace, up the flank of one mountain and then down through the valley and up the side of another. He stopped only to demand Thom open a portal. The route Traell chose was rife with sharp stones and slick shale. More than once, Thom and Puck slipped and fell. Trying not to die, Thom had no time to think about Norealle or Silmea.

At one point, Puck spoke through panting breaths. "I can't believe I'm going to say this, but I miss those faerie trails."

Thom was too out of breath to answer, but he couldn't agree more.

It was late in the afternoon when the wind picked up. Thom eyed the darkening sky with alarm. The exposed hillside they were traversing offered no protection from a storm. Their quick pace had kept them warm all day, but getting wet would change that rapidly.

"We need to find shelter." Puck shouted as he took the lead, the gale threatening to carry off his words.

Traell squawked as the first raindrops began to pelt down.

Tugging up his hood, Thom bowed his head against the wind and followed Puck. Lightning exploded overhead. They scrambled across the uneven mountainside, rain pouring down as if a giant knife had cut the heavens like a massive waterskin, dumping its contents right onto their heads.

"Here!" Puck ducked beneath an alcove in the rocky face.

Thom and Traell crammed in close to Puck, huddling under the scant outcropping. It did little to shield them from the slanting rain. The giant droplets pounded against their bodies and formed rivers down their faces and arms. Thom blinked, trying to see out as he pressed closer to the rock. Thunder shook his bones, and a flash of lightning illuminated a peak in the distance. His mapmaker's mind fixated on the outline, and he squinted through the rain. It looked strangely familiar.

"Some storm," said Puck, his words catching on the wind and whipping away.

"Aye!"

Once before, Thom had watched a storm like this, but from the comfortable confines of his library with a warm cup of tea in hand. From the safety of his chair, he'd marveled at the raw power. But right now, misery eclipsed marvel. He was soaked, and he could feel water trickling down his skin beneath his wet clothes. Undoubtedly, every item in his pack was equally drenched, and he prayed the oilskin that he'd wrapped the map in was keeping it safe and dry.

Subdued before the power of the storm, they took refuge against the rock. The mighty thundering gradually moved south down the valley, and the flashes of lightning retreated after it. The sky above cleared.

Thom dragged a hand through his wet hair and shoved the dripping strands off his forehead.

"Traell wet." A voice grumbled from the ground. Traell, with his fur soaked and water dripping off his snout and ears, looked like they'd fished him out of a river.

"Me too." Puck groaned.

They're actually agreeing on something?

Thom shivered. "We need to get dry."

They were all dangerously soaked, and night was not far off. Heavy fog, a parting gift from the storm, had already settled over the tops of the mountains and was flowing quickly down into the valleys. Concern spiking, Thom scanned their surroundings for shelter. The odd shriveled tree dotted the craggy valley below, but apart from that, it was all rock.

Thom watched the advancing wall of fog with mounting worry. "Let's move. Once that fog is here, we won't be getting down the rest of this hillside."

"Aim for those trees down there," said Puck. "We need wood for a fire."

Moving as quickly as he dared, Thom picked his way down the wet rocks. The fog swept over them as they reached the narrow valley floor.

Puck took charge. "We don't have much time before it'll be dark as pitch. Thom, Traell, find wood."

Thom tossed his pack against a large rock and hunted for anything that could be used to start a fire. The trees growing in the harsh valley were sparse with short, rubbery branches covered in brittle needles. Thom hurried to the nearest one.

It'll have to do.

Pulling out his sword, he sawed off branches until he'd nearly stripped the tree of limbs. Traell darted about, harvesting an armful of small twigs from the ground.

Together, Thom and Traell hustled over to where Puck was digging a small hole and lining it with rocks. Shivers wracked Thom's body, clanking his teeth together. He dumped the armful of sawed-off branches beside Puck's firepit.

"Yikes, those are awfully wet and green." Worry filled Puck's voice.

Traell threw down his armful of smaller twigs. "Make fire! Traell cold!"

Puck snatched up Traell's offering. "These might light."

Encouraged, Traell zipped back and forth, bringing a few small sticks with every flight as Puck crouched down and carefully began building the fire the way Thom had seen him do many times before in his father's great oven. He used the larger sticks first and then stacked Traell's twigs in a crisscross fashion until he had an airy little tower. Last, he took a bit of dry moss that he'd collected earlier that day and set it beneath his carefully stacked wood.

Puck struck his flint in quick succession. Sparks scattered. The tension in the small camp mounted with each failed attempt. Finally, a tiny tendril of smoke trickled up from the damp pile of kindling. There was no time for rejoicing. Puck bent down, his hands cradling the infant spark, and blew, gently coaxing it to life. Thom hovered, ready with extra twigs in his hands if Puck needed them.

The wisp of smoke faltered and died.

We need that fire.

Puck struck the flint again. The spark landed and smoldered. He gave a gentle breath. A flame flickered to life.

Thom let out a whoop. "Well done!"

Puck hovered over his fledgling fire. "Sticks," he ordered between breaths.

With utmost care, Thom added the thinnest and driest pieces to the fire. Puck continued to feed it air, one slow breath at a time. They worked doggedly until a small fire crackled, and flaming tongues licked at the damp wood.

"More wood." Puck ordered.

Thom hurried into the mist. Not daring to go far, he hacked at the trunk of the first scrawny tree he found. It was scarcely taller than he was. Felling it, Thom dragged it into camp. When he returned, Puck was sitting on his pack, diligently feeding sticks to the hungry flames and arranging the wet wood to dry. Thom set the tree down beside the fire.

"The wood won't last long," Puck warned. "Try and dry out as much as possible."

Thom removed his wet boots and set them by the coals before tugging off his socks and draping them over the drying wood. Puck did the same.

"Let's see if anything stayed dry in here." Thom dug into his pack. To his surprise, the interior was moist, but not soaked as he'd expected.

"How's it look?"

"Only a little damp." *Thank the Creator.* Thom rummaged a little deeper and found the cloth wrapped food parcel. "Anyone hungry?"

"I could eat something," said Puck.

Traell, already curled up by the fire, lifted his head. His ears perked forward.

Thom unwrapped their rations of dried meat and two crusty biscuits. He split the meat in half and gave a portion to Puck. Two packets of food remained. Tomorrow, they'd have to figure something out or prepare to go hungry.

"Watch you don't light your fur on fire." Thom tossed a biscuit to Traell who promptly began gnawing on it. The little beast's paws were nearly in the hot embers, and steam unfurled off his soggy pelt.

Unenthusiastically, Thom broke the biscuit in half and took a bite. Dry pastry crumbled across his tongue. He chased it back with a few gulps of water. "Gah, that's awful."

Traell finished devouring his biscuit and belched. With an excess of snuffling noises, he curled up in a little ball and snored—loudly.

Puck and Thom studied him as they worked on their jerky.

"He snores like a grown man," Puck mused, "and I still can't decide if he looks more like a rat, a squirrel, or a bat."

Thom smirked. "A bit of all three, I guess. What was that he called himself—a faergo?"

"I can't remember."

They fell silent for a bit before Puck randomly chuckled. "I'm staring at him, but I still can't wrap my head around the fact that any of this is real. And you," he shook his head at Thom, "the guy who doesn't want to try brown sugar on his oatmeal because he knows he likes cinnamon, now has magical powers and is hiking through the wilderness."

"Careful. Cinnamon is amazing." Thom deadpanned, but his lips twitched.

Puck laughed under his breath and then sobered, clearly still marveling at their situation. "Thom, we're looking for a mythical kingdom, following a chubby, flying bat-squirrel, walking on magical faerie trails, and trying to save the world from monsters. This is crazy."

Thom knew exactly what his friend was feeling. "It's hard to believe. What annoys me most is that all of this existed our whole lives, and we're just now finding out about it."

"Makes you wonder what else we haven't been told."

"Exactly."

Traell's snores provided a steady backdrop to their low conversation.

"What's your plan?" Puck asked.

Thom reached inside his shirt and pulled out the leather-wrapped map. The fog was lifting, and there was just enough moon and starlight for him to see if he squinted. "Nothing major. Find the Key Keeper. Save our realm. Go home."

Puck took a bite of his food. "Sounds simple enough. Should be home for dinner, right?"

"Totally..." He grimaced and rubbed his stomach. "I miss Ma's cooking."

Puck groaned. "Don't you dare talk about it, or I'll hit you. This stale bread is torture."

Thom couldn't agree more. With care, he unrolled the parchment, relieved to find it dry. "There has to be something here."

Puck peered at it while gnawing on another piece of jerky, content to leave Thom to the parchment.

Thom studied the three spheres depicted on the map. Left to right, they lay: first The Hidden Realm, then The Human Realm, and finally The Realm of Zakar.

Silmea must be the Hidden Realm, nothing else makes sense. Unless there is a fourth realm...

Frowning, Thom inspected the Hidden Realm. It had no distinguishable roads, settlements, or cities, but many detailed lakes, rivers, and mountains. What kind of world was it? Were the people nomadic? Was it sparsely populated with settlements too small to be noted on a map?

He shifted his focus to Zakar. The sphere held several dark blotches on it, but no names were written beneath them. What could they represent? Like the Hidden Realm, there were no cities, towns or roads depicted. Was it a primitive place, populated only by mindless beasts?

Thom's eyes skimmed the Human Realm. He had worked on hundreds of maps detailing the kingdoms of Knor and Abadonia. This mapmaker's rendition was out of date but still reasonably accurate.

"Getting anywhere?" Puck asked.

Thom shook his head. "Not yet."

He examined the map, searching for anything that didn't quite fit or simply felt important. Did the placement of the realms mean anything? Was the Human Realm truly situated between the other realms? The Hidden Realm was slightly larger than the others, was that important? Thom's focus snagged on the black rim drawn around each sphere. The borders were not evenly sketched but decorated in unequal patterns of thick and thin lines. Curious.

Why hadn't the mapmaker simply drawn a consistent outline around the realms? Why the random pattern?

Every map had a key. The key could be in the words, the placement, an actual diagram, or even a puzzle. His gut told him the latter was probably the case in this scenario. Thom lifted the map up to see it better. The firelight flickered behind the thin sheet of parchment, highlighting the thickened strokes around the spheres.

Hmmm, possibly? His lips pressed into a thoughtful line.

Thom carefully folded the map, using the firelight to guide him, so that the Hidden Realm was directly above Zakar. Another fold, this time to place the Human Realm in alignment. Holding the map up to the firelight, Thom gazed through all three layers.

Interesting.

When overlaid on top of each other, the thick borders formed a nearly consistent circle, except for one spot that remained etched in thin ink. An entry, perhaps? Thom flipped the map open, noting with his fingers where the border had remained thin. Beneath his digit, a large mountain lay on both the Hidden Realm and the Northern Mountains in the Human Realm. He re-folded the map to ensure the location and note the place on the Realm of Zakar—not even a splotch appeared to indicate any significance in Zakar.

Thom carefully smoothed the map and let it lay across his lap. Unbidden, his mind drifted to the craggy slope that had caught his attention during the storm.

"I think Eldehein was right. There may be a connection to the Hidden Realm in these mountains," Thom said finally.

Puck wrapped his wool blanket around his shoulders. "Hopefully there is an inn or two in this direction then."

Thom stared at the endless lines of mountains on his map. There was no inn anytime soon. "Maybe," he hedged.

Puck slid him a sideway glance. "That's a no, isn't it?"

"Probably."

"Fantastic."

Thom folded the map and tucked it away, his thoughts drifting back to a certain dark-haired girl with searching brown eyes. He absently touched his chest, his mind recalling the brush of her fingers and the surge of awareness that had coursed through him. Did she even exist beyond his visions?

Thom dozed off beside the crackling fire and awoke in another vision. He was standing on the flank of a mountain. His eyes scanned the imposing crags that surrounded him on all sides.

Where was she?

As if his thoughts had summoned her, Norealle blinked into existence beside him. Thom yelped, startling violently. For her part, she didn't look nearly as surprised to see him.

"I was starting to think you wouldn't come tonight," Norealle stated bluntly, as she tucked a thick lock of hair behind her ear.

"Believe me, I don't know how any of this happening," Thom grumbled, embarrassed at the unmanly yell that had leapt from his mouth. He released a forceful breath, still recovering from the shock of her abrupt appearance.

She frowned, her head tilting to the side as she studied him. Without warning, Norealle stepped closer, lightly touching his cheek. Thom stilled, his breath catching, as her soft fingers grazed the stubble of his jaw.

"You look tired. And pale." Concern filled her voice, and Thom could see the questions in her probing gaze.

He swallowed hard, alarmingly aware of the way her dark eyelashes swept across her fair cheeks when she blinked and how the breeze stirred her hair. Her pink lips parted, and Thom's mouth grew dry.

"Thom?"

Thom jerked his eyes back up to meet hers, heat crawling up his neck to warm his face. "We've been hiking. A lot. And it's cold," he finally answered.

Her fingers fell away.

"Could you take this back with you?" she asked, unclasping her thick cloak. A blast of cold mountain air buffeted them, nearly snatching the garment from her hands.

Thom hurriedly grabbed the cloak, shocked at her unselfish act. Awkwardly, he settled it over her shoulders, his heart giving an extra thud as his knuckles grazed her neck. "Thank you...but please keep it. I'll be all right."

Her dark eyes lifted to meet his, the genuine kindness shining from the depths rocking him.

"Are you sure? I have another."

She's going to be the death of me.

Women had always unsettled Thom, but none quite like Norealle. If she wasn't scaring him half to death, she was lighting his nerves on fire with her touch or scrambling his brain with unprovoked kindness. A tremor, that had nothing to do with the cold, passed through Thom's hands as he gently took the clasp from her and refastened the cloak.

"Puck is pretty handy at getting a warm fire going," he assured her, hardly recognizing the unevenness in his own voice.

Her eyes lit with curiosity. "Who's Puck?"

A safe question. Thom stepped back, settling his hands deep into his pockets. "My best friend and travel companion."

"Is he human too?"

What?

"Yes," Thom answered with a startled laugh. "What else would he be?"

She shrugged, her cheeks turning rosy with a slight blush. "A friend can be anything."

Another stiff gale slammed into them, and Norealle wrapped her cloak tightly around her body. She raised her voice to be heard over the wind. "Did you really *just* become a Realm Walker?"

Clenching his teeth against the cold, Thom fought back a telling shiver. "Yes." He paused. "Why do you ask?" As quick as it had arrived, the temperamental wind died back down. The mountain was as unruly as a spoiled child.

Norealle pulled up her hood, settling it over her head. "My father said it is very unusual for a Realm Walker to be strong enough to travel here, even in a vision."

Thom grew alert, hungry for information. "What else did he say?"

"That was all, really. Just that you must be strong to be traveling here and then pulling me into your dreams."

Disappointment settled into his heart. He'd hoped for something more than that from her father. Perhaps a hint on how to enter the Hidden Realm? Or advice on searching for the path?

Thom tried to infuse some optimism into his voice. "I keep opening portals trying to find a path to the Hidden Realm, but I can't. Did your father know where one might be?"

Norealle bit her lip. "He said that if El'Ohim wanted you here, that He would show you how."

Thom fought the urge to groan out loud. He pondered her answer for a moment before slowly responding, "So, there is a way. We aren't chasing a fool's errand."

"He did tell me that Silmea is called the Hidden Realm by your kind," Norealle offered, clearly sensing his frustration.

At that, Thom couldn't help but smile. "Thank you. That's helpful."

They were both silent for the space of several heartbeats before Thom spoke again, "There's something about this mountain." He traced his gaze across the craggy, unforgiving contours.

Norealle's voice softened, "My father says he feels closest to El'Ohim here."

Thom could understand that. There was *something* about this place.

"Maybe we can explore from here and find your path." Norealle offered, willingness glimmering in her brown eyes.

"All right." Thom agreed, then quipped mildly, the corners of his mouth tipping up, "but I thought you said El'Ohim would help me find the way if I was meant to."

An almost cheeky grin curved her mouth. "Yes, but no one said I couldn't assist."

Thom chuckled. "I would never refuse your help."

The delight that lit her eyes was reward enough for his acceptance, and Thom had the distinct feeling that he'd be hard pressed to deny her anything.

Norealle grabbed his hand, tugging him a few steps up the mountain slope. Too shocked to do anything else, he stumbled after her.

"Come on, let's start with this side of the mountain," she urged.

It was hard to focus on anything other than her warm fingers threaded through his. This was why books were far safer than women and adventures. The combination of the two was a confounded disaster for his normally logical thoughts.

Utterly distracted, Thom hurried to keep up to Norealle's nimble steps, his brain blanking as to *why* he was tripping and struggling up the mountainside. The terrain grew rougher, and Norealle dropped his hand. His thoughts finally unscrambling, Thom called for her to stop.

"Why here?" She scanned the rock-covered cliffside for something remarkable.

Winded, Thom dragged in a few deep breaths. "I need to check for a path." He could see the questions swimming in her eyes but was grateful when she didn't voice them. It was enough just trying to breath. He felt for his magic, smiling as it leapt forth.

Norealle scrambled away as the green orb appeared. "What is that?" she cried out.

Thom darted a quick glance at her stunned face and dared a grin. "Portal magic."

She edged closer to him, positioning her body behind his as she peered around his shoulder. Her nearness did not help his concentration. Trying to ignore the sweet scent of flowers that drifted off her skin, Thom somehow managed to open a portal to The Inbetween. Traell would have been proud—he'd done magic with a very substantial distraction present.

Sadly, as in his world, the sphere was empty. A growl rumbled up Thom's throat, and he withdrew his power.

"Nothing." Disappointment slammed through him. He'd hoped it would be different here.

"That wasn't nothing!" Norealle protested in amazement.

Thom sighed and then explained, "The portal was empty. There's no path."

"But you're the Realm Walker. Can't you make a path? In the old stories, some Realm Walkers used to do that."

Thom shook his head. "I don't know how."

"Have you tried?" she challenged.

"No," Thom admitted.

She gestured at the empty space where the sphere had been. "Well, you should." She looked at him, expectation written all over her face.

Her confidence was endearing, but she had no idea what she was asking.

"Norealle, I only learned how to make portals two days ago. I wouldn't know where to start."

"Well..." She considered him for a moment. "Can you make a portal *inside* the portal? Maybe that would work?"

Thom started to say no, but at the hopeful look on her face, he paused. It wouldn't hurt to try. Would it? He quickly reformed the portal. Norealle's warm hand slipped into his as she watched eagerly. Heat flooded through him.

"You can do it," she encouraged.

Her hand was not helping him focus.

Thom snuck a glance at her face, but she was staring into the portal, her face eager.

Well, here goes nothing.

He drew out a piece of magic from within and pushed it into the portal with a prayer. When had he become so reckless?

Creator, El'Ohim, please don't let me drag us into The Inbetween. I don't want to die in that emptiness.

To his astonishment, the piece of magic unfurled like a coil of rope and stretched into the endless abyss. It floated there like an untethered string being cast to and fro by the waves of an invisible ocean.

"It...needs an anchor," Thom mused out loud.

Norealle bounced on the balls of her feet, her enthusiasm tangible. "Do you have a powerful artifact or place in your world that you could anchor it to?"

Thom studied the drifting ribbon of magic. "No," he answered thoughtfully, "but I think the Northern Mountains are significant."

"Mountains are always places of power. Especially this one."

"The first time I came here, this mountain was almost alive," Thom shared.

"I remember."

Without warning, Norealle's face blurred. Thom tightened his grip on her hand, groaning. *Not yet!*

Her fingers slid through his.

"Look for an anchor in your world, Thom!" she called after him.

Thom desperately clung to the vision even as his body fell away. He willed the experimental portal to close a split second before Silmea vanished. He sat up stiffly in the shivering reality of his own realm and knew what woke him.

Chapter 16

A Treacherous Climb

Snowflakes coated Thom's body. The small fire they'd struggled so hard to light was nothing more than darkened, smoldering ash. Puck and Traell were asleep, but even in sleep, their bodies shivered. A thin layer of snow covered their prone bodies. Bone-deep cold cut through to Thom's core. He flexed his numb fingers. With effort, he pushed himself to his feet and forced his frozen legs to move. He stumbled over to Puck and shook him.

"Puck, get up!" Puck groaned but didn't move. Thom shook him again. "Get up!"

Puck opened his eyes, and for an alarming moment, Thom could see that his gaze wasn't focused. Slowly, his friend sat up.

"Snow," Puck mumbled.

"Aye, we need to get moving, or we're going to freeze to death out here."

Thom had read about men falling asleep and never waking again as the cold stole them away in their sleep. Stomping his feet, he moved over to Traell, nudging him with his toe.

"Traell, get up. It's snowing."

Traell batted his toe away with a paw. He blinked his large, black eyes and shook his furry body, creating his own little flurry as the white flakes flew everywhere.

"Not good. Not good," Traell puffed himself up into a ball Thom had begun to recognize as his warming state.

"We need to find better shelter and somehow get another fire going," Puck spoke through chattering teeth as he climbed to his feet.

"I think I know where to find the path," Thom interrupted.

Two sets of eyes swung to stare at him.

"I've been seeing a mountain every night in a dream," he kept his words vague, "and I saw the same one during the storm." He pointed into the night.

"You want us to hike through the mountains, on snow-covered rocks, in the dark?" Puck asked, his voice incredulous.

"We can't just lie here and freeze to death," Thom argued. "Let's pack up. We'll go slow. At least the movement will keep us warm."

"Lie here and freeze to death, or plunge over a cliff and die." Despite his words, Puck bent down and rolled up his mat.

Thom moved to his own supplies. His fingers were numb, and he struggled to get his mat strapped to his bag. He hefted his pack, the snowfall mercifully slowing. Moonlight streamed down and illuminated the sparkling landscape.

Thank you. The prayer drifted through his mind as they left their camp.

Thom moved carefully across the rough terrain with Puck close behind. Traell, hunkered down on Puck's pack, let out an indignant squawk every time Puck stumbled on the snow-slick rocks. They traveled in focused silence, and no one challenged Thom on his route. The odd cloud drifted across the moon, and in those minutes, he would pause to wait until the moonlight was once again lighting the way before moving forward.

Finally, they crested the flank of a mountain, and Thom saw the familiar outline he'd seen during the storm. His gaze raked across it, noting every detail. *It's the same mountain*—identical to the one he'd climbed with Norealle. He was sure of it.

"Why'd you stop?" Puck spoke from beside him, his gaze darting left and right.

"That's where we need to go."

Puck grunted. "It's big. And steep."

"Yeah." Legs protesting, Thom began the arduous trek, testing each footstep before planting his weight. It had snowed just enough to make the journey treacherous. By the time they reached the hip of the mountain, the early rays of dawn were painting the landscape golden. The skin on the back of Thom's neck prickled.

Traell flapped to Thom's shoulder and let out a high-pitched trill. "Traell feels magic!" He bounced, jarring Thom's balance.

"Careful."

A strong sense of *rightness* washed over Thom as he retraced the steps that he and Norealle had made. They didn't climb far. Something in Thom's gut told him he didn't have to. He stopped and formed a portal, nearly fumbling the act in his anticipation. His heart pounded as he opened it wide and studied the emptiness of The Inbetween. Norealle had told him to find an anchor, and the unshakable feeling that he'd found it settled deep in his bones.

It was the mountain. It had been the mountain all along.

He pulled out another ball of magic and sent it into the void. It behaved the same as it had in his vision, unfurling into the emptiness, but this time, Thom focused on the mountain's replica in the Hidden Realm. The ribbon of magic flattened into the unmistakable image of a path.

Traell let out a shrill cry as he flew in a series of dizzying circles. "The skinny Realm Walker did it!"

Thom stared at his work, speechless. A green path stretched into The Inbetween. It was there, as real as anything he'd ever seen.

"Is there a path?" Puck asked quietly from beside him.

"Aye, there is."

Puck fidgeted. "I was hoping I'd be able to see this one." His voice roughened. "But it's just black and empty."

"It's there." Thom gripped his forearm in a quick squeeze. "Just hold on to me, like on the faerie trails, ok?"

Puck grasped Thom's bag. "I'm ready."

"Now?"

"No point waiting. If we're going to die in there, we might as well get it over with."

Traell squawked and landed on Thom. "Let's go, Realm Walker!"

"What, no dumb-dumb this time?" Thom asked, stalling. The ring of magic shimmered, flowing like a living thing around the edge of the portal.

"You still dumblehead Realm Walker." Trael tugged his hair, but the gesture was less violent than usual. "Traell wants magic path. Go!"

Thom approached the opening to The Inbetween. His stomach churned as he eyed the slender path and the cavernous darkness surrounding it. He grunted as Traell's claws dug into his flesh.

Pivoting, Thom shoved Traell in Puck's arms. "Wait here."

Don't think. Just do.

He leapt.

The hair on the back of his arms stood on end as he passed through the portal. His boots touched down on something solid. The magical path, blazing like a torch, held firm beneath him. A relieved laugh broke past his lips, the sound echoing as if in an empty room. Thom glanced back through the portal. He could see Puck's mouth moving angrily, but he couldn't hear a word. Swiping his damp palms on his pants, Thom strode several more steps down the path.

We did it. Thom turned back to the Human Realm. He could see Puck through the center of the portal, waving his hands wildly. His skin tingled as he left The Inbetween. The inundation of sound was instant.

"What were you thinking, jumping in there?" The veins in Puck's temples pulsed within his flushed face.

"Testing it. And don't tell me you wouldn't have done the same."

"I don't give a flying hoot what *I* would have done! Don't *you* ever do that again."

Thom raised his hands in surrender. "All right. Fine."

"I mean it," said Puck. "Brother or not, I'll knock you flat." His nostrils flared. "Next time, send the flying squirrel."

Traell let out an indignant squawk. "Faergo eat flying squirrel and big dumb-dumb." He snapped his teeth at Puck and flapped onto Thom. "Send big dumb-dumb!"

"That's enough. Both of you."

Sullen, Puck grasped the back of Thom's bag.

Thom sighed. "Don't let go."

"I'm not the one with a death wish."

Fine, stay mad. Thom strode into The Inbetween without another word. When he was several paces in, he glanced over his shoulder. Puck's face was as white as Pa's flour. He lengthened his stride, eager to find the exit.

"Pretty path. Pretty path," Traell chanted, his furry body jostling Thom's head as he spun in a circle.

Thom gnawed the inside of his cheek. *How far do I need to go?* His gaze darted to the sides as he sought any indication that they'd gone far enough. "Do you think this leads all the way to the other realm, or do I need another portal?"

Puck's voice pitched, "You're asking us?"

"Traell?"

The little beast made an odd chirping noise. "Don't know. Don't know!"

Thom drew in a deep breath and willed an orb of swirling magic into existence. *Focus on the anchor.* Locking an image of the mountain in his mind, Thom expanded his magic until a portal sat perfectly on top of the path. Through its center, clear as anything, sprawled the stunning valley he'd visited every night in his dreams. In the center stood the proud form of the towering peak that existed in both realms.

"Land!" Puck let out a joyous whoop and clapped Thom on the shoulder.

Heart leaping, Thom jumped forward with Puck on his heels.

Chapter 17

Consumed

"How?" A simple question. The only one that Slager could formulate in that moment.

Triumph gleamed from Titus's blue eyes. "Breaking part of the wall had *some* usefulness, it would seem." To partly negate his words, he toed the enchanted chain that still tethered him—a failure that he never ceased to throw in Slager's face.

Slager bit his tongue. *Only some? Have I not led dozens of errgoths from this land through that hole? Brought you slaves? Led a war in your name?* Irritation burned, but he kept it carefully veiled behind an expressionless mask.

Either oblivious or ignoring Slager's inward chafing, Titus continued proudly. "A portion of my power has returned, and with the human blood," Titus eyes glowed with mad, maniacal glee, "I have created life!"

Slager followed his gaze to the vast plain. Mounds of misshapen forms filled the landscape. Some were mere hills, others had the vague shape of various beasts, and others... Slager watched as a lifelike image of stone and clay shifted, a giant wing flexing and breaking free of its molding as it threw back its gnarled head and sliced the air with an ungodly shriek. Errgoths. Thousands of them. No longer would Titus be limited to the scant remnant leftover from his era of creation hundreds of years before.

This changes everything. An image of the relentless havoc delivered by a mere score of errgoths flickered through Slager's mind. *They will devour the Human Realm in its entirety.*

A withered seed of humanity within his soul flinched at the thought, and trepidation tentatively touched his conscience. Slager swallowed, his mouth growing dry as he rasped, "How will I control that many?"

Titus crossed his arms, still proudly staring out over his handiwork. "I will give you a portion of my power."

What? Shock spasmed through Slager, and his heart accelerated, anticipation slicking his palms. *Finally!* He rested a trembling hand on the hilt of his sword. For years, Titus had dangled the hope of increased power before Slager, but he had never delivered.

Titus's face hardened as he muttered, as if speaking only to himself. "I will rule the Human Realm, and this time, El'Ohim will not stop me."

With the speed of a viper, Titus wheeled and struck Slager with vicious ferocity. His dagger sliced through bone and muscle as it drove into Slager's heart before wrenching free.

With a strangled cry, Slager's knees buckled. Blood spurted. Pain seared. Disbelief seized upon horror.

Titus fisted Slager's shirt and hauled him bodily to his feet. "Stand!"

Blood gushed from his wound. Slager choked, a copper tang filling his mouth. Titus gripped him roughly, forcing him to remain upright.

The landscape tilted.

Slager's vision wavered.

Pain seared.

He was dying, his lifeblood splashing onto the hard ground and seeping through the uncaring grains of sand. Vaguely, he was aware of Titus staring at him, drinking in his pain. Enjoying it.

"Fail me, and I will do much worse," the master of Zakar crooned, and then Titus stabbed his fingers into the gaping wound.

Slager's entire body jolted, his head snapping back. Raw power seared into his frantically beating heart and spread like lava through his veins. A soundless scream gaped his mouth wide. Titus yanked his fingers out of his heart. With an almost reluctant wave, he passed his hand over Slager's chest, knitting the torn flesh back together.

Slager stayed upright but barely. Bile joined the taste of blood in his mouth. He could feel the inky taint of his master's ambition and insatiable lust for revenge seeping through every pore of his body. Power, raw and pulsating, beat through him.

Addicting.

Drowning the last residuals of his humanity.

Titus watched him, dark knowing gleaming in his icy gaze. "Conquer the Human Realm. Bring me slaves. Bring me victory."

Slager nodded, hatred for the realm of his birth burning through him.

"Yes, master."

No trepidation remained. The Human Realm would bleed, and it would fall.

Chapter 18

An Arrival

Thom stared. They had made it to the Hidden Realm. A green valley stretched out before them like an emerald blanket draped upon the feet of the majestic mountains that towered on either side. Their rocky robes and snow-capped crowns emitted a magnificence that made a mockery of the triangular shapes sketched onto his map. Waterfalls cascaded from their lofty shoulders and disappeared into the delicate mist that hung suspended over the valley far below like a billowing skirt. For a long moment, neither Puck nor Thom moved as they absorbed the wild beauty. Even Traell was silent.

"Where do we go now?" Puck finally spoke, his tone thick with emotion.

"That depends entirely on who you are," a feminine voice spoke from behind them.

Puck spun, his blade ringing from its scabbard, but Thom stilled. He recognized that voice. It was *her*.

There was a thud. Then a grunt. Thom turned. Puck was on the ground with a thin blade at his throat and a boot on his chest. Thom lifted his gaze from the prone body of his friend and found himself looking into Norealle's brown eyes. A slow smile spread across his lips. "Norealle."

"Hello, Realm Walker. You made a way."

"I did." His soul lifted, lighter than it had been in days.

"Umm...a little help down here?" Puck's throat bobbed beneath the tip of the sword.

Traell, who had ducked out of sight the moment Norealle had first spoken, burst out of the grass by Puck's head, cackling, "Stick the big dumb-dumb!"

Rolling his eyes, Thom gestured for Norealle to lift her blade. "Norealle, this is my friend Puck. The one I told you about. And that imp is Traell."

She removed her leather boot from Puck's chest and sheathed her sword. Puck scrambled to his feet and aimed a failed kick at a snickering Traell. "I'm going to turn you into a sausage!"

Traell winged out of reach and stuck his black tongue out at Puck.

Puck muttered a curse under his breath and faced Norealle. His eyes widened, and Thom recognized the familiar light of appreciation that lit his friend's gaze. A strange sense of possessiveness grabbed hold of Thom, and he took a subtle step forward, partly placing himself between Norealle and the interested gleam in Puck's eyes.

Puck's gaze bounced between them, and Thom saw the moment realization dawned. "Wait, you two know each other? How?"

"Norealle's been helping me."

Puck's brows pinched together. "When? How?"

"In my dreams." Thom glanced at Norealle, who was nodding.

"In your *dreams*?"

Thom chuckled, the incredulity in Puck's voice perfectly suited to the situation. "You act like that's the craziest thing you've heard lately."

Puck muttered something unintelligible under his breath.

Norealle faced Thom. "I still can't believe you're here!" she marveled, wonder filling her voice. "What was the anchor?"

Thom let his gaze travel over her face, absorbing every detail of her smooth skin, the small upturn of her pert nose, and the excitement dancing in her brown eyes. She was *real*. "The mountain."

A satisfied grin curved her lips. "That makes sense."

Gratitude welled deep within Thom's heart. "Without you, we'd still be stumbling around in the ice and snow."

A loud cough sounded to Thom's left as Traell hovered into view and bowed deeply midair. "My lady. Traell is most happy to meet your beautifulness."

Thom wanted to swat the besotted look off the little imp's face. What was with his companions?

Norealle laughed and waved him off. "Go find your folk, young one. Look in the forest on the far side of the lake, just beyond the meadow. They like the rocks and older trees there."

Traell's eyes lit up, and he bowed low once again. With wings beating faster than Thom had ever seen before, he shot off down the valley.

"Good riddance," Puck grumbled.

Thom glanced at his friend. Puck was staring at Norealle like a man seeing the sun for the first time in weeks. Now that he didn't have a sword at his throat, Puck's swagger was rapidly returning. An easy grin spread across Puck's face, the same way it did with all the maids back home. Thom gritted his teeth, feeling oddly vexed.

"Puck Pearcely," Puck introduced himself.

Norealle dipped her head in greeting, her eyes flickering over him, but not lingering. "Well met, Puck Pearcely," she replied politely. She pivoted to Thom and held out her hand. "Come, Thom. I want you to meet my father."

Relaxing, Thom grasped her smooth hand, his fingers folding gently around hers. Puck gaped as he stared from Norealle to Thom. He mouthed an incredulous "what?" to Thom, but Thom merely shook his head. He'd explain later.

Norealle began to walk, and Thom willingly followed. "My father is going to be shocked to see you."

Thom slid a sideways glance at her. She sounded a little too thrilled at the prospect of surprising her sire. "Do you want to go warn him before we march into his home?"

"No, it's fine." She tossed her hair over her shoulder. "He probably already knows you're here."

She led them a short distance into the valley, their route hugging the base of the mountain. The dampness of the long grass soaked Thom's boots, and the mist from the waterfalls clung to his hair. An odd sense of contentment settled over him. The cold no longer bit at his skin, and jagged mountain rocks didn't threaten to send him sprawling with every step. They had made it to the Hidden Realm; the first step of their impossible journey had been accomplished.

"This way." Norealle gave his hand a little tug and steered him up the hillside.

Thom's breathing deepened as the climb grew more difficult. "You live on the mountain?" There was no need to specify which one. There were mountains all around, but only one had served as their anchor to another realm.

"Yes. It's not too much further," she encouraged.

"Where are you taking us?" Puck questioned from behind them.

Thom turned guiltily. He'd almost forgotten the presence of his friend. Puck ignored him, completely occupied with Norealle.

"You'll see," she answered lightly, guiding them further up the slope until rocks replaced grass, and they found themselves on a path. It stretched far ahead, the well-worn trail snaking over the gnarled terrain.

"Watch your step," Norealle warned. She released Thom's hand, taking the lead.

The path narrowed into a mere ribbon along the craggy slope and angled sharply upward. Thom found himself focusing on every footfall, lest he misstep and take a nasty tumble down the slope. Up ahead, Norealle climbed nimbly, her footfalls light and sure as she navigated the trail with enviable ease. For the thousandth time that week, Thom rued his lack of physical fortitude as he gulped in air, struggling to keep up with her. The only satisfaction he felt was that he could hear Puck panting behind him.

Finally, Norealle slowed as the trail reached a dead end at the base of a rock wall. To Thom's shock, she propelled herself up over the ledge with a jump and push of her hands.

Not a chance. Thom bent over, planting his hands on his knees as he gulped in air. Sweat trickled down his face and puddled beneath his heavy pack.

"That girl can climb," Puck huffed, his face red from exertion.

Thom nodded, too busy breathing to respond. He slowly straightened with a groan. "This is the second time today I've had to chase her up a mountain."

Before Puck could form a response, Norealle's voice called from somewhere overhead, "Thom?"

"Coming!" Thom drew closer to the wall and realized there were small steps carved into the surface. Using the steps and whatever handholds he could find, he heaved himself up over the rock ledge. To his surprise, he found himself on a flat surface. It was roughly the size of three wagons, and its stone surface was worn smooth. At its far end, against the chest of the mountain, stood the ominous mouth of a cave. Ruing the weight of his pack, Thom climbed laboriously to his feet.

Puck appeared beside him a moment later, eyeing the cave where Norealle had presumably disappeared. "Wait, Thom. We don't know her, and we don't know what's in there."

A flash of annoyance coursed through Thom, but he bit back a retort. He *did* know her, even if Puck didn't. He stepped forward, but Puck's hand clamped down on his arm.

"Thom," he growled. "Use your brain. She's gorgeous, I'll give you that, but you can't just walk in there."

Thom shook Puck's hand off and was about to argue when Norealle reappeared in the entrance. From the dark, another figure approached. A giant of a man ducked through the entrance of the cave and straightened. He towered over Norealle, the top of her head only coming to his chest. Long, straggly gray hair tumbled from his face and continued in a beard that reached his waist. A thick animal hide was belted to his body, held in place by a golden clasp larger than Thom's fist. The man had the same brown eyes as Norealle, but his gaze pierced straight through Thom, directly into his soul. It probed and searched, leaving him feeling utterly exposed.

"I felt your arrival, young Realm Walker," the imposing figure finally said, "and that of your companions."

The giant's focus shifted to Puck, and Thom sagged with relief as the heaviness lifted from his mind. To his side, Thom watched as Puck visibly fidgeted beneath the intensity of the giant's stare. Subtly, Thom swiped his damp palms over his pants, trying to shake the uncomfortable feeling that Norealle's father had somehow been inside his head.

Finally, the man spoke again. "I am Keifor, Norealle's father. Come, you must be tired from your journey." He left them on the ledge and disappeared into the cave.

Norealle hesitantly approached Thom and Puck, her face apologetic. "I'm sorry. I should have warned you. My father is gifted with the Sight. He can perceive the hearts of those he sees."

"Was he reading our minds?" The idea did not sit well with Thom.

Norealle shook her head. "No. He can get a sense of your intentions and the nature of your spirit."

What was there to say to that? Thom grimaced. "I see."

"There is nothing to be afraid of. Well, unless you mean us ill." She had the nerve to smirk, before spinning on her heel, her hair swinging about her hips. "Come!" she called, her voice drifting back to them as she disappeared inside the cave.

Puck eyed the entrance to the cave warily. "Thom, I don't know what that fellow did to me. But a man should ask before looking at someone like that." Puck crossed his arms over his chest. "It felt like he was flipping through my thoughts like a book."

"It was unnerving," Thom admitted.

"You're still going in there, aren't you?"

Thom shrugged. "We've come this far. And what choice do we have?"

"Who are you, and what have you done to my boring friend?" Puck groaned but followed Thom inside.

The cave had a narrow entrance which was lit from outside, but once they were several feet in, the natural light faded and was replaced by glowing yellow stones embedded in the walls. The effect spread a warm light, illuminating the gravel path. The tunnel was short, and it opened into a cavern the size of a small home.

Thom took in the room. Despite the rock and lack of outside light, it was inviting. He could feel the warmth from a large fireplace that looked like it vented up through the rocky ceiling. In front of the fire, three wooden chairs rested. Their placement told a story, and Thom could almost picture Norealle and her father sitting in those seats, warming themselves and talking about their day. His heart sank as his gaze faltered on the third chair. Was that her mother's? Or did she have other siblings?

To the left of the fireplace stood a tall countertop with shelves pounded into the cavern wall above it, each stacked with an assortment of dried food and herbs. A few steps away from that sat a hand-hewn table with three stools. Against the far wall there was a single bed draped with animal skins and covered in a hand-woven blanket. A man-sized rock wall cut off one corner of the cave, and Thom assumed it led to a private room. It was a crude home, but Thom sensed that it was diligently cared for.

Keifor stooped beside the fire and gave the spit a turn. The smell of cooking meat and spices filled the cave. An assortment of dirty root vegetables lay spread across the table, and Thom watched as Norealle lifted a bucket of water onto the surface.

As if sensing Thom watching her, she met his gaze. "Lunch will be ready soon. I assume you're hungry?" Norealle dunked the vegetables into the bucket and scrubbed the dirt off.

His stomach growled. "Very."

The promise of food drew Thom further into the cave with Puck at his heels. Thom dropped his bag on the floor and pulled out a stool opposite Norealle. He grabbed what looked like an overly large potato and cleaned it.

Puck stopped beside the table and asked, "Where do you want our bags?"

Norealle pointed. "Over there by the wall. Thank you."

Puck picked up Thom's bag and headed in the direction she'd indicated.

Thom selected another vegetable, speaking as he worked. "Did you ask your father anything more about the Key Keeper? Or Realm Walkers? Or Zakar?"

Norealle's fingers paused, and she arched a brow at him in amusement.

"I've had a lot of time to think." Thom explained, giving a half chuckle, the sound self-deprecating.

"Then why only three questions?" Norealle teased.

Thom's own humor rose to the surface. "I'm also wondering how the dreams worked and how we were both in them. How magic within a portal turns into a path. If there are other anchors other than the mountain—"

Norealle burst out laughing and held up her hand. "Okay, stop!"

From across the cave, Puck called, "Don't get Thom started. When he gets talking about brain stuff, he can really ramble."

"I like it." Norealle stated, her tone softening as she regarded Thom.

The way she was looking at him made Thom feel like the only person in the room. He drew in a breath, trying to calm the alarming sense of awareness that was zinging over his skin. She leaned forward, and all Thom's thoughts evaporated as she answered the question he no longer cared about. "I didn't get a chance to talk to my father much after last night, but now that you are here, you can talk to him."

Great. I can sit there while he sifts through my mind and realizes that I can't keep my eyes off his daughter. The thought was not a comforting one, and Thom hoped his unease didn't show on his face.

"Good idea," Thom answered, trying to infuse confidence he didn't feel into his voice.

Norealle gestured with a carrot, her tone thoughtful. "We were right about one thing though, Thom. The dreams were meant to help you find your way here."

Thom felt himself relax as he regarded her, respect kindling in his gaze. "*You* were right about a lot of things," he replied humbly. "And the dreams would have meant nothing without you in them."

Norealle's cheeks flushed. She ducked her head, deftly slicing the carrot as she spoke from behind the curtain of her dark hair. "I believe it was El'Ohim's doing. I'm just glad I was a part of it."

Keifor's deep voice rumbled from near the fireplace, jarring Thom back to realization that they weren't alone. "El'Ohim uses all of us, if we are willing to follow where He leads."

Thom could feel Keifor watching him, so he turned in his seat, meeting the giant's unnerving gaze. Unlike the first time Keifor had studied him, Thom didn't feel laid bare.

Keifor continued to speak, "I can feel His design deeply on you, young Realm Walker."

Thom's gaze dropped to the vegetable he still held in his hand. "I am nothing, sir."

A deep chuckle rumbled from the man's barrel of a chest. "Aye, isn't that a wonderful place to start? We are all nothing. From the dust we came and to the dust we will return. His mighty power blazes most brightly through the weakness of His followers."

Puck approached the table, smirking. "If weakness is what He's after, He'll be able to blaze pretty bright in you, Thom." He elbowed Thom.

Thom frowned and shifted on his stool as he selected another vegetable.

Norealle stopped working. She straightened, her dark eyes narrowing at Puck. "Is that how you talk to your friends, Puck Pearcely?"

Puck leaned back and threw his hands wide. "Hey, I didn't mean anything by it. Right Thom?"

Thom hesitated. "Right." He scrubbed harder at the brown spud. Jabs like that weren't typically Puck's style. *I should have told him about Norealle and the visions.* It was too late now. They'd have to talk. Later.

Escaping the conversation, Thom addressed Keifor, "Sir, do you know where the Key Keeper lives?"

"He roams the land as he pleases and goes wherever El'Ohim guides him," Keifor answered without hesitation.

"Well." Puck sank down on a stool beside Thom. "That's going to make it hard to find him."

"Why do you wish to find him?" Keifor asked, but Thom had a feeling that he already knew the answer.

Puck jutted his chin toward Thom. "The Realm Walker here is supposed to get his help. He needs to shut a wall or something. Not that he tells *me* anything."

Thom flinched.

"Beasts from Zakar are attacking our country of Lomair, in the Human Realm," Thom said quietly. "I was told that the Key Keeper might be able to help me lock them back in Zakar, and that I'd find him in the Hidden Realm." He glanced at Norealle. "Though, if your realm is as big as ours, finding one person isn't going to be easy."

"It's big," Norealle confirmed. "Where are you going to start?"

Thom gestured above his head. "These mountains, I think. They seem to hold a lot of answers."

Norealle's father sat on one of the chairs in front of the fire. His large frame dwarfed the piece of furniture. "Why else do you seek the mountains?" he inquired.

Thom hesitated a moment, then reached inside his vest and drew out the map. He brushed bits of food off the table before spreading it out. He was keenly aware of Norealle abandoning her stool and moving to stand behind him to watch over his shoulder. Thom offered her a quick smile.

"If you look at these spheres here," he tapped the map and then traced the dark outlines, "the borders are inconsistent. If you rotate and overlap them on top of each other, you'll see that they make a complete border." His finger moved to the bottom left of the Hidden Realm sphere, the top right-hand corner of the Human Realm, and the far right of Zakar. "But not at these spots. We left the Human Realm where this gap indicates, and I think we entered the Hidden Realm here." He tapped the spot. "This mountain exists in both our realms and was the key to being able to form the path."

Thom glanced up to see an approving light sparkling in the giant's eyes. Puck grunted beside him.

"Very good. Very good indeed." Keifor looked thoughtfully at Thom. "Now, why do you think the Key Keeper you search for is also in these mountains?"

Thom shrugged. "I was told to find the Key Keeper and close Zakar. I'm assuming, by his name, that the Key Keeper holds the keys to the realms. And if I were such a person, I'd want to be near the gate of my realm, which I think is this mountain."

Puck peered down at the map. "Or as far away from it as possible."

Thom wasn't convinced. He felt a hand rest on his shoulder, and he glanced up at Norealle.

"El'Ohim has His ways. If it is His will that you find this person, you will."

The truth of her words settled deep into Thom's heart, and he felt peace wrap around his soul. She was right.

Dinner was the heartiest meal Thom and Puck had consumed since they'd left Knor. Both young men ate ravenously. Their hosts graciously kept placing food in front of them until they were satisfied. Keifor asked about the Human Realm—which kingdoms ruled and the state of the land. Thom and Puck took turns describing the war and everything that was currently happening. Norealle asked how Thom had become the Realm Walker, and he told them about Eldehein. The conversation reminded Thom of home and the many meals he'd shared with Puck and his family. Keifor left the cavern shortly after lunch finished, and Thom helped Norealle clean up while Puck sorted through his supplies.

"Do you want me to show you around outside?" she asked.

Thom smiled ruefully at her. "As much as I want to do that right now, I think we need to rest. A bad storm raged all night in our world, and we didn't get much sleep. We ended up walking most of the night to keep warm and find the mountain."

Norealle grimaced. "Sounds cold."

"It was."

"You can set your mats up over there." She pointed to the far side of the cave near the lone bed.

Thom stifled a yawn. He badly needed a few hours of decent sleep.

Puck and Thom settled down on their mats while Norealle quietly drifted about the cave tidying up.

"Hey, Puck." Thom kept his voice low.

Puck didn't look at him. "What?"

Thom sighed. "I'm sorry. I should have told you about the visions I was having and about Norealle."

Puck picked at a piece of mud that had dried onto his wool blanket. "Yeah, you should've."

"I know."

Puck abruptly looked up, his blue eyes filling with hurt. "Why didn't you?"

Thom clenched his fists, his nails digging into his palms. The pain in Puck's eyes was far worse than his anger. "I thought you'd think I was crazy." The excuse sounded lame, even to his own ears.

Puck snorted. "Yeah, well, I'm getting pretty used to crazy." His voice lowered. "I would've listened."

"I know, and I'm sorry. I don't know what else to say."

"Say that the next time you have dreams with beautiful girls and other realms, you'll tell me. Got it?" A hint of Puck's usual humor lightened his last words. Thom recognized the deflection for what it was. Puck was forgiving him and moving on.

Thom smiled slightly. "If I have any more visions, I'll tell you."

"Don't forget the part about the beautiful girls," Puck warned.

Thom punched him in the shoulder, and Puck hit him right back. They shared a grin.

"We good?" Thom asked.

"We're good."

Feeling like a load had been lifted off him, Thom laid his head on his arm. Across the room, Norealle busied herself by the fire. Fatigue weighing his eyelids down, Thom sleepily observed how the firelight danced through her dark hair and highlighted the profile of her face.

Puck nudged him.

Thom rolled over to face his friend. "Yeah?"

"She's a pretty picture, that one."

"She's more than that."

Thom struggled to keep his voice even. He didn't want to watch Puck flirt with her as he did every other maid. Norealle was smart, perceptive, and kind. She deserved to be honored and respected, and the thought of Puck flirting with her was enough to make Thom's fists clench.

Puck was still watching her.

"Puck," Thom growled, feeling his ire rise.

His friend turned to him, a flash of knowing amusement in his eyes. "Aye?"

"Stop ogling her."

"Steady, Thom." Puck lifted a placating hand. "You like her. I'll stay out of the way."

Puck flipped over on his mat, and Thom was left staring at his back. Slowly, the tension drained from his body, and Thom let out a long sigh. What a day it had been. He'd found a way to the Hidden Realm using magic that he still didn't understand. Somehow, the enchanting girl from his dreams was real and sitting in the same room as him. And, even faced with Puck's charm, she still seemed to like...him. Food, warm and fresh, filled his stomach, reminding him of home. It was almost too much. In one day, his impossible quest had changed.

There was hope.

Chapter 19
A Testing

A clatter woke Thom some time later. He groggily blinked his eyes open, and the rock ceiling of the cave came into focus. So, it hadn't been a dream after all. He was in the Hidden Realm.

Thom sat up and scrubbed a hand over his face, grimacing at the feel of stubble. He needed to shave. On the mat beside him, Puck was still snoring deeply. Another clang sounded, and Thom turned to see the source of the noise. Norealle was wrestling a large log onto the fire and using a metal prong to leverage it in. Thom kicked the blanket off and hurried over.

"Here, let me help." He kept his voice low.

Norealle blew a lock of dark hair out of her face and handed over the tool. Using the fire iron, Thom wedged the section of tree trunk further into the belly of the fireplace. It would have taken a giant to carry such a massive piece of wood up the mountainside.

Where was Keifor?

Thom set the metal hook down, glancing out the entrance of the cave. He gaped. It was dark outside.

"Did we sleep all day?" Thom asked, his voice hushed.

Norealle nodded.

Thom watched as she unhooked a finely tooled scabbard containing her sword from a hook on the wall. She buckled it around her hips and tilted her head towards the outside, an unspoken request in her eyes.

Brow furrowing, Thom hesitated for a moment before retreating to his bedroll, grabbing his sword, and strapping it on.

"Puck, I'm going outside." Thom gripped his shoulder, giving it a brief shake.

"Harrumph," Puck mumbled in his sleep and snored on, oblivious to everything around him.

Norealle moved stealthily into the tunnel. With one final glance at Puck, Thom followed. Moonlight bathed the entrance of the cave, and a thick blanket of stars covered the heavens, much like it had the first night he'd seen her in a vision.

"This way," Norealle lifted her voice to a normal volume and began to deftly climb.

Thom stared after her. *What is she doing?*

The clouds parted, and the moon shown on a nearly invisible path chiseled into the rock and arrowing straight up the mountain. Norealle was already several paces up it.

Warily, Thom followed, placing his booted feet with care. "Norealle, where are we going?"

He'd already scrambled over several dark, ice-covered mountains the night before. Repeating the experience did not appeal. Norealle halted to wait for him, pressing herself against the cliff. They were above the cave, and the mountainside was jagged and alarmingly steep.

"Where are you taking me?" Thom repeated as he stopped just behind her, his fingers digging into a cleft in the sheer rock wall.

"To watch the stars," came her sweet response.

What? Thom eyed her incredulously. Was she serious? "I'd really like to do that with you, but..." He stumbled over his words, his throat bobbing as he swallowed hard. "I'm just really tired, can we maybe—"

Her laughter wrapped around him, easing his worry. "I'm only teasing you, Thom. You said you wanted to meet the Key Keeper."

Oh. "You could have led with that."

She grinned, revealing a side of mischief he hadn't yet seen in her. "I could have," she conceded.

Thom shook his head at her but couldn't help smiling.

Norealle sobered. "My father and I spoke while you were sleeping. He said I could bring you. I'd hoped to climb during the day, but you slept a long time."

Thom eyes warily followed the dark, treacherous trail ahead of them. "You should have woken me."

"You were sleeping soundly. It's okay. We'll take it slow."

It didn't feel like a good idea, but Thom reluctantly agreed. They climbed carefully for what felt like hours. The spray from the waterfalls crystalized on the rocks, freezing and forming a slippery layer of ice. Thom could no longer move his feet without first making sure he had a firm handhold on the rocky face. The heavy chill in the air cut through his clothes to his skin, but he said nothing as he followed where Norealle led. The moon continued its pilgrimage across the sky, and Thom prayed it would not fall behind the neighboring mountains before they reached the end of their journey. It would spell certain death trying to traverse the icy mountain without any light.

His skin cold and clammy, Thom stopped on a small ledge to catch his breath. A sudden clatter of stone jerked his eyes up, and the dark form of Norealle pitched and began to slide. Thom lunged forward without any thought of his own footing. He grabbed her, snatching her back against his chest. His feet slid on the loose shale. Thom stumbled, slamming into the rock wall.

Norealle's fingers dug into his shoulders as they fought to regain their balance. Thom held her close as he secured his footing, one arm locked firmly around her waist.

They stared at each other, shocked. Finally, Thom spoke, his voice rough even to his own ears. "Are you okay?"

"That was...close," Norealle choked out.

His heart was still pounding. "Very," he answered grimly. *If I hadn't looked up at that exact moment...*

He tightened his grip on her as he stared down the cliff that Norealle had nearly plunged over. It would have been a fatal fall.

"I'll not have you dying for my quest," he rasped, the realization of what had nearly happened straining his every word. "We'll wait here until the sun comes up."

Norealle braced her hand against his chest and carefully found her own footing. "We're almost there."

"No," Thom spoke through gritted teeth.

"Truly, it's just around the corner. It'll be safer to wait up there." Her words cajoled him.

Thom reluctantly let her go, the temptation of safety the only thing convincing him to release her.

Norealle moved cautiously ahead and then paused. "Be careful, it gets really steep around this bend."

A snarl rumbled out of Thom's chest. "I thought you said it would be safer?"

"We'll be fine."

Nerves taut, Thom followed her up the rough terrain, his eyes on her as often as they were on his own footing and handholds. He climbed close, ready to yank her to safety if need be.

Together, they scaled the mountain, the cold air biting at their scraped fingers and exposed faces. Any signs of an established trail had long since disappeared. Light wisps of cloud passed before the moon, shadowing the mountain but never completely blocking out the light. They finally made it to the peak, and to Thom's surprise, there was a relatively level area where they could rest. Legs trembling from the strenuous climb, Thom paused. He watched as Norealle paced around the summit, clearly looking for something or someone. Thom's concern mounted. Where was the Key Keeper?

The clouds shifted, and moonlight flooded the area, illuminating the valley far below. Amazement eclipsed his worry, and Thom strayed to the cliff's edge. He looked down, and his stomach plummeted. How high were they?

A terrified scream exploded from behind him.

Thom spun, his heart leaping into his throat as his feet slipped on the loose rock. "Norealle!" he bellowed, scrambling across the peak of the mountain.

She was gone.

"Norealle!" Terror sliced through him as his eyes frantically probed the darkness, trying to spot any sign of her.

She'd been *right there*.

"Norealle!"

There was no answer. Thom threw a searching glance down each flank of the mountain. He yelled her name into the foreboding night. There was no sign of her. She was no longer on top of the mountain. As fast as he was able, Thom scrambled down the route they'd just climbed, desperately shouting her name.

A flash of red light, blinding in the darkness, flared in front of him. Thom stumbled and nearly toppled off the narrow precipice. The blaze of crimson solidified into a woman—a beautiful but terrible form. Her eyes, lidless hot embers embedded in her skull, bored into him. Scarlet hair, alive with flame, hung to her hips, and a gown of burning coals cloaked her body.

Thom retreated a pace as a black sword materialized in her hands. She bared her teeth at Thom, her canines piercing her lips. Thom stared, frozen in horror, as twin droplets of blood pooled on her lips before her tongue swept them away.

"Looking for something?" she crowed, and the tip of her sword dropped. Thom followed its descent as it touched a dark form on the ground.

"No!" The word ripped from his mouth as he lunged, yanking his sword from its scabbard. Thom swung wildly, knocking the witch's blade away from Norealle's crumpled form. A blaze of heat blasted him, and she hissed, reaching a gnarled hand toward Norealle's pale face. With a snarl, Thom clenched his blade in both hands and drove his weapon straight for her gut. She didn't even bother parrying the blow, and Thom stumbled off balance as his blade passed right through her. He regained his footing.

Chest heaving, Thom leveled his useless blade at the witch. "Get away from her!"

"Silly boy," she screeched. "Did you think that trinket could kill me?"

Thom's blade glowed red, and a scorching heat traveled up the weapon and into his hands. He clenched his teeth against the pain and swung again at the witch.

"Back away!" he bellowed, stepping over Norealle's motionless form and planting himself between her and the fiery abomination. The heat radiating off his blade turned scalding, and Thom felt his skin beginning to burn. With a cry, he dropped the weapon to the ground where it clattered over the edge.

The witch laughed, the sound like a death knell on the cold mountain air. Her eyes narrowed into snake-like slits. "Give up your quest, Realm Walker, and I will let her go."

"Not...a...chance," Thom gasped, the heat from the witch burning his face. He bent down and picked up a rock. "Get away from her!"

She cackled, seemingly pleased by his refusal. "I will end you, Realm Walker. You will never close Zakar."

Her mouth yawned wide, revealing rows upon rows of razor-sharp teeth. Thom threw himself on top of Norealle just as a blast of fire hit him, scalding his skin and burning his flesh. A scream ripped from his throat. Pain like nothing he'd ever felt before ravaged his body.

Darkness blessedly took him.

He heard his name, as if through a dark tunnel. "Thom!" A dank, musty smell assaulted his nostrils. "Thom!" The voice was desperate and louder this time.

Why did it sound familiar?

"Thom, get up, we have to go!" The voice pleaded.

The sounds of water dripping echoed in his ears. Thom blinked into the mottled darkness. He couldn't see anything. "I...I can't see," he cried, panic gripping him.

"Hold on to me. We have to hurry."

The voice was familiar, but it couldn't be. "Eldehein?" Thom gasped.

"Yes." Tension filled the warrior's voice. "Come on!"

Thom stumbled, grappling in the dark as Eldehein seized him by the elbow and hauled him to his feet. "Wait! Where's Norealle?"

"Who?"

"The girl!" Thom exploded, desperation edging his voice. "Dark hair, brown eyes...the witch had her!"

"There's no girl here," Eldehein answered grimly. "We're in a cave. But your enemies are coming. We need to move!"

What? No! Where's Norealle?

Eldehein's steely fingers tightened on Thom's arm as he dragged him into a stumbling run. "Hurry!"

Every step into the black unknown felt like it was going to be Thom's last. Heart wrenching, he ran. The sounds of yelling and pounding feet reverberated through the darkness behind them, echoing along the cave walls. Eldehein urged Thom faster. Giving up all hope of self-preservation, Thom sprinted, completely trusting the other man not to guide him to his death. The shouts grew louder.

"We aren't going to make it," Eldehein panted. "Form a portal, Realm Walker!"

"I can't! I'm blind!"

Words tumbled from Eldehein's mouth. "You don't need to see! Feel the magic!"

"I have no anchor!"

"Yes, you do! Your mind is the anchor." The shouts were nearly upon them. "Quickly!"

Panic strangled his focus, and Thom grappled within himself to find his magic. He yanked it outwards. He envisioned the green sphere opening and forming a portal, and then called forth more power, casting it through his imagined portal. Frenzied, he pictured the only thing that came to mind: the beautiful meadow in the Hidden Realm.

"You did it!"

Thom felt himself being dragged forward.

"Close it!" Eldehein barked.

Thom reached for his magic and to his shock, felt it return to him. The sounds of pursuit instantly ceased. They were in The Inbetween—nowhere else had such a complete deprivation of ambient sound and smell.

"Create an exit portal," Eldehein ordered.

Thom obeyed. The scent of grass filled his nostrils, and warmth from the sun caressed his face—or at least he assumed it was the sun. Thom took a cautious step and felt his feet sink into something soft. Was he in the meadow?

Eldehein released his elbow. "This is where I leave you," he announced.

"Wait! Eldehein! I can't see!" Thom yelled, alarm flaring hot within him.

There was no answer.

Heart pounding, Thom strained his eyes. There was nothing but darkness. Nausea churned his gut. He took a hesitant step forward, his hands swiping the air.

"Eldehein!"

"There is no one here but you, boy," a crone's craggy voice droned from somewhere in front of him.

"Who...who are you?" Thom stuttered, feeling utterly defenseless as he pivoted in the vague direction of the voice.

"I am no one, really," the voice replied. "But I can give you your life back, young man. Your sight. That pretty girl you lost on the mountain."

Thom's neck prickled as he became aware of the owner of that voice walking in a circle about him. He stiffened. "How do you know about her?"

She ignored his question, and her voice continued to move as she orbited him. "I can put it all to right again. I can send you back to your realm. Far away from the war and back to your library. I can make it so that you remember none of what has happened to you."

Thom's breath came in panting gasps as he turned, his fists clenching and unclenching, trying to face the voice as it moved. "Are you friend or foe?" Thom growled.

The voice chuckled. "That's a matter of perspective, my boy. What matters is that I can help you. So would that make me your friend?"

A cold finger slid down his arm, and Thom shuddered, pulling away. "Do you follow the Creator?"

There was a beat of silence, and then the voice replied, tone smooth, "I know of him."

"Not the same thing," Thom snarled. "Leave!"

The voice laughed. "Leave you? Here? Blind and alone? Is that wise, young one? Imagine sitting in your library, tea in hand, your maps in front of you... I could even throw in the girl. She'd make a pretty gift, wouldn't she?" The voice coaxed, but the temptations were not enough to drown out the warning in his mind.

"Leave," Thom ordered, his voice shaking. "Leave now."

There was a blast of air, then stillness.

"Hello?" Thom shouted.

Nothing stirred. He was alone. Thom lifted his voice and called again into the quiet. Silence greeted him. Heart pounding in his chest, Thom took one slow step and then another. He didn't know where he was going, but he couldn't just stay in the middle of nowhere.

With cautious steps, Thom waded through the grass and tripped over barren, rocky patches. Branches and bushes slapped against his outstretched arms and stung his face. He walked until his mouth was parched and his feet ached. Gradually, he became aware of the heat from the sun fading and the coolness of dusk taking its place. Was it nearly evening? Defeated, he stopped.

Grief punched through him. Norealle. Puck. His sight. All gone.

A familiar but distant sound reached his ears. He strained to listen. Was that running water? Hopeful, Thom shuffled forward until he reached what sounded like a slow stream. With a groan, he dropped to his knees and plunged his hands into the cool wetness. He scooped up the water and slurped greedily from his hands. The refreshing liquid slid down his throat, bringing life back into him. Once satisfied, Thom rocked onto his heels, his dripping fingers dangling between his knees as he crouched beside the water.

"El'Ohim..." Thom groaned the name, staring straight ahead at the utter blackness that consumed him.

Why has this happened? What did I do? I'm blind. I am utterly and completely blind and lost, and I don't know what to do... The fumbled prayer ached through his tired mind.

Fear clawed at his heart, along with a crippling sense of abandonment. Thom buried his face in his hands and hauled in a deep breath. Self-pity obscured any helpful lines of thought. Why had the Creator chosen him to do this impossible task if he was just going to abandon him in the middle of nowhere? With no one. Blind!

Thom fisted his hair. He wanted to scream, but he didn't dare. What if a predator was lurking nearby? He bitterly speculated that getting eaten might be a blessed relief. At least he'd be done with this cursed journey.

A warm breeze stirred against his body, and Thom dropped his hands from his face.

A voice spoke. "Thom."

Thom's heart exploded in his chest, and he leapt up, spinning blindly, his hands lifting in front of himself. He hadn't heard anyone approach.

"Thom," the voice spoke again, authority reverberating through the air and stilling Thom's fumbling movement.

"Who's there?" he called out, false bravado making his voice tremble.

"It is I. Did you not call me?" The voice came from every direction at once, and the skin on Thom's arms and neck tingled.

An overwhelming sense of utter horror mingled with awe burned within Thom. *It can't be...*

"And why not?" the voice replied to Thom's unspoken words.

Thom wordlessly sank to his knees, his head falling forward to touch the ground. "El'Ohim," Thom gasped, his body trembling against the earth.

"Lift your face." The voice ordered, though not unkindly.

Thom swallowed the immovable lump in his throat and obeyed.

"Why did you call me?"

His mouth grew dry. The Creator knew, didn't He? He knew the angered and frustrated thoughts that had been stomping through Thom's mind.

"I..." Thom's voice faltered, and he gripped a handful of earth in his fingers, seeking courage. The breeze stirred about him again, warm. He let out a shuddering breath. "I'm alone. I don't know where I am. I'm blind. Norealle is probably dead." He gripped the earth harder. Would the Creator simply burn him where he knelt for his insubordination?

"Are you alone?" the voice pressed.

Thom gulped and answered in a small voice, "No."

"Have I ever left you?"

Thom's shoulders drooped. The temptation to say no was strong, but... "Often."

He expected at any moment to feel fire burn his flesh from his bones. Frustration bubbled up through him, and he twisted, turning his blind face in the general direction of the voice. "I've prayed to you all my life. I've never heard you answer. Now I'm this 'Realm Walker,' and I don't understand the half of it. Apparently, horrid creatures are going to kill everything I know and love if I don't close this magical door to a kingdom I don't even know how to get to. I'm not strong like Puck, and I don't have a knack for weapons. I'm not experienced like Eldehein. I don't know what I'm doing or why I'm the one who has this job. I'm the wrong person! And now I can't even see!"

His chest heaved as if he'd just sprinted across the field. There was a long silence, and Thom glared, daring the voice to smite him. He was done anyway.

"Who do you think guided your footsteps to the Pearcelys' door so you'd have a family to love you? Who gave you the intelligence to be chosen by your king to study at his royal academy? Who gave you a friend with strength to walk this journey with you? Who sent you dreams to guide you to the Hidden Realm? I've not left you, Thom Darkfell. I chose you for this task."

"Why me?" Thom's voice broke. "I'm nothing."

"Is anything I make inconsequential?" The voice rattled his bones, and Thom trembled.

"No," he whispered.

"Do I make mistakes?"

The ground beneath Thom's knees shook, and his heart pounded so hard he could hear it. "No."

"Then stand up."

Thom found himself lurching to his feet.

"I *chose* you for this task. Do you doubt Me?"

Thom shook his head. "No, my Lord."

"I am El'Ohim. I do not make mistakes."

Chapter 20
Hidden in Plain Sight

The blackness around him deepened, and Thom pitched forward. He threw his hands out to catch himself, but the earth fell away to nothing. A cry ripped from his throat as he tumbled through the directionless void. Gradually, small spots of light danced through the gloom. They grew in number until the dark was scattered with...stars?

The feeling of something cold and hard solidified beneath Thom's back. A bone-biting breeze cut into his exposed skin and through the lining of his shirt. He groaned, fingers scraping against rock and stone as he slowly pushed himself upright. Disoriented, he looked around. He was on top of the mountain. In the Hidden Realm. And he could *see.*

Confusion filled him.

What just happened?

"Thom?" Norealle's voice called from behind him, thick with worry.

Thom startled and scrambled to his feet. "Norealle." Her name fell from his lips in a disbelieving gasp.

There she was. Whole. Not a hair on her head singed from the witch that had tried to murder them both. *How?*

"Are you all right?" she asked.

Thom wordlessly shook his head. He strode forward and wrapped his arms around her, pulling her against his chest. She stiffened in his arms before relaxing into him. Thom burrowed his face into her hair, his breathing ragged.

"You're not hurt?" He hardly recognized the raspy grate of his own voice.

"No…"

A shudder coursed through Thom, and he slowly dropped his arms away from her. "I watched you…die."

Norealle's face grew incredulous. "Thom, what are you talking about?"

"How long have we been up here?" he asked hoarsely.

"We just arrived," said Norealle. "Thom, what's going on? You're scaring me."

You're scared? I just watched you die at the hands of a flaming demon, got burned to death, sprinted through a tunnel with a dead man, lost my vision, spoke to El'Ohim… Thom reined in his rampaging thoughts. "I think I had another vision."

They were becoming far too lifelike. *How do I tell what's real? And what isn't?* Thom eyed Norealle. *Is this real?*

There was a smattering of rockfall and Thom spun, his sword singing from its sheath without hesitation. Norealle's father crested the peak of the mountain. Thom lowered the tip of his blade—the blade he apparently *hadn't* lost over the cliff.

He felt sick.

Norealle shot him another worried look before brushing passed him to greet her father. "Father, I brought him to you, as you asked."

Ill at ease, Thom stiffened. *Keifor asked for me? I thought we were meeting the Key Keeper.*

Norealle's father approached, but Thom did not sheath his weapon. *How do I know anything is real?*

Keifor stopped directly in front of him, and Thom glared into the man's probing gaze. The moon and stars seemed to dance in his eyes, and Thom felt himself falling into the bottomless pits of those twin orbs. Unlike the first time, warmth accompanied the searching look, and Thom relaxed slightly.

"He has completed the test," Keifor rumbled, pride underlining his tone.

"What?" Norealle darted a look between the two of them. "When?"

Thom stared hard at her father, his jaw clenching grimly. "Wait. The visions? That was *you?*" he bit out.

Keifor dipped his head in acknowledgement. "I showed you three scenarios, and you did well. You chose bravery when faced with the witch. You did not give into fear when you were blinded and chose instead to trust. You refused temptation, even when all hope was lost."

Thom's eyes narrowed. "There were four visions."

Keifor's brow furrowed. "Four?"

"Yes. El'Ohim came to me in the meadow." Thom heard Norealle gasp.

Keifor's dark eyes softened with knowing. "There is no describing being in His presence, is there?"

"No," Thom answered softly.

Norealle returned to Thom's side, and slipped her warm hand into his. The feel of her skin against his lessened some of his tension. Like a slow trickle, the stress faded. He squeezed her hand.

"I told you he was the one." Norealle spoke to her father, sounding far too pleased with herself.

"Peace, daughter." Those bottomless eyes flickered to Norealle before resting on Thom. "I had to be sure. One doesn't simply hand over the key to Zakar to just anyone without taking special care."

Thom stilled. "The key?" He searched her face, both wanting and fearing her answer. That mischievous sparkle that delighted and terrified him was back in her eyes.

"My father is the master of this realm, Thom. He's the Key Keeper."

Thom's shoulders sagged with unspoken relief, and he finally sheathed his sword. "We couldn't have done this test back at the cave?" he asked ruefully.

Norealle's father—or the Key Keeper—shrugged. "I was quite certain you were the one El'Ohim had told me of, especially when my daughter spoke to me of her dreams. But I had to be sure. My power is strongest on this mountaintop."

"The visions I just saw," Thom ventured, "were they..."

"Real?" Keifor finished.

Thom nodded.

"No. The ones I sent you were not, but they felt real, did they not?"

Thom's fingers titghtened around Norealle's hand. Keifor reached into his pocket and pulled out a handful of ordinary-looking keys. Thom raised his eyebrows. The Realm of Zakar was locked by one of those little pieces of metal? Doubt skyrocketed.

Sensing his disbelief, Keifor spoke. "They are more than they appear." He selected a key stained black and handed it to Thom.

Thom took it and curled his fingers around the dark piece of metal. Curious, he eyed the remaining keys in Keifor's hand.

"What are those ones for?"

Keifor chuckled, the sound like the deep stirring of rocks on a river's bottom. "Not all mysteries are for you to know, Realm Walker."

"Here." Norealle reached behind her neck and unclasped a silver chain. She took the key from Thom's hand and strung it on the necklace. Thom stilled as she drew close. Her fingers brushed the skin of his neck as she fastened the clasp. "There. Now you won't lose it."

Thom reached up and fingered the small piece of cold metal before tucking it beneath his shirt. "Thank you." He took a deep breath and faced the Key Keeper. "How do I find the gate to Zakar?"

The Key Keeper smiled sadly. "Finding the way into darkness is never the difficult part, it's finding your way out again."

Norealle spoke from Thom's side. "I wish to go with him, Father."

Thom's attention snapped to her face, his lips parting in wordless shock.

"I know. I have seen it in my visions." Keifor's voice was resigned, but he did not argue with his daughter. He gave Thom a pointed look. "You will keep her safe?"

Norealle made a sound of protest, and Thom reached over and took her hand, giving it a reassuring squeeze before responding, "Sir, I think she can look after herself better than I ever could." Thom felt more than saw Norealle calm beside him. "I would be grateful for her help, and I will guard her best as I'm able, although," he grimaced, "I'm no warrior."

Norealle straightened her posture, her chin lifting. "I *can* look after myself, Father. And as you said, your visions foretold it."

"That does not mean you can be reckless, daughter," he chastised, but the words held little sting. The Key Keeper's eyes lifted to the heavens. "The sun will rise soon. I would bid you rest today, and tomorrow make haste for Zakar."

Rest?

The days were falling away. Could they afford to delay? Thom's thoughts returned to Lomair and the army they'd left behind. What were they facing? Every day Zakar remained unbound, the danger to his realm grew. He needed to lock Zakar, but if the first leg of the journey was any indication, he would need all his strength to finish his task. Thom was exhausted—body, mind, and soul.

The words from the Creator floated through his mind. He had been chosen. As much as his adventure had felt like a cascade of chaos and impossibilities, he had been chosen. Somehow, this would all work out—if he didn't accidently drop the key in The Inbetween or break the door to Zakar and unleash never-ending terror onto the world. Thom's mouth curled at the wry thought. He would do what Keifor suggested and rest for a single day.

"You're smiling."

Thom startled, jarred out of his musings. Norealle was watching him curiously. On impulse, Thom gently tucked a stray lock of hair behind her ear, the smooth strands gliding through his fingers. "I was just thinking that everything would be all right as long as I don't somehow fumble this mission."

"You won't," she stated, completely unconcerned.

Thom wished he had her confidence. "I'm glad you're coming along," he confided. "I'm going to need your optimism."

"And my brain," she added impishly. "Remember whose idea it was to cast your magic into a portal."

Thom chuckled. "How could I forget?"

There was something about Norealle—an innocence and a raw openness that Thom dearly wished he could guard. She lacked the coyness he often witnessed in the Human Realm, even by girls young enough to still be in pigtails. Norealle didn't play the strange feminine games that left Thom feeling confused and utterly out of place. She was simply herself.

His stomach grumbled, reminding Thom of the long trek they still had before them and the friend he'd left behind. "We should head back before Puck wakes and finds us gone." He was not looking forward to picking his way down the mountain or Puck's anger.

Norealle waved his concern away. "I told the sparrows to let him know where we were if he woke up before we returned."

Thom blinked, but his amazement only lasted a moment. Nothing truly surprised him anymore. "The sparrows? They talk?" he asked dryly.

She gave him a funny look. "Of course. Don't they in your realm?"

"No." Thom hesitated. "Or at least not in a language we can understand. They just talk, or rather, chirp at each other."

She pursed her lips. "How strange."

Thom chuckled. Strange indeed.

"Father?" Norealle called.

Keifor had lowered himself to the ground, legs crossed, and was studying the fading stars as if they held all the answers in the world. He didn't appear to hear her, so Norealle walked over and laid a hand on his shoulder. "Father, are you staying up here for a while?"

"Yes, daughter. Take the lad home. He needs rest after his ordeal."

"Are you sure you don't want to come down with us?"

He simply shook his head, his gaze returning to the heavens.

Apparently satisfied with that answer, Norealle rejoined Thom. "Ready?"

"Ready as I'll ever be," he replied honestly.

Norealle led the way, and Thom followed close behind. Dawn's light illuminated their route, making it safer than their midnight climb. However, there was still no margin for error. Placing their feet with care, Thom and Norealle descended without incident. By the time they reached the cave entrance, they were both tired and hungry.

Thom caught Norealle's arm just before she stepped into the tunnel. "Norealle."

She paused, her brown eyes lifting to his in silent question.

Thom chose his words cautiously, trying to express the burden that had grown in his mind during their trek down the mountain. "I want you to reconsider coming with us." Norealle opened her mouth to protest, but Thom held up his hand. "Please, just hear me. I was nearly killed by a Zakarian monster back in Lomair. Puck and I nearly froze trying to find your realm. You almost fell to your death so I could get the key. Nothing about this journey has been safe, and its about to get worse."

"Thom, I am coming with you." Her tone left no room for argument. She'd made up her mind.

Thom let his eyes briefly shut, internally warring against his fear and panic...and to his shame, his relief. He wanted her insight, her presence, and her skills at his side, but the thought of leading her to her death was worse than that of dying himself. The terror he'd felt when the red demon-witch had pointed her blade at Norealle's prone body would be with him forever.

"Norealle, there's a very good chance you might die," he stressed. "We all might die. The evil is real. And we're heading straight for it."

"You think I don't realize this?" Norealle's eyes flashed at him. "That evil killed my mother. I know where we are going."

Thom groaned. "I know you do. You're smart and strong and more capable than I will ever be." Angst punched through Thom, and he cupped her face in his hands, earnestly trying to make her understand. "I couldn't protect you in the vision, Norealle, and I'm afraid I won't be able to in Zakar either."

"That is what this is all about? Keeping me safe?" An unreadable look passed over her face, and then Norealle leaned forward and brushed her lips across Thom's shadowed cheek. "You are not El'Ohim, Thom. My fate is not up to you. Stop worrying."

She strode into the cave, leaving Thom standing on the ledge, her kiss branded on his skin and her words seared into his mind.

Chapter 21
Exploring Silmea

When Thom entered the cave, Puck was standing by the fire, and Norealle was hovering by the tunnel entrance, clearly waiting for Thom. From the strained look on Puck's ruddy face, he'd not received the message from the birds.

"Where were you?" Puck growled, pushing away from the fireplace and striding toward them. Norealle shared a wide-eyed look with Thom and darted around Puck's frame, hurrying to the kitchen. Puck ignored her, glaring at Thom.

I can't deal with this right now. The fatigued thought flew through Thom's mind followed immediately by the knowledge that he had no choice. "Up the mountain," he said tiredly. "I tried to wake you, but you were passed out."

"You must not have tried very hard," Puck snarled. "Which I suppose makes sense if you were out on a lark with your lady friend."

"It was nothing like that!" Thom protested. A headache pressed behind his eyes.

"Then what was it? I wake up, and you're gone!" Hurt flashed across Puck's face. "You just went on a midnight hike for fun?"

"No!" Thom's voice pitched, his own temper rising. "I went looking for the Key Keeper!" Thom forced his voice to lower. He paused, taking a moment to breathe, before replying evenly. "I didn't mean to worry you."

Puck dragged a hand through his blond hair. "I told you. I can't watch your back if I don't even know where you are. For all I knew, you'd been kidnapped!"

Norealle's words from minutes before nudged Thom. *You are not El'Ohim, Thom. My fate is not up to you.* The irony was not lost on him.

Thom groaned. "To be honest, I didn't know we'd have to climb the whole mountain or that we'd be gone so long, but we did find the Key Keeper."

The anger drained from Puck's countenance and shock took its place. "You didn't."

"We did." Thom relaxed a bit as he sensed Puck's agitation fading. "It's Keifor."

Puck dropped onto a stool. "Keifor? As in, Norealle's pa?"

"One and the same."

"And he couldn't have told you down here?" Puck asked, incredulous.

At that, Thom smiled slightly and sat. "I said the same thing. But there were tests, and he needed his power, which is apparently strongest on top of the mountain."

Puck shook his head. "And here I thought you were just off trying to figure out how to kiss, leaving me to worry like an old granny."

Thom snorted. "We weren't."

"Bet you wish you had been."

"You're a cad."

Puck chuckled and held out his hand. "Well, let's see this thing we literally traveled to another realm for."

Thom pulled the chain out, the dark key resting against his shirt.

Puck's jaw dropped. "You've got to be joking. That's it?"

"I thought the same thing, but apparently there is more to it than what we can see."

Puck reached forward, rubbing the dark metal between thumb and forefinger. "I sure hope so. Can't see us locking the gates of anything with that little thing."

"At least it's easy to carry."

From her spot by the fire, Norealle caught Thom's eye, a subtle question in her gaze. He nodded, letting her know everything was once again all right with Puck. In response, she padded over and set a loaf of bread between them. Her fingertips grazed Thom's hand, and his heart squeezed. "Thank you."

"You're welcome." Norealle touched Puck's shoulder. "I'm sorry too, Puck. Neither of us meant to worry you."

Puck shrugged off her apology as he reached for the bread. "Thom explained. It's fine."

"Keifor suggested we stay here for the day. Rest." Thom glanced at Puck, gauging his friend's reaction.

Puck's eyes lit up, creasing at the sides as his cheeks lifted. "Yeah? I was hoping we wouldn't just leave right away. This place is incredible." He stuffed the bread in his mouth and closed his eyes, a moan rumbling out of his chest. "This is so good."

Thom chuckled, smiling at Norealle as she sat beside him. "That's high praise coming from him. He's a bread snob."

Norealle's eyes sparkled. "I'm glad you like it." She braced her elbows on the table. "I'd like to show you some of my favorite places and introduce you to my friends."

Puck grabbed another piece of bread. "By all means! If they are half as pretty as you, I can't wait to meet them."

"I think you'll enjoy them," Norealle said, a glint of mischief in her eyes.

"Let's go," said Puck, standing.

"Now?" Thom groaned. His legs were sore, and his feet ached from the trek up the mountain.

"Oh." Norealle's face shadowed. "We can wait."

"He's fine!" Puck shouted, already outside.

We hiked most of the night. How is she not tired?

"I thought we were going to rest." Thom pushed off the stool.

"If I don't show you now, we might not get the chance," Norealle said.

He tilted back his head and exhaled. *Toughen up.* Squaring his shoulders, Thom faced her. "All right, let's go."

The smile that lit up Norealle's face was all the reward he needed. Mimicking Puck, Thom took another slice of bread and followed her into the sunshine. Norealle led them down the hillside and into a forest. Dappled light shown through the leaves, and the cheerful calls of morning birds greeted them.

Puck's brows furrowed as his hands planted on his hips. "Your friends live in the woods?"

Norealle pointed. "Here's one now."

A flash of reddish brown dropped from a nearby branch and bounded across the ground. The squirrel halted a stride away and straightened up onto two paws. Thom realized instantly that this was no regular squirrel. His black eyes gleamed with intelligence, and he had a bag slung across his back filled to bursting with acorns.

"My lady." The squirrel bowed. "I heard talk of strangers." He looked carefully from Puck to Thom then back to Norealle.

"Loupe, this is Thom, the new Realm Walker, and his companion, Puck," Norealle said.

Her fingers whispered against Thom's, and he caught her hand. The warmth from her touch travelled up his arm and straight to his core.

The squirrel gave a formal nod to Thom and Puck, but his black eyes remained trained on Thom. "It is well met."

Thom dipped his chin, fascinated by the human-like creature. "The honor is ours."

Puck ignored the introductions, too busy gawking. He turned to Norealle. "Do all the animals around here, you know, talk?"

Thom sent a swift elbow into Puck's side.

Puck grunted. "What?"

"They do." Loupe's tail bristled. "They are even taught manners."

Thom chuckled. "You deserved that."

"I meant no offense."

Loupe's coat smoothed, his attention shifting to Thom. "It has been a very long time since one from your realm has come to our lands."

Norealle nodded, picking up where he left off. "Hundreds of years."

"Puck and I didn't even know there were realms outside of our own until a few days ago," Thom admitted.

The squirrel's snout curled into what could only be described as a smile. "And yet here you are."

Thom scanned the forest. "That we are."

Norealle turned to Puck. "To answer your question, no, not all of the citizens of our realm are like you and me. There are dumb creatures who have no words, but they dwell outside of this valley. The animals in this part of the realm are very intelligent."

Puck frowned. "But don't you eat meat?"

"Yes."

"Aren't you worried you're going to accidently eat, you know, a talking beast?"

"We take care to hunt outside the valley," Norealle patiently answered.

"That seems mighty inconvenient. What do you eat if you can't manage a hunting trip?" Puck persisted.

Thom groaned. The urge to smack his insensitive friend was growing by the second.

"Fruits. Vegetables. Herbs." Norealle answered wryly.

Puck frowned, clearly thinking up his next line of questioning.

"That's enough, Puck," Thom muttered under his breath. Puck started to protest, but Thom sent him a sharp look. "I'm sorry. Our lands are very different." Thom smiled at Loupe, then added to Norealle, "I'd enjoy meeting more of your friends."

Loupe bowed to Norealle. "Blessings on your day, my lady."

"You won't be joining us?"

"No, I promised Loupe Junior we'd skip rocks at the lake after I foraged breakfast."

"Oh! Fun." Delight sparked in her eyes. "Tell Lilly I said hel-lo."

Thom lifted a hand in a wave. "It was a pleasure to meet you, Loupe."

"You as well, sir." He dipped his head to Puck. "And you, strange one."

Puck grinned. "See you later, squirrel."

Loupe chuckled and bounded away.

Puck crossed his arms and shot Norealle a suspicious glare. "Are all your friends animals?"

"Mostly, yes." She smirked. "Though sometimes I walk down to the river to talk to the river nymphs."

"River nymphs!" Puck rubbed his hands together delightedly. "Now that sounds more like it!"

Thom rolled his eyes.

"Is he always like this?" Norealle marveled. She slipped her hand into Thom's, and he squeezed it in return.

"Afraid so."

"Do you blame a fellow?" Puck protested, falling in step on Norealle's other side. "I'm not holding the hand of the pretty girl."

Norealle's cheeks pinkened.

Thom snorted. "You're incorrigible, Puck."

"I'll take that as a compliment...whatever it means."

"How ever did the two of you become friends?" Norealle asked, amazement coloring her tone.

"Says the lady whose best friend is a squirrel," Puck shot back.

"You've got to give him that one," Thom agreed.

"No stranger than the two of you." She laughed. "You're smart, thoughtful, insightful..." She looked to Puck. "And you're big and strong, but devoid of any tact at all."

Puck sent a wry look to Thom. "I think she has us figured." He shrugged. "I do the heavy lifting, and Thom does the thinking. I get the women, and he takes the books. It works."

Norealle pursed her lips together. "I suppose it would."

"And I can always use his hard head to smash down doors, if need be," Thom smoothly added.

"Hey now." Puck laughed.

They continued to walk through the forest, and as Thom listened closely, he could hear that the birds weren't just chirping, they were *singing actual words*. He marveled. This was a place he could spend the rest of his days.

Norealle guided them expertly through the forest, but apart from the birds, they didn't see any other creatures. They returned to the meadow, and Thom was once again struck by the vastness of the land and its endless beauty. A rabbit bounded by, saw the three of them, and stopped dead. It stood on its hind legs, its nose quivering as it scented the air.

"Good morning, my lady," its voice rang out, high and feminine.

"Good day, Lucille," Norealle replied.

The rabbit stared at Thom and Puck with unabashed curiosity. "What are those, my lady?"

Thom swallowed a laugh. "We're humans. I'm Thom, and this is Puck."

"The new Realm Walker and his companion," Norealle added.

"Ah." The rabbit's brown eyes widened, the explanation clearly meaning nothing. She leaned in, scenting them. Thom fought to keep his face neutral as he struggled to win the battle against his amusement.

"You smell strange," Lucille stated frankly.

Thom gave up the fight and chuckled. "I'm afraid you're probably smelling days of travel and dirt. We've come a long way."

The rabbit looked up at Norealle. "You should take them to the spring."

"That's a good idea." Norealle began to walk again and called over her shoulder. "Happy foraging, Lucille!"

Thom followed, waiting to speak until they were out of ear shot. Uncertain of how far a rabbit could hear, he leaned in and kept his voice low. "Do you know all the animals that live here?"

"In this area, yes. I've spent my life here." She gestured, the motion encompassing the vastness of the land. "But not everywhere, of course."

"They call you 'lady.' Why is that?"

"My father is the master of this realm."

"Is he the king, then?" Thom pressed.

She shook her head. "No, El'Ohim rules our land. My father receives visions from Him at times, and he has been trusted with keeping the entrances to our realm safe. He is very respected here."

Thom's voice softened. "Could you tell me about your mother?"

Norealle's eyes glimmered with unshed tears. "She was a daughter of the stars."

"Ah, that would explain your radiant beauty," Puck chimed in.

Thom wanted to smack him.

"You do enjoy compliments, don't you?" Norealle drew in a deep breath, steadying herself. "My mother was very beloved, both here and in the heavens. She loved to walk through the forests, and she always had time to help anyone who needed it." A tear trickled down her cheek, and she hastily brushed it away.

Thom's heart clenched. "You don't have to say anymore, Norealle."

She sniffled. "No. It's good for me to talk about her. I don't want her forgotten. She was the kindest soul I've ever known."

"Like her daughter," Thom replied gently.

Her smile wobbled, and she gripped his hand tighter.

"Is there a chance she's still alive?" Thom ventured.

Norealle shook her head. "No. The other stars told my father that when my mother saw the wall that contains Zakar being breached, she descended to defend it. She was lost in the battle."

It was Puck who responded, his voice solemn, "Your mom was brave. That's something to be proud of."

Norealle swiped another tear off her cheek. "I am." She straightened her spine. "Come, let's go to the spring like Lucille mentioned." She looked askance at them. "She was right. You both smell."

The air about them lightened. No one could argue with that.

"Good plan," Thom agreed.

The three of them made their way across the vast meadow and into a poplar grove. The white and black bark dappled the trunks of the green-leafed trees. The grass here was shorter, but far greener, and Thom could feel the moisture squelching beneath his feet. Water gurgled nearby, and sure enough, Norealle led them down a loamy bank and onto the pebbled beach of a slow-moving stream. Crystal clear water bubbled up out of the ground at the head of the pool.

"I'll leave you both for a bit." She released Thom's hand and moved into the depth of the trees. Thom and Puck wasted no time shucking their outer garments and wading into the crisp water.

"Whew!" Thom shivered as he eased in up to his knees and stopped. Heavens, did he ever want to get clean, but this was no warm bath.

"Best just to jump in." Following up his words with action, Puck dove under the water. He burst through the surface a second later, water pouring off him as he let out a loud whoop. With a wicked grin, he sent a shower of water cascading over Thom.

"Hey!" Leaping forward, Thom swept his arm through the water and sent a curtain of spray over Puck. He laughed and disappeared under the surface. Thom dunked himself next and scrubbed his hair. When he surfaced, Puck was climbing out of the shallow pool. Thom followed.

"Feels counterproductive putting on our dirty clothes." Thom's teeth knocked together as shivers rippled over his goose-bumped flesh. He tugged on his travel-worn garments, fumbling in his haste.

"Well, at least we're clean," Puck said, shaking his head like a dog and peppering the foliage with water droplets. With a roll of his shoulders, Puck began swinging his arms back and forth.

Thom lifted his arm and sniffed. Smoke, sweat, and the scent of wet wool filled his nostrils. He grimaced. The water may have washed the worst of the grime from his skin, but nothing other than a bar of lye soap was going to remove the odors of travel. Straightening his damp shirt, he combed his fingers through his dripping hair.

"You really like her, don't you?" Puck asked. Movements un-hurried, he shrugged on his shirt before pulling on his pants.

Thom threaded his belt through the buckle, tightening it to hold up his loosening pants. The metal prong slid into an unused hole. The lack of nourishing food and extensive hiking were showing. "What's not to like?" He shoved his feet into his boots. Dropping into a crouch, he tied them with nimble fingers.

Puck considered him for a moment before nodding. "Good point," he winced, "but I will say, when her friend turned out to be a squirrel..." He sucked in a breath through his teeth, his expression pained.

Thom laughed, the sound joining the pleasant gurgling of the creek. "Not quite what you expected?"

"The water nymphs sound more promising, but now I'm scared to get my hopes up." Puck threaded the rawhide laces of his boots, notching them securely around the sturdy eyehooks before knotting them. Standing, he slapped his hands against his thighs, his attention shifting to the surrounding forest.

Thom followed his gaze, taking in the thick tangle of vegetation crowding the bank and sprawling between the willows and birch trees. "Just think of all the hearts you'll break back home if you come back taken." He nudged him in the ribs. "Half the kitchen maids are in love with you."

Puck's eyebrows shot up. "Only half?" he asked.

"You're impossible."

"Try not to be too jealous."

The mere thought of the gaggle of females, with their verbal drivel and obsessive matchmaking, made Thom's stomach churn. "Oh, I'm not."

A branch snapped, and Thom pivoted towards the entrance to the overgrown trail. His face lit up as Norealle appeared, her hands pushing aside the dangling branches and legs parting the bowed bushes as she made her way over to them.

Puck spoke under his breath. "Besotted."

Thom ignored him. Tilting his head toward the creek, he smiled at Norealle. "That was chilly."

Her eyes twinkled. "Were you expecting a warm bath?"

"No." Thom rubbed his arms ruefully, the water's chill still clinging to his skin. "Just not glacial temperatures."

Her gaze traveled from his boots up to his eyes, and Thom fought the urge to squirm beneath her scrutiny.

"I should have thought to bring you both clean clothes," Norealle said.

"Oh well. Hopefully, we smell a little better."

With an impish grin, Norealle gave a teasing sniff, her face drawing close to Thom's neck. He froze. Her flowery scent overwhelmed his senses, and her loose hair brushed the column of his throat sending arrows of awareness slicing through him. Tension tightened his shoulders as his lungs forgot to breathe.

A throat cleared behind them.

Norealle leapt away from Thom and into a curtain of leafy limbs. A pink flush highlighted her cheeks as she fumbled to loosen her hair from the grasping branches. Puck slapped Thom on the back as he strode by, eyes dancing with mirth. "Let's go find those water nymphs."

Thom shook his head and closed the space between him and Norealle. Voice husky, he said, "Just hold still for a second." Deftly, he loosened the strands, focusing on his task and not their proximity. "What kind of creatures are these water nymphs?"

Norealle eased free of the branch before smoothing a hand over her hair. "They have long flowing hair, luminous eyes, beautiful singing voices...and they are about this big." She held her thumb and forefinger about four inches apart.

Thom burst out laughing. He gestured for Norealle to take the lead, and she headed down the path. *She has a mischievous side I wouldn't have expected.*

Ahead of them, Puck yelled, "What's so funny?"

"Nothing." Thom called back.

"Uh huh." Puck walked backward, risking life and limb, as he studied them both. "Which way, my lady?"

"There's a wider path just up ahead. Follow that down to the lake."

True to her word, they found themselves on a well-established path a minute later. Thom forgot about his sore feet, his damp clothes, and the dangers that would stalk them the next day as they trod through the forest, listening to Norealle explain her homeland. The towering mountains, the fresh air, the birds, the peaceful stillness...it would be so easy to pretend that his world wasn't teetering on the brink of ruin and that dark forces weren't gathering to end everything he'd ever known.

They stepped out of the forest onto a small beach, and Thom shook his head in silent wonder. The lake was narrow, but it glimmered like a diamond between the forest walls. The snow-capped mountain at its end cast a perfect reflection across the icy blue water.

High-pitched laughter and chattering voices greeted his ears, and Thom's gaze sought the source of the sound. Small girls with flowing hair and shimmering scales lounged on the stones and splashed in and out of the crystal-clear water.

Puck's mouth dropped open. "Water nymphs?" he finally asked, his shoulders drooping.

Norealle grinned at him, clearly basking in the success of her subterfuge. "Not what you were expecting?"

Puck just shook his head and flopped down on a rock. He crossed his arms above his head and closed his eyes. Thom and Norealle joined him, sitting side-by-side as they watched the tiny nymphs frolic. A few of them glanced at the trio, but otherwise, they were completely ignored.

The sun gradually rose high above them, and they stretched out on the smooth boulders. Warm and content, Thom drifted off to sleep.

Norealle's voice eventually woke him. "Thom? Time to wake up. We should head back soon."

Thom blinked against the bright sunlight and sat up. He scrubbed a hand down his face, slowly coming to alertness. The sun was cresting the tips of the western trees. It was well past high noon.

"Did you have a good rest?" Norealle questioned from where she sat, dangling her bare toes in the water. A short distance down the pebbled beach, Puck was skipping stones across the water.

"Very." He stifled a yawn. "I wish we had more time to see your realm." Thom mused wistfully as he drank in the scenery.

"After we've locked Zakar, you'll have to bring me home." Norealle stood. "And I will show you everything then."

From your lips to El'Ohim's ears. It felt like too much to hope for, but Thom merely replied, "I'd like that."

Norealle called to Puck, and once he joined them, they followed Norealle home to her cave. They spoke little, everyone lost in their own thoughts. For his part, Thom simply took in everything around him. He couldn't get enough of the craggy, snow-capped mountains, emerald-infused fields, and sprawling forests. His fingers itched for his quill and parchment. He wanted to be the one to properly map this land. Everything about it called to him, but it wasn't to be.

Tomorrow, they would leave for Zakar.

Chapter 22

The Crib

The Lomairians fled. From every battle and skirmish across their land, they ran in panicked retreat. With targeted attacks, Slager herded them toward their precious capital. Like ants dodging a bird's pecking beak, they scattered beneath the errgoths' savagery, scuttling to Knor.

Helpless fools.

They would find no safety there.

Upon Knor's proud walls, Slager would unveil the full breadth of his power, displaying the might of Zakar to the mockery of El'Ohim—the absent god who had not once appeared to protect His precious humans.

El'Ohim. Abhorrence burned through Slager.

With Titus's powers had also come his hatred—a loathing as deep and vast as the endless darkness within The Inbetween. It pulsed, joined to Titus's power, and flowed like blood through Slager's veins.

Dark fantasies festered and brewed in the corrupted mire of Slager's mind. It would only be days now. Soon, his errgoths would devour Lomair's men, tearing them limb from limb and feasting on their dying bodies. The women of Knor would watch from the gates as he destroyed their defenders, splattering their entrails against the walls of their beloved city. The screams of fear and horror from Knor's inhabitants would fill the air, serenading his senses. Then he would bind their gates closed, and he would burn the city down with every remaining man, woman, and child left inside. The scent of burnt flesh would rise from the land, a mocking tribute to their failing god. Slager would smash down their high places of worship and grind every stone to dust. Knor and its people would be no more.

Soon. So very soon.

Slager was restless. The dormant, sulfuric air of Zakar swirled up his nostrils as he drew in a long breath. He paced, eyeing the new horde of errgoths slowly birthing from Titus's Crib. Overhead, the newly emerged but full-grown errgoths circled, their maws gaping as they split the stagnant air with piercing shrieks. As Slager watched, a misshapen beast broke from its stone womb and beat its singular wing. It crashed into a neighboring mound and plowed its scaly snout into the earth as it vainly struggled to take flight. Like the vultures that circled the human battlefields, the errgoths soaring above locked on to their struggling comrade. As one, they plummeted from the sky, their teeth and claws biting and tearing apart their flawed brother. Slager laughed, the sound joining the cacophony of shrieks from the dying errgoth below.

Soon, they would be ready. Oh, so very soon.

With a thought, Slager opened a portal and cast a path to the Human Realm. The errgoth hatching was taking too long. Titus needed more human blood to fuel his magic. Somehow, even in the basest of El'Ohim's most prided creations, remnants of El'Ohim's power still lingered.

Human blood would give life to Titus's creations—creations that would, in turn, destroy the humans. Slager's lips twisted cruelly.

Delicious irony.

Chapter 23
A Deep Inhale

The scramble up the hillside after Norealle left Thom and Puck breathless. As before, Norealle was hardly winded, and Thom suspected she could probably climb to the peak of the mountain again without breaking a sweat. She was a marvel.

"We have a lot to prepare before we leave tomorrow." Norealle spoke without breaking stride as she led the way into her rocky home.

Puck leaned close to Thom. "I have a feeling she's about to get bossy like Ma."

Thom bit back a smile, but he didn't dare say anything lest her hearing was as good as Keifor's.

Puck was right. The moment they stepped into the cavernous room, Norealle started giving orders. "Puck, there are some pails of water there. Hang them over the fire so we can get them heated. We need to wash both of your clothes." She beckoned to Thom. "Thom, let's see what you have in your bags."

Her tone brooked no argument, and Thom found his feet moving to obey before his brain even registered what she was asking. She followed at his heels, and Thom unceremoniously dumped his dirty, damp, and haphazardly packed belongings onto the bedrolls they'd spread out the night before.

A musty scent hit him in the face, and he instantly wished Norealle wasn't standing right there smelling the dirty socks he'd shoved in the bottom of his bag, the damp sweater that he'd stowed in there after the storm, and the remnants of three-day-old food.

"Oh my, what died in there?" Norealle retreated, holding a hand over her nose.

Thom flushed. From across the cave, Puck laughed. "That, love, is the scent of men."

Norealle gagged and pointed to a wooden tub. "Thom, fill that with water and"—she picked up what looked to be a homemade ball of soap and tossed it to him—"scrub everything." She backed away. "I'll go gather some food."

Grinning from ear to ear, Puck dumped a bucket of barely warm water into the tub. "Told you she was about to get bossy."

"We need it." He dropped his soiled garments into the tub. A suspicious brown leached from the clothes into the water. Leaning over the edge, Thom scrubbed awkwardly. He'd seen Puck's ma doing laundry plenty of times, but he'd never actually done it himself.

"The water even stinks." Puck shook with mirth. "Here, let's do this outside, then we can empty it over the edge."

"Good idea," Thom grunted.

Together, they hefted the washbasin and carried it to the rocky ledge where they dumped everything out, including the half-cleaned garments. Puck added fresh water, and Thom started scrubbing again. It took the better part of an hour and a good deal of effort to clean all the clothes they weren't currently wearing.

Norealle reappeared just long enough to carry an armful of vegetables inside the cave and toss them both some clothing that was far too large with an emphasis to wash *everything* before disappearing again.

They did.

Puck and Thom had just finished hanging their last items up to dry in front of the fire when Norealle returned. A relieved smile curved her lips as she took in the freshly laundered clothing. "That's better."

"Well." Puck chuckled. "It might smell good now, but no promises by tomorrow night."

She shook her head. "You're very strange, you know that?"

Thom choked on a laugh.

Puck planted his hands on his square hips and leveled a mock-severe stare at her. "I hope you realize you are the first woman who has ever declared *me* the strange one over Thom."

Norealle glanced at Thom, her brow wrinkling in confusion. "Are you odd in your country?"

"Very odd," Puck assured her.

Thom shot a dark look at Puck. "Thanks, friend."

Norealle looked between the two men. "Your women have strange taste."

Puck reeled back as if wounded. "Our women have *wonderful* taste!" He flexed his bicep, and Norealle arched a brow, unimpressed.

Thom cleared his throat. "Let's get this gear packed."

Norealle sorted through the supplies, and Thom was content to let her decide what he needed or didn't need. Puck, on the other hand, took personal offense to every one of her suggestions. Not wanting to get caught in the crossfire as Norealle and Puck argued, Thom took his map and drifted over to the fire. He sat down and unfolded the worn pages. The warmth of the fire chased the chill from his body while he examined the sparse landmarks in the Zakar sphere.

At the sound of footsteps, Thom looked up to see Norealle's father entering the cave. Keifor hung his cloak on a peg in the cave wall, took one look at where his daughter and Puck were debating what food they would need, and headed in Thom's direction.

Thom lowered the map into his lap and straightened in his chair, preparing to stand.

Keifor waved him back down and sat. "How was your day, young Realm Walker?"

Thom's memories automatically swung from the eerie events of the night to the tour Norealle had given them. "Interesting."

Keifor glanced over as Norealle's voice rose, a hint of amusement in his eyes. "She doesn't get many opportunities to boss anyone around other than me."

Thom chose to keep his mouth shut.

Keifor continued, "She's quite in her element at the moment."

Thom bit the inside of his cheek to keep from smiling. In fact, Norealle did *not* look like she was enjoying herself at all. Her cheeks were pink, and a scowl creased her brow as Puck shoveled food into his pack, arguing that he did indeed need to take all their stale rations along. Her eyes sparked at Puck as she gestured wildly with her hands.

"She...is..." He wanted to say "magnificent", but Thom was talking to her father who happened to be large enough to crush him. "Very efficient," Thom finished quietly.

Keifor settled more deeply into his chair. "That she is." He paused. "She is my only child, and the only piece left of my beloved."

Those dark, bottomless eyes rested on Thom, and he felt trapped in his chair. Creator help him, but was Keifor trying to read his mind regarding Norealle? Thom focused hard on keeping his thoughts blank. A sheen of sweat formed on his brow. The warmth of the fire no longer felt comfortable.

"She is very like her mother. Strong, smart, independent, and loyal," Keifor reflected, "and she has taken to you, Realm Walker." His gaze bored into him again, and Thom had to fight the urge to squirm...or flee.

"I...I am not worthy of her, sir," he stammered.

"No. You are not." There was an awkward moment of silence before Keifor sighed. "But is any man worthy of the love of a woman?"

Thom chose his words carefully. "I've never met anyone like her, sir."

A memory flitted across Keifor's expression. "I thought the same thing when I met her mother." His tone grew firm. "You will honor and respect my daughter, Realm Walker."

It was not a question.

"Of course, sir." Thom glanced over at Norealle, who now had her hands on her hips. She and Puck were nose to nose, still arguing. "I don't think she'd allow anyone to do anything she didn't wish for anyway."

Keifor chuckled, also watching the exchange. Norealle was not relenting, even though Puck was twice as wide and towered above her.

"I better go intervene before Puck gets a black eye." *And before this conversation gets any more awkward.*

Thom approached the duo cautiously, more than a little relieved to leave the conversation with Keifor, even though it meant jumping between his best friend and Norealle. Puck held a crumpled wad of bundled food in his hand, and Norealle was grasping a bedroll like it was a weapon.

"You don't need all this! It will slow us down!" Norealle huffed, clearly exasperated.

"What if we have to spend a few days, hmm? You planning on starving? Sleeping on the rocks?" Puck challenged, reaching to tug the bedroll out of Norealle's hand.

She held on grimly. It was the oddest standoff Thom had ever seen. He edged in. "Hey guys, if this is about those stale buns, it's not worth fighting over."

Neither of them so much as glanced at him. Thom chuckled nervously and went to take Norealle's hand, but then thought better of it and instead planted a hand on Puck's chest, pushing him back a step. Two sets of eyes swung to glare at him.

"She wants us to leave everything behind!" Puck blustered.

"You overgrown man-child!" Norealle snapped. "We have to move fast. I said to leave the bedrolls and take a thick cloak. We can always make a fire."

"And sleep on the rocks?"

"We can use branches!" she shouted back.

"What if there are no trees?"

Thom eased himself further between the two of them. "Puck, can you go see if our clothes are dry by the fire?"

His friend stomped away, muttering under his breath.

Norealle's eyes flashed daggers at Puck. She faced Thom, seething. "He drives me crazy."

Thom chose safety and decided not to respond. He pointed to the scattered gear. "Care to show me how you would pack for this trip?"

"All right." Norealle huffed and crouched down, reaching for the flint.

"Did you ever see Zakar when you visited the stars with your mother?" Thom inquired.

"I just saw a lot of red dirt and rock. We were a long way off."

Thom picked up his cloak and handed it to her. She placed it in the bag. A thought occurred to Thom. "Can stars travel through The Inbetween?"

Norealle shook her head. "No. The stars stay within our realm, but our heavens mingle with the other realms in some places, so its possible to cross over." Norealle looked up at Thom, her gaze far away, seeing a memory that Thom wasn't privy to. "My mother said that the light from our stars could be seen everywhere."

Absently, Norealle wound a strand of dark hair around her finger. "She would hold me in her arms and take me up to the sky, where she would shine so bright I'd have to keep my eyes closed. And she'd sing the most beautiful songs with the other stars..." Her voice trailed off. She lifted a hand and dashed it across her eyes.

"You have beautiful memories with her," Thom spoke quietly.

"Yes."

Surprising himself, Thom blurted out, "I...lost my mother too. When I was eight." He couldn't remember a time he'd spoken of his life before the Pearcelys—if he ever had. Puck's Ma had asked a few questions when he'd first come to live with them, but when Thom had refused to share, she'd stopped asking.

"What happened?"

"I don't know exactly. I was young...but I remember her always being sick. The nights were cold on the streets, and she was always coughing. And she never ate much. She was too worried about making sure I had enough." Thom kept his voice low and busied his hands by lining up his belongings.

Norealle's brow furrowed. "Where was your father?"

"Dead," Thom answered bluntly. "He was a mapmaker and traveled a lot. Honestly, I don't remember much about him. When he didn't come back from one of his journeys, we lost our home."

Norealle looked confused. "How did you lose it?"

"In the Human Realm, if you owe people money and you can't pay them, they can take something you own in repayment."

"That's terrible!"

Thom shrugged. "It's life."

"What happened after they took your home?"

Thom's lips pressed into a hard line. "We traveled through all the small towns and villages of Lomair, doing odd tasks for a meal or begging. We never stayed in the same area for more than a couple days before moving on."

Troubled, Norealle asked, "But where did you sleep?"

"A shopkeeper's door, an alley between homes, or maybe a stable with nice straw if we were lucky."

"That's awful," Norealle whispered.

Thom could tell Norealle didn't completely comprehend what he was saying, but she understood enough to be upset. He handed her his bedroll, and she set it to the side.

"Why couldn't you just stay with someone or make a new home?"

"We had no money, and my mother was too scared to stay in one spot. She was always looking over her shoulder," Thom spoke evenly. Time had faded the memories and the emotions attached to them, but he remembered her fear. The cold. The hunger.

Norealle's brow pinched. "What was she looking for?"

Thom shrugged. "She never said, but I know she was scared. Maybe she thought the creditors would use us as indentured servants to pay off the remaining debt or have us sent to debtor's prison."

He handed Norealle his water canteen, which she placed in the bag. "She died while we were in Knor. I found a bakery and slept in its doorway because the air coming out was always warm from the ovens, and it smelled so good." Thom tossed her a wry smile. "It also didn't take long for me to notice that Puck's ma left food on her step every night. And she caught on quick that I never missed a dinner and began leaving out food for breakfast and lunch too. Pretty soon, I had a bed beside Puck, and she was sending us both off to school."

Norealle's eyes had softened as Thom explained how he'd come to join the Pearcelys' family. "That's why you and Puck are so close. You're like brothers."

Thom nodded.

"I'd like to meet Puck's ma. She sounds wonderful."

"She's that and more," Thom agreed.

"Why did she leave food out?"

Thom relaxed, warming to this part of the tale. "In Lomair, it's part of our worship of the Creator. As a gesture of thanksgiving and to make sure that widows and orphans are provided for, followers of the Creator leave meals on their doorsteps every evening."

"That's beautiful."

"It probably saved my life," Thom admitted, shocked to find himself a bit choked up. "Anyway…" He gestured to his bag. "Is that everything?"

Norealle had placed his flint, a small bundle of dried sticks, a thick woolen cloak, the water canteen, and a wrapped bundle of fresh bread in his bag.

Thom eyed the items left behind: a thick wool blanket, the animal hide they'd slept on, and the remains of the jerky and biscuits. He picked up the jerky and tossed it in.

Norealle handed him the packed bag. "We'll bring our weapons, of course."

"Of course." He frowned, eyeing the bedding. "Are you sure it's not worth the weight?"

"I think the faster and quieter we can move, the better. We get there, we lock the wall, we get out."

"Something tells me it won't be that easy."

Norealle grimaced. "No. It probably won't be." She touched the chain around his neck that held the key. "Magical keys and their gates are horrendously unpredictable."

"And you're sure we shouldn't pack more?"

"It's up to you."

Thom sighed and closed his bag. "Let Puck bring whatever he wants. He's strong as an ox, and a few extra things won't slow him down." He pointed to his clothes hanging by the fire. "However, I am bringing an extra pair of socks."

She laughed. "Whatever for?"

Thom shrugged. "I hate wet feet. What if we cross a creek or something?"

She shook her head. "You're funny."

"He really isn't," Puck interrupted as he returned, and directed his attention to Thom. "Did you talk sense into her?"

Norealle tilted her head back, eyes crinkling, and smirked. "He agreed with me."

"You didn't." He stared at Thom, accusation all over his face. "Just because she's a pretty girl!"

"No," Thom defended. "I mean, yes. She is pretty." He could feel red creeping up his neck. "She made a good point. We will need to move fast. So yeah, I'm going to leave a few things behind, but you can bring whatever you want."

Puck grunted.

"So, everyone packs their own bag. But be able to run. Got it?" Thom gave them what he hoped was a stern look.

They both nodded.

Thom sighed. "Good. Okay." He grabbed his pack, strapped it down tight and then swung it on his back. It was definitely lighter than what it had been. He'd be able to move quickly, if need be.

He caught Norealle watching him, and he smiled. Her lips curved in response, and his heart give an odd thud.

Abandoning the supplies, Norealle headed to the table and started prepping food. Her father leaned over and said something to her. She shook her head.

Thom set his pack down and picked up his sword. "Puck, can we practice?"

Puck looked up in surprise. He was stuffing his pack...with everything. When he caught Thom looking, he growled, "I'm twice as strong as both of you. A blanket and a hide won't slow me down."

Thom touched his hilt. "Sparring?"

Puck grinned. "In the mood to get knocked over?"

"Nah, I was thinking it was your turn this time."

"Brave words." Puck snorted and strode from the cave. Unlike Thom, he'd worn his sword all day. Thom quickly strapped his weapon around his waist before hurrying after his friend. Puck stood outside, arms crossed, staring out over the valley.

When Thom reached his side, he spoke, his voice low, "Thom, doesn't all of this seem a little too easy? How do we know we can trust them? And Norealle..."

Thom frowned. "I trust her."

"Of course you do." Puck let out an exasperated breath. "She's the first woman who's ever shown interest in you, and she's gorgeous."

Thom glared at him. "Give me one good reason why we shouldn't trust her then if I'm so blind."

Puck threw his hands in the air and stalked a few steps away. He wheeled around. "I don't know." He unsheathed his sword. "I just...have a bad feeling."

"Because she isn't falling all over herself for you?" Thom supplied.

Puck laughed despite himself. "It's not natural, Thom."

Snorting, Thom drew his sword and took a swing at Puck. Puck parried it to the left. Thom let his blade flow to the side then curved it down and around, stepping forward quickly to stab at Puck's now exposed chest. Puck blocked the blow. Their movements weren't fast, but they were steady as they parried, blocked, and attacked each other.

"Your footwork is getting better," said Puck.

"Thanks."

Thom gripped the hilt with both hands to block a hard blow from Puck. He grunted at the impact but didn't lose his weapon. They hadn't had a lot of time to practice, but Thom knew he was getting stronger. The hiking and climbing had seen to that.

The sword, which had felt so unnatural in his hands a mere week ago, was becoming familiar. He was growing used to its weight and how much muscle he needed to lift, swing, and jab it. Thom hefted his blade as Puck carved his sword down, and the weapons crashed together with a clang. The impact set his teeth on edge as the force reverberated through his bones. He fought to hold the block, but his muscles trembled as Puck leaned into the blow. Thom's arms gave way, and his blade was forced down. Puck swept up his sword and pricked him in the chest.

Thom groaned, and Puck punched the air with gusto.

"Again," Thom ordered.

Puck's eyebrows shot up. "Who *are* you?"

They continued until dusk had settled over the valley, and Norealle appeared at the entrance of the cave. She watched Puck bat Thom's sword out of his hand before clearing her throat. "Dinner."

Flushed and sweaty, Thom picked up his fallen blade and swept his hair off his forehead. They both sheathed their swords and followed Norealle into the cave. A delicious aroma filled their noses, and Thom sniffed appreciatively. "That smells so good."

Puck was already by the pot, lifting the lid to sneak a taste. Norealle waved the spoon at him. "Get back, you beast!"

Puck laughed and raised his hands in defeat. "I'm hungry!"

Thom looked around the room. "Where's your father?"

"He went to pray for our journey. He'll be back later."

Thom frowned. "I didn't see him leave."

Norealle simply smiled again and filled three bowls with a hearty stew. They all sat and ate. *Delicious.*

"I wonder what happened to Traell," Puck spoke around a mouthful of stew.

"Missing him?" Amusement flashed in Thom's eyes.

Puck snorted. "Hardly. Just curious."

Thom turned to Norealle. "Do you think we could get a message to him? Let him know we are leaving tomorrow?"

"Are you serious?" Puck spluttered. "We don't need that name-calling, hair-pulling, biscuit-stealing little freak!"

"El'Ohim sent him to me. I think we should at least give him a chance to come—if he wishes."

Puck groaned.

Norealle's fingers brushed Thom's arm. "I'll try and get word to him."

"Thank you."

After dinner, Thom and Puck helped Norealle clean up before changing into their clean clothes. Norealle packed a small bag of supplies for herself while Thom studied his map, worry needling him. What would they find in Zakar?

Darkness deepened outside the cave, and they all settled into their beds for the night. Thom laid on his animal skin beside Norealle's cot with Puck on his other side. Concerns peppered his mind. Would he be able to open a portal to Zakar? How did the key work? Would they encounter foe? In his vision, El'Ohim had told him he'd been specifically chosen for this task...but what if he failed?

Norealle dropped her hand over the side, and Thom wordlessly took it, his thumb stroking small circles over the back of her hand. They were silent for a long while, and eventually Puck's gentle snores joined the crackling of the fire.

"Are you nervous?" Norealle's voice spoke softly from her bed.

"Yes," Thom answered with barely a beat of hesitation. He stared at the shadows dancing across the cave ceiling. The reasons behind his fear were more than he cared to recount.

"Me too."

Something in her tone caused Thom to prop himself up on his elbow so he could see her face. She rolled over to face him, her lower lip catching between her teeth as she worried it.

"El'Ohim has gotten us this far," said Thom. The words, meant to encourage her, were equally for himself. This second stage of the mission was as impossible as the first. They had no choice but to trust.

"I know..." A wistful expression flitted across Norealle's face. "I always wanted to explore another realm. I just wish it was your world we were going to instead of Zakar."

She wants to visit the Human Realm?

Thom's eyes lit up, pleasure coloring his tone. "Would you truly like to see the Human Realm?"

"I've dreamt of it since I was a little girl," Norealle admitted.

Thom shook his head, a disbelieving chuckle rumbling out of his chest. "It isn't nearly as beautiful as here, and our animals can't talk."

"I want to see the cities. I can't imagine a place where hundreds of people all live together."

"It's smelly," Thom deadpanned. "And crowded."

"You don't like it?" She asked with surprise.

"I like my library. It's quiet and full of books."

Norealle frowned. "What are books?"

"Norealle, please tell me you are kidding."

She shook her head, and Thom groaned. "All right, now you *must* come visit the Human Realm. I'll show you my library and..." His eyes brightened with anticipation. "I can teach you how to read, if you wish."

She smiled. "I think I would like that."

"And I can introduce you to the Pearcelys."

"Yes, please!"

Satisfaction filled Thom. "It's a promise. When we finish in Zakar, I'll show you my home."

"I'll hold you to that promise, Realm Walker."

Thom leaned forward and bestowed the barest touch against her lips. "Good."

Chapter 24

Into Darkness

"Thom. Wake up."

Thom grunted and burrowed his face deeper into his rolled-up cloak.

"Thom!" The voice was getting exasperated.

Thom groaned and blurrily blinked his eyes open. Norealle was crouched beside him, a hand on his shoulder. "Are you always this hard to wake?"

Thom sat up, still half asleep as he retorted blurrily, "Only when I hike up a mountain the night before."

Norealle was already bending over Puck, calling his name.

Puck sat up, his eyes enviously alert. "Is it time to go?"

Norealle shoved some bread into each of their hands. "Yes. Eat. My father says it's time."

Thom scarfed the food down while tugging on his boots. He laced them snugly, taking care with the knots. Puck strapped on his sword, and Thom hastened to do the same. He noticed that Norealle already had her small pack slung across her shoulders. She wore a baggy shirt, snug black pants, and sturdy boots. At her hip was the same thin blade she'd held on Puck the day they'd arrived, and her hair had been tied into a thick braid down her back. She looked gorgeous...and fierce.

Appreciation washed over Thom. He strode to her side and ducked his head. His lips grazed her ear. "You look beautiful."

A pretty blush bloomed on her cheeks.

Norealle's father marched into the cave, and Thom straightened. Keifor threw a large log on the fire. Sparks burst forth, and the tang of smoke filled the air.

He faced them, his eyes grave. "The way between here and Zakar is quiet. You need to go." He focused on Thom. "Part of the magic of the key is that it responds differently to every user. I cannot tell you how to close the breach in the wall, but trust your instincts. Above all else, try and pass through unseen. The three of you are no match for the enemies you may encounter in that land."

His words given, Keifor wrapped Norealle in his strong arms, swallowing her lithe frame within the barrel of his chest. "Be careful, daughter."

She stood on tiptoe and pressed a kiss to his bearded cheek. "I will, Father. We will be back by nightfall."

"I will pray and keep watch for you."

Taking the lead, Thom walked outside the cave. The crisp air, carrying scents of trees and snow, filled his nostrils. Overhead, the stars still covered the heavens. The moons had yet to relinquish their heavenly stage to the morning sun.

He turned to Keifor and lent voice to a thought that had refused to leave his mind all night. Well, at least when he wasn't thinking about the brief kiss he'd pressed to Norealle's lips. "Sir, have you been to Zakar?"

"I have. Twice." Keifor's voice was grim.

Relief flooded Thom. "Would you...is there a chance you could come with us? None of us have ever been there."

"You don't know what you ask of me. My responsibility is to this realm, and I cannot leave. Not again." A dark, pain-filled shadow fell over his face.

Thom swallowed his disappointment, but sensed there was a dire tale behind Keifor's refusal. After a moment of respectful silence, he carefully spoke again, "I don't have a lot of experience with portals. I was able to come here because of the mountain. Norealle and I realized I could use it as an anchor to set a path between our realms. I have nothing to anchor to Zakar..." His voice trailed off.

Keifor paused thoughtfully before speaking. "I knew one other Realm Walker with an ability like yours. A long time ago. A clever, ambitious young man." Renewed sadness flickered across Keifor's face, but it was gone a moment later. "He needed to only picture a location in his mind, and he could go there. I have a feeling you are much the same." Keifor laid a hand on Thom's shoulder. "Close your eyes. I will give you a vision of a location near where I believe the breach is. That should be enough."

Doubt tugged at Thom, but he closed his eyes and abruptly gasped. He was in a barren desert. Red and brown rocks with jagged edges dotted the endless gravel landscape. Small hills, really just mounds of sharp stones, broke up the flat horizon. The sky was murky orange, and no sun or moon hung in the heavens. The light was dim, like in the last minutes of dusk. Thom took in the unforgiving view. His eyes settled on a formidable black wall that towered beyond what his straining eyes could see.

"Do you have it in your mind's eye?" Keifor's voice jarred Thom from his staring.

"Yes."

Keifor lifted his hand, and Thom was instantly back at the entrance of the cave in the Hidden Realm. He blinked.

"Whoa, that's…" He exhaled. *Bizarre. Terrifying. Fascinating.* "How do you *do* that?"

A subtle smile tugged at the corners of Keifor's mouth. "It is just one of the many gifts El'Ohim has granted His servant. Now, you should go."

Thom squared his shoulders and took one last look at the starlit fields and mountains of the Hidden Realm. He hadn't even left yet, and he already missed it.

"You've got this," said Puck.

A shrill voice rent the air. "You'd leave without Traell?" A familiar, squat figure flapped over the edge of the cave, his black eyes glaring at them as he flew directly at Thom's face. "Where are you going?" he screeched.

Thom ducked beneath the assault. "Zakar."

Traell buzzed by barely missing Thom's head.

Thom straightened and tried not to laugh. Somehow, Traell had managed to make himself look even more ridiculous than before. He had a colorful flower necklace looped multiple times around his fuzzy neck.

Traell landed with surprising agility on Thom's shoulder and tugged his hair before draping his furry body over the top of Thom's pack. "Well?" He gave an imperious wave. "Continue."

Thom arched a brow. "I thought you wouldn't go there. Stinky, ugly, yucky, and all that."

Traell harumphed. "Dumb-dumb Realm Walker needs Traell."

Puck rolled his eyes. Norealle coughed to cover up what sounded suspiciously like a laugh.

"Fine. Are we *all* ready now?" Thom asked dryly.

A chorus of "ayes" mingled through the air. Thom used his magic to form a portal and widen it to human proportions. Black emptiness yawned before him. He threw another strand of magic into the portal and a long, whip-like tether unfurled from his body. Thom focused on the image Keifor had given him of Zakar.

Please, El'Ohim, let this work.

The tether snapped taut and widened into a solid path. Thom released a breath he hadn't consciously held.

"Amazing!" Norealle exclaimed, and Thom shot her a startled look.

"You can see it?"

"Of course I can, I'm not blind."

"Well, of all the…" Puck grumped. "Am I the only one who has to stumble through all this magic ridiculousness completely blind?"

Thom chuckled. "It would seem that way. Hold on to me, Puck. Norealle, stay close, please."

With a groan, Puck grabbed on to Thom's right arm. Thom walked out onto the path. His stomach plunged down to his feet as he left the Hidden Realm and entered the bottomless emptiness of The Inbetween. Puck's fingers clenched painfully into his arm.

"Ease up there, Puck."

"Sorry." Puck's grip loosened a touch.

"This is extraordinary," Norealle's voice came from behind them. She didn't sound the least bit perturbed by the fact that they were walking on the equivalent of a forest pathway above a literal chasm of nothingness. Perhaps soaring through the heavens with her mother had prepared her for this.

They had not walked far when the path began to change beneath their feet. It squelched. Slime wrapped around Thom's ankles. "Not good," Thom muttered out loud.

"What? What's happening?" There was no hiding the panic in Puck's voice.

"Eww, what is this? Thom, is this normal?" The first hint of concern edged into Norealle's tone.

"Hang on, I'm going to open the portal out of here," Thom muttered. He let the portal behind them close and redirected his magic to the spot Keifor had shown him.

El'Ohim, keep us safe. Let this work.

Thom funneled his magic into a small portal. The strong odor of sulfur burned his nostrils. He could hear Norealle and Puck gagging behind him. He peered through the portal. It looked just like what Keifor had shown him: a vast, rocky wasteland. If they ended up staying the night, Puck was going to gloat over having a bedroll to sleep on. Thom grimaced and eased the portal bigger. Puck's fingers dug into his arm. Reaching behind him, Thom found Norealle's hand in the dark and led them both out of The Inbetween and into desolation.

He shut the portal.

Silent, they took in their surroundings. An impossibly tall wall stretched as far as Thom could see to the left and to the right. Geysers of steam gushed from the fissured earth, and the darkened sky was burnt with singes of molten red and orange. In the distance, an eerie shriek rent the air.

"Errgoths," Norealle supplied grimly.

"We need to find the breach." Thom's fingers nervously gripped the hilt of his sword. "Which way?"

A quivering voice from behind Thom's head spoke for the first time since they'd left the Hidden Realm. "East."

"Which—"

A small hand swatted the left side of his head. "That way, dumb-dumb."

Thom could feel Traell's body trembling. It did nothing for his own confidence.

"All right," he muttered the word, more to himself than to anyone, and began to walk.

Norealle fell in step behind him, and Puck took up the rear. Thom's booted feet crunched over the shale-covered ground. The loose shards made silent passage an impossible feat. He winced and prayed that there was nothing within earshot. Lengthening his stride, Thom trained his attention on the massive wall to their right. It towered upward into the darkness far beyond the range of his eyes.

The earth rumbled beneath his feet, and a moment later, a geyser of boiling steam erupted into the air not nearly far enough away. Puck let out an oath as hot air—not enough to burn, but hot enough to be uncomfortable—hit them.

Thom chose a wide berth around the geyser and hurried onward. Another shriek in the distance raised the hair on the back of his neck.

"Traell." There was no response. "Traell," Thom growled. "I need you to scout ahead. You're small and you can fly. Go."

"You're small," Traell mocked, but his voice was missing a large degree of its usual sass. "Snack-sized small. No. Staying here."

"Traell," Norealle's soft voice interrupted Thom's reply.

She plucked Traell off Thom's pack, cuddling him in her arms. Thom and Puck gaped as the impudent little creature burrowed his face into the crook of her elbow. Traell would have undoubtedly bitten their fingertips off if they'd tried to hold him like that.

"You are such a brave soul," Norealle soothed. She stroked a finger between his overly long ears and down between his bat-like wings. A rumble came from the little beast, and it took Thom a moment to realize Traell was purring, not unlike a cat. He had to fight to keep his chuckle to himself.

Norealle shot him a warning look. He sobered.

"We need you, Traell. We can't do what you can." Her fingers glided down his fur. "Please scout ahead?"

Traell lifted his head and stared up at Norealle adoringly. His long ears flattened against his body as he stretched beneath her soothing touch. Thom shifted impatiently.

"I know you can do this, Traell," Norealle encouraged. He slowly straightened in her arms.

"For you, milady." He puffed himself up, his wings spreading.

Norealle gifted him a smile that made Thom foolishly wish he could do something to earn such a look. Traell stuck his black tongue out at Thom and Puck, and with a puff of self-importance, he leapt from her hands, his leathery wings beating hard as he took off into the dusky light.

"Well...that worked." Thom released the laugh he'd been holding in.

Norealle's eyes tracked Traell's flight. "Faergoes are prideful little creatures," she replied absently.

Traell was no longer visible to Thom's eyes, but by the way Norealle watched the sky, he suspected she could still see him. The unwelcome notion that she wasn't exactly human nudged into his brain. At the very least, she was half star and half...whatever her father was. What did that make her? He shoved the thought away as they began to walk again.

"Prideful...and hideous," Puck added, drawing Thom back to the conversation.

Norealle shot Puck a dark look. "Be nice."

Far ahead, another geyser erupted. Thom noted the location and asked Norealle a question, keeping his voice low, "Is Traell from the Hidden Realm? Honestly, he doesn't fit with what I'd expect from your world."

Norealle shook her head. "No. His kind are originally from Zakar, but some of them made their home in the Hidden Realm before the realms were separated."

That was concerning. Thom frowned. "Are they good or bad, then?"

"That's a hard question to answer about anyone. Aren't we all a mixture of both?"

"You know what he meant," Puck interjected.

They had reached a rough band of rocks about ten feet high. Norealle nimbly climbed up and over, a feat that Thom envied as he clambered awkwardly over the obstacle.

She waited for the men to join her before answering, "Faergoes can be influenced for good or evil."

"He's probably off consorting with some monster right now," Puck muttered.

"He hasn't done anything to make us doubt him," Thom defended.

Being the most surefooted, Norealle took the lead over the jagged landscape. Thom diligently noted where she placed her feet and followed precisely behind her. The last thing they needed was for one of them to slip and begin to bleed—an obvious beacon to any predators nearby. Thom was exceedingly grateful he'd taken Norealle's advice and packed light. He couldn't imagine trying to navigate the difficult terrain with a fully weighted pack.

Sweat trickled down his face, and Thom could taste salt when he moistened his lips. The stench of sulfur was only getting stronger, and his eyes burned. Where was the breach? He unclasped his waterskin and took a modest drink. The liquid was no longer fresh and cold, but it still tasted clean. Beside him, the others halted and followed suit.

"Where is that blasted gate or hole or whatever?" Puck squinted into the steam-filled haze in the direction Traell had long since flown. "And I think the winged imp has ditched us, Thom."

"Who are you calling a winged imp?" Traell's voice snarked from above their heads, and even Norealle jumped.

Puck cursed. "Fates above, Traell! Why do you always have to do that?"

Traell landed on a rocky outcropping and pulled a face at Puck. A geyser erupted nearby.

"Enough," Thom snapped, anxiety lending his voice a rare edge. They had been in this realm far too long already. "Traell, what did you find?"

Traell glanced at them all, ensuring everyone's attentions was adequately focused upon himself before he spoke. "I flew and flew, and then my wings hurt so I stopped." He paused his story to inspect his wings for a moment.

Thom cleared his throat.

Traell sniffed at him and then continued importantly. "I flew some more, and then a group of nasty-smelly errgoths came out of a biiig hole in the wall." He gave his wings a small flap and snickered. "Traell thinks Realm Walker isn't going to be able to fix it. Nope. Too big. Realm Walker too small."

Thom was not a violent man, but he had a sudden urge to shake the smirk right off Traell's face. They didn't have time for his nonsense. "How far, Traell? An hour? Two?"

Traell stroked his wings. "Hard to tell with your slow feet."

Puck let out a growl, and Traell cast a slightly worried glance at Puck, whose fingers were twitching on his sword hilt.

"About two miles, I think," Traell threw out.

Thom nodded sharply. "Traell, keep scouting ahead. Let us know if more errgoths or anything of the sort are coming and we need to take cover."

Traell took off. Thom glanced at his companions. They both looked hot and tired. Thom tenderly brushed a stray lock of hair off Norealle's sweaty forehead that had worked its way loose from her braid. His eyes traced her dusty face with concern. "Are you doing all right?"

Norealle leaned against Thom's chest, her head resting against his shoulder. "It's hot here."

Compared to the coolness of her home, it was. Thom wrapped his arms around her and pressed a kiss to the top of her head. With one arm around her, he unclasped his water and gave it to her. "Have a drink."

He watched as she took the tiniest sip and handed it back, clearly not wanting to use his water. "More," Thom ordered gently.

She gave him a withering look that made him grin and took a healthy swallow before firmly pressing it against his chest. "I've got my own water, Thom. You need to drink too."

"I will." He took a small sip to appease her and clipped it to his bag. Thom glanced at Puck. "How're you doing?"

Puck grimaced. "This place sucks."

"Aye, it does." With one final glance at them, Thom continued walking. The hot, sulfuric air burned his throat with every breath. Puck was right, this place did suck. They needed to close the gate and get home. Zakar was not a land designed for humans.

With the black wall on his right, Thom maneuvered them through and sometimes over countless outcroppings and around the steaming geyser holes. It was hard to gauge distance. How far had they traveled? A mile? More? Thom's shirt was soaked with sweat, and his eyes burned nearly as badly as his throat. He longed for the cool springs of the Hidden Realm and the fresh mountain air.

The trio's pace gradually slowed as they all struggled, laboring against the heat and the oppressively toxic air. They walked for what felt like five miles, not two, before Thom finally saw the breach in the wall. The sight almost knocked him to his knees.

"El'Ohim, help us," Thom breathed.

Horrified, he took in the jagged rip that had torn the endless wall. Massive creatures that reminded Thom of a cross between a dragon and a giant bat streamed from the breach and lumbering monsters shuffled after them on foot. Traell quietly rejoined the group.

"Where are they all going?" Thom spoke, not really wanting the answer to the question he innately knew the answer to.

He hauled himself a little further up the rock to get a better look. That's when he saw the portal in the distance. It was rimmed in red and large enough to accommodate the winged, hoofed, and clawed monsters trekking and flying toward it. Mute, Thom could only stare. The portal was a dozen times bigger than anything he'd ever made. The beasts disappeared into the portal one after the other.

"El'Ohim..." Agony cut into his soul. *Have mercy on my realm.*

The full realization of what was about to descend upon his fellow humans crashed into Thom in a wave of grief. They were about to meet with the embodiment of their nightmares. The Human Realm could not last against such a force.

"Fates above," Puck gasped.

"I know," Thom whispered hoarsely. "We must close the wall. Now."

"I fear... I fear it may be too late," Norealle choked from beside him, her dirty face streaked from sulfur-induced tears.

Thom clenched his teeth as he watched score after score of ergoths and nameless monsters head toward his world. "It doesn't matter. I have to close it."

No one said anything, but Thom could hear the raspy breathing of both Puck and Norealle. "I want you both to go back to the Hidden Realm." He faced Puck and Norealle, gaze resolute.

Puck scoffed. "As if that's happening."

"Puck..."

"No." Puck glared at Thom, hurt in his eyes. "I didn't come all this way with you just to turn back at the first sign of conflict."

"Puck's right," Norealle wheezed. "We're coming with you."

"Fools," Traell muttered. He turned eagerly to Thom. "You can send me back."

A shriek from somewhere overhead stole Thom's response. Acting on pure instinct, Thom hauled Norealle to him and rolled them both beneath an outcropping. A few feet away, Puck scrambled under a rocky shelf while Traell dove beneath some rocks. A gust of hot air buffeted them as a shadow swept over their hiding place. Another shriek sliced the air. Norealle buried her face into his shoulder, and Thom tightened his grip on her.

There was a skitter of gravel and loose rock as four enormous, clawed feet landed near their hiding place. Scales covered the creature's body, and a horrific reek emanated from its flesh. Thom leaned deeper into the small shelter and pulled Norealle flush against his body. He could feel the hammering of her heart. A gust of hot air blasted from the nostrils of the creature as it swiveled its head, looking to the right and the left. Thom didn't even dare breathe.

The seconds passed slower than any he'd ever lived before. Claws scraped against the stone as the beast took a few slow steps forward, its bladed tail dragging behind it. Thom's vision blurred with sweat, and he feared that his own heart would fail. Another shriek sounded a short distance away, and with a guttural snarl, the beast abruptly leapt back into the air, spitting dirt and gravel at them, and flew off.

Thom sagged against the rock. "Merciful Creator," he gasped.

Norealle let out a shuddering breath, and Thom leaned his cheek against her hair. For a long moment they just breathed together.

"That was too close."

"Aye."

Across the narrow way, Puck crawled out on his hands and knees. Once clear of his shelter, he dashed over in a crouched run. "I'll never complain about bears or wolves again." Puck's voice shook despite the attempt of bravado in his tone.

"You've never even seen a bear or wolf," said Thom.

"What was that *thing*?"

"An errgoth." Norealle eased out of their rocky nook and away from Thom. "A general name for all the creatures that come from this place."

Thom clenched his fists to hide his shaking hands and climbed to his feet. "Are you sure you won't go back?"

"I will!" a squeaky voice called from somewhere beneath a rock mound.

Puck raked his fingers through his grit-filled hair and growled, "Stow it, Thom."

Turning away, Puck crept toward the fissure in the wall. Thom swore under his breath and crawled after him with Norealle at his heels. As a unit, they moved carefully until they were only a short sprint away from their target. They stopped, their bellies pressed against the rough earth.

Determination hardened within Thom. "All right, we wait for a gap in the monsters and then make for the breach. I need to see it up close."

Puck and Norealle nodded in unison, their faces set in grim lines. A group of about ten errgoths winged through the break in the wall. Thom waited. A few seconds later, a lone errgoth flew from the gate, its wings beating rapidly as it struggled to keep up with the others.

No others followed.

Time to go.

Thom sprang to his feet, arms pumping as he leaned into a full sprint. There were few times in his adult life where he'd been forced to run. Thom could hear Puck and Norealle's feet pounding behind him. There was no going back now. They were out in the open. Exposed. The air above them remained quiet, and no monstrous forms appeared in the gateway. Thom reached the wall first but skidded to a stop a stride away as an odd sensation washed over his body.

"Don't touch it!" He swung his arm out to physically block Puck as he barreled up behind him. Faint red lines flowed through the liquid-like blackness of the wall. Thom's heart pounded as he drew in several deep breaths.

"I...I think it might be a portal."

Chapter 25

The Breach

Slager yanked on the chain fastened to the slave's collar. The man, an Abadonian captain, stumbled forward with a grunt. His men, their collars linked to his, staggered to keep their balance as the chain jerked. They had been stripped to their loincloths, and their tanned bodies dripped with sweat beneath the gray-orange sky. The captain lifted steely eyes to glare at Slager, defiance flashing bravely in their depths.

Slager snorted. *Bravery won't save you now, human.*

"How many did you bring?" Titus strode toward him, his hands dripping with blood from the humans Slager had brought him just that morning.

"Twenty more," Slager answered, his voice devoid of any inflection.

The Abadonian king had been livid when Slager had seized two score of his men, but with over a hundred errgoths now at Slager's command in the Human Realm, there was little the irate king could do.

"Excellent. Bring them to the Crib."

Slager smirked. Crib. A fitting name for the birthing fields of Titus's horde.

The Abadonian captain let out a vicious snarl and leapt at Slager, his fist smashing into his jaw. Slager's head snapped back with the force of the blow, and the tang of blood filled his mouth. The captain's hands gripped his throat, and Slager snarled, wrenching the dagger from his belt and driving it into the man's stomach. Desperation flamed in the captain's eyes as he struggled to maintain his suffocating hold on Slager's throat. Sneering, Slager twisted the blade, and the man arched in pain, his fingers loosening. Pulling the blade free of the captain's gut, Slager swiped it across his throat. Blood sprayed. The captain's body fell to a bloody, lifeless heap. His men staggered, their own chains tightening under the weight of their dead commander.

"March," Slager ordered, and the men shuffled awkwardly, their fallen captain dragging with them.

Slager swiped his sleeve across his blood-splattered face and absently rubbed his sore jaw. A foreign sensation itched beneath his skin. He paused, an old memory tugging at his mind. The feeling continued, and Slager glanced around, a distant awareness nudging at him. He'd felt this before. But it had been years.

Another Realm Walker.

But how?

Slager's posture grew rigid. "My lord. Another Realm Walker has entered your realm." It was impossible, his mind protested, but the feeling was distinct. Despite the years that had passed since he'd last sensed another Realm Walker's portals, he remembered the sensation.

The entirety of Titus's cold focus centered on Slager. "Are you sure?"

Slager glared. "I am."

Titus's eyes flashed, anger biting. "You told me Eldehein was inept. His blood diluted. Useless."

At one time, Slager would have cowered before his master's wrath but no more. He focused on the feel of the other Realm Walker. The impression was different than Eldehein's. That bumbling fool was incapable, his abilities nearly useless. This held...raw strength.

"It's not him. It's someone new." Of this, he was certain.

Titus spat on the ground. "You swore to me there was only one bloodline left."

Slager's eyes narrowed, power crackling through his veins. "There was. I made sure of it."

"I should cut *you* to pieces next," Titus threatened, and his blade flicked between his fingers.

A cold smirk curled Slager's lips. "You could try."

He pivoted. The Realm Walker was east. Near the hole he'd created in the wall. Anger flared, and without comment, he snapped open a portal.

Whoever the new Realm Walker was, he would not interfere.

Chapter 26

The Stench of Evil

Thom dragged in ragged breaths, muscles in his neck cording taut as he fought to fill his lungs. The distance between their hiding place and the wall gap had been further than he'd thought. Swiping his sleeve across his dripping brow, Thom extended his hand toward the barrier, his skin prickling with awareness. Streaks of red spasmed over the coal-colored surface. *Magic.*

"Look for a keyhole, but don't touch the wall!" Thom's eyes flew across the surface, searching for a place to put his key.

A red flash. Searing light.

Thom flung up his arm, shielding his face as white dots streaked across his vision.

"I thought I felt another Realm Walker," a voice said, contempt dripping from the words.

Thom forced his watering eyes open. His jaw dropped, heart flagging. A flaming red portal burned several strides in front of him, and a man stood framed by the ring of magic. Black cloak stirring about his muscular frame, the stranger descended from the portal, chest thrust out and hand resting on the hilt of his sword. His boots crunched on the Zakarian gravel as his gaze swept over them.

Thom found himself staring into twin black orbs that swirled with more malice than he could comprehend. Foreboding crashed upon him, drowning his hope beneath a swell of dismay. He took a step back. The crimson portal still blazed, raw power crackling along its edges. It stood as a mocking tribute to Thom's own inexperienced magic. His mind grappled to make sense of what he was seeing. Dread grew like an anchor in Thom's stomach. "Who are you?"

Chest out, the stranger planted his feet squarely, his mouth slanting down. "I will ask the questions, seeing as you are trespassing."

Behind him, Thom heard the familiar sound of steel ringing from its scabbard.

"Thom, be careful," Puck said, his voice more snarl than actual speech.

The dark Realm Walker's fierce gaze shifted to Puck and Norealle. "If I wanted you dead, human, you would be."

"Don't talk to them," Thom growled, jutting out his chin. Sweat trickled down his forehead and over the pulsing arteries in his neck.

A harsh laugh grated from the dark Realm Walker's throat. He tilted his head, observing them like a hawk watching its prey. "I will speak to whom I wish, *filth*."

"Who are you?" Thom's fingers tightened on his sword hilt. *Please, don't let it be Slager.*

The dark Realm Walker prowled forward several steps, but Thom grimly held his ground. Out of the corner of his eye, he saw Puck move up to flank him, naked steel in hand.

"Leave." Puck lifted his blade and pointed it at the cloaked stranger, authority that Thom had never heard him use deepening his voice.

The stranger halted, the tip of Puck's sword touching his chest. He arched a single brow. "You think you can command me?"

The red portal behind the black-cloaked man sparked and expanded. Distracted, Thom reacted too late as the dark Realm Walker parried Puck's blade to the side and wrapped his vice-like fingers around Thom's bicep. With inhuman strength, he hauled Thom to the portal.

Thom dug his heels into the dirt and wrenched his body to the side. He landed a punch on the dark Realm Walker's jaw that had no effect on his foe and only sent pain shooting through his hand.

With a bellow, Puck charged, blade swinging in aggressive but ineffective slashes—blows the stranger easily blocked.

"Let him go!" Norealle darted between Thom and the portal, brilliant white light blazing from her eyes.

A shout tore from their enemy. "A star!" He released Thom, shielding his face from the attack of light.

"Run!" she cried.

The pure starlight radiating from Norealle purged every other color from existence, and Thom stumbled, half blind, through a world of white. "Norealle!"

Shielding his eyes, Thom could see the bent form of the dark Realm Walker. Throat constricting, Thom watched as the man straightened and plunged into his portal. The ring of red magic vanished.

Norealle's light blinked out, and she wavered on her feet. Thom rushed forward and grasped her elbow, steadying her. Her now-brown eyes lifted to his, fear widening them. "We need to get out of here. Find the keyhole!"

Thom's chin jerked in a swift nod. He spun, gaze darting over the wall. *Where is it?* The black, undulating surface yielded no secrets. *Where is it!*

The wall flared crimson.

Strong hands snapped through the forming portal and dug into Thom's shoulders, pulling hard.

"You should've run," said the dark Realm Walker.

No, no, no! Thom drove his hand down onto his attacker's arm, trying to break his hold. Portal magic crackled and blazed on all sides. Thom smashed his palm against the man's face, forcing his head back. The Inbetween loomed.

A blade swished past Thom's elbow, slicing his shirt, and plunged into his foe. The fingers digging into Thom's flesh loosened as the dark Realm Walker let out a roar of pain. Thom wrenched himself free. Norealle, with bloodstained sword raised, heaved him away from the wall-turned-portal.

Bleeding profusely from his chest, the dark Realm Walker abandoned his portal and stepped fully into Zakar. Eyes blazing with fury, he swung his blade at Norealle's neck. She ducked, barely avoiding the lethal blow, and thrust her steel forward. He parried, the power behind his block causing her to stagger.

Manic energy roaring through his veins, Thom drew his blade.

Puck caught him by the back of his shirt and shoved him hard toward the breach in the wall. "We got this. Go!"

For a horrible moment, Thom stood, muscles tensed, torn between completing his mission and aiding those he loved.

"Go!" Puck plowed into the fight, his sword hacking at the dark Realm Walker in frenzied but powerful strikes.

Like a dancer, Norealle moved between Puck's cleaving blows, her slender blade sneaking through their enemy's defenses as he was forced to parry Puck's unhinged attack.

Thom bolted for the gap in the wall, his eyes frantically scanning for the keyhole.

"Here!" Traell's panicked cry sounded from above Thom's head. "The keyhole! Traell sees it!"

Sure enough, floating in the void, where the wall should have been, glowed a red keyhole. Thom snapped the key off its chain. It pulsed and grew until it was the size of a dagger. A cry of pain rent the sulfuric air. Thom spun, key heavy in his hand. Puck lay sprawled on the ground, his prone form unresponsive to the fight that raged above him.

"Puck!" Thom's knees threatened to buckle, bile surging up his throat as fear clenched his pounding heart. The dark Realm Walker drove Norealle back, wielding his blade like a master.

"Dumb-dumb!" Traell shrieked.

Ripping his fevered eyes from the fight Thom sprinted, leaping for the suspended keyhole. With hand outstretched, he thrust the key into the keyhole. Momentum carrying him forward, Thom felt his body plunge into a congealed mass of air. His arm sank into the keyhole, finger joints locking around the key. He struggled, his mouth forming a soundless yell as he hung within the reforming barrier. Magic, burning and biting, slid around his trapped arm, tugging it and the key deeper in.

He could feel the wall's single-minded purpose...*Bind! Keep!*

Thom thrashed, struggling to free his arm. The magic lashed, burning his skin. It wound tighter, encompassing his whole body and forcing the breath from his lungs. Realization settled over Thom.

It won't let go.

Lungs screaming for air and vision blurring, Thom set his jaw and drove the key *and* his arm deep into the yawning keyhole. The magic responded, pulling them deeper in. The wall was reforming, with Thom in it. Force crushed him on every side. Magic burned up the full length of his arm and licked at his neck. Embedded up to his shoulder, Thom struggled to turn the key. Black spots swam before his vision. *I'm not going to make it.*

Thom thrust his other hand into the keyhole and grasped the expanding black key. The magic raked his arms, stretching and pulling. A roar filled his ears and blackness closed in.

Thom felt the key turn.

Magic exploded.

Chapter 27

When Success Feels Like Failure

The dark Realm Walker made a vicious swing. Norealle ducked as his sword sliced through the air, a breath away from the top of her head. She parried, both hands on her sword hilt as she battled her powerful foe. He was alarmingly strong, and he wielded his blade with brutal efficiency. Her hands already ached from the ringing force of blocking his attacks.

Puck roared at Thom to go.

The Realm Walker, momentarily distracted, turned his head to follow Thom's mad dash. Seizing her opportunity, Norealle thrust her blade hard toward his exposed chest. Realizing his peril at the last possible second, the man twisted to the side and smashed his blade against hers. The edge of her sword cut into his side, but it was not enough.

With a guttural snarl, the Realm Walker bolted after Thom. Puck tackled him to the ground. Both swords clattered out of their hands and into the rust-colored dirt. Norealle gripped her blade, balance shifting to her toes, as she tried to find an opening. The two men thrashed about, raining punches down on each other with feral ferocity. The sounds of their labored breathing and fists connecting with bone and flesh filled the air. Puck was bigger, but the Realm Walker was burly and fought like a man who knew no pain. They grappled in an endless tangle of arms, legs, and devastating blows.

A glint of steel caught Norealle's eye. Her heart stuttered. "Watch ou—"

Puck let out a yell of pain as the Realm Walker drove a blade into his gut. Puck punched the Realm Walker in the face and cracked his dagger-wielding hand against a rock. The blade clattered away. With a howl of rage, the Realm Walker seized Puck by the hair and smashed his head against the rocky ground.

There was a sickening thud, and Puck's body went limp. Norealle's stomach heaved. The Realm Walker surged to his feet, snatching up his sword. He wheeled on Norealle just as a flash of blinding light burst from the wall, followed by a mighty blast that knocked them both to the ground.

A loud ringing filled her ears. Norealle lifted her face off the rough ground, coughing on the thick cloud of dust. She scrambled to her feet. The wall was rapidly reforming, but she couldn't see Thom anywhere.

"Thom!" Norealle screamed.

The Realm Walker shoved himself up. Ignoring Puck's prone form, he stalked Norealle, hatred blazing from his eyes. Her eyes widened and her mouth grew dry as she retreated, raising her blade defensively.

Behind him, the wall sealed.

Thom crashed into the unforgiving ground. Gravel tore at his hands and ripped his clothing as he skidded. He blinked blurrily, fighting to keep conscious as he wheezed in one breath after the other. The stale air flowed over his tongue and into his starved lungs. With a groan, Thom rolled over, spitting dirt from his mouth.

Norealle. Puck.

Thom staggered to his feet, the horizon tilting as he took an unsteady step. His eyes widened. The tear in the wall was twenty feet away, but it was changing. The gap was solidifying—and he was on the wrong side.

Thom broke into a lurching, stumbling run. He could see Norealle battling the other Realm Walker, but his bold attack was driving her back at a concerning pace. Puck's body lay on the ground. Unmoving.

No, no, no!

The wall was closing. Ignoring his pain, Thom sprinted with all his might. *I'm not going to make it!* Thom lunged for the wall and slammed into an unyielding surface. Pain surged. The wall had reformed, hard as granite. No portal lines moved on its surface, and no magical current shimmered across it. Thom kicked it. Pounded his burned and blistered fist against it. "Puck! Norealle!"

I'm coming, just hold on. Thom struck the wall with his blade. The sword rebounded, reverberations traveling up his arms. He wrenched his power forward. It surged beneath his desperation, but no portal formed.

A snarl ripped from Thom's throat. *Come on!* He reached again for his power and yanked harder, trying to force it out of his body. Nothing happened.

"Norealle!" Desperate grief tore from his soul as he slammed his bloody fist against the wall. He'd left her with that monster!

"Puck!"

With a cry of despair, Thom threw all his will at forcing a portal to appear, but not one spark of magic left his body. He tried again. And again. And again.

Nothing. No magic.

I can't get back.

The realization sank deep into his mind, and Thom staggered, numb.

A bellow of rage rent the air as the dark Realm Walker charged Norealle with renewed ferocity.

"It's over!" Norealle yelled as she blocked his blow and took a quick step back, struggling to stand under the onslaught. She was used to sparring against the formidable strength of her father, but this stranger was battling like a man possessed.

"Over?" His lips curled into a sneer. "Only for you, little star."

He drove Norealle back. She fought to keep her footing on the uneven ground while fending off the brutal blows. Fear kindled in her heart, and she called forth the last of the power of her mother's blood. *I'll only have a second.* Blinding light shot from her eyes.

He threw up his hand.

She lunged, driving her sword through his chest. It made a sickening crunch as it sliced through bone and flesh. The dark

Realm Walker screamed. Her starlight blinked out. Crimson liquid squirted from his wound, splattering her face and torso.

Norealle leapt back.

Blood bubbled in a frothy river down his shirt. His breaths rattled. "This is not over." Clamping a hand over his wound, the injured Realm Walker summoned a portal and limped through, unfurling a path as he went.

Choking on a sob, Norealle stumbled to Puck's side. "Puck!"

She dropped her blade and fell to her knees beside Thom's friend. A circle of blood stained his shirt over his abdomen. Pressing her fingers to his throat, she felt for a pulse.

He groaned. "Did you kill him?"

"Puck!" Norealle sagged. "I thought you were dead."

"Where's Thom?" Puck struggled to push himself up, his eyes glazed and unfocused.

"I don't know," Norealle's voice shook. She pressed against his chest to stop his movement. "Stay still."

"I'm fine." Puck grunted. "Find him."

Norealle's gaze flew to the reformed wall. The dust was settling, but there was no sign of Thom. And Puck was bleeding. Her breaths quickened. Sweat trickled down her face and into her eyes. She swiped it away, agitated, but mind made up.

"I need to see how bad your wound is." Her fingers lifted the hem of Puck's shirt.

Puck swatted her hand away as he drew himself up on one elbow. Focus was returning to his blue eyes. "I'm fine! It was the hit to the head. Dazed me for a second. Find Thom!"

"He almost killed you!" Norealle snapped, her nerves raw. She shoved up his bloodied shirt, ignoring Puck's protests. His sword belt had been sheared in half by the Realm Walker's dagger...but there was only a shallow cut in his flesh. Crawling to his head, she probed his skull, fingers sinking into his blood-matted hair. Puck groaned as her fingers prodded a swelling lump. Norealle parted his hair and exhaled, shoulders losing their tension.

"You have a nasty cut, but your head is intact." She stood. "You'll be fine."

"Told you. Go!" Wincing, Puck eased himself into a sitting position.

Lurching to her feet, Norealle forced her shaking legs into motion and made for the wall where Thom had disappeared.

"Thom!" She ran along the unending barrier. It towered above her, solid and unbroken. Her gaze searched the surrounding ground, probing every shadow. "Thom!" *Where was he?*

There was no sign that the breach had ever existed—or of Thom. Light from the orange sun reflected off an object. Norealle bent down, tears springing to her eyes. It was her necklace. The one that had held the key. With trembling fingers, she picked it up, cradling the broken chain in her hands. Numbness stole over her body and an invisible band tightened around her chest, making it hard to breathe.

"Thom!" Puck's voice carried to her ears.

She caught sight of him, limping towards her using his sword as a cane. Norealle fisted the chain and returned to her search, her eyes scanning the wall and rocky terrain for other signs of Thom. Tears blurred her vision.

A scuttering noise snatched her attention. Norealle stiffened. A small form crawled out from between several boulders. *Traell.* His eyes were as round as the biscuits he loved so much, and tremors shook his debris-covered body.

"Traell," Norealle choked out his name. She hurried over, scooping him into her arms and cuddling him against her chest. "Are you ok? Have you seen Thom?"

"Nasty, horrible, ugly, stinky place," he wailed. "Dumb-dumb Realm Walker is gone!"

Puck drew near. Perspiration beaded on his brow. "Did you find him?"

He did not look well. Norealle mutely shook her head and un-curled her fingers to reveal the severed necklace.

Puck's face drained of color.

Traell fidgeted in Norealle's arms, his ears flat against his skull. "Nasty wall spat him out. On other side."

No. Norealle forgot to breathe. Her horrified gaze lifted to the ominous barrier.

Puck's entire body grew rigid. "We have to go after him."

"How?" Norealle's lips trembled. "We have no portals. The wall is impenetrable." She hated the hopelessness staining her tone and strangling her heart, but if Thom was on the other side, there was nothing they could do.

Puck's eyes steeled. "We find a way."

With uneven steps, he hobbled to the wall. His motions chaotic, he kicked and beat at it with his sword. The sound of metal striking stone filled the sulfuric air. A roar, brimming with grief, erupted from Puck.

A sob caught in Norealle's throat as she drew alongside him, Traell still clutched in her arms. "Puck." His face was ashen and eyes wild. Blood trickled down his neck from the wound on the back of his head. "Please." Norealle gripped his arm, her expression pleading.

Puck stilled. His expression stony, he slumped to the ground and put his back against the wall. "Thom's smart. He'll be back."

She didn't say anything. Her torn necklace bit into her palm as she squeezed it hard enough to hurt.

Puck closed his eyes. "We wait. Right here."

Norealle sank down beside him with Traell in her lap. "Puck...your head..."

He grunted. "Just a scratch. Save your worry for Thom."

Far in the distance, Norealle could see the giant red portal that had ferried the Zakarian horde to the Human Realm. From ground to sky it still burned bright, its giant center empty. No more monsters would fly or lumber through it to wreak savagery upon the humans. Thom had completed his task. The wall around Zakar was sealed. Whatever horrors remained within Zakar were once again trapped inside El'Ohim's barrier.

As for them...Norealle glanced at Puck. They languished on the slender border of land that lay on the outside of the wall. An uninhabited territory denied to Titus when El'Ohim had first constructed the wall.

Tears trickled down Norealle's cheeks. It didn't feel like a success.

Chapter 28

Tears of a Star

Thom sank to his knees at the foot of the wall. Gutted. *I've failed them.*

The wall was closed, but Norealle and Puck were on the other side, trapped on the outskirts of a poisonous realm with no way to get home. The Human Realm might yet survive, but Thom mentally staggered beneath the price he'd paid. Would Puck and Norealle be left to suffer until they died in the wasteland beyond the wall?

"El'Ohim, get them home. I beg you," the hoarse whisper fell from his chapped lips. He didn't bother throwing out a prayer for himself. He was locked within the depths of Zakar; hope felt like a dream too extravagant to wish for.

The shriek of an errgoth pierced the grayish gloom, and Thom's focus swung to the sky. In the distance, he could make out the dark forms of the winged monsters rapidly approaching.

With a curse, Thom scrambled to a nearby group of boulders and threw himself behind them. Not more than a minute later, an errgoth charged the sealed gate. At the last second, the creature reared back, its wings beating madly as it abruptly arrested its flight. A scream of fury surged from its beastly chest. From nearby, another cry answered, and within seconds, the wall was swarming with a dozen errgoths. They flew up and down the barrier, probing and searching for a way to escape. Thom watched with grim satisfaction. Those beasts would never see his realm. Their jaws would never tear into human flesh...unless they found him.

Eventually, the errgoths gave up and winged off. Thom waited until he was sure they were gone before standing, their cacophony of angry cries still ringing in his ears. He swiped a tattered sleeve across his sweaty brow and eyed the reddened, blistered skin of his arms. They hurt, but he was alive. With stiff, swollen fingers, he pulled out his map.

According to the aged parchment, the wall encircled the entire realm, which made sense. Thom wasted a quick glance upward. Getting over the wall would be impossible. Not even the winged errgoths had attempted that. More than likely, going under was out of the question as well. His gaze fell to the map, and he eyed the dark blotch near the center of the realm. It was as good of a destination as any other at this point.

Thom tucked the map away. He'd head inland. Perhaps there would be something near that blotch that would give him a clue on how to get out of Zakar. At the very least, he could hope and pray that he'd find water. Honestly, his most pressing issue was soon going to be dehydration.

El'Ohim, if you can hear me from this cursed place, I could really use some help.

Thom waited, but his silent plea went unnoticed or unanswered. He scanned the rocky landscape dotted by jagged outcroppings of stacked boulders. Was there even water in this realm? He hadn't seen a single plant since they'd entered Zakar, but surely the errgoths had to drink?

Gritting his teeth, Thom set out from the wall. His footsteps crunched on the dry ground, breaking the unnerving quiet. Apart from the occasional hissing of geysers, there were no sounds. It was eerie. Even a silent night in the Human Realm was filled with at least some noise, now that he thought about it. The crickets would chirp, voices from the neighbors would carry through his bedroom window, and sometimes he'd even hear the odd hoot of an owl.

Here, there was...nothing.

As he trudged further from the looming wall, Thom was struck with how isolated he truly was. He was uncannily aware of the empty space beside him where Puck usually walked and the lack of Norealle's hand in his, a new addition to his life he'd quickly become attached to. Not even Traell was present to snark in his ear.

He was alone.

Thom walked until the wall behind him was a mere shadow on the horizon and his feet ached. It was impossible to tell how much time had gone by. The light never changed from the dull grayish orange that muted the sky. Was there even day and night here?

He eased himself down on a rock and unclasped his water flask. He carefully dribbled a few precious drops onto his swollen, dehydrated tongue. It took every ounce of his self control not to immediately guzzle it all and splash some on his burned skin. The water spread over the surface of his tongue like the most blessed balm, and for a moment, it cooled his raw throat. With utmost care, Thom screwed the lid back on. With nothing to lose, he tried for his power again, but it refused to leave his body.

He stood and continued walking. Rocks. Dirt. Steam. More rocks. It all looked the same. Twice, Thom heard an errgoth-like call in the distance, but somehow, his passage through the land went unnoticed. He pushed on until the throbbing in his feet demanded he stop. Thirst raged through his body, and it hurt to breathe.

Spent, he collapsed amongst a small cluster of rocks and set his back against one. He untied his boots and gingerly removed them. Small bits of grit and rock clattered to the ground as he shook them out. He tugged off his socks, shook them out, and with a soft groan, flexed his tired feet.

For a few blessed minutes, Thom allowed himself the small comfort of going bootless. He took a sip from his water canteen. The splash of lukewarm water did little more than wet the inside of his mouth and tease the sulfur-induced burn in his throat. He rummaged through his pack and retrieved his cloak and the wrapped piece of bread Norealle had made the night before. Or was it two days before? How much time had passed?

He took a small bite, and the crumbs swelled in his dry mouth, lodging in his throat. Eyes widening in alarm, Thom coughed hard. With shaking fingers, he grabbed his water canteen and took another sip to dislodge the moisture-stealing bread and force it down his parched throat. Apparently, he was too dehydrated to eat.

Disgusted, Thom threw the bread into his pack, slid his feet into his boots, and wrapped his cloak around himself. He wished he'd listened to Puck and brought the sleeping mat and blanket. Propped up between the boulders, Thom eventually drifted off into a fitful form of half-sleep.

He did not dream.

When he awoke some time later, the sky was the same orange-gray, and his feet still hurt. What had changed was his head—it pounded with a vicious headache. With a sigh, Thom climbed to his feet. A wave of dizziness spun the world in front of him.

He needed to find water. Soon.

Shrugging on his pack, Thom continued his lonely march. Gradually, the terrain around him changed. The flat landscape turned into parched hills, sand replaced rocks, and the geysers became fewer and fewer until they stopped altogether. In the distance, a shadow on the horizon began to take on a more definitive outline. Was it a line of mountains? For some reason, the sight gave him hope, and Thom lifted his dragging feet with a bit more effort as he steered himself toward the dark outline on the horizon.

Norealle's body ached from sitting on the hard ground with her back against the wall. Her eyes drooped. She strained, forcing herself to stay alert. They'd been waiting for hours but hadn't seen a single living thing other than Traell, who still slept in her lap. Beside her, Puck raked a hand through his blood-crusted hair for what felt like the hundredth time. It was beginning to irk her, but she didn't have the heart or desire to tell him to stop. Miserably, she stared at the red portal in the distance, her bloodshot eyes burning.

Puck picked up a stone and threw it. It clattered onto the hard ground. Norealle watched listlessly as it rolled and came to a stop. She was so thirsty, but only a few drops of water remained.

"I don't think he's coming back," Puck said, his hoarse words breaking the long silence.

"Don't say that." Her voice scratched from her raw throat.

Puck rose laboriously to his feet and held out his hand to her. Norealle stared at it but made no move to take it. He bent down and cupped her elbows, drawing her to her feet.

"Come on," he murmured, his voice thick. "Thom wouldn't want this."

Tears blurred her vision as her throat tightened. "What if he comes back here looking for us?"

"He's smart," Puck rasped. "He'll find us." He dropped his hands away from her.

"Are we going to the portal?" Unbidden, her eyes found the blazing red ring in the distance. Traell huddled against her neck, his nose cold on her skin.

Puck's broad shoulders bowed. "It's the only plan I've got."

Too heart-sore and drained to care, Norealle sighed. "Me too."

Neither of them had any extra words to give. Puck leaned his forehead on the wall and pressed a clenched fist against its blackened surface. Norealle could see his lips moving but couldn't hear what he said. He straightened and caught her watching.

"Puck?" Her fingers tightened on her necklace.

Puck's red-rimmed eyes held hers. "Thom isn't just my friend," his voice cracked, "he's my brother."

A tear slid down her cheek. "He said the same of you."

Puck's mouth tightened into a thin line as he struggled to maintain his composure. Surprising her, he took hold of her bag. "Let me carry this."

Norealle shook her head. "No. It's fine. I've got it."

"Give it to me."

Norealle looked up, the raw pain in his eyes wrenching. She silently slipped off the pack, and Puck took it, slinging it across his back to join his.

Voice gravelly, he spoke. "I'm not letting anything happen to my brother's girl."

Stunned, Norealle watched as Puck marched off. With one parting look at the place where the breach had been, she caught up and fell in step beside him, her heart and body heavy. Together, they walked across the barren landscape in the direction the monsters from Zakar had traveled.

"Have you ever been through a portal before Thom's?" Puck eventually asked Norealle some time later.

"No." She brokenly repeated what she'd told Thom. "Stars cannot travel The Inbetween, but there are places in the heavens where the borders of the realms meet. In those spots, my mother could move between the different heavens of the realms, and she took me with her sometimes." Her throat thickened as she fought back tears.

"If I wasn't here, could you get yourself into the sky and home?" Puck asked.

"No." Sadness wrapped its aching arms around her heart. "Not without my mother. I am only half star, and my abilities are limited."

"The light thing you did with your eyes was useful."

She shrugged. "I can only do it for a few seconds. It takes days for me to build up my power between efforts." Norealle sighed. "I didn't inherit much from my mother."

They stopped, and Norealle lifted her water flask to her lips. Only a drop landed on her tongue. She wanted to weep. Wordlessly, Puck took her flask and pressed his into her hands. She stared at him.

"Drink," he ordered.

"Puck..."

The look he gave her froze any further protest. "Until Thom returns, I'm keeping you safe. Understand?"

There was an almost desperate glint in his eyes, and Norealle took a small sip of his water. Not much remained. Anticipating that he'd refuse to take it back, she kept it.

Not far ahead of them, the portal burned. Unlike Thom's green-rimmed portals that reminded Norealle of the meadows back home, this portal reminded her of blood and the deadly Realm Walker. It was huge.

"That Realm Walker...who was he?" Norealle asked out loud.

"Someone who's been doing this a good while, I'd gather." Puck glanced over at her. "Eldehein thought a man named Slager was making portals to this place." His fists clenched. "He's a dead man if I ever get my hands on him again."

Norealle kept silent. Fresh memories of their recent battle with the dark Realm Walker filled her mind. *I doubt he will be the dead one if we run into him again.*

She nibbled her lower lip. If what she remembered from her parent's stories was true, Slager was immortal. That meant, if it was him, the wound she'd delivered likely wasn't a killing blow. Her heart sank a little further.

They reached the edge of the portal. Norealle crossed her arms tightly over her chest. A red path cut through the oppressive blackness of The Inbetween. A shudder traveled down her spine. She heard Puck draw his blade and turned quickly. "What's wrong, Puck?"

"Can you see anything?" He faced the open portal, sword in hand.

Realization struck. "There's a path."

"Traell sees path too," a glum voice answered.

Despite the short time Norealle had known him, it was strange to hear Traell so subdued. Unbidden, he leapt from her shoulder and slowly crept onto the path, his fur bristling.

"Is the path red like the portal?" Puck asked.

"Yes, blood red," Norealle said.

"Of course it is." Puck raked his fingers through the rutted furrows in his hair. He hesitated. "What if it closes while we are in there?"

Norealle's chest squeezed as he voiced the question running through her own mind. "I think we'd be trapped." Nausea stirred in her stomach, and she hugged herself harder.

Concern darkened Puck's gaze. "Part of me would rather be stuck here than in the black hole."

"We need to at least try and get out of here." She lifted his water canteen. "We're almost out of water. And if this portal disappears, we have no other way out unless Thom comes back."

"I know." A muscle in his jaw pulsed, and his face flushed. "I hate magic. Everything was a lot simpler before Thom became a Realm Walker."

A few replies leapt to Norealle's mind, but she held them in check.

Puck shifted restlessly. "Let's go."

"Are you sure?" Norealle asked quietly.

Puck barked out a strained laugh. "What could go wrong?"

What indeed? *El'Ohim, please let us pass safely through The Inbetween and reach the other side. Please. And be with Thom. Wherever he is.*

Puck grabbed her hand, and she gripped his fingers tightly. Traell watched them from where he waited on the path. Supressing her own nerves, Norealle stepped through the portal, her skin prickling. Her foot landed on the path, and it held firm. Puck joined her. She glanced up at his face. His eyes were set strictly ahead, jaw clenched, and stance wide.

"Lead on, star girl."

Puck was a lot of different things, but respect kindled in Norealle's heart. It was hard enough crossing The Inbetween with a visible path. She couldn't imagine what it felt like for Puck. For all his annoying tendencies, he was brave...and maybe even honorable.

Traell slunk forward, leading the way. Norealle followed carefully behind. The path remained empty. Eventually, the exit portal appeared, and Traell leapt through. Norealle hesitated, and then felt Puck's hand on her shoulder.

"Be ready."

Chapter 29

Fatal Greetings

Thom stared at the formations he'd originally mistaken for distant hills. They were statues. Thousands of them, scattered at random, as far as his eyes could see. The hair on the back of his neck stood on end as unease prickled his skin. The place reeked of evil. He approached the nearest statue and stopped at its base. It was one of the smaller forms, but it was easily twice as tall as he was. Reaching out, Thom touched it. The surface was rough and brittle. His fingers came away covered in an odd, chalky dust. His brows pinched together. *What was this place?*

Thom hesitated. *Could he go around?* His parched tongue dragged over his chapped lips, his throat grating as he swallowed. Finding an alternate route could take hours, assuming there was another way.

With halting steps, Thom passed the first line of grotesque statues. They boasted bulging features and the most bizarre assortment of limbs, heads, and disfigured body parts—manifestations that Thom wouldn't have imagined during his worst nightmares. His eyes darted. No two were identical. While some of the statues were unrefined clay, like the first one he'd touched, the deeper he moved into the bizarre field, the more lifelike and larger they became.

He paused in front of one such statue. Its likeness to the errgoth that had destroyed Eldehein was nerve-wracking. Sweat beading on his brow, Thom nearly jumped out of his skin as a low rumble sounded from the errgoth's stone belly. The statue shuddered, and a rockfall of clay from its scaly back shattered the silence. Thom bolted. Up ahead, a stone-encased errgoth with an array of spiked tails moved its head. Rocks cracked around its neck, and a scaly leg broke free of its clay encasement.

Thom forgot all his soreness, fatigue, and thirst. He bolted, finding a speed he didn't know he was capable of. A chorus of shrieks cut the air, and a horde of small creatures plummeted from the statue to his left. Their wings snapped out, and they collided with Thom feet first, their claws raking across his shoulders. He felt his shirt tear, and pain pierce his back. He yanked his sword from its sheath and slashed it back and forth, up and down, as they pelted upon him like a hailstorm.

They were faergoes like Traell, but the malice gleaming from their beady eyes ended all similarities. Their merciless fangs and claws ripped at Thom's clothing and skin. It didn't matter how many Thom cut down—ten, twenty, thirty—they just kept coming. Blood seeped from his countless wounds. His muscles burned, his weakened body slowing. The swarming about him intensified as the creatures sensed their prey flagging.

There was no fighting them.

Head down, Thom barreled through the faergoes. Their claws sliced his back and tore at his hair. The weight on his shoulders grew as they fastened themselves to his pack. A set of teeth sank into his neck, and he shouted in pain. Thom ripped the creature off, hurling it against a hulking stone errgoth, and kept on running.

An ear-splitting screech rent the air, and the faergoes scattered. By the hundreds, they fled to the statues. Thom looked up to see a massive errgoth diving straight for him. He sprinted for all he was worth, jerking between the crumbling statues in a zigzag fashion. Tails twitched, limbs broke free, and jaws snapped. The field of clay figures was coming alive.

A roar gusted above him.

The statue beside Thom lurched sideway, and Thom fell, gravel biting into his knees and his palms as he skidded. The earth heaved as the errgoth landed behind him. A gnarled claw batted him to the side. Thom struck the base of a nearby mound of clay. Pain exploded across his side, and he cried out, his left arm instinctively wrapping around his injured ribs as he struggled to regain his footing.

There was no time. The creature was on him. It lunged, its taloned feet pinning Thom. The weight crushed his muscles and forced the sulfuric air from his lungs in a whoosh.

His eyes bulged. He was going to die.

The claws contracted, wrapping around his body like a vice, then lifted. With two powerful strokes of its wings, the errgoth cleared the tops of the highest statues, pumping higher into the orange sky. Stomach hollowing, Thom hung there like a dead fish. His heart thundered, the frantic beat pounding through his ears. If the beast dropped him from this height, he'd be nothing more than a collection of scraps for the faergoes below.

Completely at the mercy of the beast, Thom dangled from the errgoth's claws. The miles passed by below. Thom's head lolled, his vision clouding as he struggled to keep conscious. Pain. So much pain.

Without warning, the beast tucked its wings and dropped from the sky. A yell tore from Thom's raw throat, but the sound was swallowed by the rushing air. The ground surged. Thom slammed his eyes shut, his hands fisting as he braced. The errgoth's wings snapped wide, arresting their descent. Vomit sickened his mouth as they glided into the middle of a walled courtyard. Wingtips skimming the cobblestones, the beast released him before landing with an earth-shaking thud.

Thom crashed to the ground and tumbled. He heard bones crunch as the brunt of his landing was absorbed by his left hand. A cry of agony ripped from his mouth as his body came to a stop on the cold stones. He drew his knees up, curling around his broken wrist. The taste of blood joined the vomit in his mouth. Thom slammed his eyes shut, a groan grinding past his clenched teeth.

"I told you to bring him to me undamaged!" a male voice said.

A resounding crack snapped through the air. The errgoth shrieked. There was another loud crack, and the shriek came again. Spots swam through Thom's blurred vision. Through the haze, he watched as the errgoth dragged itself to the corner of the courtyard, one clawed leg tucked awkwardly against its belly as blood trickled from a nasty cut across its limb.

Thom spat, clearing vomit and blood from his mouth. Movements halting, he tilted his head back and blinked up at his defender. A man towered above him—eight feet of terrible, unearthly beauty. A barbed whip dangled from his long fingers. In an instant,

Thom knew that this man was no savior. Bracing his broken hand against his chest, Thom forced himself to his feet beneath the penetrating stare of the stranger. Their gazes locked. Icy blue eyes, filled with untold horrors, weighed Thom with cold calculation.

While he had the form of a man, that was where the similarities ended. His face was intricately carved, with glass-smooth skin and hair so blond it was nearly white. He held the whip with lethal confidence, his relaxed stance radiating danger. A flash of light drew Thom's attention to a dazzling diamond chain resting on the cobblestones. It was locked around the man's ankles.

Thom's gaze darted about the courtyard. He was surrounded by stone walls and locked gates.

"Admiring the view?" the man asked, sarcasm dripping from his voice. "Or looking for an escape? You'll not find one."

Thom took an unsteady step back as the god-like man advanced. The chain on his ankle dragged through the dark stones, and two dog-like gargoyles raced to his side, excited snarls ripping from their throats as they jostled at his knees. Their black eyes locked on Thom as saliva dripped from their toothy jaws. They clawed at the cobblestones, their intent clear.

Thom reached for his sword and groped at empty air. Of course. He'd lost the blade when the errgoth had snatched him.

"Not yet, my pets," the man crooned, and he reached down to stroke the head of one of the creatures with a pale hand. Jagged teeth slashed, and he chuckled. His arms crossed as he silently assessed Thom for a long moment before arching a brow. "So, *you're* the Realm Walker that has re-locked my kingdom?"

"Me?" Thom forced out a laugh, but it came out too high pitched and cracked at the pinnacle of the mortifying sound. "I'm just a librarian."

Azure eyes slashed at him like shards of cutting glass. "Indeed." The towering man lifted a hand and snapped his fingers.

Two figures materialized from the dark shadows near the wall. They shuffled close, rusted shackles linking their legs. Thom gaped. They were men. Matted hair clung to their dirt-smeared brows, and rags scantily clad their skeletal frames. No emotion flickered in their empty gazes. Their bony fingers wrapped around Thom's arms, wrenching his injured limb from its cradled nest against his body. He grunted against the pain as he was dragged forward with surprising strength.

"Don't damage him further!" said the god-man. "Clean him up. Then bring him to me."

The words brought little comfort to Thom. The slaves did not respond but hauled Thom's battered and bloodied body across the courtyard and up some stairs. Thom stumbled between them, struggling to keep up with their pace. They did not look healthy enough to move as quickly as they were, but he supposed keeping the man below waiting was probably an unwise choice.

Thom was brought to a windowless room. The walls were made of stone, and the floor bare except for a worn mat. They pushed him inside. The decaying wood door slammed, and a metal bolt clanged with distressing finality.

With a pained groan, Thom gingerly lowered himself onto the mat. He hurt. Everywhere. His hand throbbed, his side where he'd been swiped by the errgoth was burning, and his back, arms, neck, and legs blazed from the dozens of cuts and bites he'd suffered from the teeth and claws of the faergoes.

Thom leaned his head against the wall and closed his eyes, shoulders slumping. Pain washed over him in waves, eclipsing his panic over his unplanned capture. His body sagged to the side, and darkness claimed him.

Slager snapped the portal closed and sank onto the crimson path that he'd laid through The Inbetween. Wheezing, he pressed a hand against his gushing wound. He could already feel Titus's dark power knitting his flesh together, the pain slowly muting. Livid, he glared into the darkness. That little usurper, a mere whelp of a human, had somehow managed to close the wall!

Hundreds of years of work! Gone!

There had been something oddly familiar about the young Realm Walker. Slager couldn't settle on what had given him that impression. Was it his look? The feel of his magic?

It doesn't matter.

Rage burned as Slager sat there fuming, waiting for the magic to finish its repair. Tendrils of an idea entered his mind, and he stilled.

Titus may be trapped in Zakar...but I am not. He could feel Titus's power sliding across his skin. *I have his power and hundreds of his errgoths at my command.*

The idea took shape.

The Human Realm could be mine.

Thom awoke to something wet being thrown over him. He pushed himself up, coughing and spluttering as he swiped at his eyes. Moisture dribbled over his cracked lips and into his mouth. *Water!*

A slave stood over him holding a dripping leather bag.

"Wait!" Thom croaked and reached weakly for the strange waterskin. The slave handed it to him, and Thom chugged straight from the leather rim. It tasted earthy with an unfamiliar tang, but Thom didn't care. The water washed over his swollen tongue and down his raw throat. He drank until his stomach distended and he couldn't physically swallow another mouthful. Reluctantly, he lowered the waterskin but kept hold of it. The slave grabbed it and tugged, but Thom refused to let go. There was a brief, wordless tug-of-war, but the slave finally relented and gestured to his companion. The second slave, who'd been guarding the door, approached with another waterskin and unceremoniously dumped its contents on Thom's head.

The lukewarm water washed over Thom's bloodied and scraped skin. He cradled his broken hand against his stomach as the second slave took a rough scrap of cloth and mercilessly scrubbed at Thom's blood-crusted neck. The first slave tore off the remains of Thom's shirt and scoured his back and arms. The ruthless ministrations relit the flames across Thom's skin, and a few of the cuts began to bleed anew. He bore the treatment in silence, knowing it was necessary and grateful for the unexpected care.

"What is this place?" Thom ground out, his voice still hoarse from the many hours of dehydration and breathing the sulfuric air.

The slaves did not answer, but he could tell from the way their red-rimmed eyes flickered to him and back to their tasks that they'd heard him.

Thom cleared his throat. "I'm Thom. Who are you?"

Neither of them answered.

A lumpy bar of soap was shoved into Thom's right hand. The slave mimed scrubbing his body. Thom obeyed. Another bag of water was tossed over him. Spluttering, Thom pushed his dripping hair off his forehead.

The first slave approached with a long length of black cloth. Thom's eyes narrowed. The slave reached for Thom's injured arm, but he instinctively held it tighter against his abdomen. The malnourished man mimicked wrapping the cloth on his own arm. Thom slowly held out his injured wrist. With surprising care, the slave bound the cloth snugly from Thom's palm all the way to his elbow. It formed a strange support, and he was pleasantly shocked to find that it felt noticeably better.

"How long have you been here?" Thom asked quietly.

The man simply looked at him.

"Your whole life?"

The man shook his head no.

Thom's heart clenched as realization hit him hard. *That other Realm Walker must be bringing humans to Zakar.* "Are you from the Human Realm?"

The man glanced at the second slave, then slowly nodded.

Thom's jaw clenched. "How many people are here?"

The slave made an odd guttural noise, frustration and despair washing over his face.

Thom tried a different question. "Is there any way to escape?"

The slave took a quick step back from Thom, fear flaring in his eyes as he threw a terrified glance at the door. He grunted and gestured for Thom to be silent. Thom obeyed, not having to wonder who the men were afraid of. Both slaves were now eyeing him warily.

"Guess you're not allowed to talk," Thom grumbled.

The slave nearest him glared. Leaning forward, the man shoved his face right up to Thom's and opened his mouth wide. Mortification punched through Thom as he stared at the hacked-off stub of a tongue. The man's eyes wordlessly challenged Thom to make another comment. Nausea curdled through Thom's gut as his brain struggled to comprehend the level of debased evil that would make someone do such a thing to another living being.

Thom closed his mouth and didn't ask any more questions.

In silence, the two mute slaves helped Thom clean up his bloody legs. One of them took out a jar of ointment. When he unscrewed the lid, a foul stench overtook the room. Thom waved him away, but he swatted Thom's hand to the side and proceeded to liberally apply it to his wounds. Despite the odor, it was incredibly soothing. Once that task was done, they gathered up their supplies and left Thom sitting in the wet cell, alone with his racing thoughts.

Shivering, Thom pulled his legs up to his chest and simply sat there. A few minutes later, one slave returned. He handed Thom a worn set of black clothing and left. The bolt thudded shut. Thom rose and gratefully shucked what was left of his wet, tattered clothes and dressed in the borrowed garments. They fit surprisingly well.

Exhausted but too unnerved and edgy to sleep, Thom sat down in a dry corner facing the door and simply waited. That was all he *could* do. His magic had abandoned him.

Chapter 30

Truth or Lies?

It was hard to know how much time had passed, but Thom's door finally reopened, and two new slaves entered. They were just as withdrawn as the original two but even thinner. Thom stood, his battered body protesting the movement.

Wordlessly, they led him from the room. They made an odd trio as they shuffled down the ridiculously long hallway. The shackles binding the slaves' ankles together clanked with every step, and Thom's aching body moved stiffly between them. Several hallways and turns later, they led Thom into a cavernous room. The walls were stark, and the lack of adornments made it feel hollow, unalive. Their footsteps and clanking chains echoed unnervingly. The slaves forced Thom to his knees.

Time passed by inconsequentially as Thom knelt on the cold stone floor. His mind drifted.

What's become of Puck and Norealle?

Have the errgoths reached Knor? Is the city even still standing?

How do I get out of here?

Finally, clipped footsteps approached from the far side of the room. The god-man from the courtyard strutted in. His contemptuous gaze raked over Thom, and his mouth pinched.

Puck's voice slipped through his mind, a memory from their first day as soldiers. *"Don't let them see you as weak. Shoulders back. Chin up."*

Thom lifted his chin and squared his posture. *Don't cower. Don't let him know you're afraid.*

A ghost of a smirk twitched up the sides of the man's mouth. "Did my servants treat you to your satisfaction? I will have them whipped if not." There was an undercurrent of mocking in the man's imperious tone that suggested his words held no true caring for Thom's well-being.

"Your human servants?" Thom's voice hardened. "Or the winged brute that brought me here?" His gaze didn't waver. "I didn't care for being carried here like a piece of meat, if that is what you're asking."

A bark of laughter burst from the man, and his eyes gleamed as he leaned toward Thom. Not the response Thom had expected. Discomfort slid down his spine, but he refused to show his unease. Spine straight, he did not cower.

"You didn't care for it..." The man snorted and shook his head. His face hardened.

Thom's muscles tightened as he tensed. *His moods are like a pendulum.*

"Tell me, Realm Walker, how did you close my wall?" The question rang through the empty room like a hammer against an anvil.

Thom kept his mouth shut.

Irritation flared in the man's eyes but then vanished behind an almost welcoming smile. "What am I thinking?" the god-man muttered under his breath. He paced, the chain trailing after him.

He turned sharply toward Thom, a wild look in his eyes. "I haven't even introduced myself yet."

Thom subdued a shudder. *He's mad.*

His lips curved ruthlessly, revealing perfect teeth. "I am Titus, lord of these lands."

Ice sloshed down Thom's back. Titus…Zakar's evil master who'd tried to take over the Human Realm hundreds of years ago. Thom stared at the diamond shackles, recollection dawning. *He's chained to this realm.* He swallowed hard but held his silence.

Anger flickered across Titus's face, and the muscles in his jaw tightened. "Perhaps some food will loosen your tongue, hmm?"

Thom stilled at the word "tongue." He did not want his tongue *loosened* by the man in front of him.

Titus flicked a finger at the two slaves, and they quickly hauled Thom upright. His feet were numb from kneeling, and sharp pins and needles erupted across the soles of his feet. He took a painful, limping step forward. Titus still watched him, missing nothing.

"Take him to the dining hall." Titus spun on his heel and strode out, the chain gliding through the floor behind him.

The slaves gripped his elbows, and sternly led Thom up the long corridor. Clattering and a mix of different noises reached his ears from a wide-open doorway up ahead. Thom's steps slowed as they passed. Inside, a well-staffed kitchen bustled with at least a dozen human slaves. At the rear of the kitchen, he spied a door ajar to the outside.

"How are there so many people here?" Thom asked, but the slaves did not respond. *Are they all mute? Has Titus mutilated every soul here?*

They tugged Thom passed three closed doorways before leading him into an expansive dining hall with a long, rectangular table. It was set for several dozen people, but all the seats were empty. Explicit tapestries hung across every wall. The threads wove bloody scenes of terrifying and downright revolting acts. One of the slaves shoved Thom into a chair near the end of the table. The slaves shuffled to their positions near the door, but they did not leave the room.

Restless, Thom shifted on his seat. Minutes ticked by. Eventually, he heard footsteps. Titus breezed into the room with two gargoyle-type beasts shadowing him. They sat by the door as their master moved to the head of the table, several places down from where Thom had been seated.

A dagger appeared in Titus's hand, and he drove the tip into the surface of the table. It stuck there, quivering. "Give me your name."

Thom did not quail. *If I am to die here, I will not die a coward.* He lifted his chin. "Will you cut out my tongue too if I refuse to answer?"

Titus chuckled coldly. "Oh, my slaves? The voices of human filth grate on my nerves."

Thom leaned back and crossed his arms, eyes narrowing. "Yet you speak to me."

"But you are not quite human, are you, Realm Walker? Give me your name, before I etch a pretty picture on your flesh." He picked up his dinner knife.

Thom paused. "Darkfell."

A keen flash of interest, rabid in its eagerness, lit Titus's eyes. "Now that is interesting."

The way Titus's gaze slid over him left Thom feeling violated. He pressed his lips together.

Titus snapped his fingers. Slaves shuffled in with platters balanced on their hands. Thom willed himself not to react as a large plate was placed in front of him and the lid removed to reveal a heaping mound of steaming food. His mouth watered, his stomach clenching in hunger. Slices of an orange vegetable, like a yam but not quite the same, were heaped on one side. Slabs of medium-rare meat filled most of the plate. Unease slid through him. *What kind of meat does a monster prepare?*

Titus stabbed a piece of meat and sank his teeth into it. He chewed, a dark challenge in his eyes. "Eat."

Thom hesitated, then reached for what looked like a vegetable and took a tentative taste. The flavor was odd, but the hunger pangs in his stomach encouraged a second bite.

Titus smirked. "Delicious, yes?"

Thom used the excuse of another bite to avoid answering. It was all a game. Titus, the predator. Thom, the prey.

"How did you close the wall, Realm Walker?"

Thom focused on his plate. His heart pounded as he carefully selected another root vegetable, slowly chewed, and swallowed. He could feel the impatience radiating off Titus. "Ask Eldehein."

Titus let out a chuckle. It was not an inviting sound. "I have it on good authority that he is dead. But fascinating that you knew about him. That fool and his family liked to hide their little secret."

Thom looked up. The dark light gleaming in Titus's eyes made Thom want to squirm. He resisted, fighting to keep his tone impassive. "I met him a couple times." Creator above, but he'd rather be just about anywhere than at this dinner table with this man.

"Oh? Such a brief acquaintance, and yet he shared his talent with you." The unspoken questions and insinuations hung in the air, like oil to trap a fly.

Thom shrugged, feigning nonchalance. He discreetly swiped his sweaty palms on his borrowed pants. "Wrong place, wrong time, I suppose. I saw him appear through a portal."

"Is that so?" Titus murmured. "How shocking for you. But then again, you are a Darkfell, so nothing you hadn't seen before, I'm sure." He took a bite of meat, his icy gaze never leaving Thom.

Using his food as an excuse, Thom selected another vegetable and ignored Titus's strange taunt. What did being a Darkfell have to do with anything?

"Human flesh is quite tender, is it not?" Titus lifted a morsel of dark meat to his mouth and took a slow, scornful bite.

Vomit surged up Thom's throat and he retched, the vegetables he'd just eaten splattering on the stone floor by his feet. Trembling, Thom swiped his arm across his mouth, mortification flooding through him. True fear cracked his composure. *I'm in the presence of pure evil.*

Titus braced his weight on his forearms, drinking in every detail of Thom's reaction. Thom reached for a glass of what looked like wine and took a sip. He coughed as the bitter liquid hit his tongue. *El'Ohim, help me.*

Titus took a slow sip of his own wine. "My subjects are suffering in this dry, forsaken land." He gestured at a window far across the room. Thom followed the movement to the barren landscape outside. Simmering rage built in Titus's voice. "It never used to be this way. A vile, unfair curse turned it from a paradise into a wasteland." He speared Thom with a venomous look. "I need that cursed wall removed." He paused. "You *will* reverse what you have done."

Thom's nails bit into his palms, his mind landing on the one comment that he believed would distract Titus from his demand. "What do you mean, a curse was placed on this land?"

Titus spat. "The one your kind call the Creator could not stand the fact that I had improved Zakar's creations and made something spectacular. He banished me behind the wall and cursed everything I'd made until all that was left is what you see."

Thom kept his face impassive. "Why would he do that?"

"Jealousy?" Titus sighed, an imitation of sadness settling over his countenance. "I just want freedom and the ability to restore my realm."

Thom shifted on his seat. Despite the hunger that still gnawed at his belly, he had no intention of touching his food again. He had to keep Titus talking. "How do you plan to do that?"

Titus stood. "Come with me."

Not good. Thom had no choice but to follow Titus. He quickened his steps, struggling to keep up with the man's giant stride. The halls were empty, and Thom noticed that Titus's ever-present creatures and slaves had not followed him. *Odd,* he thought.

They entered a shadowed room lit by a single torch. Titus took the torch and ignited several others. The soft glow of firelight flickered through the room, illuminating walls lined with books and countless small tables that each featured a vast array of different items. Thom felt himself relax slightly. His eyes roved the books hungrily, his fingers itching to reach out and touch them. He scanned the bindings. Some were written in languages he knew or at least recognized from home, but others were completely foreign.

Thom flicked a glance at Titus before taking a step toward the displays. Titus didn't stop him, so Thom circled the tables curiously. Most of them held glass vases with the dried remnants of beautiful flowers and other plants. They looked like the slightest touch would crumble them into a thousand pieces. Beside each vase was a glass jar filled with seeds. He raised questioning eyes to Titus.

Titus walked over. His fingers hovered above a blood-red flower, but he did not touch it. "Mere shadows of what were once my beautiful gardens. The land was covered in plants such as these." He picked up the jar of seeds. "I can revive Zakar, but not while trapped behind this infernal wall."

Thom stared at the plants. Even dead, they were lovely. Had this place truly been a garden of paradise? Had the Creator honestly destroyed such beauty out of spite and jealousy? *No. It made no sense. But...*

Thom hesitated. "But the creatures here..."

"Why are they grotesque, misshapen figures?" Storm clouds rolled across Titus's face. "They were disfigured by the curse. My children were as beautiful as these plants once were."

Thom frowned, resenting the seed of uncertainty in his mind. "Why are you showing me all of this?"

Titus set the jar of seeds down, his gaze boring into Thom's. "Because," he stated flatly, "I know you are a Realm Walker. One powerful enough to create a path to my realm and relock the gate to my prison." His voice reverberated with command. "I need you to reopen the wall."

Thom straightened his spine. "To what end? Why do you want the Human Realm?"

Ire flashed across Titus's face. "I never said I did."

Thom's eye caught on a dull, blue object sitting off to the side on a worn table. Unlike the other objects on display, it was not protected by a glass cover. He moved closer to it, using it as an excuse to step away from the conversation.

It looked like a rock. A very smooth, symmetrical rock. Thom frowned and reached out to touch it. A current traveled up his arm, and he paused. It wasn't unpleasant, but it was certainly there. Slowly, he brushed his fingers over the surface. It was rougher than it looked. The current intensified, and the scent of clean mountain air filled his nose. A hum rang in his ears, and a deep yearning grew within him. For what, he knew not.

Thom removed his hand and the sound faded, the odor of sulfur returning to his nose. "What is this?" He pointed to the object.

Titus glanced at it dismissively. "An old relic from an ancient age."

Thom stepped away, and the whisper in his mind grew almost desperate. Titus drifted to another section of the room and gestured him over. Obediently, Thom followed. They halted in front of a map. Thom caught his breath. The details were magnificent.

His eyes drank in the details, appreciating every stroke of the excruciatingly detailed and beautifully painted map. It showed everything from the giant wall to the statues he'd stumbled upon right before his capture, to the keep he was currently held in, to a thousand other details throughout the land. But what struck Thom was the lack of other dwellings noted in Zakar. Was this castle truly it? A harsh line surrounded the entire perimeter of Zakar. Beside the red-hued realm lay an artist's rendition of the Human Realm and the Hidden Realm, penned "Silmea."

"Why attack the Human Realm and not here?" Thom tapped the Hidden Realm.

Titus shook his head dismissively. "It is not suitable."

"How so?"

"I have certain *requirements* that the Human Realm better provides."

Unbidden, the image of the slaves sprang into Thom's mind. He kept his face calm and returned his attention to the map.

Titus touched a blue haze beautifully painted around the Human Realm and the Hidden Realm. "Your Creator's blessing." He sneered.

Thom took the dangled bait. "What is it?"

"The giver of life." Titus paused for effect. "Water."

"Ah."

That did make sense. Thom hadn't seen a single plant during his march across the desert, which led him to his next question. "How do you all survive here?"

Titus smirked, his shoulders squaring proudly. "I devised a system to pull water from the ground. Every drop is used carefully and reused endlessly. We heat the water over the steam vents to purify it."

Thom's mind flashed back to the water that had been carelessly thrown over him. Clearly the slaves didn't care as much as their master.

"Like a well?" Thom asked.

Titus pursed his lips. "Of a kind."

"It never rains?"

Titus's face grew stormy. "Never. The curse stole the water from our skies."

Fascinating. "Is water the reason you are trying to leave this realm?"

"Not *leave* this realm," Titus countered. "I want to rekindle it, and to do that, I must link the Human Realm with mine. If I can bind them together, your people would have protection against the Creator who could curse you at his whim, just as he did us. And we would be able to bring life back to our realm with your resources."

It all sounded good, if on a superficial level, but Thom had seen what Titus's creations were capable of. They were the embodiment of nightmares. Plus, there was the unanswered question as to why Titus wanted the Human Realm in particular. What other resources beyond water was he after?

Thom studied the map. "But you've already opened the wall once, why do you need a Realm Walker to do it again?"

"Why do I need you?" His eyebrows slanted down into a scowl. "Because my Realm Walker only partially completed the job and took hundreds of years to do so."

"Oh?"

Titus thrust his foot forward, and the diamond chain flashed against the cobblestone floor. Contempt dripped from his voice. "Slager is inept. When the gate is properly brought down, the wall will dissolve entirely, and my curse will be lifted."

Thom moistened his lips. *He thinks I know more than I do. If I have no value to him, he will kill me.* "That is a large request."

Titus smiled coldly at him. "I'm sure a few days in one of my cells will give you proper motivation to start thinking about ways to go about it."

Fear tightened around Thom's chest. What horrors would a man like this invent for his prisons? Sweat beaded on Thom's brow, and by the hard smirk on Titus's face, the man noticed his distress.

"You could." Thom's mind scrambled. "But my best thinking doesn't happen when I'm under distress." He tried to force an edge of confidence into his voice, like Puck would have. "Give me three days to try and work out a plan. Somewhere comfortable." *And safe! Time enough to figure out how to get out of here.*

Titus guffawed, the sound like claws on stone. "I think not." He smirked. "My experience is that humans become very pliable under duress."

An image of the slave's tongueless mouth leapt into Thom's mind. He swallowed hard. *I need time.*

"I can't access my power in your realm. I will be better able to help you once I leave," Thom said.

"That is because your power is from the Creator, and you are in *my* realm." Titus placed a hand on Thom's shoulder, his fingers digging into the damaged muscles. Thom stiffened. Promise lurked in Titus's eyes as he continued, his voice taking on a smooth, tempting cadence. "I can reinstate and magnify your abilities, but you will have to bind your soul to mine."

"That is a big commitment." Nervousness swelled.

"Swear your allegiance to me, Darkfell, and you will have power beyond anything you ever imagined."

If I say no outright, he'll kill me. Thom's eyes rested on the map. The peaceful blue rims of the Hidden and Human Realms called to his aching heart. "I need time to think."

Titus's fingers tightened. "Then think. I will ask you again in three days, Realm Walker. But I will not ask again after that."

Titus pushed Thom toward the door. As they passed the blue stone, the hair on the back of Thom's neck stood on end as the current buzzed over his skin. Thom's own power suddenly lurched forward. On impulse, Thom urged it forth. An orb, pale and weak, flickered in the dim light of the library. He frantically tried to force it bigger, but it didn't respond, instead fading out of existence.

Titus laughed softly, the tone approving. "Good try, young Darkfell. You see how weak El'Ohim's power is? Join me, and you will discover how mighty you truly are."

Flushed, Thom was forced through the door. His thoughts were a chaotic, roiling mess. Titus barked out orders in a language that Thom did not understand, and a cluster of monsters and slaves hurried toward them. Titus spoke to the monsters in a guttural language, and they bounded off. The slaves grabbed Thom by the elbows, their fearful eyes on their master as they awaited orders.

"Throw him in the dungeon," Titus commanded. "Do not give him food or drink."

The slaves dragged Thom down the hall. Thom could feel the man's cold eyes boring into his back as he was led away.

Titus's voice rang after him, like the knell of funeral bells. "Think about my offer, Darkfell. But do not take long. I am not a patient man."

Chapter 31

The Human Realm

Norealle's heart pounded in her chest. How many childish afternoons had she spent playing in the forest, imagining that a burrow or creek could magically whisk her away to the land of humans?

She crept closer to the edge of the portal, and Traell's claws dug into her shoulder. The magical path ended on a slight hill overlooking a vast, trampled field. They were on the border of a large encampment, and errgoths streaked across the blue sky overhead.

But this is not how I'd hoped to see it. Thom's promise to bring her to his country and show her his books ached through her heart.

"Get down!" Puck said.

Norealle dropped to her stomach and crawled free of the red portal. Dry, broken stubs of grass poked through her wool clothing and scratched her knees.

Eyes wide, Norealle gaped. Across the field, she could see a fortified city wall. She recognized it for what it was thanks to her father's stories, but it was far vaster than what she'd pictured in her mind. Strange buildings of all different sizes and angles filled the land guarded by the gray stone walls. In the city's center she could see a towering structure, its spires reaching far higher than any other building around it. Her lips parted. There was so much to see. In front of the city walls, thousands of soldiers dressed in brown stood in lines. Their metal spears and shields glinted in the sunlight.

"Keep going. This isn't our encampment!" Puck's low voice held a desperate edge and urged her to stop staring. "Look!"

Not far off, men dressed in scarlet were gathering on the field. Scores of monsters from Zakar prowled through their ranks, and the lines of the army wavered as the men jostled away from the snapping jaws.

"Abadonians," Puck said, the word falling bitterly from his mouth. "We need to get to Knor."

Her eyes widened. *How?* Two armies and a vast field lay between them and the city.

From within the red-cloaked ranks, the beating of drums began. Puck swore, panic flashing in his eyes. "The battle is about to start. Get to that tent!"

Staying as low as she could, Norealle clambered over the trodden dirt to the nearby enemy camp. The beating of the drums intensified. Errgoth shrieks filled the sky, setting her teeth on edge and making her want to clamp her hands over her ears. The snarls of the land-bound monsters and the shouts from the humans added to the cacophony. Traell took off like a shot.

"Bloody useless little rat..." Puck snarled from behind her. "Faster, Norealle!"

On hands and knees, she scrambled across the remaining distance and threw herself behind the fringe tent. Puck was at her side an instant later. Norealle's heart pounded in her chest, fear mounting as the roar from the battle lines intensified. A soldier raced by, but he was too focused on his destination to notice them.

"We need to hide." Puck's eyes darted.

"Puck." Norealle's voice wavered as she gripped his elbow, her gaze on the hulking, lumbering form of a Zakarian monster. A long, reptilian tail trailed behind the beast, and its black tongue flicked over jagged teeth. The monster stared right at them.

"Move!" Puck cried.

Norealle leapt to her feet, darted to another tent, and crouched behind it with Puck right beside her. A regiment of soldiers approached. Norealle and Puck dropped to their bellies, squeezing tight to the edge of the tent. The regiment passed by.

Puck held up his hand, motioning for her to wait as he crept forward. Without warning, a soldier in full battle dress hurried around the side of the tent with a dozen men at his back. He halted as his eyes fell on their prostrate forms. The soldier drew his sword, yelling a command in a language Norealle didn't understand. Puck leapt to his feet as men surged forward. In a second, they were surrounded, trapped against the tent wall and vastly outnumbered.

With a roar, Puck swung his blade in a powerful arc, shocking their captors as they swarmed him. Using the distraction, Norealle snatched her dagger from her belt and thrust it up the fabric wall behind her and scrambled through.

Puck leapt in front of the escape she'd just made, bodily placing himself between her and their enemies. He drove his blade through a soldier's chest and landed a solid kick to another's gut. Norealle hesitated.

"Go!"

She ran across the empty tent and slit the rear canvas. Bursting through, Norealle plowed into a red-cloaked chest. The man grabbed her. She stabbed her knife into his arm and ducked around him. With a curse, the soldier tackled her to the ground. Her head smacked against the dirt. His weight settled on top of her, and Norealle bucked beneath him. A torrent of aggravated words she couldn't understand streamed from his mouth. Glaring, Norealle struck at him again with her blade. The soldier caught her wrist and slammed it hard against the ground, trying to break her hold on the dagger. Norealle gritted her teeth against the pain and drove her knee up into his groin. The man rolled off her with a guttural groan. She drew back her arm, her knife poised to strike.

A sword pricked her neck.

"Get. Up." The words were spoken in a strong accent, but she understood well enough.

Her eyes wide, Norealle climbed slowly to her feet. A firm hand seized her bicep in a ruthless grip. The bleeding soldier she'd stabbed and kneed snatched her dagger from her hand. With a hateful glare, he shoved it in his own belt before reaching for Norealle's sword. Without hesitation, she kicked him in the shin. The soldier grunted. The sword bit into her neck.

"Enough." A hot, stale breath seethed against her cheek.

The soldier she'd kicked confiscated her sword. Puck, flanked by a half dozen men, stumbled around the corner. Blood dribbled from his nose, and one eye socket was already turning blue. He cast Norealle a lazy grin. "These fellows here were nice enough to let me practice a few moves on them."

"No talk," said the guard holding the blade to Norealle's neck. He barked out a guttural command to his companions.

Norealle caught Puck's eye. "What are they saying?"

"No clue."

A new guard with a thick beard grabbed her arm. The sword lifted from her neck only to prod her in the back a second later. The command was clear, and Norealle reluctantly moved forward. She could hear Puck and his guards following close behind. They were escorted deep into the enemy camp. A large, luxurious tent draped in purple and blue fabrics came into view. One of their guards broke away from the group and approached a broad-shouldered figure in a black cloak who stood near the entrance. Norealle's heart pounded. The cloaked figure turned, and her stomach dropped. *No.*

She'd stabbed him. In the chest! Norealle watched with disbelief as the dark Realm Walker approached them, a grin spreading across his ruthless face. He appraised Norealle, an anticipatory light gleaming in his eyes.

"What? Did you think you'd killed me, little star? I am Slager, mightiest Realm Walker that has ever lived." He chuckled at the look on her face, and the sound made Norealle's blood run cold. He lifted a finger and trailed it down her cheek. She twisted her head and bit him. With a foul curse, Slager withdrew his hand.

"Feisty. I like that." Lust burned in his eyes.

"Hey! Leave her alone!" said Puck.

Slager smirked. Grabbing her chin in a painful grip, he pressed a bruising kiss to her lips. Norealle whimpered. Her captor's sword pricked into her back, warning her not to fight. The man's vile taste filled her mouth. She gagged. Slager pulled back, and she spat on his boots. He laughed, the sound filling her with more terror than anything she'd ever heard in her life.

To his soldiers, the dark Realm Walker sneered, "Blindfold her and bind her in my tent. Throw him in a cage with the other prisoners!"

Panic roared through Norealle. The bearded soldier tightened his grip on her arm. Ignoring the sword at her back, she punched his hairy jaw. Pain streaked up her hand. She jerked, trying to get free. A second man leapt forward, seizing Norealle's free arm. She thrashed. Together, the soldiers wrestled her inside the tent. She heard Puck frantically yell her name. A third man joined in, wrapping burly arms around her waist as she was dragged into the depths of the dark Realm Walker's tent and bound.

Chapter 32

A Light in the Darkness

Thom had no choice but to stumble along as he was hauled down a short flight of stairs into a cellar-type room. The first slave, a man with an empty eye socket, pushed on the door at the end of the small room, and it creaked open to reveal nothing but blackness. The smell of dank soil and mustiness hit Thom square in the face.

They stood in the doorway as the second slave, a man with a tattoo across his scarred back, lifted a torch off the wall and set to work lighting it with a piece of flint he'd taken from the small ledge beside it. A minute later, the torch smoldered to life, and thick, tarry smoke tumbled forth. Thom coughed as his eyes watered. The two men nudged him through the small door.

I'm going to die here. The thought entrenched itself in Thom's mind, and every step he took felt like the slow closing of his own life's story.

The torch offered only a scant amount of light, but what it did illuminate was unremarkable. The tunnel was nothing more than a dug-out shaft through the ground. It reminded Thom of the mining tunnels he'd read about in his library. It was narrow, forcing them to travel single file. Thom had to walk bent forward to avoid scraping his head on the low, dirt ceiling.

His heart pounded as they descended deeper and deeper into the depths of the earth. Panic dug its claws into his chest, and he struggled to breathe as the man with the tattoo prodded him forward. The knowledge that a few words of agreement would return him to the surface lurked in the corners of his mind.

Thom gritted his teeth. *No!*

El'Ohim, let me die well. Keep me from Titus. Please.

A faint, soft light spilled into the dank tunnel as they rounded a sharp corner. Its glow warmed the dirt walls, illuminating a long row of cells that stretched down the length of the dark tunnel. Both the slaves visibly relaxed. For reasons he could not explain, Thom felt his own tension melting away as comfort replaced fear.

They came to a cell door, and inside was a woman. She shone with radiance. Every pore of her skin emitted light as pure as the morning sun. Thom stopped and stared at her. She rose gracefully from where she'd been sitting on a stone bench and smiled at Thom. Her eyes were warm as honey and filled with kindness. She shifted her focus to the slaves on each side of Thom, her gentle countenance exuding love and warmth.

Tears trickled down a single cheek of the one-eyed slave as he reached through the bars. The woman didn't hesitate to take his grimy hand in hers. A shudder traveled through the man, and slowly, an expression of peace filled the slave's mutilated face.

"Please. Let me stay near the light," Thom begged, his eyes shifted to the darkness beyond the woman's glow.

The tattooed slave grunted in disagreement. What proceeded next was an odd mixture of grunting, hand gesturing, and tugging at Thom. Finally, they agreed on the cell next to the woman. They unbolted the door and shoved it open. The hinges squealed in protest.

Thom was thrust into the cell. Stale air filled his lungs, and his boots sank into the damp dirt floor. The door clanged shut, blocking out most of his neighbor's light. Only a few slivers of light through the top bars of his cell remained.

Thom listened as the slaves shuffled back up the dark tunnel toward the surface. Wanting to know his surroundings, he edged to the rear of the cell, his fingers drifting along the dirt wall for reference. The cell didn't extend from the door very far at all.

Thom's foot caught on something hard. He stumbled, the rattle of metal breaking the eerie silence. Bending down, he groped along the floor until his fingers closed around a metal chain. He tugged, and it came loose. A set of shackles. Thom frowned and let them fall to the floor. In two steps, he crossed the cell and leaned against the door. The soft light from his neighbor filtered through the bars and soothed his nerves.

A lyrical voice spoke into the silence. "I am Ethereal."

Tension drained out of his body at her voice. "Thom."

"Hello, Thom. I'm sorry you're here, but I am glad for your company. It gets very lonely."

"How long have you been down here?"

A light laugh, filled with genuine amusement lit up the air. "I dearly wish I knew. It is hard to tell. But it feels like a long time."

Of course, she wouldn't be able to tell how much time had passed. Thom felt like the "dumb-dumb" Traell liked to call him.

"The master of this realm usually keeps his human slaves above ground. What have you done to make him so angry?" she asked, her voice like a fresh mountain breeze.

"I'm not his slave." *Yet.* Thom pushed the thought away. "He's...giving me time to think about an offer."

There was a beat of silence.

"Be careful, child. Offers from him have many dangerous edges."

Thom sighed. "I know."

She didn't probe any deeper or offer further advice.

"Who are you?"

She laughed, the sound reminding Thom of the bell choir he used to hear from the balconies of the Creator's high place in Knor. "I'm Ethereal. But I think you mean *what* am I, is that right?"

Embarrassed, Thom nodded.

"I am a star from the Hidden Realm."

A star! "I know a star!" Thom pushed away from the wall and grabbed on to a bar with his good hand, excited. "Or at least, she's half star."

"There are not many of those." Thom could hear the warmth in her voice. "What is her name?"

"Norealle."

There was a stark silence, and then the woman's voice spoke again, urgent. "Did you say *Norealle*?"

"Yes. She's from the Hidden Realm too."

"That...that is my daughter's name."

Her daughter? Thom's heart thudded. "Her father is Keifor."

A delighted cry came from the cell next to his, and the light grew so bright that Thom was forced to draw deeper into his cell.

"My husband! And my daughter!" Ethereal's joy covered every word. "Are they well?"

Thom gulped. *Do I tell her I led her daughter to Zakar and left her stranded?*

"Your husband was strong and well when I saw him a couple of days ago," he confirmed, dreading her next question.

"And my daughter?"

Thom drew back to the door and let his forehead rest against the bars. "She came with me to Zakar."

There was a beat of silence. "Why would she do that, Thom?"

He bowed his head. "She wanted to help me close the wall because errgoths were entering my realm. But when I put the key into the gate, it threw me into Zakar and sealed itself. Norealle and my friend Puck are still out there. On the other side."

A soft moan came from the neighboring cell. "Oh, my sweet girl."

Thom gritted his teeth, his fingers tightening on the bars as his own heart ached anew. "I'm so sorry." Thom's voice broke. "I never meant to hurt her."

"Norealle has always loved adventures, ever since she was a child," Ethereal spoke gently, the forgiveness in her tone almost too much for Thom to bear. "She always wanted to join me in the heavens."

Thom spoke around the lump forming in his throat. "She told me that."

"Are you two...close?"

Thom hesitated. He'd only known Norealle for several days, but it already felt like he *knew* the heart of her, and what he saw captivated him. Norealle was kind, brave, and intelligent. She made his heart pound and made him wish there was something he could do to be worthy of her. "I've never met anyone like her," Thom said, repeating the same answer he'd given her father.

"You are human, yes?"

"I am."

"How did you meet my daughter? Have I been gone so long that the paths between our realms have been restored?"

"Not quite. I met her in my dreams after I became a Realm Walker." Thom smiled to himself at the memory. "She helped me find a way into the Hidden Realm."

"I see. Do you know how long I've been gone?"

Thom wished he could see the woman he was speaking with. It was difficult to tell what she was thinking with only her words and soft tones to guide him. "Three months."

She sighed. "Truthfully, it's felt longer." For the first time, pain edged Ethereal's voice, and the light from the neighboring cell faded.

The shadows lengthened, and Thom shivered, wrapping his arms around himself. "What happened?"

"I was in the heavens near the border of Zakar. A red light burst from the wall, and I watched as dark creatures poured from the break. I knew El'Ohim's wall had fallen, and I fell from the sky with several other stars to chase the darkness back where it belonged, but the Realm Walker Slager was there. He used his portals and monsters to defeat us. I was too injured to return to the heavens, so I was taken captive and brought here."

"You were there when the gate was opened." His memory latched on to a different conversation he'd had a week prior. "Slager. That's the Realm Walker who sided with Titus hundreds of years ago, right?"

"Do not speak his name. Names have power, and his brings darkness to the light. But, yes, that is the same man."

"I think I saw him," Thom stated grimly. "How is he still alive?"

"He made a pact with the master of this realm in exchange for immortality."

"Oh."

"Yes, be careful what deals you make. He is cunning and his true motives are cleverly concealed."

The burden of his own impending choice weighed heavier on Thom's mind. "How do we get out of here?"

"I have been kept below ground to hide me from the light. The evil of Zakar mutes my strength, but being completely cut off from the light altogether has weakened me greatly."

"I can't form a portal here either." Thom exhaled, long and slow. "There was an old artifact in Ti— I mean, the master's library. It seemed to help my magic."

"It must be an object from the Hidden Realm then, and a powerful one if it has managed to maintain an essence of El'Ohim's power throughout its captivity," Ethereal mused. There was a pause, then she spoke again, "Thom, I'd like you to get some rest. When you wake, I will try to give you some of my strength. Perhaps it will be enough for you to form a portal. We need to get you home so you can rescue my daughter."

Thom stiffened. "I'm not leaving without you."

"You may not have a choice, dear one."

Dear one. Tears pricked at the back of Thom's eyes, and he blinked them away. He did not deserve her grace.

There was no way he was leaving Zakar without Norealle's mother.

Thom's mind flickered to the human slaves and their desperate situation. They could not be abandoned in Zakar either. Sinking to the cold floor, Thom leaned his head against the door, trying to ignore the pain that radiated from all over his battered body. He'd thought that closing the wall was the totality of his mission, but reality was rapidly changing that perception.

Ethereal's light filtered comfortingly through the bars as he struggled to formulate a plan. Words could not express how grateful he was for her light. Without Ethereal, the dark would have been complete and beyond terrifying. Thom idly wondered if Titus knew that his slaves had put him next to the only source of comfort in his dungeon.

Chapter 33
Dragon Daughter

Thom tried to rest propped against the wall, but sleep wouldn't come. He had no desire to lay on the cold dirt—what manner of insects and rodents existed in these tunnels? The idea of something crawling over his face was enough to keep him upright. He fidgeted, trying to ease the aching of his body. His bandaged arm pulsed with pain. Tortured thoughts of Puck and Norealle marched continuously through his thoughts. Had Slager injured them? Or worse, killed them? If they were still alive, did they still have water? Had the explosion of the wall harmed them?

Thom pushed himself to his feet, injured hand tucked against his stomach. "Ethereal?"

He heard movement in the cell next door. "Yes, Thom?"

"I need to find Puck and Norealle. I can't just wait here."

"Come to the bars. Try and reach my hand."

Thom obeyed. The bars were at head height, so he was only able to reach up and get his forearm out. He rose on tiptoe to extend his reach. His fingers only touched wood.

"It's too far," Ethereal said. "We will have to wait."

"No." Thom gritted his teeth. "Shine brighter. I need to see better."

Light flared. Thom examined his door. His eyes fell on a piece of iron bolted over the hinges. It looked brittle. Picking up the shackles, he wedged the manacle under the iron casing and began to work it loose. Hindered by the use of one hand, it took longer than it should. Finally, the casing clattered to the floor, revealing a simple rusty peg holding the door in place.

"What are you doing?" Ethereal asked.

"Getting out of here."

Using the manacle as a hammer, the cell filled with loud clanging as Thom beat the peg up and out of its keepers.

"Got it!" Thom set his shoulder against the door and shoved. The bottom part shifted, but not enough for him to crawl through. "I've got the first hinge off, but I need to do the second one. Can you keep the light going?"

"I can. Good work, Thom."

The second covering was better secured than the first. Thom used his knee to apply force to the manacle. Struggling with only one usable arm, he worked the manacle back and forth until the casing popped free. Ignoring his bloodied knuckles, Thom set to work banging the final peg loose. It finally lifted clear, and he shoved his prison door. It crashed to the ground. He was free.

Thom hurried to Ethereal's door. He slid the bolt free and swung her cell open. Light poured into the tunnel, and Thom grunted, shielding his eyes.

"My apologies," she gasped. The light dimmed.

Thom blinked as his eyes adjusted. "Whew, that's bright."

"I was trying to send enough light that you would be able to see in your cell." Ethereal took a small step forward. "Are you all right?" Her pale hand touched Thom's cheek.

"You did a good job," Thom said ruefully and swiped at his still watering eyes.

"Well, I am a star." She smiled. "Shining is what we do."

"I wouldn't have gotten free without your light."

Ethereal held out her hands. "Here, let's see if I can help you form a portal."

Thom gripped her fingers, and Ethereal began to shine. He closed his eyes. Warmth flowed up his arms and to his core. He exhaled, feeling the tension ease from his stiff neck and taut shoulders.

"Try your portal, Thom."

Reaching inwards, Thom sought his magic. It responded, thrashing at an invisible barrier as it fought to leave his body. Ethereal's light brightened, the heat in his hands growing painful, and a small tendril of magic escaped. Thom squinted. A faint green orb, hardly more than a mist, hovered in front of him.

"Come on…" He tried to coax it open, but there wasn't enough magic to form a usable portal. With a groan of disgust, he let it go. The magic instantly disappeared. He released Ethereal's hands, disappointment radiating through him. "It's not enough."

She grimaced. "I am weak. I need to get to the surface. I may be stronger up there."

"Let's go."

With Ethereal's light leading the way, they hurried up the dirt tunnel. When they reached the wooden door, they found it closed.

"Dim your light," Thom whispered, slipping past Ethereal. He set his palm against the wood and pushed. It eased open, and no guards or slaves charged them. He glanced around. The hall was empty. Exhaling a sigh of relief, they crept from the tunnel, and Thom eased the door shut behind them.

"No point advertising that we're gone," he said.

Together, they crept up the stairs the slaves had led Thom down only hours before. When they reached the top, Thom carefully peered into the hall. It too was empty.

Right goes to the library and the dining hall. But first, past the kitchen and the door out of here, he reminded himself, grateful for his innate ability to map and remember places.

With quiet steps, Thom turned and crept toward the kitchen. Ethereal, on bare feet, glided silently behind him. Pots and pans clanged, and the smell of food cooking assaulted his nostrils. Nausea churned his gut.

The familiar scrape and rattle of chains hit his ears. Thom froze. A slave, accompanied by two gargoyle-type creatures, rounded the corner. The slave stared at Thom and Ethereal, his eyes widening with shock. The creatures charged. Their clawed feet skittering on the stone floor, teeth bared.

Thom and Ethereal bolted. Snarls and strange yips echoed off the walls as they sprinted down the hall that Thom knew dead-ended in the library. With jaws snapping at his heels, Thom wrenched the library door open, and they leapt through. Spinning, they threw their backs against the door, muscling it shut as the gargoyles hurtled themselves against the other side. Thom slammed the bolt home. Pain thrummed up his injured arm. Ethereal grabbed a table and braced it against the door. The yipping on the other side reached a crescendo, and Thom could hear them frantically clawing at the door. It cracked.

Thom's heart thundered, his gaze darting about the room. A rush of cool mountain air filled his senses. *The rock!* Thom ran to the wooden table and snatched it up, cradling it awkwardly against his side. It was shockingly heavy. A current zipped up his arms.

"A dragon's egg," Ethereal gasped.

Thom's eyes widened. The door shook. "Your light!"

A man's voice shouted from down the hall. *Titus!* Sweat slicked his hands.

"Focus," Ethereal commanded, and light blazed from every pore of her body. Heat flared from the egg, and Thom felt his power leap inside him. He yanked it forth, and it came easily.

"Break it down!" Titus's voice roared from the other side of the library door.

Thom formed a portal.

The egg cracked beneath his palm.

He pictured the wall where he'd left Norealle and Puck and hurled his power into The Inbetween. A path snapped into place as the library door splintered. Thom grabbed Ethereal's hand and tugged her into The Inbetween.

The library door came crashing down, and Titus appeared, rage contorting his features. "Stop!"

Norealle sawed her hands, up and down, using the wooden post for friction. Splinters from the pole bit into her back. Her wrists burned as she struggled to fray the rope. Desperation drove her frantic movements. She needed to escape. Memory of the dark Realm Walker's vile kiss filled her mind and fueled her efforts.

Troops marched outside her tent, and in the distance, she could hear battle. The enemy had only sent part of their forces into the first wave of battle—a grim sign for Thom and Puck's people. She forced her arms to move faster.

Night would soon fall, and she didn't want to imagine what would happen to her then. Death would be more favorable than what the dark Realm Walker undoubtedly had planned.

Thom snapped the portal shut, chest heaving. The silence within The Inbetween was deafening, and the faint green light from Thom's path and the white glow from Ethereal were the only sources of light in the bottomless darkness. Thom adjusted his hold on the warm egg, cradling it in the nook of his uninjured arm, and exhaled a shaky breath.

"That was close," he said.

"Are you all right?" Ethereal was watching him, motherly concern shining in her face.

The slaves. He hadn't been able to save a single one. Thom swallowed and turned away. "I'm fine. Let's find Norealle and Puck."

The egg tucked under his arm was beginning to cool. *You can't help everyone,* he lectured himself as he trudged down the path. *Puck and Norealle come first. And Ethereal. And Knor, if it's still standing.*

Thom grimaced and formed an exit portal. Sulfuric air burned his nostrils. "We should be near the breach," he warned Ethereal, "or rather, where it used to be."

Ethereal drew alongside him, her brows slanting into a frown as she stared out over the empty, geyser-dotted expanse. The wall, whole and impenetrable, towered beside them. Thom left the portal, and when she was clear of the green rim, he withdrew his magic. The portal vanished.

Thom turned, eyes roving over the surrounding landscape. There was no sign of Puck or Norealle.

"Can you search from the air?" Thom asked.

Ethereal shook her head. "Not yet. I can feel my strength returning, but El'Ohim's light is so far from here. My strength is not yet renewed."

Thom bit back a groan. "They could be anywhere."

He'd pictured the tear in the wall when he'd formed the portal, but truthfully, the wall looked the same here as it did everywhere else along its unending length.

"Puck! Norealle!" His voice carried over the barren landscape, but there was no answer.

Ethereal and Thom searched and called until their voices grew hoarse. They found no sign of Puck, Norealle, or the dark Realm Walker. In one regard, Thom was relieved that no bodies lay broken in the dirt, but the lack of information was driving him mad. Had he come to the right place? If so, where had they gone? What direction had they chosen? He halted, despair growing in his heart.

"Is there any way they could have gotten home?" Ethereal asked. Her fingers twisted anxiously through her hair.

"No. I closed my portal."

A horrible thought struck him. *No. They wouldn't have...would they?* "Except..." His throat bobbed, not even wanting to speak his thought out loud. "There was another portal. Slager's."

"But would they have taken such a dangerous path?" Ethereal's voice bordered on incredulous.

Thom clenched his jaw. *They didn't have a choice once I left them.* "If they were hurt or had run out of water. Then, yes." He paused. "We need to get to my realm."

Ethereal held out her hands. "Give me the egg, Thom. If that is who I think it is, we can use her help."

Thom handed it over. And Ethereal carefully took it. He watched, curious, as she set it on the ground.

"Give me some room and close your eyes. This will be bright."

Thom backed a few steps away. Ethereal looked at him and arched a brow. He turned and strode a dozen paces off. Light blew past him and streaked up the towering wall, nearly turning it white in its intensity. Thom stumbled.

A song, in a language he did not recognize, reached his ears. It arched and soared, the notes bringing beauty and joy to the desolation of Zakar. Thom stood entranced, his back to Ethereal and the egg, as the notes wound around him. Time stood still as Ethereal sang. The notes faded away and so did the light.

"Can I turn around?" Thom called.

"Yes."

He turned but did not approach. The egg was shimmering between shades of blue and purple. A glow pulsed from deep within the egg. Thom stared, transfixed. Ethereal joined him by the wall.

Eyes wide, Thom watched as the glow intensified and the egg rocked back and forth. A fissure cracked down its side. White light flashed.

The egg exploded.

A wall of heated air knocked Thom flat on his back. He fell hard, a shout tearing from his throat. He lay there, pain spasming through his bruised ribs, and stared up at the orange-gray sky. Fates above, but he was about finished with being knocked over, dropped, clawed, and whatever else this horrible place could think up.

With a groan, Thom sat up. He shook his head to clear the odd ringing that filled his ears and blinked. There, in a heap on the ground, was the form of a woman.

The figure moaned.

With a wince, Thom pushed himself to his feet and limped toward her.

Ethereal joined him, brushing red dirt off her stained dress. "Give her a moment, Thom. I think it has been a long time since she was awake."

Hearing their voices, the woman lifted her head. Long, blonde hair tangled across her face. She had sharp features and glowing, golden eyes that reminded Thom of a cat. She blinked at them.

His movement slow, Thom crouched in front of her. "Are you hurt?" She stared at him. He hesitated, searching for understanding on her face. "I'm Thom."

Ethereal knelt beside Thom and offered her hand to the woman. "And I'm Ethereal, from the heavens above Silmea."

The woman ignored Ethereal's hand and slowly, almost painfully moved to her knees. Thom shifted a little closer, preparing himself to catch her if she listed to the side. Her lips curled as she hissed at him. Thom jerked back. Unassisted, the woman labored to her feet. She wavered unsteadily, but Thom held his distance. She silently observed the barren landscape and the towering wall. Thom was struck again at the feline aspect of her eyes. She was so human, but those eyes...

"Where am I? What year isss it?" Her voice, unused for who knows how long, cracked.

"As counted from the Human Realm, Year 3591." The answer was quick on Thom's tongue. It was not something most people would know or care about, but as a scholar, such things were important.

"And you are in Zakar," Ethereal said softly. She reached out and lovingly grasped the woman's arm.

"Zzzakar?" A lone tear trickled down her porcelain face. "I...three hundred yearsss..."

She staggered then, and Ethereal caught her. They were about the same height, but the woman folded into Ethereal like a child. Her face burrowed into Ethereal's shoulder as she sobbed. Ethereal stroked her back, murmuring gentle words.

Thom fidgeted. Rubbing the back of his neck, he turned, giving them privacy.

I need to find Puck and Norealle.

Agitated, he found a smooth boulder and sat down to wait, his back to the women. Gradually, the sounds of her weeping subsided, and Thom could hear them speaking.

"Ssso long...why did no one wake me sssooner?" asked the woman from the egg. Every word was laced with pain.

"I am so sorry, dragon daughter. But we just found you today," said Ethereal.

"Where did you find me?"

"The young man found you in Titus's library."

Hearing his cue, Thom stood. Two feminine faces swung towards him. Distrust lit the dragon-woman's feline eyes. "Are you a ssservant of Titusss?" she challenged, her stance growing almost predatory.

Thom shook his head "No. I was captured after I resealed the wall around Titus's kingdom."

She bared her teeth. "Who are you?"

"I'm Thom"—he held up his hands in the universal sign of peace—"a Realm Walker from the Human Realm."

"I am Ranele, daughter of the King of Dragonsss." Ferocity edged her reptilian words as she straightened to her full height. "Tell me. What isss happening in the realmsss?"

Thom glanced at Ethereal. She nodded to him, gesturing for him to speak. He supposed he *was* probably the most up to date, considering one of them had been stuck in a dungeon and the other in an egg.

How is this my life?

"In short? The Realm Walker Slager has brought errgoths to the Human Realm to join the Abadonians in their war against the Lomairians," Thom said. "Titus plans to conquer the Human Realm and use its resources to strengthen Zakar."

"And Sssilmea?" Ranele asked hesitantly.

"It appeared fine to me." He looked to Ethereal.

Ethereal shrugged. "I was captured months ago, but when I left, our realm was secure."

Ranele let out a long breath. "Good. That isss good. And the dragonsss?"

Ethereal hesitated. "We have not seen any sign of them in a long time."

Ranele moaned, fists gripping the sides of her head. Without warning, flames erupted from her skin. Thom jumped back while Ethereal merely looked on. An inferno engulfed Ranele until she was completely lost from sight. There was a burst of light, and suddenly, he was confronted with a massive dragon.

Throwing back her mighty head, the dragon let out a roar that vibrated every bone in Thom's body. Fury and pain raged through the sound. Her golden wings snapped out, her powerful haunches flexed, and she leapt into the sky.

"She'll be back," Ethereal said, lowering herself to a boulder to wait.

Thom's hands clenched and unclenched as he stared up at the retreating form of the dragon. "We're wasting time. We need to find Puck and Norealle."

Ethereal pressed her lips into a line but did not respond.

He pulled on his magic, preparing to open a portal.

"Wait," Ethereal said. "When she returns, we will ask her to search. She can cover vast distances in minutes."

He wanted to yell and beat his fists against the wall, but instead, Thom sat, spine stiff. Minutes passed, and Ranele's dragon form winged back into sight. Thom shuddered—the similarity of her flying form to the errgoths was unsettling. She plummeted from the sky and landed with a spray of gravel. With a flash of light, she transformed back into a woman.

"Dragon daughter, I feel your grief, but I must ask for your help," Ethereal said, stepping forward.

Ranele lifted her bowed head, her golden eyes pinched with suffering. "I owe you a life debt. What do you need?"

"My daughter and the Realm Walker's friend are missing. They may yet be in this area. Can you search for them?" Ethereal asked.

"And if we can't find them, then in the Human Realm," Thom said.

"Thisss I can do." There was another flash of light as Ranele retook her dragon form. She reared up and stretched out her wings, each as long as two full grown men. Her golden scales, stained red by the Zakarian sun, glinted. She kicked off and shot into the sky.

Thom paced as the dragon flew back and forth across the plain, her powerful wings eating up the distance. "You weren't kidding," said Thom, pausing his restless movement to address Ethereal. "She's an *actual* dragon."

Ethereal smiled. "I do not tease about such things, Thom."

"Puck is going to have a fit." Thom dropped onto a rock. He cracked a rueful smile. "We already have a faergo with us that drives him crazy."

Ethereal laughed, and Thom marveled at her ability to express such joy with her daughter missing. Ranele dove and landed in front of them. This time, Thom anticipated the shower of gravel that hit him. A bright light blazed off the dragon as its size diminished and Ranele reformed into her human self.

"I sssearched far. They are not here," Ranele said. A feral grin stretched across her severe face; her countenance lighter than when she'd returned from her first flight. "It isss good to fly." She rolled her shoulders, and Thom half expected wings to reappear.

Then they took the portal. Thom's muscles grew rigid and he stood.

"Follow me." Thom did not wait for them. He formed a portal and crossed the magic threshold. Ethereal and Ranele, in her human form, entered after him.

If the letter he'd read in Drayen's tent had been accurate, then the Abadonians and their errgoth counterparts would be attacking Knor about now—either at its gates or at the Great Woods. He'd try the gates of Knor first.

It was time to find Puck and Norealle.

With single-minded focus, Thom hurried down the green pathway until instinct told him he'd gone far enough. With a flick of magic, he opened a portal and startled.

They were in the sky. And far below, Knor was burning. Smoke rose from within his city's walls, and thousands of men fought in the giant field that had been home to their recruitment camp. Soldiers in red clashed with those in brown. Catapults hurled giant stones and tar-soaked missiles into the city. Errgoths peppered the sky, plunging in and out of battle.

Emotions rocked through him, and the edges of his portal undulated wildly.

"Calm yourself, Realm Walker!" Ranele's voice commanded from behind him.

Thom forced his portal to steady, but could not tear his eyes from the conflict below.

"Abominationsss," Ranele hissed from beside him. Thom swung a glance her way. Her face was fierce, and a predatory hunger gleamed in her eyes as she stared down at the attacking errgoths.

"We will battle together, Realm Walker. You with portalsss. I with tooth. And claw. And flame." Her teeth bared, then shrewd eyes fell to his wounded arm. "But not like thisss."

Without asking, she reached out and grasped his injured hand. Thom jolted as flame curled over his skin.

"Hold ssstill," Ranele said.

Thom's muscles coiled, but he froze. The flame swirled over his body, but it did not burn. Stunned, Thom watched as the swollen flesh of his arm slowly shrank to its normal size, and the bruising faded to pale white skin. The slicing pain in his back disappeared, and within a few moments, Thom felt like a new man. He tore off the bandage, gawking at the restored hand. Awed, he flexed his fingers. "Thank you."

Ranele's attention was already on the city. "Are you ready, Realm Walker?" She did not turn to face him. Her body held a fighter's stance, and she glowered straight ahead.

What is she about to do? "No?"

"Ssstraighten your spine, Realm Walker. Now, for courage. For your realm. For your friends. Through the portal!"

"But we are in the sky!" Thom protested.

"And I am a dragon!" she roared, flames licking at her skin.

Thom beseeched Ethereal, "I am not being modest when I say I am no warrior! I need to go find Norealle and Puck, not join the battle!"

"You cannot find anyone until the fighting ends, Thom." White light streamed from her eyes, making her impossible to look at.

"Battle firssst. Sssearch later," said Ranele. She shoved him from the portal.

Thom shouted as he plummeted toward the battle raging below. He could see men from his army fighting desperately against the hulking creatures from Zakar and the Abadonian warriors.

He hoped that he splattered to death on top of one of the monsters. At least he could claim a single kill...or maybe injure the thing. A rush of air sent Thom tumbling sideways through the sky, then Ranele, in full dragon form, swept beneath him.

Chapter 34
A Daring Rescue

In full scales and fiery glory, Ranele soared up beneath Thom. He crashed onto her back. A beam of light shot passed them as Ethereal descended to the battlefield cloaked in terrifying brightness. Light blazed from her eyes incinerating those in her path.

Heat blasted from the dragon's mouth as she banked toward a three-headed-serpentine creature. Thom flung his arms around her neck. Her fire overtook it, and the smell of charred flesh stung Thom's nostrils as the errgoth fell from the sky. He watched over her scaly shoulder as the monster smashed to the ground below in a cloud of dust.

She rolled, and Thom gripped her scales as his body slipped. He found a notch just above her wing joints to lodge his calves, and he wedged himself in as she climbed. Ranele pumped her wings hard, and he could feel her scales heating beneath his body. Without warning, she dropped into a dive.

He was going to die.

She dove down on top of a swarm of creatures that were viciously ripping apart a defense tower on Knor's wall. Her fire consumed them in an inferno.

"Put me down!" Thom beat her neck with his fist, but she ignored him.

To the eastern side of the battle, a white light burned through the enemy. Ethereal. Ranele dipped her right wing, pitching her body to the side. Thom held on with a white-knuckled grip. Movement caught the corner of his eye.

"To your left!" Thom yelled.

Ranele banked, fire blasting from her throat. A fearsome beast with curved horns protruding from its skull let out a scream of agonized fury as the flame glanced off its wing. It feinted hard to the right, its maw gaping wide, and a volley of *something* shot from its grizzled throat. Ranele twisted, but not fast enough. A roar ripped from her throat as several black spikes thudded into her body.

"Portal!"

It took a second for Thom to realize that Ranele's voice had hissed into his *mind*. Her wings pumped hard, and she rolled, covering the giant beast in flame. It dodged out of the way.

Mentally fumbling, Thom opened a portal several dragon lengths in front of Ranele.

She tucked her wings, diving like a loosed arrow.

"Wait!" Thom wrenched his power, frantically throwing it outwards as she sliced through the opening. A path formed just as her claws skidded onto the magical surface. The pursuing errgoth didn't slow. With a yell, Thom slammed the portal shut, severing the monster's head from its body. The head rolled across the path and tumbled into the abyss.

Thom slapped Ranele's scaly neck.

"What were you thinking!" His anger mingled with battle-field-induced terror. "You can't just fly into The Inbetween without a path!"

He heaved in one rapid breath after another. *She almost killed us!*

Ranele let out a loud chuffing noise, and to Thom's disbelief, he realized she was laughing. *"Open the portal, little Realm Walker! I will tear. I will burn the flesssh of your enemiesss!"*

Shuddering as the inhuman voice rocked through his brain, Thom suppressed his quaking nerves and formed the portal out. Without hesitation, Ranele bounded across the green pathway and plowed into the battle. Thom called his magic back, and the air sizzled as it snapped shut behind them.

Ranele poured fire down on the troops of the enemy. Shrieks from the Abadonians rent the air, and cheers from the men of Knor completed the battlefield chorus. Ranele attacked the eastern flank, her flame joining Ethereal's light as they burned the creatures to ash.

Thom clung to her twisting form as he tried to watch the sky. A swarm of errgoths was flying straight for them.

"Ranele. From the north!"

She shot upward like an arrow. Every vile thing with wings erupted from the battlefield in pursuit.

Thom readied his magic. Ranele flew high, and as the strongest of the enemy reached her, she flipped in the air, nearly unseating Thom, and sent a blast of flame through their ranks. Half a dozen creatures fell, but there were ten dozen behind them. She slanted hard to the right, and Thom threw every bit of his strength into exploding a dragon sized portal and anchoring a path into existence.

She landed in The Inbetween, and Thom shut the portal behind her. Blessed silence descended as the sounds of battle and death were cut off.

Ranele's sides heaved from exertion. *"Just. Take. Sssecond."*

Thom's legs shook. He couldn't unclench his locked fingers from her scales.

"Now fly." She straightened and leapt out the portal he'd created near the city.

They soared the sky west of Knor, stalking the rear of the errgoth horde. Thom studied the battlefield grimly. To the south, an unending ocean of red-cloaked men and errgoths were flooding the battlefield. The tide of battle, which had been turning in their favor, shifted against them once again. Even though Ranele was larger than the biggest errgoth, she was only one against many.

Far below, Thom could see Ethereal battling, but her light was fading. "We need to help Ethereal!"

Ranele dropped into a dive. Extending her talons, she snatched Ethereal from the battlefield. Thom nearly fell from his precarious perch on the dragon's back as Ranele cut through their foes, but he managed to hang on long enough to open a portal and get them all into The Inbetween.

Thom tumbled from Ranele and hit the green path, his heart beating so hard he feared it might rupture. *I'm still alive. How am I still alive?* Shaking, he lifted a hand and raked it through his hair.

"The spikesss. Pull them out," said Ranele through the mental link.

Thom staggered towards the dragon, every logical part of his brain demanding he run from the ferocious, bloodthirsty creature. Shapeshifting woman or not, she was terrifying. Two black spikes were embedded in her shoulder. The flesh was mangled, and blood oozed down her leg. Thom felt his already motion-sick stomach lurch, and he barely made it to the side of the path before heaving.

"I will help her," said Ethereal. With surprising strength, she grasped the bolts and tore them free of the dragon's flesh.

Ranele let out a roar and her tail slashed angrily. Unphased, Ethereal tossed the weapons over the edge of the path. To Thom's shock, the dragon's flesh knitted itself together.

"I will go to the stars for reinforcement. If you can portal me back to my realm, I will gather them, and we will fly from our heavens to yours," Ethereal said quickly.

"Of course." Thom wiped his mouth, the vomit taste souring his stomach. Thom turned to Ranele. "Are you going with Ethereal?"

She grunted, smoke rising from her flared nostrils. *I fight with you, Realm Walker.*

Thom nodded, attention already shifting to his magic. "I've never created a new path while already in The Inbetween. Give me a moment."

Closing his eyes, Thom pictured the entrance to Norealle's cave and unfurled his magic. He mentally pressed it into the path at his feet. To his amazement, it snapped taut.

"I think I got it." Cautiously, he stepped onto the new path with one foot. It held firm. "It's good. Come on!" He ran along the path until the familiar tug alerted him to the fact that it was time to cast the exit portal. He did so, and the sweet scent of fresh air wafted up his nostrils. Through the portal's mouth, Thom could see the mountain-rimmed valley and radiant sun.

"Well done." Ethereal blew past him, her white form streaking for the heavens.

He closed the portal and faced Ranele. "We're returning to the battle, but you're putting me down."

She puffed a small cloud of smoke into his face. "*We fight together.*"

Thom coughed and waved the smoke away. "I need to find my friends!"

"*This is unwise.*"

He didn't really care.

Brushing past Ranele, Thom returned to the portal site that exited over Knor. Ranele crouched down, and he clambered up. He opened the portal.

Ranele surged through and plummeted with blinding speed. Grappling for a hold on her scales, Thom managed to wedge himself back into place. Ranele smashed into the rear of a horde of errgoths flying low over the battlefield. With tooth, flame, and claws, she delivered destruction on a scale Thom had never beheld. Black blood splattered off her sides and covered him.

The body of a faceless beast glanced off her neck and hit Thom hard in the chest. His fingers fumbled for purchase on her bloodied scales, but he was too far off balance. Thom toppled from his perch. Ranele's talons snatched him out of the air, and she swooped down, her wings skimming the field, and dropped him. Thom landed hard in the mud.

The breath knocked out of him, Thom staggered to his feet, wheezing. A spiked tail swung at him, and he ducked, nearly losing his head. Breaking into a sprint, Thom dashed for the edge of the battle. Stumbling, ducking, and weaving, he made it to where a regiment of Knor's soldiers were fighting. They appeared to have the upper hand in this small corner of the battle.

He spotted a familiar figure with blue epaulets on his shoulders. "Drayen!"

The Lieutenant Commander's head turned in Thom's direction, and his eyes widened in amazement. "Thom!"

Thom ran, jumping over corpses as he dodged his way to the commander. Drayen grabbed him and hauled him against his chest in a fierce embrace as he thumped him hard on the back.

"Creator be praised! I thought you dead!" he shouted, ruddy face beaming. "Did you bring the fiery beast that aids us?"

"Aye. Ranele!" Thom grinned, heart thundering in his chest as energy pulsed through his alert body. "And the gate is closed!"

"Well done!" Drayen bellowed as joy lit his face.

An Abadonian warrior charged them. The lieutenant commander pushed past Thom and engaged in battle. A second red-cloaked soldier barreled towards Thom with an axe raised over his head. Thom grabbed for his sword, his fingers closing on empty air. He had no weapon. The warrior was almost upon him. Thom dove behind Drayen. A swift battle ensued as Drayen held both attackers at bay. With alarming skill, he cut down his opponent before skewering the axe-wielding maniac.

Sweat dripping off his brow, Drayen used his bloodied blade to finish off the dying enemy at his feet. His eyes raked over Thom. "Where's your weapon?"

"Lost it!"

"Well, grab one!" Drayen yelled, incredulous.

Pillage the dead?

A press of enemy soldiers closed in, making the decision for him. Bending down, Thom lifted a sword out of a dead man's hands, an apology on his lips, and flanked the lieutenant commander. Overhead, Ranele was holding her own, but her attackers were many.

"I need to find Puck and a girl." Thom swung his blade, blocking a savage pike-wielding Abadonian. "They...may be...captured." Thom jabbed his sword, trying to stay alive.

"They are..." Drayen surged forward and stabbed his blade into the man's gut, "holding prisoners...in the middle of their camp." Drayen drove his sword through the Abadonian's chest as the bloodied warrior struggled to raise his pike one last time.

Thom staggered, bile burning up his throat at the sight of the carnage.

"Get out of here." Drayen hefted his blade, bracing for his next foe.

He didn't need to be told twice. With a thrust of his magic, Thom escaped into The Inbetween. The portal slammed shut behind him. He sheathed his sword, his hands shaking so badly he nearly cut himself. Covered in battle gore and mud, Thom took one deep breath. *Don't think about it.*

He ripped open a portal and plunged onto the far side of the battlefield near the Abadonian encampment. A wounded warrior, draped in a red cloak, charged. Thom barely got his sword up before their blades clashed. The man let out an animalistic roar and parried Thom's blade with enough force to rattle his bones.

"Dumb-dumb!" A high-pitched shriek cut the air. A familiar furball zipped past Thom and into the enemy's face, biting and scratching.

The man let out a howl, and Thom stuck his sword into the man's thigh. The Abadonian fell to one knee with a string of vile curses. Wide-eyed, Thom backed away.

Traell tugged his hair. "We must hurry! Quick, quick! Traell has a path!"

Sword clutched in his fist, Thom sprinted after Traell through a blessedly unpopulated section of the battlefield. He could see the blurred form of a faerie trail up ahead. Traell flew into it and vanished with Thom only a few steps behind. The world grew murky, and the sounds of battle faded away as magic wrapped around them.

"Where are Norealle and Puck?" Thom asked, panting for breath.

"Captured. Hurry!" Traell flapped his wings twice and left the path on the other side.

Thom jumped after him—straight into a sea of enemy tents.

Chapter 35
Unexpected Resistance

I should have driven my sword through his heart the moment I first saw him!

The embers of Slager's ever-constant rage flared with fury as he watched the dragon tear through his errgoths. An inferno raged from the gigantic beast's maw as its expansive wings propelled it across the battlefield in a path of unfettered destruction. The small figure clinging to her back, wielding portals to aid the dragon's escape, had disappeared a few minutes ago. Slager's eyes searched the battlefield.

Where are you, little Realm Walker?

He had no doubt that the dragon and the blasted star, who was blinding and burning his forces on the ground, were both additions brought by the young Realm Walker.

Without turning, Slager addressed the Abadonian captain at his side. "Send the rest of the troops in."

The captain saluted and strode off without question. Slager's lips twisted into a dark smile. After reaping a collection of troops for Titus's pleasure and the rebirthing of his errgoths, the Abadonians had become compliant. The king had to die, of course, but that was a small matter. The rest of his forces had willingly followed

Slager's commands after he'd fed the king's beheaded corpse to his errgoths—one piece at a time. After that demonstration, what little resistance had remained within the Abadonian ranks had been soothed away by promises of Lomair's riches and women.

Humans. Their minds, so pliable. Their souls, so easily bought.

Crossing his arms, Slager flared the dark power coursing through his veins. He could feel every errgoth and land-bound monstrosity on the battlefield. He flexed his magic, bending the minds of his errgoths to his will. The dragon swooped low. Slager's winged horde accumulated, circling in a maddening frenzy.

Attack! With a thought, he sent them hurtling toward the dragon and returned his attention to the rest of the battle. The star and the dragon were unexpected complications, but what were two warriors against the might of Slager?

Chapter 36

Traell's Moment

Traell led Thom through a deserted camp.

"Where is everyone?" Thom whispered.

"Chopping, slicing, stabbing." Traell flew in a tight circle, the dark light in his eyes filled with panic. "Faster, dumb-dumb! We must help the lady!"

"I won't be any help if I get caught." Thom lengthened his stride. *I'm coming, Norealle.*

Bent in half, he skirted from tent to tent following Traell's black form. He could still hear the shrieks of the errgoths and the cries of men from the battlefield, but it was a background to his pounding heart.

"Down!" Traell slammed into Thom's chest.

Thom dropped. A messenger sprinted past.

"*That's* why I was going carefully." Thom pushed himself off the ground.

Traell grew frenzied. "No time, No time! Nasty Realm Walker has the lady!"

"What? You could have led with that!" Thom broke into a run, forsaking all caution for speed as he sprinted past the sprawl of tents.

Traell landed on Thom and yanked his hair. "Stop!"

With a growl, Thom dodged behind a tent and crouched down.

"In there," said Traell.

Thom peered around the tent, swiping sweat from his forehead. Two guards stood outside a large white tent draped in luxurious blue and purple fabric. The colors of royalty. They had spears in their hands and were dressed in full metal armor, unlike the common soldiers on the battlefield.

"Slager has her?" Thom kept his voice low.

The faergo made a distressed sound and bobbed his head.

Thom's aversion to killing evaporated as his eyes bored into the tent. Slager had Norealle.

Traell shoved him. "Kill them!"

Thom grabbed the impudent little creature. "Hush!" He set Traell on the ground, his mind racing. "They'll likely kill me, not the other way around. I'll portal in."

Traell's eyes grew round. "Too bright! Too hard!"

"Easier than battling two warriors," said Thom grimly.

Traell let out an annoyed huff. Before Thom could say anything, the crazy rascal dove straight for the guards. With wild abandon, Traell latched on to one of their helmets. The stoic guard let out a yell and jumped forward, swatting at his helm. The other guard swung his spear. Traell leapt off the first helmet and clawed at the face of the second guard. Thom crept toward the tent, eyes locked on the fight. Cussing and yelling, the guards did battle against the little tyrant as Traell brilliantly led them several paces away.

With the guards otherwise engaged, Thom managed to slip inside undetected. The flap fell closed behind him. He spotted

Norealle. She was bound to the center pole of the tent with a blindfold tied around her eyes and a filthy gag around her mouth.

"Norealle!" Thom sprang to her side, unknotting the rags they'd tied about her head. His fingers fumbled in their haste. Fury like he'd never known pulsed through him. How *dare* Slager touch her? Bind her? The blindfold dropped to the ground.

Norealle blinked up at him, eyes wide.

Thom threw the gag. He cradled her face in his hands, his thumb brushing across a swollen bruise on her cheekbone. A muscle in his jaw pulsed. "Are you injured?"

Her lips trembled and she shook her head. "No."

Thom released a shuddering breath he hadn't realized he'd been holding. "I'm getting you out of here."

He used his sword to sever the rope binding her arms around the pole. Dropping to his knees, Thom swiftly untangled the knots around her wrists. Her skin was raw and bloodied, and her whimper broke his heart. The bonds fell away and she curled forward, flexing her fingers. Tears pooled in her eyes.

Clenching his jaw, Thom pulled her against his chest, his fingers sinking into her soft hair as he guided her head to his shoulder. She curled into him, her body shaking. He rubbed her back, struggling to subdue the hammering of his heart as fear and anger spurred it on.

"The guards are still outside," he murmured against her hair. Drawing in a deep breath, Thom spoke the question that was driving him half mad, "Did he...hurt you?"

Norealle shook her head, her face flushing. Thom nodded, nearly sagging with relief. He wanted to hold her forever, but they weren't safe in Slager's tent.

Reluctantly, he eased back. "Can you stand?"

"I think so."

Thom grazed a kiss across her forehead, unable to keep from touching her. He'd found her—alive and relatively unharmed. He whispered a prayer of thanksgiving to El'Ohim and helped her to her feet. "Take it slow." His hands braced her elbows as he hovered, ready to catch her if she fell. *How long was she tied?*

"I need a weapon." She lifted her chin, courage wrapping around her like armor.

Pride burned in Thom's chest as he took her in. "Here." He handed her his bloodstained blade, knowing she could wield it far better than he could.

Snatching a sharp knife off a food plate that had been left on a short table, Thom headed to the rear of the tent. He could hear the guards outside, still cursing at Traell.

Sword gripped in her hand, Norealle joined him.

"Do you know where they took Puck?" he asked.

"He's with the other prisoners."

Thom's gut clenched, and revulsion washed over him anew. Norealle was brought to Slager's tent for only one reason. As much as he hated violence, the knowledge of Slager's intent made Thom want to rip the man's heart out with his bare hands.

"I'm taking you home," Thom uttered through clenched teeth, barely managing to keep his voice low.

"Don't you dare." Norealle's eyes flashed at him.

"I found your mother. Let me take you home. Please."

"My mother?" Shock slackened her jaw, but a second later she jutted out her chin and glared at him. "I'm coming with you. We have to get Puck."

"Norealle…"

She glared at him.

Thom groaned and pressed his lips to the side of her head before grabbing her hand. "Fine." At the entrance, the tent flap stirred, and Thom froze.

The guards' voices carried through the fabric. "What was that thing?"

"It nearly took my eye out!"

Norealle lifted her sword and sliced through the heavy fabric. The sounds of nearby battle covered the noise. They slid from the tent, and a moment later, Traell joined them. He flew into Norealle's arms, and she caught him. Together, they snuck through the camp and didn't speak until they were a good distance away from Slager's quarters.

"Where's Puck?" Thom asked Traell, keeping his voice as low as possible. A thought, growing in urgency, pressed through his mind. *I need to get back to Ranele.*

"This way." Traell shot off to the right.

Thunder boomed from the clear sky. Thom and Norealle startled. Blazes of white light plummeted from the heavens toward the battlefield.

"The stars!" said Thom.

Norealle's hand pressed to her mouth as she watched the explosions of light ignite the air above the battlefield. Another volley of stars streaked through the sky, followed by a crash of thunder. A blood-red portal exploded into existence directly in their path. The stars plunged through the red vortex and blinked out of existence. Another white light fell, and the crimson portal consumed it before it hit the ground.

"No!" Norealle cried, hands stretching towards the sky, agony written across her face.

"Slager." Thom spoke the name like an oath. He tore open a portal, his magic leaping to his call. He hesitated, conflict warring in his eyes. "Can you free Puck?"

Fierceness burned in Norealle's eyes. "Stop him, Thom."

His portal flickered behind him, but his feet refused to move. *I'm leaving her. Again.* His heart clenched.

Before he could think better of it, Thom closed the distance between them and slipped his fingers into her matted hair. Dipping his head, he covered her lips with his own. Norealle froze, her mouth unmoving beneath his. Thom stilled. *Fool!* He straightened, heat creeping up his neck in mortification.

She stared up at him, shock widening her eyes.

Thom's hands fell away, but before he could form the words to apologize, Norealle reached up and traced the stubbled line of his jaw. His breath caught. Her hand curled around the back of his neck, and Thom didn't move as her gaze searched his. Slowly, she raised herself up and touched her sweet lips to his.

Every nerve in his body ignited.

Her lips moved again, and Thom's fingers ghosted across the soft skin of her neck. She shifted closer. Wrapping his arms around her, he drew her close. They kissed, each hesitant touch growing bolder. Norealle's body molded into him, eliciting a groan from the depths of Thom's soul.

Pulling back was one of the hardest things he'd ever done.

Breathing uneven, Thom tenderly smoothed her dark hair off her face. His heart clenched as he stared into her wonder-filled eyes. He never wanted to let her go.

Norealle fisted his shirt and pressed a final kiss to his mouth. "Be careful."

Thom reluctantly let her go. "I will." He swallowed, hardly recognizing the husky pitch of his own voice. He shot a pointed look at the faergo. "Help her, Traell."

"Go," said Norealle.

Thom plunged into the portal.

Chapter 37

An Endless Fall

Thom formed a portal hundreds of feet above the battle raging below. Standing on the edge of his magical path, he scanned the battlefield. Righteous anger burned through him.

Where are you, Slager?

The battlefield was a chaos of men, monsters, and stars. Red portals appeared, seemingly at random, trapping one star after another.

"Slager is here!" said Ranele, the venomous words erupting in his mind.

Thom's shoulders sagged with relief. She was still alive. He spotted her, winging powerfully in his direction. Thom jumped, and Ranele swept up beneath him.

He landed hard on her spiny back and let out an oath as his eyes watered. Up ahead, a red portal burst into existence. Without being asked, Ranele flew hard toward it.

Thom's eyes probed the battle. *Where are you, Slager?* Portals didn't simply manifest on their own. As if power beckoned power, Thom found him. A nondescript figure in a black cloak standing to the side of the battle. "There!"

"I see him," she answered grimly and changed course.

"El'Ohim, help us," Thom prayed—perhaps the most fervent prayer of his life.

Like a thrown javelin, Ranele hurtled through the sky. Her scales heated beneath Thom's body, and a torrent of fire shot forth, aimed at Slager.

But the flame never reached their foe.

With a flick of his wrist, Slager summoned a portal, and Ranele's inferno blazed harmlessly into The Inbetween. An instant later, the air shimmered directly in their path.

Thom leaned. "Pull back!"

Ranele stretched her wings, but it was too late. They streaked through the red portal, into the pathless void, and plummeted. Ranele writhed, unseating Thom.

Arms flailing, Thom tumbled. Terror sliced through him. Magic exploded out of him in a scattering of useless green orbs. He grappled with his power, struggling to halt their endless descent, but the laws of The Inbetween did not allow it.

"El'Ohim!" His maker's name tore from Thom as they fell through the abyss.

No matter what lies Titus had spewed into his mind, Thom knew whose name to call. There was only one God worth following, and it wasn't Titus.

"Thom." His name, spoken with unbelievable power, was breathed into his mind.

Out of nowhere, light surged through the emptiness. Sparkling like crystals, the lights streaked through the darkness from every direction. They weren't just green. They were crimson, emerald, sapphire, diamond, violet—every color Thom could imagine, and some he would never be able to conceive a name for. They flowed together to form a straight path that coalesced beneath Ranele's claws and Thom's feet. Their endless fall ceased, and the glimmering outline of a portal appeared.

Ranele's entire body trembled and with a flash of light, she transformed into a woman. "I never want to do that again." She glared, her yellow eyes flashing at him.

Thom fell to his knees, his breathing ragged. He stared at the opalescent path and its accompanying portal as they reflected every color imaginable back at him. Thom bowed his head. *Thank you, El'Ohim.*

The raw beauty of El'Ohim's power burned away any last seeds of doubt left lingering in Thom's mind. Titus and Slager were authors of destruction, chaos, pain, and grief. The desolation of Zakar and brutality of its inhabitants were a direct reflection of who they were. No promise from them could manifest into anything good.

El'Ohim was life, compassion, and protection, and the Creator of all things good and beautiful. *Thank you,* Thom repeated. Standing, he strode toward the portal, the light from the gems casting a radiant glow that not even the darkness of The Inbetween could quench.

It was time to end Slager.

"Coming?" Thom threw over his shoulder at Ranele.

With a burst of fire, she transformed into her dragon form. Ranele crouched, and Thom sprang up onto her back.

"Go ahead," said Thom.

She trotted forward, her lofty dragon strides carrying them through El'Ohim's portal. Thom had no idea where it led, only that it would take him where he needed to be.

Norealle slipped soundlessly through the tents, artfully avoiding detection as she and Traell made their way closer to the prisoners. They were being held in iron cages with three to five men to an enclosure. Her lips trembled as she took in the caged men baking beneath the hot sun.

Norealle counted the guards. *Six.*

Too many for her to face alone. She clenched her teeth. Somehow, she'd have to sneak to Puck's cage without being detected. *El'Ohim, please help me.*

Norealle reached up and stroked Traell's fur. "Traell, can you find Puck?"

"Big dumb-dumb easy to see. Traell find him." With that boast, Traell promptly took off. He circled high, and Norealle watched as he flew back and forth across the enclosures, his form looking like a bird.

He landed on Norealle. "In the middle is the big one," he said proudly.

"Good job." She stroked his fur. "Let's go get him."

Using every skill she'd ever learned stalking prey, Norealle crept past the guards and into the rows of cages. Her presence caused an immediate stir. The prisoners grew agitated, grabbing bars and whispering far too loud. Their eyes were wild with fear and desperation. Norealle held her finger to her mouth, her own eyes silently begging them to be quiet, but it did no good.

"Hey! What's going on over there?" a guard yelled.

She'd been discovered. Norealle followed Traell, dashing through the cages. *Where was Puck?*

"Star girl!" Puck bellowed.

Norealle spotted him, standing a foot taller than any other man in his enclosure. Ducking around a guard, she bolted toward Puck. She could hear the pounding footfalls of the soldier behind her, and he was gaining. She careened past Puck's cage and threw her sword to him before somersaulting forward. The guard tripped over her, and Norealle kicked up with all her might, her feet knocking the air out of the man's lungs. She surged to her feet. The soldier regained his footing faster than she had expected and brandished his sword.

"You little..." He spat out a foul name, advancing.

To her left and right, other guards approached. Norealle let out a squeak as her spine hit a cage. She was trapped.

There was a sound of metal striking metal, and Puck's cage door clanged open. With an enraged roar he sprang forward, driving his dented blade through the soldier's chest. Norealle leapt to the side as the guard fell. Puck was there in an instant.

Face grim, he grabbed the sword out of the dying man's fist and shoved it into Norealle's hand. Traell flew straight into the faces of the oncoming guards, scratching, biting, tearing. More guards poured in, alerted by the yells of their fellow soldiers.

"Let's go!" said Puck.

He was a battering ram. With his fury and his size, he cut through the soldiers like a farmer slicing through wheat. Puck battled like a wild animal, slashing, stabbing, and punching as he cut down their foes. Right behind him, Norealle made up for her lack of size with skill, cutting down those who came too close.

An animalistic roar boomed through the air. The prisoners cried out, flattening themselves in their cages, and the soldiers fell back. Puck didn't slow. Another roar shook the ground, but this one was right overhead.

"Errgoth!" said Puck.

"No...dragon!" Norealle had heard enough stories from her parents to know that the fire-breathing monstrosity flying overhead was no errgoth. The dragon roared again as it swept low over the cages. Prisoners screamed, and the soldiers fled.

"Norealle! Puck!" a familiar voice yelled from the dragon.

The giant beast landed, dust billowing around its scaly feet, and Thom jumped from its back. Puck let out a whoop and covered the short distance between them. They collided, pounding each other in joyous greeting. For a moment, the very real thought that Puck was going to break Thom's back flashed through Norealle's mind.

All around them, chaos reigned as prisoners broke free of their cages and guards struggled to contain them. Men ran in every direction. Shouts punctuated the havoc. But everyone gave the fiery beast a wide birth.

Following Puck, Norealle ran to Thom. He turned just in time to catch her as she threw herself into his arms. He crushed her against his chest, breathing her name. She wound her arms around his neck, staring at the mountain of hulking muscle and golden scales.

The dragon lowered its angular head, its voluminous yellow eyes staring unblinking at her. *"Hello, Star Daughter."*

Norealle's eyes widened. "Thom…"

Thom turned them to face the dragon but kept his arms around her. "Norealle, Puck…this is Ranele."

Norealle swallowed hard, then dipped her head. "It is well met, Ranele."

"And you, Star Daughter."

Thom drew her to the dragon's side. "We have to return to the battle. Climb up. Both of you."

Strength and a confidence that Norealle had never seen from Thom radiated from his eyes. With a sharp nod, Puck braced his boot on the dragon's knee and hoisted himself up on her scaly back. Thom wrapped his fingers around Norealle's waist and boosted her up behind Puck. A moment later, he scrambled up behind her.

"What do I hold on to?" she shrieked as the dragon spread its wings.

"Me!" Puck let out a whoop as the dragon sprang off the ground.

With a cry, she threw her arms around Puck's waist. Thom reached around her, gripping the scales right in front of her thighs, holding her legs in place. She felt his chest press against her back. "We've got you, but squeeze tight," said Thom.

Norealle hunkered down.

Thom raised his voice to a shout. "Take us to Slager, Ranele!"

Chapter 38

A Reckoning

Slager wielded his portals unchallenged. Thom watched the red rings blinking in and out of existence, stealing their warriors right off the field of battle.

"How are you going to kill him?" Norealle pitched her voice to a scream to be heard over the din.

"I don't know!" Thom shouted.

"Thom, I already stabbed him. It didn't work!"

Thom's thoughts raced. *Slager traded his soul for immortality. Can he be killed at all?* The skeleton of an idea formed in Thom's mind, and he uttered a silent prayer to El'Ohim to somehow keep his foolish hide intact.

He released the dragon scales and wrapped his arm around Norealle's waist, squeezing her to him in a quick hug. "Stay with Ranele!" Tucking his body, Thom rolled off the flying dragon.

Fear no longer had a hold on him. He'd literally fallen through The Inbetween, and El'Ohim had plucked him from certain death. What was one Realm Walker? Thom plummeted through the sky, his gaze focused on Slager, still manipulating the field with his weaponized portals. Snapping open his own portal, Thom unfurled his magic and hit the path running.

He exited directly behind Slager.

Lunging, Thom grabbed Slager by the shoulders and yanked him backward. *Let's see if your trick works on you.* Slager stumbled, caught off guard by Thom's attack, but he did not fall into the portal as Thom had hoped. Slager pivoted, and they grappled on the edge of Thom's portal.

There was a loud bellow, and a second later, Ranele landed. Puck came flying over her head and slammed his foot into the middle of the Realm Walker's back, propelling him and Thom through the portal.

The portal shut, and Thom leapt to his feet. Slager stood, and the two Realm Walkers sized each other up. Anger consumed Slager's face, but as he studied Thom, it morphed into a chilling look of speculation. Trapped in his line of sight, Thom took a few steps backward to give himself some space. A smile slid across Slager's features, cracking his face unnaturally.

"You escaped The Inbetween." His voice was calm. Calculating. "That is...unexpected." He took a step toward Thom.

Thom retreated.

"You are young," said Slager, and advanced another step. "Untrained."

"That's far enough." Thom held up a hand.

Slager chuckled but stopped. He cocked his head, his posture reminding Thom of the serpent heads he'd seen on some of the errgoths.

"I could teach you...much. You are more skilled than your father ever was," said Slager.

Thom stilled. "What?"

"Didn't you know?" Slager arched a brow. "Your father was a Realm Walker. It took me a while to figure out why you looked familiar." A cruel chuckle rumbled out of Slager's chest as he eased closer "I hunted for you after I'd gotten rid of him."

Understanding dawned on Thom. "*You* were what my mother was afraid of."

Slager sneered. "Aggravating woman. I should have known better than to leave a strand of Darkfell's line still breathing. But..." He trailed off, contemplating. "Perhaps losing track of you wasn't such a bad thing. You are strong, and I can show you power beyond anything you ever dreamed."

Thom's fists clenched. "I don't dream of power, and I think I have the job about figured out." Thom readied his magic. "And you're trespassing in my realm."

"Am I? I quite like it here." He paused speculatively. "We could rule this world with what I could teach you."

Thom shook his head, his voice hardening to flint. "My task is to help bring peace, not to conquer and rule."

"Naïve fool," Slager spat, his lips curling in derision. "You squander power that is unmatched, except by me, on protecting ignorant humans and serving a pathetic god."

"How I use my magic is my business."

Slager lunged. Thom dodged and sprinted down his path to try and give himself a few extra seconds. He yanked open a portal and leapt onto the battlefield.

Behind him, he could hear Slager laughing. "You think that will trap me here, boy?"

Thom slammed his portal shut, praying that Slager would not be able to portal out of a path made by another Realm Walker. Lomairian warriors swarmed all around Thom, shouts and screams filling the air as Ranele and the stars wreaked havoc on Zakar's forces.

Slager did not reappear.

Thom dodged a red-cloaked warrior and brandished his sword.

"Realm Walker! I'm coming!" Ranele's voice whipped into his mind.

Thom slashed at the Abadonian, trying to keep the man away.

"Behind you!" The cry leapt into Thom's mind too late.

Agony exploded. He staggered, staring down at the dagger buried in his side. Rough hands grabbed his hair and jerked his head back. Thom grunted as Slager's face swam into view. The dark Realm Walker grasped the dagger and twisted the blade, cruelty raging in his eyes.

"Choose, young Realm Walker." The blade turned again. "Join me, and I will heal you." The blade plunged deeper, and Thom's legs buckled, Slager's grip on his hair the only thing keeping him somewhat upright.

"Never." Thom grunted through clenched teeth, panting against the pain.

"THOM!" Puck's voice roared from overhead.

The blade ripped out, and Slager slammed it into Thom's chest and through his heart. The blade tore his flesh, and blood spurted from the fatal wound.

Thom slowly blinked, black spots obscuring his vision. *It's over.*

Pain seared. The world tilted. One last resolve took over. Wrapping his bloodied fingers around Slager's arm, Thom let himself fall backward into The Inbetween.

Slager pitched after him with a yell, his arm clutched fast by Thom, and his own hand still clenched on the dagger embedded deep in Thom's heart.

They plummeted.

Slager wrenched away from him, and Thom watched as he bucked and kicked, sparks of vile red power splintering off him but never forming a solid portal.

Thom closed his eyes, letting the darkness embrace him as he fell through the endless abyss. *"I tried, El'Ohim. I tried."*

It was over. He was dying.

"Do you choose me, Thom Darkfell?"

"Always." Thom could feel himself fading from life, but to his surprise, he wasn't afraid.

"Do you trust me?"

"Your way is best." Peace washed over him. He was tired. Consciousness drifting, Thom cracked his eyes open one last time. He could no longer see Slager. There was nothing but blackness, but somehow, he knew he wasn't alone. His eyelids closed, and he let the darkness take him.

Ranele landed hard on the charred, body-littered ground. She threw her head back and released a soul-wrenching roar. Everything near her, friend and foe, fled. Norealle sagged on the dragon's back, her tears soaking Puck's shirt. She'd seen the dark Realm

Walker stab Thom through the heart and had watched as they'd tumbled into the void.

Grief shook Norealle's frame. Puck didn't move, his entire body held taut as he stared at the place Thom and Slager had disappeared. Long seconds ticked by. Neither Realm Walker reappeared. All around them, the remaining stars wreaked havoc on the residual errgoths, and the Lomairians put flight to the Abadonians. Slager and his weaponized portals were gone. The tide had shifted. The battle was nearly over.

But...Thom.

Norealle slid off the dragon, heaving sobs wrenching from her soul as she fell to her knees. Ranele released another long, mournful cry, the sound echoing the breaking of Norealle's heart. Puck still hadn't moved from Ranele's back. He sat. His face ashen.

It wasn't fair. Thom had done everything he'd been sent to do. He'd saved everyone—except himself.

"Daughter?"

Norealle lifted her red, tear-streaked face. A glowing white figure glided towards her and caught Norealle in her arms.

"Mother," she wailed as she sank into her mother's embrace. Tender fingers stroked her hair, but the loving touch did nothing to dull her pain.

"My darling girl," her mother crooned, tears thickening her voice. "My sweet, brave, beautiful girl."

Norealle curled in on herself, weeping. *He was gone. Thom was gone.* Any joy she should've felt at being reunited with her mother was eclipsed by her loss.

Tears fell from Ethereal's eyes. "He was an honorable man."

Denial surged to the surface, and Norealle shook her head, hating the single-word summary of the man she'd gifted her heart to. Honorable did not do him justice. Thom was kind and thoughtful. He was loyal and strived to do the right thing. Thom was tender. Considerate. Self-sacrificing.

"Take me home." The words were brittle. There was nothing left for her here. Any dreams she'd ever had of experiencing the Human Realm had died with Thom.

"You're leaving?" Puck dropped from the dragon and trudged toward her. His expression gutted. He stared at her, betrayal galloping across his face. "You can't go. Thom needs you."

Tears poured down Norealle's cheeks as she faced Puck. "Thom is *dead*, Puck. Slager killed him."

Puck reeled back like she'd punched him. He shook his head madly. "No. He's not dead. He isn't dead. Thom's smart. He'll figure out a way."

Norealle pressed her fist against her mouth. Slager's dagger had plunged into Thom's body—not once, but twice—before they'd fallen into the void. "I can't stay here. Not without..."

Puck's lips trembled, and he hauled in a deep breath. "Not without Thom," he finished hoarsely. He trained bloodshot eyes on Norealle's mother. "You're a star?"

"Yes, I am her mother."

Puck's eyes widened for a split second before pain shattered his gaze. He grabbed Norealle's hand. "Wait for him. Please."

A sob lurched out of Norealle's chest, and she tugged her hand free. "I...I can't. He's dead, Puck." Norealle fell into her mother's embrace. "Take me home."

With a flash of light, they shot into the sky.

Chapter 39
El'Ohim's Country

Thom's fingers twitched and stirred through something soft. He was lying down, the surface cool against his back and legs. Slowly, he rolled his head to the side. He was on grass.

How? He'd been stabbed and fallen through The Inbetween.

"I must be dead." He pushed himself up. No pain accompanied the movement. He touched his chest. His shirt was bloodied, but no blood spurted from the wound. Thom searched the flesh beneath. It was whole.

"Not dead," a warm voice intoned heartily, and Thom startled as a man settled down beside him.

He had the sturdy build of a farmer and a pleasant enough face, but he wasn't particularly handsome or notable. What captured Thom's attention were his eyes. They were filled with endless compassion and quiet strength.

I know him.

The man simply sat there, a knowing smile curving gently across his mouth.

"El'Ohim." The name fell from Thom in a reverent whisper, and as he said it, he knew it was true.

His eyes crinkled at the corners as His face lit with joy. "My children always know Me."

Peace filled Thom, and he threaded his fingers through the grass, content to just sit in the presence of his Creator. "Is Slager gone?" he eventually asked.

"Yes, he has fallen."

To Thom's surprise, grief clouded El'Ohim's eyes. "You're...you're sad."

"Yes," He responded simply. His breath stirred the grass through the endless meadow. "He was once My child, and I made him just as I made you."

Thom moistened his lips. "And Titus...will he be locked in Zakar now? Is my realm safe?"

"For now, yes, but Titus is clever, and his lies ensnare many." Despite his grim words, El'Ohim smiled at Thom once again. "You did well, Thom."

Warmth and gratefulness saturated Thom's heart. He settled more comfortably against the soft green grass. His thoughts drifted to Puck and Norealle, but sadness could not find a purchase on him. They would be all right.

He closed his eyes and let the sun bathe his face. "Was my father really a Realm Walker?"

"Oh, yes. He served Me for many years."

Thom rolled his head to the side and met El'Ohim's loving eyes. "What will become of Puck and Norealle?"

El'Ohim laughed kindly. "I'll let you find that out for yourself."

"Really? How?"

"You didn't die, Thom."

"But...I was stabbed. And I fell into The Inbetween."

El'Ohim just smiled. "Did I not make you *and* The Inbetween? Your work is not yet done, Thom Darkfell. I have more for you to do."

Confused, Thom watched his Creator climb to His feet. Thom followed, sensing that their meeting was over. A deep sorrow welled within him.

"Will I see you again?" Thom asked.

"Yes, but not for a time."

Thom's heart fell.

"However," El'Ohim continued, and Thom looked up. "I will be with you, just as I have always been." El'Ohim placed His hand on Thom's head, and the field disappeared.

Thom stood in the middle of the battlefield. Brown-uniformed soldiers from Knor hauled bodies through the gore-filled muck to a large burning pile. The stench of burnt flesh assaulted his nostrils, and Thom gagged. Black smoke filled the sky, but no errgoths circled overhead. Disoriented, Thom picked his way across the trampled battleground toward Knor.

He found a road that led to the city. Stepping around bodies, burned catapults, and other carnage, Thom approached the main gate. The large doors hung haphazardly on their hinges, the wood charred black. No one stood guard. The hair on the back of his neck prickled as he walked under the stone archway. Finally, a tired-looking guard pushed away from the wall. A sling cradled his arm across the chest of his bloodied uniform.

Thom stopped. "When did the battle end?"

The soldier cocked a brow, considering him. "The battlefield cleared about six hours ago."

"Where are all the soldiers?"

"Some are on mop-up duty out there, and they've sent several regiments after the remaining Abadonians."

"And the rest?"

"Infirmary. Barracks. Tavern." He narrowed his eyes. "You have a lot of questions."

Thom rubbed his neck. "I blacked out near the end. I need to find my friends."

The guard allowed him to step through. "Good luck. I hope they made it."

"Me too." Thom's feet bore him across the city toward the Pearcelys' Bakery. It was a fool's hope, but if he were Puck, that was the first place he'd go.

Every window Thom passed was lit from within, and he could see men and women tending soldiers or serving them food. The street was busy as men, women, and military personnel passed by. Thom finally reached the Pearcelys' gate. As if in a trance, he flipped the latch and pushed it wide. He walked down the cobblestone path, up the two steps to the door, and paused. There, on the step, was a plate of food. Smiling, he bent down and picked it up. He inhaled, the smell of fresh bread and thick meat gravy tantalizing his senses. Thom took a bite and strained his ears. He could hear voices inside.

Setting his hand on the knob, he started to turn it, then hesitated and knocked. A moment later, heavy footfalls strode to the door, and it opened. Puck's pa stood in the doorway, utter shock spreading across his face.

Jaw slack, Pa staggered forward and threw his arms around Thom's neck, hauling him close. "My son."

"Pa." Thom blindly set the plate on the railing and wrapped his arms around his Pa.

"Is it Thom?" a familiar voice cried from the kitchen.

Thom heard a chair clatter to the floor, and a second later, Puck barreled around the corner. His eyes locked with Thom's, and he let out a holler that was probably heard in every corner of the city.

"I knew it!" He dragged Thom into a fierce hug, then froze. "Are you hurt?"

Thom shook his head. "Healed."

"You scared the life out of me!" Puck accused, his voice grating like gravel. He blinked away what looked suspiciously like tears and thumped Thom on the back. "Don't ever do that again."

Thom winced. "I don't plan to."

Behind Puck, Ma stood, tears streaming down her face, and beside her was Ranele. Moisture even glimmered in her catlike eyes.

But where was Norealle?

Thom's heart thudded.

"Puck." His grip clenched around Puck's arm. "Where's Norealle?"

Puck's joy faded. "She left, Thom. She thought you were dead. She went home to her realm."

What?

"I'll be back." He jumped off the steps.

"You just got here!" Ma cried.

Thom shook his head. "I'm sorry, Ma. I have to go."

Her face fell. On quick feet, Thom dashed up the steps and caught her in his arms, delivering a quick kiss to her cheek. "I'll be back," he promised, and she let him go.

"Go get your girl, Thom," Puck ordered. "And then get your rear back here."

Thom didn't need to be told twice. He formed a portal on their front landing. Pace rapid, Thom crossed The Inbetween and stepped out on the ledge of Norealle's family cave.

"Norealle!" *Where was she?*

"Thom?"

He spun as Ethereal and Keifor, hand in hand, hurried out of their home.

"Where's Norealle?" Agitation coursed through him.

"In the meadow," Keifor's low voice rumbled.

Thom spun, not even bothering with a farewell as he opened a portal. The need to find Norealle was all consuming. He burst into the meadow, his magic retracting as he pivoted on his heel, searching.

"Norealle!" He shouted her name, not even caring if she chastised him for yelling at her.

"Thom!" Her familiar voice carried from across the meadow, and Thom's gaze landed on her running form.

Thom surged forward, his feet barely touching the ground in his haste. He caught her, sweeping her up into his arms, and crushing her to his chest.

"I saw him kill you! I watched you fall!" Norealle collapsed against him, desperate tears streaming down her cheeks as she clung to him.

"I know," Thom said. "I know. I'm so sorry."

Her body shook as sob after sob wracked her body in a wrenching release of emotion. Thom sank to the ground and cradled her against him. Gradually, her weeping lessened, and she grew limp in his arms, her head resting on his shoulder. Thom gently brushed the tears from her puffy cheeks with the pad of his thumb before pressing slow kisses to her hair, her forehead, her damp cheeks, and finally, her lips.

She shuddered in his arms, and he tucked her tighter against his chest with no intention of letting her go anytime soon.

"It's done, love," he murmured, his lips drifting to her hair once more. "Titus and his monsters are trapped. Slager is gone." Thom kissed her forehead. "It's over."

Norealle let out a long, shaky breath. "What happened?"

In low tones, Thom quietly told her what had taken place as he and Slager had tumbled through The Inbetween, and how he had woken in El'Ohim's land. Norealle listened, her eyes widening with wonder. When his story came to an end, she sighed and cuddled in closer.

"What now, Thom?"

He bestowed a featherlight kiss to her mouth. "Dinner, I think. And then..." He smiled down into her dark, starlight-filled eyes and felt his heart grow wings. "And then I need to speak to the Key Keeper about courting his beautiful daughter, if she'll have me."

He lifted her hand and tenderly kissed each one of her capable fingers. Norealle tilted her gaze to his, and Thom laced his fingers through hers, marveling at the love he never expected to find in a girl's face shining back at him.

"I wouldn't have any other, Thom Darkfell."

Chapter 40

Six Months Later

Thom braced his hand against the library door and paused. It felt almost eerie to be standing in the exact place where he'd first learned that he was going to war. So much had happened. So much had changed. He slowly pushed the door, and the hinges creaked their welcome. The smell of books, parchment, and dust tickled his nose, and he inhaled deeply. He'd always loved the smell of his library, but he'd never noticed how stuffy the air was nor how dim the light. Thom shook his head ruefully. Spending months outdoors in the fresh air and under the sun and moon had altered his perceptions.

He strolled over to his workbench with a wry smile. The last six months had been so busy he hadn't had a chance to sit at his work desk. King Xerses had requested he join the peace talks between Abadonia's new king and himself. Thom had spent many hours speaking to both men about El'Ohim and the dangers that still lurked behind Zakar's wall. Beaten down, the Abadonian people were receptive to learning about their Creator and willing to negotiate peace. Needing a change, Lieutenant Commander Drayen had volunteered to serve in Abadonia as permanent representative of Lomair. Thom prayed he'd find peace and a new sense of purpose.

As for the human slaves in Zakar, Thom could only assume that the worst had befallen them. He'd traveled to Zakar with Ranele several times to attempt a rescue, but the wall kept them out as well as it kept Titus in. The people of Abadonia had made dark choices, and the sacrifice of their men to Titus was a consequence that could not be reversed. The memory of the slaves' sunken faces and the small measures of help they'd offered him haunted Thom, but he'd given his grief to El'Ohim.

As promised, Thom had shown Norealle his library and had begun to teach her to read. Not surprisingly, she was a quick learner. No trip to the Human Realm was complete without a visit to Ma and Pa. Thom's pseudo parents had embraced Norealle like a daughter. When Thom was off traveling, Ma often took Norealle under her tutelage, teaching her how to bake favorite delicacies, weave—and on some level—understand the foreignness of the Human Lands. Norealle drank it all in, her keen mind a sponge for all the information they taught her.

Thom sat on his stool and stared at the piece of parchment stretched across the desk—the map he'd left out on the day he'd been drafted. Thom blew a fine layer of dust off the map's surface and let his gaze rove over the familiar dark lines of mountains, rivers, and roads. Places he'd now traveled to and seen himself.

Thom picked up his quill. The triangular shapes of the mountains didn't do justice to the jagged peaks, the rough terrain, and the way the sunlight gleamed off the ice. His mind flooded with images as he stared at the map. It was just paper. A poor representation of what really was. With confident strokes, he carefully sketched the rugged slopes of the mountain that had taken him to the Hidden Realm for the first time. When it was complete, he stowed his quill away and stood.

Picking up a leather satchel, Thom filled it with parchment, a compass, ink, and a quill. The tools of a cartographer. Mind drifting to home, he opened a portal and unfurled a path to the Hidden Realm, an action that now came as easily as breathing. Leaving The Inbetween, Thom's feet carried him down the short path to the cabin Puck had helped him build in the forest.

"Thom!"

Smiling, Thom spotted Norealle, his wife of nearly two months, walking up the bank from the little creek that trickled by their home. A full basket of produce hung off her arm. Adjusting his satchel, Thom hurried towards her. She set the basket down and stepped into his waiting arms. Thom buried his face in the crook of her neck and inhaled her woodsy scent.

"I missed you." He mumbled the words against her skin, and felt her body shake with laughter.

"I missed you too. But I thought you said you'd be gone for a few days?"

He leaned back far enough so he could see her smiling eyes and grinned sheepishly. "The king gave me his blessing to map the Hidden Realm, if your father agrees." He patted his bag. "And I stopped at the library, but somehow, the idea of sitting inside working on those dusty, old maps couldn't compete with coming home to you." He cradled her face and pressed a leisurely kiss to her lips.

To his delight, a pink blush colored her cheeks. "Oh, you."

Thom stole another kiss from her soft mouth. "Can you blame me?"

She rolled her eyes. "Has Puck visited Ma and Pa lately?"

Thom snorted and shook his head. "He's still following Ranele around like a lost puppy. I took him to the Northern Mountains yesterday."

Norealle laughed. "She'll never have him. I don't know what he's thinking."

"He's besotted."

"Just like you." Norealle shot back, but the love in her eyes told the whole truth.

"Yes." He smirked, even as his heart filled with joy. "Just like us, my love."

Bonus: Ranele & Puck

She was wind. She was fire. She was *free*!

Ranele banked sharply and cut across the skies of the Hidden Realm. She'd been searching the Northern Mountains for months, looking for any sign of her kin. To her sorrow, there had only been false leads and crushed hopes. A flash of green light caught her attention, and she dove straight for it, recognizing the portal for what it was.

"Welcome, Realm Walker."

Thom strode from the portal, wearing confidence like a cloak about his shoulders. He'd grown much over the last months, especially after marrying the Star Daughter. Following close behind Thom was his sandy-haired companion.

"Have you found any recordsss in your library?" Ranele asked as she landed, gravel spraying from beneath her taloned feet. Thom had promised to do some research and see if he could find anything to help her locate her missing family.

Thom shook his head. "Not yet. But I will keep searching. Norealle is helping too." The Realm Walker gestured to Puck. "I brought you another set of eyes, though."

"He isss too slow." Ranele puffed a cloud of smoke into Puck's face.

The incorrigible man grinned. "Aww, did you see that, Thom? She missed me!" He winked at Ranele, and she snapped her teeth an inch from his face. He was nonplussed. "Every time I see you, you become more radiant."

Ranele let out a chuff of smoke, unwilling to admit that she liked his compliments. Subtly, she arched her neck a little.

Puck approached and ran a callused hand over her flank. "Magnificent."

Thom shook his head. "Did you know, he almost peed his pants when he met Traell for the first time?"

"I did *not* pee my pants." Puck growled. "Plus, Traell is a little freak. Ranele is *splendid.*"

Ranele preened. She supposed that there were worse companions to have around than Puck, and the months spent alone in the mountain were growing lonesome. Not that she'd ever admit that to Puck.

"If you need a break from hisss prattling, I can take him off your handsss for a few days," she conceded, golden orbs only looking at Thom.

Puck scowled. "You know I can hear you, right?"

"I'll come get him in three days." Thom glanced at Puck. "Behave yourself."

The image of innocence, Puck spread his hands wide, palms up. "Don't I always?"

Ranele chuffed out a smoky chortle.

Puck grinned, leaning up against her flank as he crossed his arms. "Get back to your wife, Thom. We're fine." Without asking permission, Puck vaulted up on top of Ranele's back.

A growl rumbled up from her throat. *"You know I could eat you."*

Puck leaned down and patted her. "But you wouldn't. Deep, deep down, you love me too."

Ranele snorted, a puff of hot, white smoke blasting from her nostrils. Thom shook his head, and Ranele was pretty sure she heard him mutter "besotted idiot" under his breath. Her golden eyes followed El'Ohim's newest Realm Walker as he disappeared through a portal.

Acknowledgements

To my wonderful people,

I can't believe I have a book in this world. This pile of words, printed on a stack of paper, is a dream come true. I've wanted to be an author since I was a little girl, galloping through the bush on my pony imagining stories of dragons, talking animals, and heroic maidens who save the princes. I can't ever remember a time that I didn't want to write.

Stories like Redwall and Narnia shaped my early reading, and you don't have to look far to see their influences in my stories today. To the hundreds of authors who wrote the thousands of books I've consumed, *thank you* for feeding my love of story and teaching me how to craft my own.

To my Creator. My El'Ohim. My Jesus. I wrote this book during one of the hardest years of my life, and you were there. I felt your presence as I wrote. I felt your love. I felt you take my anguish and turn it into a prose that I could then turn around and understand my own life better with. Thank you for speaking to me through this story, and for giving me a creative outlet. This gift of writing brings me impossible joy, and I thank you for that.

To my hubby, Cody. Thank you for being patient with the amount of time I've spent writing and editing Darkfell. I know you don't understand why I want to write or the crazy imagination that runs through my brain, but you love and support me anyway (you are honestly the best). I know I tend to mentally drift off into my story worlds and sometimes you have to call me quite a few times to get my attention...thank you for loving me as I am. Your support means the world. I'll never forget how I came home from work to find that you'd made me a writing desk so that I'd have a place to craft this story. Or when you surprised me with tickets to Realm Makers, a conference that you knew about because you listen to my ramblings and care about things that matter to me. I. Love. You. You are the reason I can write romance.

To my kids, Miss Bean and Little Dude. You two are such a massive blessing. Thank you for cackling along with me as I wrote Traell and bringing that winged imp into the family like he's a real person (scary thought). Your innocent love of my stories encourages me so much. Thank you for letting mommy write. I can't wait to see the story God has written for your lives. I love you both to the moon and back. And Little Dude, you inspired Thom. You are so quiet and thoughtful, yet with the biggest heart. I know life can be daunting, but just like Thom, I know you will grow up to be a man of courage and a man of God. And Miss Bean, the fact that you are proudly drawing and writing your own books has me in awe. I have a feeling I'm going to be reading your stories soon. Can't wait to hear them. I am so proud of you, my spirited girl. Never stop loving life. I love you both so much.

To April Skelly, my crazy-awesome publisher and dear friend. Thank you for taking on an unknown writer and guiding me along this wild journey of publishing. Best of all, thank you for the hilarious road trip and all the laughs we shared. You are an incredible woman and friend. I am so excited to see where God takes you and your writing. Keep making me swoon!

To Jenni Frankovic, you were the first person to welcome me into the writing community when I logged on to the Realm Sphere. I felt like an imposter, and you swung that around and made me feel like I belonged. Your kindness shines out of your beautiful soul, and I am so grateful to know you. You never fail to put yourself aside to help others, and you are so generous with your many skills and talents. Thank you for doing an amazing job editing my book and cheering me on. You are a wonderful friend. I can't wait to read more of your wonderful stories.

To Brittany Eden, you are a classy lady and a beautiful writer. It is lovely to know you, and thank you for your sharp eye on my developmental edit.

To J.J. Fischer, you saw my vision. When I handed you the disgusting mess that was my first draft (I'm sorry!), you gamely took it on and understood what I was trying to do with this story. Thank you for your kind words, your encouragement, and your expertise. Your friendship and editing skills are so valued. I look forward to working with you on my future projects.

To all the realmies I met at the 2024 Realm Makers event. Thank you for making me feel so at home and for encouraging me to dream. I can't wait to read all your stories and cheer you all on.

To Sir Gunner (yes, the horse). My goofy, four-legged friend. Thanks for fueling my muse. Writer's block doesn't stand a chance with you hurtling through the bush. Thank you for not killing me.

Nikki, you are such a fabulous cheerleader. Every time I felt doubtful about my work, I texted you. Your enthusiasm for this story and its characters always lifted my heart. Thank you for always being such a good friend. Can't wait to climb more mountains with you one day.

To my family. Thank you for a wild life that has led to more experiences than I could ever put into words. It makes writing easier when I have real life scenarios to draw on. Thank you for taking me to the library, and always giving me so much time to read as a kid.

To Brigitte. Thank you for proofreading my work and making sure that the Canadian (British) spelling was fixed. Who knew how weird Americans spell...

To Laura. Thank you for being my writing buddy for so many years. You kept me in practice and taught me how to write dialogue. I hope you finish that terrifying medical thriller you started all those years ago. It still gives me goosebumps.

It's 2am as I write this, and I'm realizing that I could probably add another two pages of "thank-you" notes, but I don't think Madame Publisher wants to print my long-winded explanations. So, I'm buttoning it up. To everyone who was part of this journey, thank you!

About the Author

Amanda Wright lives in picturesque Canada with her amazing husband (who made her believe in love at first sight) and their two children (who think Traell is the best character ever). Between running a business with her husband, homeschooling, and chugging way too much coffee, Amanda is forever crafting new tales of magical adventure and romance. Her debut fantasy, *Darkfell*, was awarded the 2025 Christy Award for First Novel. To stay up to date on all of Amanda's upcoming novels, sign up for her newsletter at www.awrightauthor.ca and follow her on Instagram!

Instagram & Twitter: @amandawrightauthor
Substack: https://amandawright.substack.com/

thing he knows for certain is that Ranele Firewing is unlike any woman he's ever met before...even if she does have a habit of dropping him from the sky and singeing him with her flame and ill temper. He isn't a fool, he knows she's hiding something, but surely his shoulders are broad enough to bear it?

After three hundred years of captivity, dragon shifter Ranele is free of her enchanted prison. With the race of dragon kind now nonexistent and her biggest mistake vanquished, it appears her dark secrets are safe. As her relationship with the Realm Walker's handsome, quick-witted brother grows, she realizes that guilt and shame are not so easily absolved. When danger finds those she's growing to love, Ranele knows her link to Zakar must be revealed...even if it means losing everyone that's become dear to her.

As darkness rises to reclaim Ranele, can one man's love and courage and her Creator's grace give her the strength to right an ancient wrong? With battle lines forming, time is not on her side.